THE BANDERA TRAIL

Set on rescuing their old friend Clay Duval who is trapped inside war-torn Mexico, Gil and Van Austin cross the border after him and soon discover half of Mexico's army wants them dead. Taken prisoner by Santa Anna's soldiers, the brothers make a daring escape and head into Durango country, where they stumble on a valley full of longhorns — and a chance to build a future north of the border. All they have to do now is break Duval out of prison and drive the cattle to safety. But faced with outlaws, soldiers and the cunning plans of a beautiful woman, the Austins are finding out that this isn't a trail drive, it's a war to reach the Bandera Range alive.

Books by Ralph Compton
in the Niagara Library Series:

GOODNIGHT TRAIL
THE WESTERN TRAIL
THE CHISHOLM TRAIL

RALPH COMPTON

THE BANDERA TRAIL

Complete and Unabridged

NIAGARA

Ulverscroft Group Limited
England - USA - Canada
Australia - New Zealand

COM
LARGE
PRINT

First published in the
United States of America

First Niagara Edition
published 1996

Published in Large Print
by arrangement with
St. Martin's Press Inc.
New York

ISBN 0–7089–5840–0

Published by
F. A. Thorpe (Publishing) Ltd.
Anstey, Leicestershire
Set by Words & Graphics Ltd.
Anstey, Leicestershire
Printed and bound in Great Britain by
T. J. Press (Padstow) Ltd., Padstow, Cornwall

This book is printed on acid-free paper

In Memory of Rosa Faye Compton
1936 – 1993

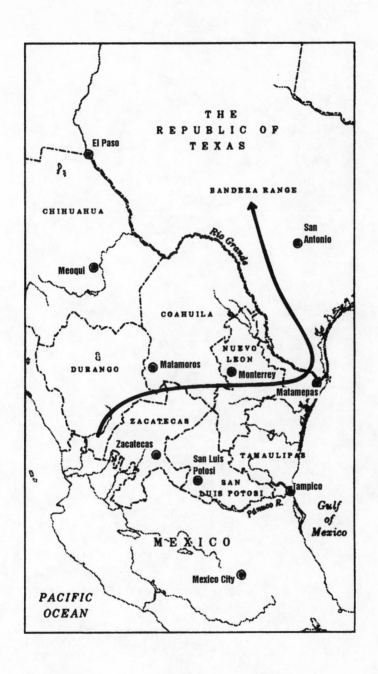

Author's Foreword

Spanish explorers found little about Texas to excite them. There was no gold or silver north of the Rio Grande. In fact, there was no abundance of *anything*, except grazing land, and there was a blessed plenty of that in Mexico. Why spend more money for soldiers, missions, and padres in a vain attempt to civilize hostile Indians who had no desire to become civilized? The missions soon crumbled, and the Franciscan padres are a memory, but they left a legacy that may have changed the course of history in Texas and the American southwest. For it was the padres, forever struggling to support their missions, who became the first cattle ranchers.

Having little interest in Texas, the Spanish Crown wasn't opposed to offering land grants to Americans willing to colonize the territory. Moses Austin, born in Connecticut but more recently from Missouri, sought and received permission from Spanish authorities to settle Americans in Texas. But Mexico declared its independence from Spain, and the newly arrived American colonists found their land grants worthless. Even as he sought an agreement with the new government, Moses Austin took sick and died. His son Stephen, then twenty-seven, had been studying law in New Orleans. Young Stephen took up his father's fight on behalf of the hapless colony, and after many months in Mexico City, persuaded the Mexican government to recognize the grants the Spanish had promised his father. In 1825 the Mexican government passed an immigration law, and for ten years Stephen Austin managed the colony his father had begun.

By the thousands, Americans came to Texas, all seeking a fresh start. A few were from the north, but most of them were southerners. There was unrest in the states. There had been a war in 1812, a panic in 1819, and an unpopular Land Law had been passed in 1820. In the United States the law demanded payment of $1.25 an acre — in cash — for a minimum of eighty acres. In Texas, not only was the land almost free for the asking, but in grants of such proportions that a man might build an empire. A farmer could secure 277 acres, but if he intended to raise stock as well, he became eligible for an additional 4338 acres! Most of the colonists, being southerners, intended to become cattlemen, and so received a maximum grant of 4615 acres. Austin had chosen the land wisely. The grants on which his American colony settled — millions of acres — lay along the Brazos and Colorado rivers. Eventually Austin's colony consisted of 297 families, and until 1836 they lived peacefully as Mexican citizens. Then came the bloody battle of the Alamo, and every man north of the Rio Grande became a Texan.

The cattle in Texas had been left there by the Spanish, but weren't very numerous. Many of the American colonists, taking the larger land grant and promising to raise cattle, had not done so. Unlike much of the West, the fertile land along the Brazos and the Colorado was as suited to farming as it was to ranching. Most of the new "ranchers" raised only enough beef for their own needs, and the Spanish longhorns continued to run wild. The cattle drifted south, across the Rio Grande, and back into the thickets of Mexico. Herds of wild horses that had once roamed the plains soon followed. The Republic of Texas had become too civilized for them.

After Mexico's stunning defeat at San Jacinto, Texans entering Mexico — for any reason — did so at the risk of their lives. By 1840 there was only a few thousand wild longhorns north of the Rio Grande, and many of these were diehard old range bulls. There were few cows, and the natural increase was small. Ironically, the millions of wild longhorns in Mexico were viewed as virtually worthless, except for their hide and tallow, and the select fighting bulls chosen for the arena. It would be twenty-five years — in the aftermath of the American Civil War — before wild longhorns would be plentiful in the thickets and chaparral north of the Rio Grande.

Prologue

WITH some urging from their uncle Stephen, Gilbert and Vandiver Austin came to Texas in the fall of 1833, applying for and receiving Mexican land grants as part of Stephen Austin's American colony. Austin had originally been assigned a grant of 67,000 acres for his efforts in establishing the American colony, and he arranged for Gil and Van to receive grants adjoining his own. Following Stephen Austin's untimely death in 1836, Gil and Van became heirs to their uncle's original grant. Added to their own lands, their holdings became a veritable empire, stretching eastward from the Bandera Mountains to beyond the Colorado River.

The Austin brothers had arrived in Texas when Gil was barely nineteen, and Van a year younger. With them came their fiddle-footed friend, twenty-one-year-old Clay Duval. Clay had steadfastly refused to file for a grant of his own, preferring to throw in with Gil and Van.

"That's an almighty lot of land to be responsible for," he had said, "and I ain't one to make a promise I ain't sure I can keep."

In his rough-out cowman's boots and sweat-stained black Stetson, Clay Duval was but an inch or two shy of seven feet. Shaggy brown hair curled from beneath his hat brim, and

1

his brown eyes were flecked with green. His craggy face and neck were the hue of an old saddle. Faded blue homespun shirt and trousers completed his attire.

Gil and Van Austin were as tall as Clay, but towheaded and blue-eyed. Their pinch-creased Stetsons had once been gray. Like Clay's, their cowman's boots were rough-out, their trousers worn at the seat and knees, and their old shirts faded almost white by the Texas sun. On his right hip each of the men carried a tied-down, .44-caliber five-shot Colt revolver.

While Gil and Van Austin had land in plenty, they were woefully short on livestock. Many of the longhorns abandoned by the Spanish had drifted far south, into the wilds of Mexico. Most of the stock that remained in Texas had been claimed by Americans who had begun settling in the colony as early as 1822. Taking their grants in the fall of 1833, Gil and Van Austin quickly discovered the shortage of cattle and horses. Relations between Mexico and the Republic of Texas worsened, terminating in April 1836 with the bloody battle at the Alamo. A month later, at San Jacinto, the Texans took their revenge. For a dozen years the wild longhorns and the broomtails that roamed the plains south of the border would be more of a risk than most Texans would be willing to take.

★ ★ ★

December 29, 1840. Bandera range, Republic of Texas.

2

Introducing the 2012 CC.
More power. More features. For less than you'd expect.

2012 CC / 21 city / 31 hwy MPG* / **Learn more at vw.com/2012cc**

Das Auto.

The 2012 CC looks expensive.
But sometimes looks can be delightfully deceiving.

- Award-winning 2.0L TSI® engine with 200HP and 21 city/31 hwy MPG,* standard

- 37.7 inches of rear-seat legroom—more than BMW 3 series or Infinity G37**

- Available Bi-Xenon™ headlights turn up to 15 degrees around corners with AFS (Adaptive Front-lighting System)

- Standard Volkswagen safety features like the Intelligent Crash Response System†

- Optional smart features include rear-view camera, touch screen navigation and Bluetooth®

Starting at just $28,515††

Volkswagen Carefree Maintenance‡

3 Years or 36,000 Miles of No-Charge Scheduled Maintenance.
‡ Whichever occurs first. Some restrictions. See dealer or program for details.

Learn more at vw.com/2012cc or schedule a test drive at your VW dealer today.

* EPA estimates for 2012 CC 2.0T Sport with manual transmission. Your mileage will vary.
** Based on manufacturer's published data.
† The Intelligent Crash Response System (ICRS) will only activate in a collision where the airbags deploy or safety belt pretensioners activate. Not all collisions cause airbags to deploy or safety belt pretensioners to activate.
†† Starting MSRP of $28,515 for a 2012 Volkswagen CC 2.0T Sport with manual transmission. Model shown is a 2012 Volkswagen CC VR6 4MOTION Executive 3.6L with automatic transmission with a starting MSRP of $40,390. All prices exclude transportation, taxes, title, other options and dealer charges. Dealer sets actual price.

12-5899-2900(4/11)

Das Auto.

"We need horses and cattle," said Clay Duval, "and Mexico's the place to get 'em."

"Maybe," said Van Austin, "but this purely ain't the time for a gringo to ride south. Not with Santa Anna's army on the prod."

"I'd have to agree with him, Clay," said Gil. "That Mex army's unpredictable enough, but there's bandits and hostile Indians too. Any of the bunch would consider it a privilege to kill a Texan. Every horse and cow south of the Rio wouldn't be worth that."

"I ain't riskin' anybody's hide but my own," said Clay stubbornly. "I aim to ride down to the Mendoza ranch, south of Durango. I'll hide by day and ride by night. If we're goin' to have horses, why not blooded animals? I'll have enough gold in my saddlebag to afford at least one of them Mendoza hotbloods. Ridin' at night, if I can't bring one cayuse out of Mexico on a lead rope, I'm a damn poor excuse for a Texan."

"I reckon," Gil chuckled, "but do you aim to bring a herd of Spanish longhorns out on a lead rope too?"

The lanky Clay grinned. "Only if you and Van meet me at the river. I'm bettin' we can get a herd dirt-cheap. Mexico's cow-poor. All a Mex cares about is fighting bulls for the ring."

"They'd have to be dirt-cheap," said Van. "We're land-rich, but money-poor. But it won't matter if the cows are free, if we can't get 'em out of Mexico."

"We'll make that part of the deal," said Clay. "The Mex rancher gets paid when he drives the

3

longhorns across the river."

"I'll believe that when I see it," said Gil. "After San Jacinto, you think the Mex government's goin' to allow any dealin' between us and the Mex ranchers? Santa Anna would gut-shoot his own mother if he caught her just lookin' slanch-eyed at a Texan."

But Clay Duval was determined to ride to Mexico, whatever the danger. Clay was the restless one. The three friends had joined Sam Houston's army for the fight at San Jacinto. It had been a decisive battle, but when Gil and Van had withdrawn to return to their Bandera range, Clay almost hadn't gone with them.

★ ★ ★

December 31, 1840, Clay Duval saddled his big black and rode south. Gil and Van Austin shook his hand and wished him luck, keeping their misgivings to themselves. Privately, they doubted they'd ever see their friend again. Alive, anyway.

★ ★ ★

For five months Gil and Van didn't know if Clay was alive or dead. When they were all but certain of the latter, they got word from him. The letter was dated April 1, 1841, and it had arrived on May 4. Gil read the single page and passed it to Van. He read it, read it again, and then looked at his brother in disbelief.

"He wrote that on April first," said Van, "so

4

he's got to be April foolin' us. I purely can't see old fiddle-foot Clay takin' on the responsibility of a ranch. Not when it means stayin' in Mexico, with a she-male ramrod tellin' him what to do and when to do it."

"Why not?" Gil chuckled. "Old Mendoza's cashed in, leavin' his missus with a million acres, a couple hundred head of blooded horses, and God knows how many longhorn cows. A man could do a hell of a lot worse. What don't seem right is, I can't picture Clay Duval doin' anything that sensible. With a name like Victoria, I'll bet the Senora Mendoza's the handsomest woman in all of Mexico."

"Don't bet the ranch on it," said Van. "With a stable of fancy blooded horses, she could be ugly enough to stop an eight-day clock and Clay Duval wouldn't care."

★ ★ ★

The next letter Gil and Van received from Clay Duval arrived on December 5, 1842. Again it consisted of a single page, painfully brief. It was a plea for help, offering no explanation.

"He ain't askin' much, is he?" said Van. "All we got to do is help him drive two hundred horses and five thousand longhorn cows through eight hundred miles of hostile Injuns, outlaws, and Mex soldiers."

"Don't forget Victoria and Angelina," said Gil. "He aims to bring them along too."

"Who in hell's Angelina? On top of everything else, you reckon old Clay's went stomp-down,

5

hog-wild crazy and become a daddy?"

"Wouldn't surprise me none," said Gil. "With Clay's luck, them females will be ridin' sidesaddle and carryin' parasols."

"Or maybe ridin' in a buckboard, drivin' a matched team," said Van. "I flat don't like the sound of this, Gil, and I ain't sure I'd want to be a party to it."

"You look after the spread, then," said Gil, "and I'll see what I can do. I'm with you, when it comes to not likin' the sound of any of this, but Clay's countin' on us. I get the feelin' that if there was any other way, he wouldn't be askin' for our help."

"Ah, hell," groaned Van, "I'll have to go, for the same reason you are. That's the trouble with bein' a Texan. It's less painful gettin' shot dead with your friends than bein' sensible, stayin' behind, and feelin' guilty. But if we're both goin', who's goin' to look after our spread? God knows, we got little enough to look after, besides the land, but we may be gone awhile."

"There's them three hombres that's been ridin' around lookin' for work," said Gil. "All we can offer is grub and a place to bunk, but that's more'n they got now."

"They're likely on the dodge," said Van. "I'd bet my part of the spread they're wanted in the states. You reckon we can trust 'em?"

"I'd trust them before I'd trust the rest of these jacks," said Gil. "I won't forget how they all but starved Uncle Steve to death, refusing to pay him the twelve cents an acre he was entitled to for securing their grants."

6

"You're right, brother," said Van. "Let's go find those outlaws, and see can we strike a deal."

1

DECEMBER 10, 1842. San Antonio, Republic of Texas. Gil and Van found the trio they were seeking, not far from the ruins of the Alamo, in a dirt-floor saloon. The three were conspicuous because it was a time when there were few unoccupied men in the territory. Most of those owning land grants were simply trying to survive, while others — especially the young men — had joined the militia and were clamoring for a fight with Mexico. Although it was broad daylight outside, the saloon was dark. The only light was a single guttering candle, its own wax holding it upright on a makeshift bar. There were no chairs. The tables were long X-frames, made of rough boards. The bench on each side was another rough plank, each end of which was pegged to the table's X-frame. Two of the wanderers sat with their backs to the door. The third man sat on the other side of the crude table, his back to the wall, and it was he who answered Gil's question.

"Yeah," he said, "we'd hire on fer a spell. Long as ye ain't askin' fer references."

His companions laughed. Gil said nothing. The stranger took that for agreement, and got to his feet. He was a gangling scarecrow of a man, seven feet tall without his hat. When the other two men stood up, the contrast was startling.

9

The trio followed Gil and Van outside, and although there was a crude bench at the front of the saloon, none of them sat. They stood facing one another. The tall man spoke.

"Th' scrawny jaybird, here, is Shorty. T'other, with th' bug eyes, is Banjo. Me, I'm Long John Coons. An' see that ye keep it plural. First man calls me 'coon,' I'll gut him."

For emphasis, he drew a Bowie knife from his belt. It was a terrible weapon, looked sharp enough to shave with, and was. He drew the razor-keen blade along his lanky forearm, peeling off a patch of hair. Without a word he slipped the fifteen-inch knife under his belt. Gil nodded. The five of them mounted their horses and rode out, bound for the Bandera range.

★ ★ ★

December 12, 1842. The Bandera range, Republic of Texas.

Gil and Van saddled their horses and rode south, leaving their enormous land grant in the hands of three men about whom they knew little. Long John Coons was a Cajun, and there were rumors that he had left Louisiana by popular demand.

"I'm almighty uneasy about them three," said Van. "Long John, with that blade of his, just purely scares hell out of folks."

"That's why he's our segundo," said Gil. "Remember what old Granny Austin always said: an ounce of prevention's worth more'n all the cure that's to be had. I talked to Shorty

10

and Banjo some. All they told me was, Long John's mama is a conjuring woman, and Long John's got an evil eye. Whatever *that* means."

"Maybe we're goin' at this all wrong," said Van. "I can't shake the feeling we oughta be takin' Long John and his pards with us." He sighed. "But we'd need an army to keep us alive. At the very least, we'll need a dozen good riders, if we're trail drivin' two hundred horses, and five thousand longhorns."

"Clay knows that," said Gil. "We'll have to count on him havin' a plan of his own. But you know Clay Duval; he's always long on courage, but a mite short on common sense. Once he's made up his mind, he'd bridle the devil, ride the joker without a saddle, and rake him with gut hooks all the way. I concede we could use the horses and longhorns, but we can't sneak 'em out of Mexico in our saddlebags."

"Knowin' how mule-stubborn Clay is," said Van, "I'll bet you a horse and saddle he won't leave all that livestock behind and just run for it."

"He may not have a choice," said Gil. "By the time we get to him — if we do — we'll have some idea as to the odds of any of us gettin' out alive. Remember, Alexander Somervell has an expedition somewhere along the border right now."[1]

_____

[1] Moving into Mexico, Somervell's forces captured Laredo on December 18, 1842, and then went on to take Guerrero.

"Yeah," sighed Van, "I know. By the time we get to the river, them Mex soldiers are goin' to be almighty eager to get their hands on some Texans. *Any* Texans. Especially a pair that's fool enough to ride right into their midst."

"We won't make it easy for them," said Gil. "We'll ride at night. But they'll have the advantage, knowin' the country. Ridin' in don't bother me as much as ridin' out. By the time we're ready to leave, Santa Anna will have had time to force-march the rest of the Mexican army between us and the Rio Grande."

★ ★ ★

December 24, 1842. Laredo, Mexico.

Gil and Van found the town tense and virtually deserted. The inhabitants peered nervously from their log-and-mud huts. Seven horsemen rode wearily along the bank of the river, approaching the town from the east.

"Hey," cried Gil, recognizing the lead rider. "That's Ben McCulloch!"

Gil waved his hat, and the lead rider veered the little column toward them. Benjamin McCulloch was from Tennessee, and had been a close friend to David Crockett. McCulloch had been at San Jacinto, with Gil, Van, and Clay fighting under his command. Only recently had McCulloch begun scouting for the Texas Rangers. McCulloch halted his column and trotted his horse forward to meet Gil and Van.

"Cap'n Mac," said Gil, "what're you doing here?"

"Gettin' the hell out," growled McCulloch, "while I can. Take some good advice, the pair of you, and ride back the way you come."

"I wish we could," sighed Van, "but we got business in Mexico."

"I hope it's worth your life, then," said McCulloch.

Gil explained their mission, and the Ranger shook his head. With some bitterness, he spoke.

"Son, when you see the Rangers backin' off, it's time to call in the dogs and ride. Somervell had six hundred men, managed to take Laredo and Guerrero, but he's ordered his troops to head for home, by way of Gonzales."

"Have they?" Gil asked.

"About two hundred of them have," said McCulloch. "The rest of them have left the command, elected William Fisher as their leader, and aim to attack the Mex settlements across the river."

"Sounds like a fool move," said Van. "Is that why you're pullin' out?"

"Damn right," said McCulloch. "The Rangers are here on orders from Sam Houston, as scouts for the Somervell expedition. But I don't figure we owe Fisher and the rest of these damn fools anything. We done all we could. We rode across the river to Mier and reconnoitered the town. The Mex army is gathering there, and I warned Fisher. He ignored my warning, and yesterday they had a look for themselves. Tomorrow, they aim to cross the river and attack the town."

"But you don't think they can take it and hold it," said Gil.

13

"No," said McCulloch. "They'll be killed, or taken captive."

"Then we can use that as a diversion," said Van, "and get into Mexico without being seen."

"You likely can," said McCulloch, "if you're hell-bent on going. It's about ninety miles to Mier, and you'd best ride well beyond there, before you cross the river."

Gil and Van rode until past midnight before making a cold camp.

★ ★ ★

At first light, Gil built a small fire, while Van brought in their picketed horses. They cooked and ate their meager breakfast, put out the fire, and mounted up.

"Merry Christmas," said Van.

"Yeah." Gil grinned. "What do you want, most of all?"

Van sighed. "To get back to Bandera range without havin' my carcass shot full of Mex lead or Injun arrows."

"I'd settle for that too," said Gil, and he didn't smile.

★ ★ ★

They pushed their horses as hard as they dared, and it was an hour before sundown when they first heard the rattle of distant gunfire.

"Somebody's opened the ball," said Gil.

"I feel some guilty," said Van, "using their

14

fight to sneak into Mexico."

"I don't," said Gil. "I wouldn't throw in with 'em, even if we didn't have other snakes to stomp. McCulloch warned 'em. When a Ranger says back off, you back off."

"We're not *really* using their fight for cover," said Van. "It'll be dark long before we're far enough beyond Mier to cross the river. Besides, we don't know how long they've been fighting. It may all be over before we cross the river."

"Won't make any difference to us," said Gil. "If they're up against three hundred Texans, the Mex army's got a hell of a fight on its hands. When it's over, they won't be marching south for a while. They'll have to see to their wounded. Gettin' past this bunch at Mier won't be a problem. We don't know that Santa Anna ain't sending more soldiers, and if he is, we may be ridin' headlong into 'em."

But the distant firing continued, and although it was already dark, they rode wide of the river until they were well past Mier. Finally the rattle of the battle faded to silence. Reaching a point where the Rio Grande narrowed, they trotted their horses across the shallow stream.

"The easy part's over," said Gil.

"Yeah. It's hard to believe a piddling little branch like this can mean the difference between livin' and dyin'."

There was a pale quarter moon, and they rode slowly, depending on their horses to avoid obstacles their riders couldn't see. In that final hour before first light, when darkness seemed to

15

swallow the tiniest star, they paused to rest the horses.

"We'd better skip breakfast," said Gil, "and at first light find us a place to hole up for the day."

But they were destined to ride no farther. In the first gray light of dawn, Van's horse nickered, and was answered. The Texans froze, their hands on the butts of their Colts. Within seconds they were facing a line of mounted Mexican soldiers.

"They ain't armed all that well," said Van through clenched teeth.

"Maybe not," said Gil, "but there's a hell of a bunch of them. This ain't the time. Stand fast."

A soldier whose gold-braided coat proclaimed him an officer, trotted his horse within a few feet of them, careful not to come between his armed command and the two Texans. The Mexican was hog-fat, with a thin moustache, a sadistic grin on his moon face, and a malevolent gleam in his pig eyes. He spoke.

"Captain Hernandez Ortega at your service. Now move away from the horses, hombres. Slowly."

Gil and Van dropped the reins, backing away from their saddled mounts.

"With thumb and finger," said Ortega, "remove your weapons and drop them at your feet."

When they had dropped their Colts, the Mexican said, "Now, perhaps you wish to explain why you are here. Did you not see the river?"

The Texans said nothing. The cat was playing with the mice.

"Ah," said the fat man, with a smirk of anticipation. "The quiet ones, without excuses. Perhaps I should just shoot you."

"We're on our way to the Mendoza ranch, near Durango," said Gil. "We have business with Senor Mendoza."

"Senor Mendoza is dead," snapped the officer.

"Then we will conduct our business with the Senora Mendoza," said Gil.

"Ah," said the Mexican with a vulgar laugh, "I am sure the senora could accommodate the two of you. But alas! We shall never know, shall we?"

He gave an order in Spanish, and two of his company dismounted.

"Hands behind your backs, Tejanos," said Ortega.

The soldiers worked swiftly with rawhide thongs, and within seconds Gil and Van had their hands bound behind their backs. Then came the ultimate indignity, as each Texan had a rope looped about his neck, with the other end dallied around a Mexican saddle horn.

"Now," said their captor, with a chuckle, "you shall join your foolish comrades."

"You could at least let us ride," said Van through gritted teeth.

"I am so sorry," Ortega said piously, rolling his eyes, "but I cannot. Were you mounted, you might attempt to escape. It would truly break my heart, were I forced to shoot you."

They set out, Gil and Van afoot, and their

destination soon became evident. The ominous sound of distant gunfire became louder as they drew closer. The desperate Texans, foolish as their attack might have been, were taking a terrible toll. As they neared the scene of battle, they came upon the bodies of scores of mules and horses. But there were human bodies too. Literally hundreds of them. A few still lived, begging for water or for aid, but most of them were beyond all human need. Ortega halted the column, dismounted, and stood looking at the carnage in horror. Some of his soldiers turned away, their faces pale.

"Damn fools," said Van, under his breath, "but by God, Texans every one."

The fat officer heard, and turned on Van. Gil gritted his teeth. Never had he seen such hatred on a human face. Ortega swung his heavy quirt, and the butt end of it struck Van just above the eyes. He slumped to the ground like an empty sack. Furious, the soldier turned on Gil, the quirt raised for another blow.

"Go ahead," said Gil quietly, "while you can. Before we leave Mexico, you're going to die."

The blow never fell. A chill crept up Ortega's spine, and he turned away. There had been no fear in Gil Austin's cold blue eyes. Only death.

★ ★ ★

Fisher's valiant Texans held out for twenty-four hours, until, hungry, thirsty, and almost out of ammunition, they were forced to surrender. The captives were marched into a field, like cattle.

18

The wounded went untended, and the dead lay where they had fallen. Gil and Van had their hands freed, and were thrown in with the other prisoners. Suddenly, a bloody Texan sat up and opened his eyes. It was like the dead had come to life, and Gil was startled.

"I reckon," said the wounded man, "them Rangers knowed what they was talkin' about. We must've locked horns with the whole damn Mex army."

"What do you reckon they'll do with us?" Gil asked.

"Who knows? Beat us, starve us, march us to Mexico City, maybe. God, I wish I'd never heard of Mier. It ain't a name Texas will want to remember."

★ ★ ★

Mexican General Pedro Ampudia was in charge of the forces at Mier.[1] The captive Texans were

---

[1] When William Fisher's Texas command inspected the village of Mier, it was undefended. Fisher decided to take Mier, and on December 25, 1842, led 261 Texans across the Rio Grande. But Mexican forces had gathered under General Pedro Ampudia, and the Texans found themselves outnumbered more than ten to one. Thirty Texans were killed or wounded. Six hundred Mexican soldiers were killed, and two hundred were wounded.

marched on to Matamoros, where they were held until ordered to Mexico City. But the Texans had no intention of going to the capital city. Word was quietly passed from man to man. Somehow, somewhere, there would be a chance to escape.

"The rest of 'em will be going home to Texas," said Van. "My God, how I wish we could go with 'em."

"That's exactly what the Mex army will expect," said Gil. "They'll look for us all to run north. The very last thing they'll expect is for any of us to go deeper into Mexico. What better way to escape than to go on to the Mendoza spread, like we planned? Besides, Clay's countin' on us."

"Before we rescue Clay," said Van, "there's one thing I aim to do for myself. That fat bastard that cracked my head with a quirt's still here. I promise you, he'll never get to Mexico City alive."

"He took our Colts for himself," said Gil. "Notice he's got one on each hip, like a Texas gun thrower?"

"Yeah," said Van, "and that makes it even better. "Be easy to snatch 'em off his dead carcass, when I'm done with him."

★ ★ ★

February 11, 1843. Salada Hacienda, south of Matamoros Tamaulipas, Mexico.

The rain came down in gray torrents, and the roiling mass of thunderheads seemed to hang at treetop level. The march had been halted for the day. The Mexican officers huddled in tents, a few of the soldiers had their slickers, but the captive Texans were exposed to the fury of the storm. But it was exactly what they had been waiting for. It was time for the break! Word was passed along. The hands and feet of the captive Texans were bound at night, but once it got wet, nothing stretched like rawhide!

"We'll let the others go first," said Gil. "Even with the storm, this won't happen without somebody soundin' the alarm. When they do, these guards will be scattered from here to yonder. They'll be shootin' at one another in the dark. I don't aim to leave this camp without a weapon of some kind, even if it's only a Bowie knife."

"Then when it all busts loose," said Van, "let's work our way to fatso's tent. He's got our Colts, and I purely don't believe he'll crawl out in this storm to look for us, unless Santa Anna shows up to give the order. Once these greaser guards get scattered about in the dark, I'm goin' in that tent."

But the soldier guards were hunched down in their inadequate slickers, or standing on the lee side of huge tree trunks, seeking to avoid the wind-driven rain. The Mexican soldiers were alerted to the impending break only when a frightened horse nickered. There was a clatter of hoofs, a shout, and scattered riflefire. Gil and Van crept through the rainy darkness toward a certain tent. As Van had predicted, their fat tormentor had not braved the storm. Instead he had drawn aside the tent flap, had stuck his head out, and was shouting orders into the darkness.

"Do not let them escape, you peladoes! Kill them, you sons of donkeys!"

Van stepped out of the darkness and silenced his bellowing by crushing his skull with a huge rock. Then they dragged Ortega out of the tent and recovered their Colt revolvers. They took a Bowie knife from the officer's belt, and a derringer from his coat pocket. Gil grabbed the dead man's pack and saddlebags from the tent, and the Texans vanished in the stormy night. Gil and Van walked for hours, unsure as to their direction. The rain continued, becoming more intense.

"We'd best travel as far as we can," said Gil, "while the rain's coverin' our trail. Once it stops, there'll be tracks Granny Austin could follow, without wearin' her spectacles. Soon as it's light enough to see anything, we'll hole up for the day."

"I just hope that fat old buzzard has somethin' in his pack that a half-starved Tejano can eat," said Van.

As captives, their rations had been scanty enough, but when the storm had struck in the early afternoon, the little food they should have had for supper had been denied them. Sometime before dawn they came upon a fast-flowing river, and for the lack of better direction, followed it. In the gray of first light they could see a distant arroyo through which the river flowed. The higher bank became a rocky abutment, and beneath a rock shelf was what appeared to be a shallow cave.

"There's the hole we're lookin' for," said Gil.

"We don't know what's in there," said Van. "Might be a grizzly."

"Maybe," said Gil, "but I'd as soon face a grizzly as the whole damn Mexican army. Keep your Colt handy, and let's take that shelter."

2

THEIR sanctuary wasn't a cave, but a recession in the arroyo wall into which dried leaves had blown. It was less than sufficient for a hibernating grizzly, but adequate to shelter and conceal the fugitive Texans. It offered protection from the incessant wind and rain, and that was enough.

"Not much of a hidin' place, if they come lookin' for us," said Van, "but thank God, it's dry. Just let me get these boots off and rub some life back into my dying feet."

"We're concealed well enough," said Gil, "considering that the rain will wipe out any trail we might have left. We've got a few chips on our side of the table. Without Mexico's mild winter, with all this rain, we'd have been frozen stiff by now."

"I wasn't impressed with Mex grub," said Van, "but compared to the nothin' at all we had for supper last night, it wasn't bad. Let's open Ortega's pack and saddlebags and see if there's anything to eat."

Van took the pack, and Gil the saddlebags. Van whistled long and low.

"What is it?" Gil asked. "Is the pack full of gold coin?"

"Better'n that," said Van. "First thing I put my hands on was a couple pairs of clean, dry socks."

"I'm ahead of you," said Gil. "In the saddlebags there's a mess of hardtack and jerked beef. Besides that, there's flint, steel, and punk, if we're ever able to risk a fire."

"I'd risk one, if we had any coffee. My God, I'd swap my half of the ranch for a pot of good, hot coffee. Anything else?"

"Powder, caps, and balls for the sleeve gun," said Gil. "There's needles, thread, fishing line, and a map of Mexico. It's the one thing we need most of all. It's hand drawn, but it'll do. Once we know where we are, we can figure how we're goin' to get to Durango."

"I'm for stayin' right here," said Van, "until this storm's done."

"We can," said Gil, "but it won't make much difference. I once read a book about Mexico. Some Spaniard wrote it, and he said that in some parts of this country, especially the rain forests, it rains nearly every day."

"Just our luck," said Van. "With the ground always muddy, we'll be leavin' tracks. They may not know where we are, but we can't be sure a company of Santa Anna's boys won't stumble onto our trail by accident. Even *we* don't know where we are. We need the sun, the stars — something — to get our own bearings."

"Move over here where the light's better," said Gil, "and let's study this map. We can use it to get some idea as to where we are."

Crunching hardtack and chewing jerked beef, the Texans sought some point of recognition on the crude map.

"After leaving Matamoros, Tamaulipas," said

Van, "we don't even know the names of the little villages we passed through."

"That won't make any difference," said Gil. "They're not on Ortega's map. The towns don't matter that much when it comes to the movement of troops, but rivers do. See how he's drawn in the rivers? After we left Matamoros, Tamaulipas, how many rivers — not countin' this one — do you remember?"

"Two."

"See this wiggly line, south of Matamoros, Tamaulipas? That has to be the first river. There, maybe fifty miles south, is the second. Just south of the second one is Salada hacienda, where we made our break. Now look at the third river. It's just about as far south of the second one as we could have stumbled through the dark, on foot. Now do you see what I'm gettin' at, and where we likely are?"

"My God," said Van, "we followed a river that runs into the Gulf of Mexico, near Tampico. Durango's to the west, near the Pacific, and we've been gettin' farther away from it. Are we ten miles west of Tampico, or a hundred?"

"That's one thing the map can't tell us," said Gil, "but if we're figurin' these rivers right, we have some sense of direction. With the wind and rain comin' out of the west, we drifted before the storm, like cattle. So all the miles we walked, followin' the break at Salada hacienda, we've been travelin' east. But once we leave here, followin' this river in the opposite direction, we'll be headin' toward Durango."

"If we follow this river as far as we can, and

26

Ortega's map is close to right, we ought to come out somewhere south of Durango."

"We won't miss it by much," said Gil. "There ain't a whole lot between Durango and the Pacific. There's Sinaloa, and to the south of it, Nayarit. They border Durango to the west, on the Pacific. If we see or smell the ocean, we'll know we've gone too far. A turn to the northeast will take us right into the south of Durango."

"I'm glad you're so good at figurin' all this," said Van. "I like to get my bearings from the stars, but these trees grow so close together, the limbs and leaves make a roof that shuts out everything but the wind and rain."

"I believe this is what the writers call a rain forest," said Gil, "and from what I've read, it's more common to central Mexico. It should lessen as we move farther north. But you're right; with this green roof over us, we won't be gettin' any help from the sun and stars. That's why it's so almighty important that we follow this river. We'll move out after dark, rain or not."

"Then I reckon we'd better get some sleep," said Van.

Exhausted, but out of the wind and rain, they had no trouble sleeping. Gil awakened first and crept near the entrance to their refuge. While there was still enough light to see, he wanted another look at the crude map. When Van spoke, his voice was startling in the stillness.

"Got any more notions as to where we are?"

"If Ortega's map is accurate, and this is the

river we think it is, we're somewhere between Tampico and San Luis Potosi," said Gil.

"Right now, all we know for sure is east from west."

"That's the straight of it," said Gil. "The nearest town is San Luis Potosi, and Zacatecas will be somewhere to the northwest. Zacatecas borders Durango on the south."

"Once we leave the river, we're goin' to have one hell of a time keeping our sense of direction in the dark."

"San Luis Potosi and Zacatecas must be fair-sized towns, else Ortega wouldn't have bothered writin' them on his map. That being the case, there ought to be some kind of trail — maybe a wagon road — between the two towns."

"If San Luis Potosi's big enough for Ortega's map," said Van, "there may be a company of Mex soldiers there. You aim to just walk in and ask the way to Zacatecas?"

"Maybe," said Gil, irritated. "You got any better ideas?"

"Sorry, brother," said Van. "Just tryin' to look ahead at what we might be up against, so's I can be ready."

"Try to look too far ahead," said Gil, "and you're likely to stumble over somethin' close by. You can't play out a hand until you see the cards you've drawn. This is a game where we can't pass or fold; we'll have to play out the string."

"Yeah," said Van, with a grim laugh. "I know. But I can't shake the feeling there's a wild card we don't know about, that when we face up our hand, the best we'll have is a pair of deuces. So let's grab the joker — otherwise known as Clay Duval — and get his neck out of whatever noose he's got it into. Hopefully, without gettin' ourselves strung up alongside him."

Gil grinned. "You've said it all. It's dark enough; let's go."

★ ★ ★

Their second night of freedom was no better than the first. Backwater from the river had filled each depression in the land, and time after time they stumbled into leafed-over bogs, finding themselves in water above their knees. Once Van got too close, the sandy bank gave way, and he took a tumble into the river itself. At dawn they found no shelter, and had to take refuge in an oak thicket on a ridge above the river.

"I wish you'd been totin' the pack," said Van, "when I took that fall in the river. It just purely ruined the rest of the hardtack. It's nothin' but soggy mush."

"We'll have to make do with the jerked beef," said Gil. "Whatever's left."

"Not much left. Today, it's dinner or supper. There ain't enough for both."

Hungry, wet, muddy, and without shelter, they found no rest. Gil tugged on his boots and got to his feet.

"Come on," he said, "and let's be on our way. I purely don't aim to just hunker here in the drizzling rain all day, and then spend another night stumbling through the dark. We need grub, and we won't find it settin' here."

They followed the river, rested occasionally, and saw nobody. In the afternoon the gloom began to lessen, and they became aware that the rain forest was thinning out. Soon they could see the low-hanging gray clouds.

"Thank God," said Van, "the sky's still up there. I know that thicket's been good cover, but I'm glad to be free of it. I feel like I've been let out of the calaboose."

Right on the heels of his words came the braying of a mule, and the Texans froze. The wind was in their faces, from the northwest, if their sense of direction was true. Finally they heard the creaking of wheels.

"Come on," said Gil quietly. "There's a wagon road or trail close by."

They turned away from the river and, bearing north, made their way to the crest of a distant ridge. In the valley below, a trail stretched toward what had to be the northwest. Almost directly below them plodded a mule drawing a cart, its two wooden wheels creaking dismally. An old man trudged beside the patient mule, while the pigs in the crude cart grunted and squealed. But the scene below held their attention for only a moment. Their eyes were following the winding trail down which the old Mexican and his mule-drawn cart had come. Far away, rising above the tree-tops, was what appeared to be pinnacles of stone. They were twin towers, red against the gray of the sky.

"It looks like side-by-side chimney rocks," said Van.

"It's likely the towers of a church," said Gil. "Some of the churches and cathedrals in Mexico were built under Spanish rule, during the fourteenth and fifteenth centuries. The steeples we're lookin' at are in or near San Luis Potosi."[1]

"Thanks to Ortega's map," said Van, "we know where we are. Now what?"

"Soon as it's dark enough," said Gil, "we're going to follow that trail. When we reach town, we're goin' to that church and talk to the padre."

"You don't think he'll call the law on us?"

"No," said Gil. "Why should he? We need food; who else can we turn to, if not the padre?"

"I don't know," said Van, and then he laughed. "Remember what Granny Austin used to say? That neither of us would ever set foot in a church until the devil was on our trail and we had nowhere else to go?"

The church towers had been visible from miles away, and by the time Gil and Van could see the lights of town, they were exhausted. For a while they just looked at the great church, uncertain as to how or if — they should approach it. The cathedral itself was dark, except for what might have been a single interior lamp that shone dimly through its massive oval windows. Next

---

[1] The first church was founded in San Luis Potosi in 1583.

to the church was a magnificent building, no less imposing than the church itself. Gil and Van approached the massive doors that must have been a dozen feet high. On the stone wall to the right and left of the doors, a globed lamp guttered. On the left hand door was a silver plaque, upon which was engraved OBISPOS PALACIO.

"The Bishop's Palace," said Gil.

He rapped the heavy door with the big brass knocker half a dozen times without response.

"Damn," said Van impatiently, "why don't they open this door? There's never been two more perfect targets than us, right between these two lamps."

Finally there was the distant, hollow sound of footsteps. One of the big doors swung back silently, and they found themselves facing a man with the high cheekbones and obsidian eyes of an Indian. He wore a dark robe and said not a word.

"The padre," said Gil. "Take us to the padre."

Still the Indian said nothing, but stepped aside, allowing them to enter the foyer. He then closed the door and retreated down the hall.

"Maybe we're supposed to follow him," said Van.

"No," said Gil, "I don't think so. We'll wait."

"How do we know somebody won't sneak out the back way and bring the law?"

"We don't," said Gil.

But they hadn't long to wait. The little man

who came down the long hall toward them wore a long black robe that reached to his sandaled feet. Except for a fringe of hair just above his ears, he was totally bald.

"*Hablar inglés?*" Gil asked.

The padre nodded. Gil told him their names and explained their reason for being in Mexico. He told of their capture by soldiers, and of their escape. He didn't mention the killing of Ortega.

"I am Father Elezondo," said the padre, "and this is the church of Guadalupe. What do you wish of me, senors?"

"The promise of your silence," said Gil, "some food, and directions to the Mendoza ranch, in the south of Durango."

"You have my promise," said the padre, "but it is late, and the cook has gone. I was about to have some hot coffee. Aside from that, I fear I can offer you only leftovers from supper. I am sorry."

"Don't be, Padre." Gil grinned.

They followed the padre to the kitchen, and when they had seated themselves at what was probably the servants' table, he poured them steaming cups of black coffee from the pot on the stove. He then set about bringing them food. He began with a haunch of roast beef and a sharp knife, bidding them cut their own portions. He brought two loaves of bread, half a hoop of cheese, and a pot of cold boiled potatoes.

"That's all there is," said the padre. He poured himself a cup of coffee, fetched a backless, three-legged stool, and joined them at the table. He said no more. There was a twinkle in his eyes as he watched them wolf down the food.

"Padre," said Van, when he could eat no more, "that's enough to make me a churchgoin' man."

"Amen to that," said Gil. "Now, if we ain't imposin' too much, what can you tell us about the Mendoza ranch?"

"Senor Mendoza is dead," said the padre. "It was a tragedy, for he was yet a young man, with a beautiful wife."

"What happened to him?" Van asked.

"He was shot to death in an ambush. The killer has never been found."

"This friend we're lookin' for is interested in the Mendoza horses," said Gil.

"Ah," said the padre, "they are hotbloods. The military swears by them. I have heard that Santa Anna himself owns three of them, and will settle for nothing less."

"What about cattle?" Gil asked. "Did Mendoza run any longhorns?"

"I do not think so, and it is strange that you should ask. Following Senor Mendoza's death, I have heard that Senora Mendoza has begun gathering a herd of longhorn cattle. But for the hide and tallow, they are worthless. Except, of course, the fierce bulls for the arena."

"How far are we from the Mendoza spread?" Van asked.

"Perhaps two hundred fifty miles," said the padre. "A terrible journey for one afoot."

"We have no choice," said Gil. "We have

34

no money to buy horses, if they were available. Besides, a pair of Tejanos buyin' horses would attract all kinds of attention, and that could be the death of us."

"I do not believe you are in danger from my people, Senor Austin," said the padre. "I do not believe the Mejicano begrudges you your independence. It is only twenty years since we ourselves were freed of Spanish rule."

"I expect you're right, padre," said Gil, "but the *politicos* in Mexico City sing a different song. As long as they send soldiers to shoot at us, we'll be shootin' back."

"It is the radicals," said the padre. "They conscript our young men, make *zapadores*[1] of them, and force them to fight for a cause in which they do not believe. I fear there will be a great war in which many of my people will die."

"I fear you are right," said Gil, "and while we have no fight with your people, your military won't leave us be. That's why we asked for a promise of silence from you, because we don't know where the soldiers are."

"I fear for you," said the padre. "Not while you are among my people, but for the time when you must cross the river back into your country. I urge you to find your friend, if he still lives, and go."

"You think he may be dead?" Van asked.

---

[1] Soldiers

"I am sorry," said the padre. "I should not have said that. I have heard rumors of a Tejano who rode south seeking the Mendoza ranch, nothing more. What I meant to say, senors, is that these are dark and bloody times when *any* Tejano riding into Mexico may die here. The hour is late. You are welcome to stay the night if you wish."

"*Mucho gracias*, Padre," said Gil, "but we should go."

"Very well," said the padre. "Northwest of town is a wagon road — actually, little more than a trail — that will take you to Zacatecas. It is a distance of perhaps 125 miles, roughly halfway between here and the Mendoza property. I regret that I cannot offer you mounts, but we are a poor people."

"We understand, Padre," said Gil. "Are you familiar with the Mendoza brand?"

"It is the Winged M," said the padre, "known throughout Mexico."

Gil and Van departed the church of Guadalupe just after midnight. The padre had insisted they take what remained of the food, along with several more loaves of bread the cook had likely baked for the next day.

Avoiding the town, they circled until they found the trail they sought. The rain had ceased, and but for a cloud bank far to the west, the sky was fair. While there was only a sliver of moon, the starlight made the difference, and they had no trouble finding their way across the plain.

"Another two hundred fifty miles afoot," said Gil. "Ten more days, at least."

"You're figurin' twenty-five miles a day. We won't make even half that, stumbling through the dark."

"Startin' tomorrow," said Gil, "we'll travel by day. We can still follow this trail, while keepin' our distance from it. Any village along the way — such as Zacatecas — we'll approach after dark. I think the padre was right. We'll be safe enough from here to the Mendoza ranch. It's when we try to leave Mexico that hell's likely to bust loose."

"That padre didn't tell us all he knows," said Van. "My ears perked up when he said Mendoza was killed from ambush. What for? Raisin' horses? Without sayin' it, the padre believes Clay may have been killed. But I reckon you noticed that."

"Yeah," said Gil, "I caught it. He almost said Clay may have been gunned down for the same reason Mendoza was. That kind of fits what Clay didn't tell us. Something spooked him. He ain't the kind to run from a fight, but he's no fool. He wouldn't hang around to eat honey while the bees are in the hive."

"It'll be just our luck," said Van, "for Clay to have cashed in his chips, and us hoofin' it halfway across Mexico for nothing."

"Oh, it won't be for nothing," said Gil grimly. "Clay Duval had his faults, but he was a man to ride the river with. If he's dead, the bastard that done him in is goin' to pay. In spades."

★ ★ ★

Gil and Van had traveled only a few miles from San Luis Obispo before halting for the night. They started early, stopping only when darkness and exhaustion overtook them. Eating sparingly of the food Father Elezondo had given them, they limited themselves to one meal a day. Near sundown of the fourth day, they paused on a ridge overlooking the village of Zacatecas.

"If the padre was levelin' with us," said Van, "we're 125 miles from the Mendoza ranch. We still have bread and cheese. You want to make do with it, or try our luck in town?"

"We'll wait for dark," said Gil, "and pass up the town. It's too near the Mendoza spread. Until we know the situation at Mendoza's, we won't know where we stand. We may have enemies we don't yet know about, and I'd as soon they don't know we're here."

They passed wide, leaving the lights of Zacatecas behind, traveling as far into the night as their weary feet would take them. They were up before first light, plodding along the dim trail that seemed to stretch endlessly to the northwest.

"If I live long enough to fork another horse," said Van, "the man takin' it will have to shoot me out of the saddle first."

"We've been afoot so long," said Gil, "we'll likely have to learn to ride all over again."

★ ★ ★

Gil and Van were five days away from Zacatecas, and two days without food. They had reached a grassy plain dominated by creosote bush and yucca. Just ahead, a welcome ribbon of greenery assured them of water. While they paused, a cow and calf appeared briefly, then quickly vanished into the brush bordering the distant stream.

"Too far away to see their markings," said Van, "but I'd give odds we're on the Mendoza spread. We're still a couple of hours away from good dark; maybe we can get there in time for supper."

"Look over yonder," said Gil, "to the northeast. Buzzards. Something's down or dead. It's a mite out of our way, but we'd better take a look."

They reached the creek, found a shallow place and crossed. There was an abundance of cattle and horse tracks. Far to the north were irregular ridges of mountains that descended gradually to the plain, their slopes clothed with the dark green of conifers. The greasewood and yucca began to thin out, giving way to oaks and several species of trees unfamiliar to the Texans. By now they were near enough to see the circling vultures clearly.

"They're waitin'," said Van. "Whatever they got their beady eyes on must still be alive."

They came upon a coulee from the low end, and it became deeper as they followed it. Rounding a turn in the gulley, they came suddenly upon a horse and rider. The horse was a magnificent black. The animal lay on its right side, its neck twisted at an awkward angle. On its left hip was a Winged M brand, and trapped beneath it was a rider who was dressed as a

Mexican vaquero but had the distinctive features of an Indian. There was a bloody gash above his right ear, and from where they stood, Gil and Van couldn't be sure the man still lived.

"We'll need another horse and a strong rope to get that dead one off of him," said Van.

"Since we're lackin' both," said Gil, "we'll have to think of something else. Maybe we can find a pole that's long enough, and strong enough to lift the horse just enough to free his leg."

But all they could find was a dead cedar sapling that had been starved off a nearby rocky slope. Van hacked away the limbs, using the Bowie they'd taken from Ortega. When they slid down into the coulee, they found it still deep in mud from recent rain.

"With all this mud," said Gil, "he might have been spared broken bones, unless he came down on some rock."

The hapless Indian was pinned in such a position that they had difficulty getting the butt end of the cedar pole under the dead horse. Frustrated, they paused in their efforts, and found the Indian's dark, expressionless eyes on them.

"*Salvar, amigo*," said Van.

Suddenly there was an unearthly screech, not unlike the scream of a woman. A dozen feet away, on a rock outcropping overlooking the coulee, crouched a huge mountain lion! The animal's attention was focused on the prey within the ditch, its long, snaky tail twitching in anticipation.

"No sudden moves," said Gil quietly. "Ease your Colt out, and when I give the word, we'll both fire. Make the first shot count; I doubt we'll ever get a second one."

The big cat roared, and they could see the rippling muscles begin to tense beneath the tawny hide.

"Now!" said Gil. "Fire!"

3

GIL and Van fired, and blending with the roar of their Colts came the welcome thunder of rifles. The fusillade caught the lion at the start of his leap, and the big cat plummeted into the coulee, where he lay still.

"Thank God for the gents with the rifles," said Van, "whoever they are. I purely don't believe we could have dropped that big devil with our Colts."

There was the clatter of galloping horses. The riflemen were approaching. The three riders reined up their horses at the brink of the coulee, and two of them had the same Indian features as the man pinned under the dead horse. The third man seemed neither Indian or Mexican, but in other respects the trio were much the same. Each man rode a spirited, hot-blooded horse, wore a high-crowned, wide-brimmed hat, and the colorful sashes and neckerchiefs of the vaquero. They sat on ornate Mexican saddles with trapaderos, and their rough-out leather *chaparrejos* were silver-studded. Gil and Van looked first into the three pairs of dark, expressionless eyes, and then into the ominous muzzles of three rifles.

"Friends," said Gil. "*Amigos*."

The Indian rider trapped under his dead horse became aware that Gil and Van might be in some danger from the newly arrived trio. The

42

Indian lifted his hand as though to stay the rifles of his three comrades, and for the first time he spoke.

"Ninguno! Ninguno! Dos Amigos!"

It made an immediate difference. The three mounted men returned their rifles to their saddle boots, and the rider who seemed neither Indian or Mexican uncoiled his lariat. He dallied it about his saddle horn and dropped the loose end into the coulee. Gil caught the rope and knotted it around the hind legs of the dead horse. Slowly the rider took up the slack, moving the animal enough for the Indian to free himself. But for the bloody gash on his head, the man seemed unhurt. Apparently without broken bones, he struggled to his knees, and Van helped him to his feet. Gil loosed the rope from the dead horse, and was about to free the saddle, when the Indian rider shook his head. While the very last thing a Texan would have done was leave his saddle, Gil and Van made no further moves, waiting. The newly freed Indian grabbed the rope, and his companions lifted him out of the coulee. The rope was then dropped a second time for Van, and a third time for Gil. Beyond a doubt they were on the Mendoza range. Each of the three horses bore a Winged M brand. For the moment, thanks to their attempted rescue, Gil and Van had been accepted as friends. The two Texans saw nothing in the dark eyes of the vaqueros except curiosity. Finally one of the men spoke.

"Tejanos?"

Gil and Van nodded. Then, in careful Spanish,

Gil attempted to explain their reason for being in Mexico, on the Mendoza range. The vaqueros listened in impassive silence. Only once did fleeting recognition touch their dark eyes, at the mention of Clay Duval's name. Once Gil had finished, without speaking a word, the four men seemed to reach a decision. The rider who had spoken to them mounted his horse, and the Indian they'd rescued from the coulee swung up behind him. Then the second and third vaqueros mounted, one of them nodding to Van, the other to Gil. Each of the Texans mounted behind one of their benefactors, the Winged M riders sent their horses trotting toward the northwest. With the three horses carrying double, the vaqueros took their time, and it was almost an hour before they came within sight of the ranch buildings.

They approached slowly enough for the Texans to fully appreciate the massive spread. The ranch house was of cedar logs; long, low, and rambling. It was isolated from the barns, corrals, and bunkhouse by stately oaks. Far beyond the house, through the trees, they could see horses grazing behind a six-rail-high pole fence. But despite the grandeur of the spread, it was momentarily lost to Gil and Van Austin. Their eyes were on the slender woman who had stepped out the door and stood waiting on the porch.

Raven-black hair curled down to her shoulders. Except for the red brocade on her bolero, and a matching red sash, she was dressed all in black. She wore a flat-crowned, narrow-brim black hat with chin thong. The stovepipe tops of her black

44

leather riding boots were circled with red stars, and her velveteen vaquero breeches looked to have shrunk since she'd put them on. Clay Duval's decision to remain in Mexico began to make sense to Gil and Van Austin. The vaqueros reined up, dismounting only after she had nodded her permission. Gil and Van dismounted, removing their hats as the riders had. The vaquero who had first spoken to Gil and Van now spoke for them all. In rapid Spanish he explained, and when he had finished, she spoke in a low, musical voice.

"So you are the Austins," she said, in English. "I am Victoria Duval."

If she had chosen her words for shock value, she wasn't disappointed. But Gil and Van said nothing, nor did the vaqueros. They were waiting to be dismissed, and she turned to them.

"Since you've met some of my riders," she said, "allow me to introduce them. This hombre," and she gestured toward the man who seemed neither Mexican or Indian, "is an Argentine gaucho. A South American cowboy. He answers to Bola, or just Bo. He has an unusual skill that you must see to believe. This," and she turned to the Indian who had been trapped in the coulee, "is Solano. The hombre to your left is Estanzio, and to your right is Mariposa."

She nodded to the four and, dismissed, they turned to the horses. The Indian, Solano, again rode double, and they headed for a distant barn.

"Supper will be ready within the hour," said Victoria. "I will show you to your quarters. You are in need of privacy, a change of clothing, soap, and hot water."

"All of that," said Gil, "and we'll be obliged. But it'll have to wait. You know why we're here. Let's set on the porch awhile, and talk about Clay Duval. I reckon we owe him that."

"Very well. He said you would come, but I expected you much sooner."

"The Mexican army changed our plans some. Where *is* Clay?"

"I do not know. He disappeared three months ago. I fear he is dead."

"Gunned down from ambush, perhaps, like Senor Mendoza?"

"Who told you that?"

"I don't reckon that matters," said Gil. "Let's just say it's no secret the late Senor Mendoza didn't cash in from old age. Now you're sayin' Clay may be dead. I'm guessing the same hombre that gunned Mendoza likely done the same for Clay, and for the same reason. Maybe he got too close to something somebody else wanted."

"Such as?"

"You, maybe," said Gil.

She slapped him. Hard. He said nothing, but his eyes chilled to blue ice and never left hers. Shaken, she turned away from him. Finally she spoke.

"I . . . I'm sorry. I had no right to do that. Forgive me. I suppose you are entitled to your doubts and suspicions."

"You are — were — Clay's wife, then?" Van asked.

"I am expecting a child," she snapped. "What do *you* think?"

She had not answered Van's question, but put them on the defensive with one of her own. It was a frustrating situation, destined to become more so as it progressed. But the tension and the silence were broken by a petulant voice from the doorway.

"Victoria, must you swoop down on every available man in the world, without allowing lesser mortals a chance?"

She wasn't much out of her teens, if that. Her dark hair was in braids, like an Indian's, and her multicolored gown reached to her sandaled feet.

"This," said Victoria, more irritated than embarrassed, "is my sister, Angelina Ruiz. Angelina, this is Gil and Van Austin."

Beyond the introduction, Victoria had little to say, assuming a tight-lipped silence. But Angelina quickly took up the slack.

"I'm so glad you're here," said the girl. "Clay was going to take us to Texas, but got himself killed before we could go."

"Almighty inconsiderate of him," said Van. "That was one of his worst faults, gettin' himself killed just when you needed him."

"Let's put this talk aside until after supper," said Gil. "Me and Van's been too long without grub. Besides, it's time we washed up, and spent a few minutes with a good razor."

"Angelina," said Victoria, barely civil, "I will

47

show the Austins to their quarters. Please see that the cook sets extra places at the table."

There was the clatter of hoofs as Solano rode out. Again he straddled a big black, but the horse was without a saddle. The Indian was going for his own rig, taking a spade with him. When he had removed his saddle, he would cave in the sandy bank of the coulee on the big black. Although his mount was lost to him, he would spare it the final indignity of becoming food for buzzards and coyotes.

* * *

It was ironic that the clothes Victoria brought Gil and Van had belonged to Clay Duval.

"I purely hate it for Clay's sake," said Van, "but we need these duds. We were just about in rags, and I'd lay odds there ain't a six-foot-five Mejicano anywhere in Mexico with two extra pairs of britches."

"We met these females less than two hours ago," said Gil. "Maybe I'm bein' some previous in my feelings, but I can't get away from the idea they aim to use us the same as they were usin' Clay."

"You got the straight of it," said Van. "But at least Angelina's honest about it. Victoria ain't as obvious, but she's proddin' us in the same old direction. She didn't come right out and *say* she expects us to take up where Clay left off, but she didn't waste any time tellin' us she's going to have a child. Now, we can't leave old Clay's kid in this godforsaken part of the world, can we?"

48

"I reckon not," said Gil, "if we're sure it's his. But was he actually married to this woman? I could believe the child's his, if there *is* one, but I'm purely havin' trouble swallowing the idea that he'd bogged himself down in double harness for the rest of his life."

"There's just one thing I'm sure of. Our old pard's roped us into one hell of a mess. If we take up where he left off, we purely can't leave these two women here and go back to Texas. Trouble is, it'll take somethin' close to a miracle just gettin' ourselves out of here alive. Taking two females along, the odds get downright scary."

"You're only lookin' at half the problem," said Gil. "I'm not sure we've been told the truth about Clay, I doubt we can trust them if we end up with our backs to the wall, and I'm having trouble believin' Clay promised to take them with him. I think what Victoria Mendoza hasn't told us would have made a difference to Clay, and I think it'll make a difference to us."

"Then you don't aim to take them to Texas?"

"I don't know," said Gil. "I'm sayin' let's don't commit ourselves one way or the other. I got me a gut feeling that if Clay's dead, whoever got him may come after us, for the same reason."

"And you aim to give him a chance."

"Exactly," said Gil. "I think we'll pick up where Clay left off, and go on making plans for this trail drive. Before it's done, I think we'll have some answers. Such as what happened to

Clay, and why Victoria's so almighty eager to leave Mexico."

There was a knock on their door. It was Angelina, calling them to supper. When Gil and Van stepped into the hall, the girl viewed their clean-shaven faces and slicked-down hair with new interest. The Texans had long been without food, and in deference to their hunger, there was no conversation during the meal. But once it was finished, Gil had questions of his own.

"In his letter," said Gil, "Clay told us he aimed to drive two hundred head of horses, and maybe five thousand longhorns to Texas. He must have had some plan. Do you know what he had in mind?"

"The year before my husband . . . died," said Victoria, "we drove a hundred head of horses and five hundred longhorn cows to Matamoros. It is from there that Santa Anna launches most of his attacks, and it is to there that his forces return for regrouping. Captives are taken there, before being sent on to Mexico City. The horses were for officers in the Mexican army, and the cows were beef to feed the soldiers and captives. We were paid well for the horses, but nothing for the cows. It was Clay's belief that we might safely drive our herds as far as Matamoros, Coahuila by having the authorities believe that these horses and cows were again being supplied for use by the army."

"But from Matamoros, Coahuila," said Van, "it's still three hundred miles to the nearest point we can cross the border."

"Clay was aware of that," said Victoria. "From

50

there, he said we would have to make a run for it."

"My God," said Gil, "how do you make a run for it with a herd of longhorns, when you're lucky to travel fifteen miles a day?"

"Maybe not that far, with the wagon," said Angelina, all too innocently.

"*Wagon?*" Gil looked from one woman to the other, in total disbelief.

"A Conestoga," said Victoria, "and we must take it. If I'm departing Mexico forever, there are some things I cannot leave behind."

"Did Clay know this," Van asked, "that you aimed to take a wagon?"

"Well . . . no," said Victoria. "We . . . never got that far, before he . . . "

"That kills Clay's plan dead in its tracks," said Gil. "How do you aim to convince the Mexican army you're only taking horses and cows to Matamoros, when you've got a Conestoga loaded to the bows with your worldly goods?"

"I don't know," said Victoria defiantly, "but I'm not going unless I can take the wagon. I'll drive it myself. You can't travel any faster than the longhorns, and I can keep up with them."

"Damn it," said Gil, leaning across the table, glaring at her, "that's not the problem, and you know it. The problem is, we can't explain the wagon, when we're only supposed to be driving horses and cows to Matamoros."

"Damn it," she said, leaning across the table, glaring back at him, "once we're past Matamoros, Clay's plan is useless, and the presence of the wagon will make no difference.

The soldiers are marched out of Mexico City, and north along the coast. Not until they reach Saltillo or Monterrey are they marched west to Matamoros. I may have all the weaknesses of a woman, but I am not so foolish I cannot read a map. We will be traveling cross-country, and we can pass to the south of Matamoros, avoiding it entirely. The real danger, with or without the wagon, lies north of Matamoros, Coahuila, before we reach the border."

It was a standoff. Her argument made sense, and the weakness in Clay's plan — if it *was* his plan — was evident. Once they were beyond Matamoros, they still lacked three hundred miles to the Rio Grande. With a herd of longhorns — if there were no stampedes, and if they were lucky — they'd need a good three weeks. But she was right — the wagon wouldn't matter.

"How many longhorns have been gathered?" Van asked.

"Something over 2500," said Victoria calmly. "I stopped my vaqueros gathering them when . . . after Clay . . . "

"Starting tomorrow," said Gil, "let's continue the hunt. How many men do you have?"

"Eleven," said Victoria.

"In the morning," said Gil, "I want you to introduce us to them. If they're going with us on this drive, then I want to know them. Provide us horses and saddles, and me and Van will work the gather with them."

With the Texans obviously planning to trail the drive Clay had proposed, and with the taking of the wagon settled, the tension diminished.

Well-fed but exhausted, Clay and Van returned to the room Victoria had prepared for them.

"You didn't mention looking for Clay's killer," said Van.

"No, and I don't aim to. You don't look for a solution from them that may be the cause of the problem. If there's anything to be learned here, I expect it to come from Victoria's riders. After tonight, I aim for us to move into the bunkhouse. By the end of this gather, if we still don't have anything to sink our teeth into, we'll have to accept the fact Clay's dead. Then we'll head for home. North, to the Rio Grande. The Bandera Trail."

★ ★ ★

Gil and Van rose well before breakfast, and were in the dining room having coffee when Victoria joined them.

"Before we meet the rest of the riders," said Gil, "I have a question. Are they aware of the purpose of this gather, that they're to be part of a trail drive to Texas? A drive that could, and likely will, put them at odds with the Mexican army?"

"I told them before we began the first gather of the longhorns," said Victoria. "Clay said they must be told. But now . . . "

"Now," said Gil, "they must be told that we aim to finish what Clay began. I want to know that we can depend on them."

"I'll talk to them," said Victoria, "and see that they understand you and Van are Clay's

53

friends, and are taking up where he left off. Is there anything else you wish me to do?"

"Tell them we'll be bunking with them," said Van.

"Yes," said Gil. "That's important. In Texas, we don't assume the role of patron. We don't distance ourselves from our riders."

"Very well," said Victoria, "but you are making a mistake. These men are unfamiliar with customs in your country. They will still regard you as the *patrono*, and your obvious efforts to become one of them may distance you from them all the more."

"Maybe," said Gil, "but we'll risk it."

It was impossible not to be impressed with the Mendoza ranch. Near the bunkhouse was a cook shack, with an adjoining room. It was crude, with benches and rough-hewn tables, but well-constructed. The cook was an ancient old Mexican with a gimp leg, introduced only as Ghia. He nodded but said nothing. Gil and Van followed Victoria into the rustic dining room just as the riders were finishing their breakfast. The men hastened to their feet when Victoria came in, resuming their seats when she nodded. Silently, expectantly, they waited. The cook listened from the kitchen. Victoria began by introducing Gil and Van. She then told of their plans to continue the gathering of longhorns, and of the eventual trail drive. She paused, inviting them to speak, but they remained silent. The three Indian riders and the Argentine sat at one table, and the seven Mexican vaqueros at the other.

"You've met Estanzio, Mariposa, Solano, and Bo," said Victoria, and she turned to the second table. "The four hombres on the bench nearest the wall are Ramon Alcaraz, Juan Alamonte, Manuel Armijo, and Domingo Chavez. Their *companeros* on the other side of the table are Pedro Fagano, Vicente Gomez, and Juan Padillo."

Again the men rose to their feet. Gil and Van stepped forward, offering their hands. At first nobody moved, and when they did, it was with some reluctance. They were unaccustomed to such familiarity with the *patrono*. Bo, the Argentine, was the first to take Gil's hand, and then Van's. Slowly the others followed, not because they found the custom acceptable, but felt it was expected of them. Last, and most reluctant of all, were the Indian riders. Solano came first, and then Estanzio and Mariposa. Finally Gil spoke to them all in careful Spanish, striving to be as friendly as he knew how. But there seemed a wall of reserve, perhaps insurmountable, and Victoria's thin, "I told you so" smile wasn't lost on him.

"Now," said Victoria, when they faced the first rays of the rising sun, "we come to a more pleasant task. You must have horses, and you are welcome to any of those stalled in the barn. There are six that I know of, each of them Indian-gentled. It will be up to you to accustom them to the saddle, and finally to your weight. There are extra saddles in the tack room, serviceable, but without the ornamentation so dear to the heart of the vaquero. Before you begin the gather, you will need *chaparrejos*. I will see that you have them by the time your mounts are ready for the saddle."

"You say they're Indian-gentled," said Van. "Who's responsible for that?"

"Estanzio and Mariposa, in part, but mostly Solano."

Victoria seemed tired, out of sorts, and returned to the house. Gil and Van continued on to the barn, anxious to see the famous blooded Mendoza horses. They were not disappointed. There were four blacks and two grays, all fourteen to sixteen hands, none of them under twelve hundred pounds.

"I thought Clay Duval was a fool to risk coming here," said Van, "but seein' these horses, I feel like a fool for not comin' with him. My God, what won't these beauties be worth back in Texas!"

"Maybe our lives, gettin' 'em there," said Gil. "The more I see of this ranch, especially these horses, the more I want the answer to a question Victoria purely ain't going to like. With a ranch like this — these horses, and longhorn cattle for the taking — what kind of damn fool would give it up?"

"Once we know the answer to that," said Van, "I reckon we'll know why Senor Mendoza was ambushed, and probably what happened to Clay. But I don't look for any help from Victoria. Somethin' ain't right between her and Angelina, and I'm bettin' that little filly could tell us plenty."

"However we go at this situation," said Gil,

"we always come back to these females. There's one thing that's botherin' me more than the trail drive past the Mex army, back to Bandera range. Granted we get back to Texas alive, what'n hell will we do with these women? If Clay actually married Victoria, then he had a *reason* for takin' her, without Angelina bein' a threat. What reason do we have for taking either of them, except to finish what Clay started?"

Van sighed. "It's like grasping a porcupine. Where do you start, when coming to grips with such a problem? We purely don't have the edge Clay had. If he was married to this woman, then he had a claim to the horses and long-horns. We don't have that claim, brother, unless you're willin' to take old Clay's place with Victoria."

"Me? Why not you?"

"She's too old for me," said Van with a grin. "She must be pushin' thirty."

"Well, hell," said Gil, "you'll be twenty-eight in June."

"But you'll be twenty-nine in April; that gives you first claim. The firstborn has the birthright."

"I'm touched," said Gil, "but don't do me any favors. We know Mendoza's dead, and suspect Clay is, and they may have shared a common problem. They got too close to Victoria. Remember, Granny Austin always said disasters come in threes. I'm startin' to believe that."

"Then let's talk ourselves a deal with Victoria before we start this cow hunt. She finds out we want the horses and cows, but not her, she'll likely say to hell with this drive. We'll end up takin' the Bandera Trail afoot."

"I don't think so," said Gil. "Like I said, she's got some reason for leavin' here, and I don't look for her to share it with us. Remember what the padre at San Luis Obispo told us? This is a horse ranch. Mendoza never bothered with longhorns, but once he was dead, and Clay stepped in, Victoria sets about gatherin' a herd of longhorns. Why?"

"She wants the hell out of Mexico," said Van, "and she played up Clay's crazy idea of driving a herd of Spanish longhorns to Texas."

"She still wants out of Mexico," said Gil, "and for the same reason. I can't shake my gut feeling that it was Clay's planning to take her away that may have got him ambushed."

"Then if Clay's dead, we can't tie that back to Mendoza's ambush," said Van. "Mendoza wasn't planning to take Victoria away. If Mendoza's ambush ain't somehow related to Clay's disappearing, then we could spend the rest of our lives in Mexico, barking up one wrong tree after another."

"Like I've already said, if we can't reach some sensible conclusion, where Clay's concerned, then we'll just have to fold and back out of the game. But if we're taking Victoria Mendoza-Duval to Texas, then we'll make it worth our while."

"Then let's settle the price before we get in over our heads," said Van. "But we can't take her horses. What do you aim to ask for?"

"Clay came here looking for breeding stock,

58

so I think we're entitled to that. That, and the longhorns."

"I reckon that might satisfy Victoria," said Van, "but where does little sister figure into this? Does Angelina share Victoria's reason for wantin' out of Mexico?"

"I don't know, and I don't care," said Gil. "She's too young for me. You can fight with her, while I argue with Victoria. You saw the two of them clawing at one another tonight. Let's just let the situation fester awhile. It may come to a head long before we take the trail."

Their discussion of their dilemma ended when Solano came into the barn. The slatted sides of the stalls went only head high, and one of the blacks nickered a welcome as the Indian came near. Solano tousled the horse's mane and nodded to Gil and Van. Gil pointed to the black and then to the Indian.

"Him Solano *caballo*," said the Indian.

"Solano's?" Gil asked. He pointed to the horse, then to the Indian.

But Solano shook his head, pointed to Gil, then to the black horse.

"He gentled the black," said Van, "and wants you to have him."

Van pointed to the horse, then to Gil, and nodded understanding. Then he pointed to himself, and gestured in the general direction of the other horses. Was there another animal that Solano had gentled? There was. The Indian went to the third stall, and received an eager nicker from another of the blacks. He pointed to the horse and then to Van. Then, without a

59

word, he left them with their new mounts.

"We've reached Solano," said Gil, "and through him, we'll win the others."

"Maybe this trail drive ain't so impossible, after all," said Van. "Clay might have known somethin' that's just gettin' through to us. That Indian knows his horses. He'll make a damn good Texan."

4

MARCH 2, 1843. Durango County, Mexico. Gil and Van found the bunkhouse more to their liking than the Mendoza ranch house. The riders slept on thin, straw-filled ticks spread over two-inch-wide rawhide strips, latticed to a cedar pole frame. While the Austins moving into the bunkhouse had surprised the riders, there was yet another surprise in store for them. Although Ramon Alcaraz had been segundo, it was expected that Gil or Van would assume that position. But the Texans took a first step toward winning the trust of the Mendoza riders.

"Ramon," said Gil, in Spanish, "you will continue as segundo. Go ahead with the gather of longhorns. We will join you when our horses are ready."

Gil and Van spent nine days getting to know their new mounts, allowing the animals to become accustomed to their weight and to the saddles. Ramon had begun to warm to the Texans, speaking briefly to them at the end of each day's gather. While Solano rarely spoke, he seemed to approve of the manner in which the Texans treated the horses he had gentled. Once the blacks had accepted their saddles, Gil and Van took to riding the plains, familiarizing themselves with the range.

"There are thousands of wild cows in the *matorral* of Coahuila, Chihuahua, and Durango," Victoria had told them. "The beasts hide in the lagoons and marshes of the Bolson de Mapini."

To the west, paralleling one another, Gil and Van could see separate chains of mountains. The farthest they identified as the majestic Sierra Madres. But the nearest, into whose foothills the Texans rode, were not familiar. The peaks seemed to go on forever, wandering north, toward Chihuahua.[1]

The first day Gil and Van rode out to the gather, the outfit was working the Mendoza range to the west, toward Sinaloa. The longhorns sought the marshes and the brushy banks of the stream, where it was impossible for a rider to swing a lariat. Thus half the outfit rode the thickets, flushing the longhorns into the open, where other riders could rope the brutes. At noon they swapped. Those fighting the brush became the ropers, while the ropers took their turn riding the thickets. Ramon saw the Texans coming and lifted his hand in greeting. Gil and Van trotted their horses to meet him. Silently the vaquero pointed toward a pair of riders waiting for a quarry to be flushed from a thicket. The lead rider would drop a loop over the cow's horns, while his backup man would rope the animal's hind legs. The cow would

---

[1] The Continental Divide

be thrown to the ground, held helpless as the trained cow horses kept the ropes taut. With piggin string the lead rider would quickly bind the cow's front legs, while the backup rider bound the animal's hind legs in the same fashion. The cowboys then removed their lariats, leaving the furious longhorn to exhaust itself to the extent it could be led. Suddenly a longhorn burst from the chaparral, and the Texans witnessed what Ramon had wished them to see.

The cowboys lit out in pursuit of the fleeing longhorn, and the backup rider was Bo. While the lead rider prepared his throw for a horn loop, what the Argentine swung above his head was definitely not a lariat. Victoria had told them the gaucho possessed an unusual talent, and as they saw it come into play, the Texans could only agree. It was timed to perfection. As the lead rider's loop settled over the cow's horns, the gaucho device Bo had loosed snared the longhorn's hind legs, and the animal was slammed to the ground in a cloud of dust. Bo's talent was a daring alternative to a rope. But while his bola effectively caught the cow's hind legs and threw the brute to the ground, Bo lacked the safety of a taut lariat dallied about his saddle horn. While the bola entangled the longhorn's hind legs, they could still flail dangerously about, capable of crushing a rider's skull or breaking his bones. But with startling swiftness, Bo was out of the saddle. With piggin string in his teeth, he caught up the longhorn's tangled hind legs and bound them with the rawhide thong. Again their timing was amazing, as the lead rider bound the cow's front legs, finishing at precisely the moment Bo did. They allowed the longhorn to thrash around for a few moments, until the bola could safely be removed from the animal's hind legs. The gaucho waited, bola in his hand, as Ramon, Gil, and Van rode up. Ramon pointed to the bola, then to Gil and Van. Bo grinned, holding the contraption up for Gil and Van to see.

It consisted of three lengths of braided rawhide, each perhaps half a dozen feet in length, and joined at one end. At each of the three loose ends was a heavy leather pouch, each containing what appeared to be a smooth, round stone, or iron ball. Swung above a rider's head, loosed at just the right moment, it could hopelessly entangle a cow's hind legs. Gil held out his hand, and the gaucho passed him the bola. The Texan took hold of it where the lengths of rawhide joined, and almost dropped it. It was heavier than it looked, and he returned it to Bo, grinning his appreciation for the gaucho's unusual skill. Some of the other vaqueros had ridden up in time to see Gil almost drop the bola, and they seemed amused at the Texan's look of surprise. It was unexpected, unplanned, but yet another opportunity for the Mendoza riders to become more at ease with Gil and Van Austin. Ramon and the outfit returned to the gather, while Gil and Van continued their northerly ride. They reined up at a fast-flowing stream, allowing their horses to drink.

"If we're not off Mendoza range," said Van, "we will be soon. If we're to believe what Victoria says, everything north of her spread is part of the Valverde grant, and Valverde ain't the friendly, neighborly kind."

"Yeah," said Gil, "she seemed almighty anxious for us to know that this Valverde ain't one of her favorite people, and that the late Senor Mendoza was gunned down on Valverde land."

"So we're supposed to shy away from Valverde," said Van. "Why? Is she afraid Valverde will have us gunned down before we can get the Senora Victoria Mendoza-Duval safely out of Mexico? Or does she fear we're likely to learn somethin' from Valverde we're not supposed to know?"

"Maybe some of both," said Gil.

So suddenly did the Indian rider appear, the Texans were caught off guard. But Solano held up his hand, and they relaxed. The Indian nodded, trotting his horse ahead of them, looking back to see that they followed. They had ridden no more than a mile or two when Solano reined up and dismounted. There was something he wanted the Texans to see, and they swung out of their saddles. They were in a shaded valley, and the ground was soft from recent rain. The tracks were only hours old, and the single horseman had ridden south, toward the Mendoza ranch. Solano pointed south, and Gil spoke.

"*Malo hombre*, Solano?"

"Senor Valverde," said Solano.

Before they could question him further, Solano swung into his saddle and kicked his horse into a lope.

"It's a safe bet," said Van, "that Senor Valverde is on his way to the Mendoza ranch."

"So are we," said Gil. "If Mendoza was ambushed on Valverde land, then why is Valverde welcome on Victoria's spread?"

"We don't know that he is," said Van. "All we're sure of is that he's headed that way. Maybe Victoria will greet him with a shotgun."

"Somehow I doubt it," said Gil. "Solano's pointin' us toward something we need to know, something we haven't been told. I reckon it'll be to our advantage if we meet Senor Valverde in Victoria's presence."

"I expect we'll be about as welcome as a pair of bastards at a family reunion."

"I'm countin' on that," said Gil. "Let's ride."

★ ★ ★

Lorenzo Esteban Valverde rode south, his thin lips set in a grim line. He was a small man in every sense, standing but an inch over five feet. His high-heeled riding boots didn't add enough to his short stature to make any difference. He was barely forty years old, yet his hair had begun to thin on top, and he rarely removed his hat unless circumstances demanded it. He had the thin face and the furtive eyes of a weasel. His mother had died while he was young, leaving him at the mercy of a less-than-tolerant father. His mother had named him Lorenzo, and he had always hated it, preferring his middle name, Esteban. But for thirty years his father had referred to him only as Lorenzo. He always accentuated the first syllable so that it came out 'LOW-renzo,' a constant reminder of the young man's unimposing stature. When the elder Valverde had died, his only son had felt no remorse. Finally, if only by inheritance, he had become the *patrono*.

Suddenly, Esteban Valverde was jolted back to reality by the nicker of a horse. He reined up. Angelina Ruiz trotted her horse out of a stand of scrub oak. She wore pants and faded shirt, riding astraddle, like a man. She reined up, hooked one leg around her saddle horn, staring at him silently. He could read nothing in her dark eyes, unless it was contempt. He rode on, thinking of Angelina. She was a good ten years younger than her sister, possessing an innocence that Victoria would never see again. If, indeed, she ever had. Angelina was but a snip of a girl, but there were times when she seemed older, wiser, and more the woman than Victoria. When Clay Duval had disappeared, it had been Angelina who had gone looking for him. When it suited his purpose, Valverde decided, he would tell the girl what had become of the foolish Tejano. Drawing near the ranch, he put Angelina out of his mind. He had little choice. Victoria waited for him on the porch, and there was no welcome in her eyes. When he was close enough to hear, she spoke.

"Turn that horse around, Senor Valverde, and get off my range. You are not welcome here."

"I was welcome enough," he sneered, "when your sainted Antonio was haunting the bordellos of Mexico City."

"You were not man enough to steal me from him, so you had him shot in the back. You're a treacherous little beast."

"You are far short of the blessed virgin, yourself," he snapped. "Your husband was not dead a month, and you were sleeping with a gringo, a Tejano."

"He was more a man than you and Antonio combined," she said, "because I am expecting his child. You killed Clay Duval, didn't you?"

"Would it matter if I said I did not?"

"It wouldn't to me," she said bitterly. "I wouldn't believe you as far as I could walk on water. But it might make a difference to his friends. They are here to gather cattle, and if you had anything to do with the murder of their friend Clay Duval, I pity you."

"That's why I am here," he said. "Because of Duval's Tejano friends. Through your dealing with them, you are risking the ire of the Mexican government, and the gringos are risking their lives. They must leave Mexico while they can. If they can."

"I'll let you convince them of that," said

Victoria. "They're coming."

Gil and Van trotted their horses into the yard. They only nodded to Victoria. Their eyes were on Valverde. It was Victoria who spoke.

"Gil and Van, this is Senor Lorenzo Esteban Valverde. Senor Valverde, this is Gil and Van Austin. Senor Valverde brought a message, and since it concerns you Tejanos, I will allow him to deliver it himself."

The Texans eyed Valverde in silence. His saddle was silver-studded, as was his pistol belt. He wore a dark suit, white shirt, a flaming red tie, and highly polished riding boots. Ill at ease, he backstepped his horse until he faced the Texans. Then he spoke.

"I am suggesting that you leave Mexico immediately, for Victoria's sake, and for your own. The Mexican authorities will be harsh on her if she is caught harboring Tejanos."

Gil kneed his horse uncomfortably close and, as he spoke, looked the Mexican in the eye.

"You're hidin' behind a woman's skirts, Valverde, and threatening us with the Mexican army. Why don't you stand up on your hind legs and say what you really mean? That any man gettin' too close to Victoria risks bein' shot in the back by you or one of your hired gun hawks?"

It was the kind of deliberate insult a man couldn't ignore. Esteban Valverde went for his gun, but the weapon never left his holster. He hadn't seen Gil Austin's hand move, yet he found himself looking into the black bore of the Texan's Colt. Cold sweat beaded Valverde's brow, and he moved his hand carefully away from the butt of his gun. He seethed with shame and fury, for he owed Gil Austin his life. The Texan could have shot him dead. Briefly his eyes touched Victoria's, and he could see the laughter in them. Damn her, she knew what this was costing him! It was Gil Austin who broke the silence.

"You came here with a warning for us, Valverde, now I'm going to send you home with one of your own. We came to Mexico lookin' for Clay Duval. Whether we find him or not, we aim to get somethin' out of the trip. We'll be taking a herd of longhorns back to Texas, and our business here is no business of yours. We're not in the line of march for Santa Anna's troop movements, so the Mexican army shouldn't be a problem until we're near the border. If soldiers show up here, we'll know who sent them — you, Valverde, and before I leave Mexico, I'll personally gutshoot you."

"You are dead men," said Valverde, with as much contempt as he could muster. "Driving a herd of longhorn cows through the wilds of Mexico is the work of a dozen good riders."

"I have promised them the loan of my riders as far as the border," said Victoria.

"You are *still* dead men," said Valverde, with obvious relish. "Santa Anna is a vengeful man. On the eleventh of February last, 176 captive Tejanos escaped near Salada hacienda. Two Mexican officers were killed. Seventeen of the Tejanos were never recaptured, and Santa Anna will have no trouble believing the two of you are part of that elusive seventeen. Already there is a price on your heads."[1]

"We'll take our chances," said Gil. "Just see that you remember my warning. If the soldiers find us on their own, that's one thing, but if they find us with your help, you're dead. Now ride out, and don't come back. Next time you reach for a pistol, I'll kill you."

When Valverde had ridden away, Gil and Van dismounted.

"He is a dangerous man," said Victoria.

"I'd give some long odds," said Van, "that he had Senor Mendoza ambushed, and that he knows what happened to Clay."

"With that in mind," said Gil, turning

---

[1] Of the 176 Texans who escaped near Salada hacienda (south of Matamoros, Tamaulipas) all but seventeen were captured within a few days. Furious, Santa Anna ordered one man executed for each of the seventeen who remained free. Prisoners were forced to draw lots from a jar. There were 176 beans; 159 were white, and seventeen were black, for death. The 159 Texans who drew white beans were forced to watch the merciless execution. Their seventeen doomed comrades were herded into a compound, tied together, and shot in the back by Mexican soldiers.

to Victoria, "I reckon it's time you told us what your relationship is with Valverde. Since there's a better than average chance he murdered your husband, and likely disposed of Clay, why are you on a first name basis with the little sidewinder?"

"He was crushed when I married Antonio," she said, "and I felt sorry for him. Nothing more."

"Sorry," said Van, "but I don't believe that, Senora Mendoza."

"Neither do I," said Gil, "and it *is* Mendoza, isn't it?"

"Damn you," she shouted, "you're just like Clay. He — "

"He wanted to know what kind of hold Valverde has on you," said Gil.

"Yes," she said, refusing to look at him. "He said unless I . . . left here, he wanted nothing more . . . to do with me."

"Not even after you told him about the child," said Van. She kept her head down, saying nothing.

"There is no child," said Gil. "There never was."

"No!" she snapped, turning on him. "He was a perfect gentleman, damn him! Like you, he slept in the bunkhouse, and when he wasn't with the vaqueros and Indians, he was with the horses. He gave me nothing. No — "

"No hold over him," said Van.

"No!" she cried in fury. "He thought there was something between me and Esteban

72

Valverde. Only when I promised to leave here, to go with him, did he write, asking your help. He had begun to believe in me, and then — "

"Then Valverde got to him," said Van.

"I don't know," she said. "He swears he didn't shoot Clay, or have it done."

"If Valverde killed Mendoza to get to you," said Gil, "he wouldn't hesitate to kill again, for the same reason. Was that your only feeling for Clay — just a means of escaping Velverde?"

It was a brutal question, and he expected her to either ignore it or to explode in anger. But she surprised him.

"You Tejanos are very blunt," she said. "Clay was like that. He hated pretense, and now that you have met Esteban Valverde, I suppose nothing will suffice, short of the truth. I despise the man. He has hounded me since I was fifteen. I thought I was free of him, once I had married Antonio Mendoza, but I was not. Antonio ate, slept, lived, and breathed horses. So great was his skill with them, he was wined and dined in Mexico City. The military swore by the Mendoza horses, and Antonio delivered them to outposts all over Mexico."

"And I reckon Valverde took to comin' around, when he knew Mendoza was away," said Gil.

"Yes. I suppose I was flattered, but I had no intention of becoming involved with him. I don't even like him. But he refused to leave me alone. When Antonio was killed, Esteban Valverde became such a pest, I knew I must be rid of him."

"That's about when Clay Duval showed up," said Van.

"Yes," she admitted, "and when it came to horses, I saw a lot of Antonio in Clay."

"But Clay wasn't so blinded by the horses," said Gil, "that he couldn't see this problem with Esteban Valverde. You aimed to use Clay to escape Valverde."

"Of course I did," she snapped. "But I wasn't expecting Clay to do it for nothing, anymore than I'm expecting you to."

"I reckon," said Van, "it's a good time to ask what you have in mind for us, once you're in Texas."

"What do you *want*?"

Van looked at Gil, and Gil spoke.

"The horses we're riding, some breeding stock, and the longhorns."

"What choice have I, except to remain here, to be hounded by Esteban Valverde? But what of me? Is there a place for a single woman, where you are taking me?"

"You won't be a single woman for long," said Van. "There are few women on the frontier."

"But we still have to get there," said Gil, "and Esteban Valverde strikes me as a vengeful bastard. I wouldn't put it past him alerting the Mexican army, just for the hell of it."

"Don't allow him the opportunity," said Victoria. "Play by his rules. Stalk him, and when the opportunity presents itself, kill him."

★ ★ ★

The following morning, Gil and Van joined the Mendoza riders as they continued beating the brush for wild longhorns. A three-year-old bull had just been run out of a thicket, and lit out across the plains, Juan Padillo and Mariposa in pursuit. Padillo's lariat snaked out, snaring the animal with a perfect horn loop. Riding backup, Mariposa was about to cast his underhand loop for the hind legs when disaster struck. The rut was only inches deep, but the lip of it crumbled under the forefeet of Mariposa's horse. The animal stumbled, rolled headlong, and the Indian barely managed to free himself from the saddle. That left the treacherous bull caught only by a horn loop. His hind legs were free, his tail was up, and killing was on his mind. Juan Padillo could loose his horn dally, saving himself and his horse, but what of the hapless Indian? Mariposa was struggling to his feet. Gil and Van were the nearest riders, and they urged their horses into a run.

"Get another loop on him," shouted Gil, "and hold him steady. I'll come in from behind and try to throw him."

Van swung his lariat, made his throw, and settled a second loop over the bull's horns. Van's horse backstepped, taking up the slack, while Padillo's horse did the same. The furious bull bucked, bellowed, pawed the ground, and hooked the empty air with his lethal horns. Gil rode as near as he dared, dodging the bull's flailing hind legs, and launched himself from the saddle. He locked his arms around the brute's horns and slid to the ground, twisting the animal's neck. Twice the bull flung its huge head, and twice Gil's feet left the ground. A third vicious toss of the head would have broken his grip. But slowly, surely, he forced the bull to the ground, and it flopped down in a cloud of dust. Quickly, another rider secured the brute's hind legs, while Juan Padillo tied the forelegs. Gil rolled free and got to his feet, unharmed but for cuts and bruises. Mariposa joined them, leading his horse, both of them limping. The Indian had a bloody nose, but he grinned at Gil. None of them spoke, but words weren't necessary. Nobody had been seriously hurt, but with a rider down and a bull loose, every man was aware of what might have happened. It didn't matter that some of them were Indian, some Mexican, and some American. It was a thing that drew them together, further diminishing their differences, making them an outfit.

Riding back to the ranch, they came up on some enormous gray horses grazing along a creek.

"My God," said Van, "look at the size of them! They got feet as big as dishpans, and there ain't a one of the six under sixteen hands."

"B'long Senora Mendoza," said Ramon. "Wagon hoss. All wagon hoss."[1]

---

[1] Conestoga horses were bred especially to pull the Conestoga wagon. The breed, now extinct, has been traced back to Flemish stallions that carried knights in full armor. William Penn is said to have sent the first stallions to Pennsylvania to be bred to Virginia mares. The big horses weighed 1800 pounds or more, averaging sixteen hands high. A Conestoga wagon required three teams. The front team was the lead team, the middle one was the swing team, and the rear one the wheel team. A Conestoga wagon weighed 4000 pounds.

5

APRIL 5, 1843. The Mendoza ranch, Durango County, Mexico.

By Ramon's tally, their herd had grown to three thousand longhorns, more than half of which were cows. But there were other duties. The primary responsibility of the Indian riders was the gentling of horses, and each day, one of the men was excused from the roundup. When it came Solano's turn, Gil and Van left the gathering of longhorns to watch the Indian work with the new horses. While the Texans had a genuine desire to observe his skill, they were hopeful Solano might further enlighten them as to Clay Duval's fate.

Solano began with half a dozen unbroken horses, penning them in a breaking corral, so that he could get to them without resorting to a rope. Choosing the animal he wished to work with, he patiently stalked the horse, talking "horse talk." Gil and Van watched Solano spend two hours "talking" to the horse, seeking to overcome its fear. This was a big gray, who shone silver in the morning sun, and the Indian's goal seemed to be simply to get his hands on the horse. Finally Solano isolated the gray, backing him into a corner of the corral. Still the Indian had nothing but his bare hands, and he held them out, palms up, as though to reassure the horse.

The conclusion was inevitable. The animal must accept Solano's overtures, or stomp him to bloody pulp. The horse nickered, rearing, the powerful hoofs poised to strike. But Solano stood his ground, unmoving, his hands outstretched. Slowly, almost reluctantly, the big gray lowered the lethal hoofs to the ground, and stood there trembling. The Texans could see the powerful muscles twitching beneath the silvery coat.

"My God," said Van, in awe. "That took guts."

"Not really," said Angelina, who had approached silently, on foot. "One doesn't fear a friend who means no harm. The horse had the power to kill, to protect himself, yet chose not to. He recognized a friend. Only an enemy would have feared him."

The truth of her words was evident, and she said no more. Solano had his hands on the big gray, and the horse had snaked his head around, sniffing the Indian. Angelina laughed. They looked at her curiously, and she spoke.

"Victoria was always furious with Clay, because he spent every minute of his free time with Solano, usually here in the horse pens."

"Solano won't talk about Clay," said Gil. "Why don't you tell us what you know?"

"I can tell you nothing that you don't already know or suspect. Clay is beyond your help. Until you are free of Mexico, you will be riding in the very shadow of death. *Vaya con Dios.*"

With that, she was gone. The Texans looked

at one another, and it was Van who spoke.

"That young lady purely ain't plannin' to go to Texas with us."

"No," said Gil, "she has plans of her own, I reckon. Alive or dead, I'd say Clay Duval's a hell of a lot luckier than we thought."

★ ★ ★

Angelina Ruiz paused on a ridge overlooking the Valverde spread. Self-consciously, she turned in the saddle, studying her back trail. Satisfied, she trotted her horse down the hill toward the ranch house. The trail passed through a pine thicket, and when she emerged from it, there were two riders behind her. Quickly they caught up, one on her right, the other on her left. They kept pace, saying nothing. She cut her eyes to one side and then to the other, until she could see them. They were a hard-eyed pair, armed with saddle guns and pistols. Angelina rode on, looking straight ahead. Before they reached the house, hounds began baying. Beyond the house, near the barn, other riders appeared. Esteban Valverde had more riders than he needed, more than he could afford, but they enhanced his sense of power. Valverde, alerted by the hounds, waited on the porch.

"Ah," he said. "The beautiful Angelina. To what am I indebted for your presence? You have always gone to great lengths to pretend I didn't exist."

"I want to know something only you can tell

80

me," she said, ignoring the sarcasm. "Where is Clay Duval?"

"How would I know?"

"Because one of Victoria's Indian riders told me," she said. "Your men took him away, belly down over his saddle."

"He's been gone for months," said Valverde. "Why the sudden interest in a nondescript gringo?"

"Perhaps I am only now discovering that Victoria does not want him."

"And you do? *Por Dios*," he sighed piously, "what does this Tejano possess that drives women mad?"

Angelina bit her lip, restraining her anger, but said nothing.

"So one man is not enough for Victoria." Valverde chuckled. "She now has two fugitive Tejanos, and you are seeking the old one. Suppose I *did* know the whereabouts of the missing gringo; what are you prepared to offer me for the information?"

"What do you want?"

"Come into the house," he said, with an evil smirk. "Perhaps I can think of something."

★ ★ ★

April 25, 1843. The Mendoza ranch, Durango County, Mexico.

Nobody missed Solano until the outfit rolled out for breakfast. Then they discovered the Indian's few belongings were gone, and so was his horse. The outfit was finishing a silent,

81

somber meal, when Victoria came in.

"Have any of you seen Angelina this morning?"

Nobody said anything for a moment. Gil was the first to respond to her question.

"No," he said. "Have you looked to see if her horse is gone?"

"I have," said Victoria, "and it is. So are some of her clothes."

"Then she's with Solano," said Gil. "He left sometime during the night, taking his roll."

"Damn her!" said Victoria angrily. "Slipping off in the night, with an ignorant Indian!"

"We could trail 'em a ways," said Van, "and get some idea where they're headed."

"Don't bother!" snapped Victoria. "She's old enough to make her own foolish mistakes. Finish the gather, so we can begin the trail drive. I want to leave this godforsaken country."

Far to the south, Solano and Angelina trotted their horses, beginning a quest that might be in vain, and from which they might not return.

★ ★ ★

Esteban Valverde sought out two of his men he had come to rely on.

"To the south of the Mendoza ranch," he told them, "riders are working the brush around the marshes and rivers, gathering longhorn cows for a trail drive north. Watch the gather, but do not allow yourselves to be seen. When it is near the time for the drive to begin, I wish to know."

When the riders had gone, Esteban Valverde

sat with his booted feet on the kitchen table, brooding. Since the day he had taken over the ranch, he had been financially destitute, the result of his trust in a double-crossing woman. Now, he vowed, he would soon take what was his, and Victoria Ruiz-Mendoza was going to pay. He did not fault himself, that he had virtually bankrupted the Valverde ranch, systematically stealing its wealth from his ailing father. The elder Valverde had spent the last several years of his life virtually blind. Esteban, wishing to know where he stood, had taken advantage of the old man's affliction. To his horror, he had found a will naming his uncle — his father's brother — as eventual executor. And there would be no altering it, for there was a letter from the despised uncle, and he had a copy. Within that will had been a provision for Esteban to have an "allowance," doled out at his uncle's discretion! Even in death the elder Valverde had made provisions for Esteban to remain a *lacayo*.

So Esteban Valverde had taken to converting every possible asset to Mexican silver. Then he had met Victoria Ruiz. Wishing to seem resourceful and bold in her eyes, he had shared his secret with her. Victoria *had* been impressed, assured him she had a perfect hiding place for the treasure. Once the old man was gone and the domineering uncle took over, Esteban and Victoria would be married. But as long as the elder Valverde was alive, Esteban would remain at the ranch, picking its bones as clean as he safely could. But it hadn't worked out as he had planned. Just weeks before Esteban's father had died, Victoria Ruiz had suddenly married a handsome Spaniard, Antonio Mendoza. Laughingly, she had told the stunned Esteban his stolen treasure had been her dowry, that it had been spent to stock the Mendoza horse ranch!

But the worst was yet to come. When the domineering uncle took over the Valverde ranch, little remained. Esteban caught hell for something he could not, dared not, explain. He got nothing but a bunk, his meals, and a hard way to go. But cruel fate wasn't finished with young Esteban Valverde. Six months after his father's death, the tight-fisted uncle died in his sleep. Every peso Esteban had stolen would have safely, legally, been his, had he but waited a few weeks! Now he had no idea where the silver was, but he was sure Victoria still had it. He saw her as a treacherous bitch who would betray any man, so he doubted Antonio Mendoza had known of the treasure. But Victoria had felt safe with him, and when he was gone, she had turned to the Tejano, Clay Duval. There seemed no end to her resourcefulness. Now that Duval was out of the way, his troublesome friends had taken over. Victoria Mendoza was using the Austins to get her out of Mexico, out of his reach, and she planned to take his silver with her. But she would not, Valverde vowed, if he had to kill her, and every man who rode with her!

★ ★ ★

84

Solano's departure had a sobering effect on the outfit. Without saying anything to Victoria, Gil and Van circled the Mendoza spread to the south until they found the faint trail of the two horses.

"They're ridin' out on the same trail we followed from Zacatecas," said Van. "I reckon Solano knows more'n he told us, but what do you think of him and the girl lightin' a shuck together?"

"I think they have somethin' in common," said Gil, "and his name is Clay Duval. Remember what Victoria said, about Clay's passion for horses? Clay's a Texan, and Solano's a Mex Indian, but their feeling for a good horse is the same. It says something for Clay Duval that he can claim a friend like Solano."

"And a woman like Angelina," said Van. "We may never see Solano, Angelina, or Clay again, but they'll stand mighty tall in my memory."

"For once," said Gil, "Victoria said something that makes sense. The sooner we can finish this gather and get the trail drive under way, the better off we'll be."

"You aim to use a trail brand?"

"No reason to," said Gil. "It'd be just a lot of hard work for nothing. With Spanish longhorns runnin' wild and considered worthless, who's going to dispute our claim to the herd? The Mex army won't care a damn about the cows. We'll have to give Valverde credit for one truth. We're purely going to have a hell of a time convincin' the soldiers we wasn't part of that break near Salada hacienda, in February. While they won't know who we are, or that we're guilty of anything, they'll know we're Texans. That'll be enough."

★ ★ ★

After Angelina and Solano were gone, Gil and Van saw little of Victoria. It was as though she expected questions she didn't wish to answer. But the Texans left her alone, continuing the gathering of wild longhorns. There was a wagon shed — actually no more than a lean-to — built against an outside wall of the barn. It was beneath this shed that Victoria's Conestoga was kept. One evening after they'd unsaddled and rubbed down their horses, Gil and Van stopped at the shed to look at the Conestoga. So that the wagon would fit into the shed, the canvas had been stripped and the hickory bows removed.

"That's a hell of a lot of wagon to haul from here to Texas," said Van. "It'll take all six of them big puddin'-footed horses to move it."

"There's somethin' about that woman," said Gil, "that purely ain't ringin' true. She wants out of Mexico pronto, and then won't leave without taking a fool two-ton wagon. Before we're done, I look for trouble, and this thing's going to figure into it."

Van chuckled. "Maybe sooner than you think. Here comes the queen bee herself."

Victoria said nothing. She just looked at them, a question in her eyes.

"Just havin' a look at the wagon," said Gil innocently. "It'll need a good greasing, and we'll

86

have to soak and swell the wood of the rims."

"You needn't concern yourself with the wagon," she snapped. "My father was a teamster, a bull whacker, and there's nothing about this wagon that I can't handle. That includes the greasing, the driving, and when necessary, the fixing. Leave it alone."

With that, she turned and went stomping off toward the house.

★ ★ ★

The first holding pen for the rapidly growing herd of longhorns was a canyon through which ran a creek. It had been a simple matter to erect a six-pole-high fence at each end, so the poles could be let down for entry, then quickly replaced. But the time had come when they needed more room, more graze.

"Ramon," said Gil, "you know this land. Find us another canyon or arroyo, with water and graze."

The vaquero found an arroyo, but it had a shallow mouth, only deepening as it progressed. The shallow end required more fence. The outfit spent a weary two days digging post holes, cutting poles and posts, and securing the upper and lower ends of the new enclosure. They were horsemen, and anything that kept them afoot for two days vexed their souls.

"Now," said Gil, when they were finally done, "this should hold the rest of them. Come the end of the month, we'll run a tally."

★ ★ ★

June 1, 1843. The Mendoza ranch, Durango County, Mexico.

Ramon, Gil, and Van ran separate tallies and compromised on a total of 4500 longhorns.

"July first, at the latest," predicted Van.

"We'll set our sights on that," said Gil. "There's a pile of things to do. There's more than two hundred horses, and every one ought to be reshod. Even then, some of 'em will be barefooted before we get to Bandera range."

Ramon got the attention of Estanzio and Mariposa. When the Indians had reined up their horses and dismounted, Ramon turned to Gil.

"Nex' mont'," said Ramon, "they shoe hoss, gentle hoss, some each."

"Good idea," said Gil. "The rest of us will rope long horns. Way it looks right now, we'll be ready to move 'em out July first."

Ramon knew his men, and the plan worked well. Estanzio and Mariposa spent part of their day gentling the horses that were ready, and the rest of the time reshoeing those in need of it. Finally, there was the need for supplies for the trail drive, and Gil was forced to meet with Victoria.

"We travel to Zacatecas twice a year," she said, "and it is nearing the time when we normally go. Send Pedro Fagano and Vicente Gomez. They know where the pack saddles are. They will take four packhorses."

"Why don't they take the wagon?"

"*I said*," she repeated, "*they will take four packhorses!*"

She turned away, leaving Gil standing there. He stepped out on the front porch, closing the door behind him. He found Ramon, gave him the order, and the segundo went looking for Pedro and Vicente.

"Gil," said Van, "I purely hate settin' out on this trail drive with only a Colt. Since these boys are goin' after supplies, have 'em get us some rifles, if there's any to be had."

It was a good idea, but Gil doubted it would be possible in a village such as Zacatecas. When he mentioned it to Ramon, the vaquero shook his head. "No long gun," he said. "Soklados take." It made sense. The military had gobbled up all the weapons. There were no rifles and probably few other weapons to be had. They would have to make do, and might be lucky to have ammunition for their Colts. That was going to be a problem. The Texans needed percussion caps and powder. The Mendoza riders all had pistols, but some of them were foreign-made, coming from England, France, or Spain. While they all depended on percussion caps, every weapon was different. But Sam Colt offered the frontiersman an edge. Percussion caps could be dipped in varnish and waterproofed. You could swim a river and the Colt would still fire.

Gil and Van soon had reason to be thankful for having made friends with Ramon Alcaraz. Knowing they lacked rifles, and aware of their concern that they might not have sufficient ammunition for their Colts, Ramon went to the bunkhouse and returned with a canvas sack. He, too, had a Colt, and the sack was three-quarters full of the curious percussion caps the Texans were in need of.

"Thanks, pardner," said Gil, "but let's try Zacatecas first. If Vicente and Pedro come back empty-handed, we'll have to depend on you."

* * *

Vicente and Pedro rode out the next morning, each leading two packhorses. With them they took the list that Ramon and Gil had carefully made up the night before. Victoria hadn't mentioned money, nor had Gil, since he and Van had none to offer. Hopefully, the Mendoza ranch had a line of credit in the village. As far as Gil Austin knew, neither of the riders going for supplies had taken money to pay for them. Now that they were within a few days of actually beginning the trail drive to Texas, to Bandera range, Gil had that old prickly, uneasy premonition that always dogged him just before everything went to hell in a handcart.

* * *

Esteban Valverde was about to dispatch a pair of his riders to Matamoros for supplies and information.

"Without seeming too inquisitive and drawing attention to yourselves," he said, "try and find out where the soldiers will be encamped for the next several months. I also wish to know if all the gringos who escaped near Salada hacienda have been recaptured. If they have not, ask if the price on their heads still stands."

He watched the men ride out, wringing his hands in anticipation. The trail drive must begin soon, and when it did, Esteban Valverde would be ready. His outfit outnumbered the Mendoza riders ten to one, and he would have his men armed to the teeth.

★ ★ ★

Angelina Ruiz and Solano reached Zacatecas and continued riding southeast until they reached the Panuco River, a few miles west of San Luis Potosi. Solano knew the country, and led out, following the river east, toward the coastal town of Tampico. A day's ride from San Luis Potosi and they would turn south, toward Mexico City. They rode in silence, Angelina plagued with doubt. Had Valverde been truthful with her? Was there a chance Clay Duval still lived? Vivid in her mind were the terrible tales she had heard of the dungeons in Mexico City. They were infested with lice and rats, and it was more merciful for a man to fall before Mexican rifles than to face a slow death languishing behind cold, gray walls of stone. If all these grim possibilities were not enough, the girl suffered pangs of guilt for having revealed Victoria's plans to Esteban Valverde. But she had told him only what he already suspected; that in return for helping the Austins gather a herd of wild longhorns, Victoria would travel with them to Texas. Victoria was a woman capable of making her own decisions, and if she wished to leave Mexico, who was Esteban Valverde to say that she could not? Angelina knew little of Victoria's relationship with Valverde, except that Esteban seemed so obsessed with Victoria, he was unwilling to see her go. But Victoria *was* going, and what could Valverde do to stop her? Nothing, Angelina decided.

★ ★ ★

Gil and Van kept a daily tally of the gather, and when they had roped another 550 longhorns, Gil called a halt. Their total for the gather stood at 5050 head, and with the anticipated loss, it was enough. Vicente and Pedro had returned from Zacatecas and had fulfilled Ramon's prophecy. No long guns were available. They had, however, managed to find a keg of powder. Ramon eyed it with satisfaction. With his percussion caps, they could load enough shells for their Colts. The riders with other makes might have a problem, if they lacked anything but powder, but it was something that could not be helped.

With most of the horses shod, and the longhorn gather completed, there was little to be done before the drive took the trail north. Estanzio and Mariposa needed but a few days with the horses they were gentling, and once begun, it was necessary that the process be completed without interruption. They were all men of the saddle, with a horseman's appreciation of the skill of the Indians working with the horses, and they gathered near the breaking corral to watch. Gil and Van Austin paid particular attention, for they envisioned a horse ranch in Texas, begun with Mendoza breeding stock. Mariposa and Estanzio had progressed with their current horses to the point where the animals must become accustomed to a rider's weight. Beyond that — the last step — would be the horse's acceptance of a saddle.

This day there were only two horses in the corral. Mariposa approached one, and Estanzio the other. The horses stood their ground, showing no fear. The riders stroked the animals, talking the familiar horse talk. This time each of the men carried a saddle blanket over his arm. Each horse was allowed to sniff the blanket, to become familiar with it. The blankets were then placed gently across each animal's broad back. Gaining the horse's trust was not enough. The Indian understood, as perhaps few white men ever did, that what an unbroken horse most feared was *anything* on his back. It was a well-founded fear, born and bred into the animals, the result of attacks by the cougar and other predatory beasts. It was fear that must be met and dealt with before a horse would accept any burden, even a saddle blanket.

Once the saddle blankets were accepted by the horses, the animals were but a step away from being gentled to the saddle. They must yield to the weight of a rider without fear, without flinching. It was a final step in the

Indian gentling process. Estanzio and Mariposa began the day as usual, by spending some time with the horses, talking to them, and finally by placing the saddle blanket on the back of the horse. Once the animals had accepted the saddle blanket again, it was time for the ultimate test. They must learn to bear the weight of a rider. Mariposa rested his extended arms on the saddle blanket, across the horse's back. This was something new, and the animal turned its head and looked at him. Again the Indian spoke to the horse, and it seemed to relax, seeing no harm in the gesture. Finally, holding his arms rigid across the animal's back, Mariposa lifted his feet off the ground, putting all his weight on the horse. Surprised at the unaccustomed burden, the animal backstepped, turning its head. But there was only his newly discovered friend, who caused him no pain, meant him no harm. Mariposa let his feet down, taking his weight off the horse. When he repeated the action, again putting his weight on the horse, it remained calm. Repeatedly the Indian applied his weight, allowing the horse every opportunity to resist. But it did not. With startling swiftness, Mariposa was astride the horse. It side-stepped, startled, but the Indian leaned forward and spoke to it. Again the horse calmed, and when Mariposa spoke to it again, the animal took a few faltering steps. Finally, with more words of encouragement, the big horse trotted around the corral. The horse had been broken without breaking its spirit. Estanzio had progressed with his own mount in a similar fashion. The Indian riders removed their saddle blankets and, with some final words for the horses, left the corral. The rest of the Mendoza riders said nothing; they'd seen it all before. But Gil and Van Austin had not.

"My God," said Van, "that's somethin' every man who even hopes to own a horse ought to see."

"Amen to that," said Gil. "It's something I want to learn and use, if we're lucky enough to get back to Texas alive."

6

JUNE 25, 1843. Mendoza ranch, Durango County, Mexico.

"Now's the time to tie up any loose ends," Gil told Victoria. "We'll move out on July first, if all goes as planned. Until then, I aim to take the longhorns from both holding pens and bunch 'em on the north range. It's time you got your wagon ready, and loaded with whatever you aim to take with you."

He needed no response, and got none. He'd about had enough of this high-handed, independent female. She could grease the wagon, harness and unharness the teams, and anything else she took a notion to do, all without his help. He joined the outfit as they were saddling their horses. They had seen him heading for the house, and they waited expectantly. Victoria had been on the prod ever since Angelina had left with Solano, and they all wondered what had been the result of Gil's meeting with her. The Mendoza riders had become more at ease with Gil and Van, and they tried to communicate more in English. Even Estanzio and Mariposa. True, their speech was often broken and difficult for them, but it was a mark of respect and liking that wasn't lost on the Austins.

"Today," said Gil, "we're going to start moving the longhorns from the first holding pen to the north range. We'll keep them bunched until they get the idea they're a herd. Then some of us will drive the remaining two thousand from the second holding pen, and we'll combine the two herds on the north range until we're ready to begin the trail drive. If we can keep 'em bunched for two or three days, maybe they'll settle down some before we take the trail."

"Is good," said Ramon Alcaraz.

The others nodded their agreement. No part of a trail drive was easy, but the first few days on the trail with a new herd was pure hell. Not only would the bunch-quitters be constantly breaking away while the herd was moving, they were just as likely to light out after the longhorns had been bedded down for the night. One restless old cow could start a stampede that would scatter the entire herd from hell to breakfast, costing the riders as much as a week, rounding them up. The wisdom of Gil's plan was soon apparent. With the entire herd of five thousand, their task would have been near impossible. As it was, the three thousand longhorns from the first holding pen were almost more than they could handle. The weeks of captivity had done nothing to lessen the desire of the brutes to return to the wild state from which they'd been taken. Once the rails to the canyon enclosure were down, the trouble began.

"Keep 'em bunched!" shouted Gil.

Several riders had gone to the far end of the canyon and started the herd moving. Once free of the confining walls, the longhorns wasted no time exploding into half a dozen factions. But there were more followers than leaders, and it was all that prevented total disaster. Somehow, the riders managed to head the leaders, and when the brutes ran headlong into their followers, it created enough confusion to avert a stampede. The longhorns, having no leaders or sense of direction, began milling. On the north flank, Gil rode in among the brutes, popping dusty flanks with his doubled lariat. Van rode in from the opposite side. Finally they had a few longhorns lumbering northward, and the others followed. Gil and Van dropped out of the moving herd, riding opposite flanks. It was time to press their advantage. The drag riders would have to keep the stragglers moving, and Gil could hear the popping of lariats on bovine hide, sounding like distant pistol shots. Ramon and the rest of the riders were closing the ranks, moving them ahead. Dust clouds hung in the sky like smoke, seeming to dim the sun. Every rider wore a bandanna over his nose and mouth, but it wasn't much help. Gil could feel the grit against his teeth and up his nose, while sweat runneled generous portions of it into his eyes. A dusty rider trotted his horse alongside Gil's. It was Ramon Alcaraz.

"Nort'," he shouted. "Creek?"

"Creek," Gil shouted in response.

With graze and plenty of water, it would be a good place to settle this bunch down while they emptied the second holding pen. Ramon galloped ahead. The creek itself would slow the herd, inviting them to pause and drink, but that wouldn't be enough. There must be riders to head them, to start them milling. If

98

they could be made to graze, with abundant water nearby, this might become a bed ground. It could be an important step toward the herd becoming trailwise, with fewer bunch-quitters. Half a dozen miles of choking dust had built the longhorns a powerful thirst, and they seemed willing enough to pause at the creek. On the far side of the herd, Van waved his hat, pointing toward the opposite side of the creek. Two riders followed him. They would discourage any of the longhorns who might be inclined to cross the creek. Gil trotted his horse wide of the flank, allowing the herd to spread out along the creek bank. He sighed. Once the animals drank, he'd know if they were in for trouble. Thirsty cows wouldn't graze, but once they'd drunk their fill, they should settle down on the abundant grass.

Gil slowed his horse until Van caught up.

"They ain't likely to wander away from that creek," Van said. "God, I wish old Clay was here to throw in with us. For that matter, I just wish we knew he was alive."

"I believe he is," said Gil, "and I think his friend Solano has gone looking for him."

"Angelina too?"

"Why not?" Gil said. "Clay Duval's the kind whose friends would go to hell for him."

"I reckon," said Van. "Ain't we livin' proof?"

The two men Esteban Valverde most trusted returned to report on the trail drive.

"Continue your vigil," Valverde told them. "They must yet drive the rest of the herd to the creek. When Senora Mendoza rides north to join the drive, I wish to know."

"The Senora Mendoza," said one of the riders, "is preparing a *carro*."

"Ah," Valverde said, "a wagon. That pleases me. Once they are on the trail, I think we shall take the *carro* away from them."

"There are many of us," said the rider. "Let us take it now."

"No," said Valverde, "we shall wait until they've begun the drive. With thousands of wild cattle, the riders will be widely separated, with little time or concern for the *carro*. I wish to speak to Senora Mendoza of a debt long unpaid. I believe seizing the *carro* will satisfy the debt."

Gil had the outfit set up camp on the opposite side of the creek from the grazing herd. The night was divided into three watches, each consisting of four riders circling the herd. But for the yip of coyotes and an occasional faraway howl of a wolf, the silence of the night was unbroken.

"I can't believe it," said Van as they gathered around the breakfast fire. "We just bedded down this bunch, and they didn't rattle a hoof all night. It purely ain't natural."

"I'd have to agree with that," said Gil. "Let's don't crow too much, too soon. We ran this bunch hard, and when they got here, they were thirsty and ready to graze. But this mornin' we got none of that goin' for us. They ain't hungry, they ain't so dry their tongues are hangin' out, and they just might take a notion to go south. I hope I'm wrong, that they'll stay as calm today as they were last night, because most of us will have to bring the rest of the herd from the second holding pen. Van, I want you, Ramon, Vicente Gomez, and Juan Padillo to stay with this bunch. Circle them just like you were night-hawking. If this herd will behave themselves as well as they have so far, it may have a calming effect on the others."

Gil led out, followed by Juan Alamonte, Manuel Armijo, Domingo Chavez, Pedro Fagano, Bola, Estanzio, and Mariposa. They reined up at the Mendoza ranch house, and only Gil dismounted. He rapped on the door, and it was a while before Victoria answered his knock. She said nothing. Gil didn't beat around the bush.

"We're going for the rest of the herd," he said bluntly. "We'll bed them down at the creek to the north of here, and tomorrow we'll be ready for the horses. When you're ready to move out with the wagon, I want you ahead of the rest of the drive. But drive wide before you reach the creek. I don't want you crossing anywhere within sight of the herd. I don't want to risk the sight or sound of the wagon spooking those longhorns."

"Are you finished?" she asked shortly.

"Yes," he said, just as shortly.

Without another word she closed the door. Gil mounted and, with the others following, led out. Long before they reached the lesser arroyo and the rest of the herd, Mariposa pointed to the distant specks, black against the blue of the sky.

"*Busardos,*" said Mariposa. "*Muerte.*"

It was an unfailing sign of death, the circling buzzards, and they found what had attracted them, just beyond the fenced mouth of the arroyo. It was what was left of a cow.

"Cougar," said Mariposa, even before they dismounted. He swung out of the saddle and quickly found the big cat's track.

"One of you rope that carcass," said Gil, "and drag it well into the brush. The rest of the bunch may already be spooked out of their minds, but let's not make it any worse."

Gil rode to the farthest end of the arroyo, and found that he was right. When the first of the longhorns saw him, they lit out, their tails up. But there was no help for it now. He rode on toward the lower end of the arroyo, the longhorns fleeing ahead of him. He knew he had to get beyond them and head them back toward the other end, where the fence had been let down. Even when the remains of the lion-kill had been dragged away, there would remain the smell of blood and of the big cat itself. They'd be lucky not to have a stampede on their hands as soon as the longhorns hit the mouth of the arroyo. But his riders would be aware of the danger. It was up to him to keep the herd bunched, running close. Give an old mossy-horn too much daylight between himself and the brute ahead, and the old bastard was likely to lose his sense of direction and bolt left or right. Cows tended to follow other cows, but when the gap got too wide, that could change in an instant. Longhorns continued to shy out of his way, and Gil got beyond the herd. Doubling

102

his lariat, he kneed his horse into a lope.

"Hieeeyaaah," he yelled. "Hieeeyaaah!"

He didn't need the doubled lariat. The longhorns ran like the devil and all his minions were in pursuit. But they must reach the mouth of the arroyo and be through it before the cougar scent and the smell of blood spooked them out of control. He caught up to the herd, lest the tag end begin to slow, but they didn't. They left the arroyo on the run, and since they ran north, the riders didn't try to head them. Wisely, they galloped along at the flank, lest any of the brutes sought to quit the bunch to left or right. But the leaders continued north, and those behind seemed content to follow. Once they ran out their fear, they'd be easier to handle. It was rare that a spooked cow's urge to run could be utilized to a cowboy's advantage. It had almost been worth losing a cow to a cougar. The herd began to slow, and Mariposa dropped back to drag. He looked at Gil; the grin did not reach his lips, but it was in his eyes.

"*Bueno estampida*," he said.

It was the only time on this trail drive that any rider would be able to make such a claim. They kept the longhorns moving, resorting to popping their flanks with doubled lariats when those at the tag end began to slow. The longhorns bellowed in protest, but kept moving. But there was a tan-and-white-spotted bull that was determined to quit the drive. Twice Gil headed the brute, forcing him back into the herd. When he broke away a third time, Gil rode after him, shaking out his lariat. Mariposa saw

103

what Gil had in mind, and followed, swinging his own lariat as he rode. Gil looked back, and, assured he had a backup rider, threw his loop. It caught the bull by the horns, just as Mariposa snared the hind legs with his underhand cast. The Indian's horse dug in, standing fast. When the slack went out of Gil's lariat, the bull was thrown, helpless between the two cow horses. Gil left his saddle on the run, securing the bull's forelegs with piggin' string, while Mariposa tied the hind legs. The riders removed their lariats, leaving the bellowing, struggling bull to hook the air in his fury. By the time a rider returned and freed the troublesome bull, the animal would have exhausted itself, and could be led with a horn loop. It was bothersome, roping and hog-tying the brute, but better than having it continually quitting the herd. Such behavior was a bad influence, and the successful bunch-quitter soon began to attract followers.

The riders pushed the herd, swatting the stragglers with their doubled lariats. Once they neared the creek where the first bunch grazed, the second herd could slow of its own accord. Finding themselves among grazing longhorns, Gil hoped the second bunch would mingle with the first. It almost worked. A lead bull in the newly arrived bunch hooked a grazing bull on the outer fringes of the first herd. Whether accidental or intentional, the results were the same. The two brutes took an instant dislike to one another, and a horn-clacking battle ensued.

The combatants were caught between the

original herd and the newly arrived one, so the riders were unable to get to them. The drawing of blood was inevitable; when it happened, the cowboys could tell. One animal bawled in fear and confusion, and that led to a cacophony as others joined in. The riders could do little, except try and head the herd when it began to run. Gil backed his horse away, and he could see the others doing likewise. They dared not get caught in the stampede. To do so would risk a horse falling and a rider being trampled. In addition to the danger, it was impossible for riders to head a stampeding herd if they were trapped in it. Their only chance lay in outriding the running cattle and getting ahead of them. The worst stampedes of all were those when the herd split. There was no time to make decisions, shout orders, to divide the outfit. A rider's position, perhaps his life, depended on where he was when the herd started to run. When a herd split, half the stampeding cattle might run unchecked because the riders were in no position to head two herds, each taking a different path.

While the Mendoza riders were good men, Gil and Van Austin had never worked cattle with them before and didn't know the extent of their cow savvy. When the inevitable occurred and the longhorns began to run, they split along the creek. Part of the herd lit out toward the east, while the other part headed west. Gil was ahead of the bunch running west, and he was aware of riders galloping along behind him. Only a fool rode directly into the path of a stampede, depending on his presence and that of his horse to halt the running cattle. There was but one way, and that was to gradually "bend" the herd into a horseshoe, turning it back on itself until the cattle began to mill. Gil looked over his shoulder, recognizing Bola, Juan Padillo, and two more distant riders. Gil kneed his horse nearer the lead cows. He must ride close enough to turn them, but not near enough to endanger himself or his horse. When the beasts tossed their heads, a horse running neck-and-neck was in danger of having his throat pierced by a lethal horn. Closer and closer Gil rode, bearing down on the lead cows. Since they were running parallel to the creek, they'd have to be forced into it, but even that might not stop them. While the creek ran shallow in places, the banks were high enough that the longhorns couldn't readily climb out. Gil's horse knew what was expected of him, and he shouldered into one of the lead cows, shoving it into a running mate. Seeking to escape the horse, the longhorns veered to the right, nearer the creek. From the corner of his eye Gil caught glimpses of the riders behind him. They rode closely enough to prevent the running longhorns behind him from widening their ranks and running him down. Again Gil's horse pushed closer to the leaders, forcing them toward the creek. Suddenly they came to a bend where the creek turned to Gil's left, opposite to the direction the herd was running, putting the creek directly in their path. Barely in time, Gil's horse drew away as the lead cows went over the bank, into the creek. It still might not end the stampede, Gil thought grimly. The rest of the damn fools might turn away, follow the bend in the creek and keep running. But it wasn't too difficult to confuse a cow. While the leaders splashed about in the water, as though unsure as to why they were there, those who followed paused in confusion. Ahead of them, their former leaders were trying to get out of the creek, or calmly drinking from it. It was more than the rest of the bunch could comprehend, so they turned away and began cropping grass along the creek bank. The longhorns in the creek wandered downstream, seeking banks low enough for them to climb out. But there were two who weren't going anywhere. They had been first over the edge, and their necks were broken. Juan Padillo pointed to them, a question in his eyes. Gil nodded, lifting his coiled lariat.

"Pull them out," he said. "No sense in fouling the water."

"*Busardos rapido*," said Bola, pointing to the sky. Buzzards. They were birds of death, and they seemed to ride the very wind that carried the smell of it to them.

After their run, the longhorns wanted to water and graze, but the cowboys wouldn't let them. They rounded up the unwilling brutes and began driving them back in the direction from which they'd come. The herd grew as it moved along. Many of the longhorns had dropped out, likely having forgotten why they were running, and were grazing. But Gil guessed they had less than half their original gather. When they drew near their campsite, it was obvious much of the herd was still missing. Van, Ramon, and Mariposa had brought in a small bunch, but nothing like the number that had split away in a second stampede.

"The creek shallows down to nothin' up yonder," said Van. "Our bunch split again, most of 'em runnin' across the creek. We couldn't possibly head the second bunch, so we had to settle for what we was sure of getting."

"Soon as we get these settled again," said Gil, "we'll go looking for the others."

"I hope this ain't a taste of what's to come," said Van. "We ain't even off Mendoza range."

"Wagon come," said Mariposa.

"Senora Mendoza," said Van. "By God, our day's complete."

Ramon shrugged his shoulders. In his dark eyes was what might have been agreement, but he said nothing. They waited for the wagon. Whatever Victoria had to say, they might as well hear it and be done with it. She reined the three big Conestoga teams to a stop. The wagon bows had been replaced, the canvas drawn tight, and the pucker tied.

"I am ready," said Victoria. "Why haven't you gone for the horses, and where are the rest of the longhorns?"

"We've been a mite busy," said Gil. "The horses will have to wait until we round up the herd. The longhorns got restless."

"You let them run away," she said, with a hint of amusement.

"Ma'am," said Gil, struggling to hold his temper, "in Texas we refer to it as a stampede. Nobody 'lets' it happen."

The rest of the outfit rode in, pushing another bunch of cows ahead of them. Gil turned to Ramon.

"Take five men, Ramon, and get this bunch settled down to graze. Circle them like you're night-hawking, until you know they're goin' to behave. The rest of us will get on the trail of those missing cows. Van, you stay with Ramon, in case Senora Mendoza decides to take over the camp. If you have to, remind her it's a hell of a long ways to Texas, and that I'm bossin' this trail drive."

★ ★ ★

Esteban Valverde was pleased. His riders had returned from Matamoros, and yes, there was a company of soldiers there. Besides that, there had been recent word from Mexico City that Santa Anna had placed a reward of one thousand pesos on the heads of all Tejanos who had escaped near Salada hacienda. That same afternoon, one of the men he had sent to watch the Mendoza ranch had returned.

"Senora Mendoza go," said the rider. "*Carro go.*"

"*Caballos?*" Valverde asked.

"*Vaquero onico.*"

"*Mendoza caballos*," said Valverde. "*Muchos caballos.*"

"Mendoza rancho," said the rider. "*Caballos* no go."

"*Vaca?*" Mendoza asked. "*Muchos vaca?*"

"*Estampida.*" The rider grinned, spreading his arms expansively.

Valverde dismissed the man and sat down to think. So the Tejanos had to round up their longhorns a second time, following a stampede. The men at the cow camp still had only the horses they rode, which meant they still must return to the Mendoza ranch for the horse herd. But Victoria had arrived at the cow camp with the wagon. It was precisely what he had been waiting for.

★ ★ ★

July 3, 1843. Durango County, Mexico.

Running a quick tally, Gil and Ramon found they were missing almost one thousand head.

"For all the hard work we've put into this," said Van, "that's too many to lose. My God, we're not even on the trail yet."

"We'll take a couple of days and look for them," said Gil. "Beyond that, we'll have to consider the sense of it. Some of them may not stop until they're back in the swamps and thickets where we found 'em to start with, and I'm not of a mind to go back and try to make up the difference with a new gather."

Leaving six men with the newly assembled herd, Gil took five riders with him and went

110

looking for the missing longhorns. The first day, they found more than half. The animals had retained some sense of having belonged to a herd, and grazed in bunches. It was an advantage Gil hadn't dared hope for.

"Another day like this," said Van, "and we'll have them all."

"Yeah," said Gil, "but we won't have another day like this. I expect the rest of 'em to be scattered from here to yonder. They may have made it as far as their old stomping grounds, to the south of Mendoza range."

The second day's search turned out about as Gil had predicted. The bunches of grazing longhorns became smaller and fewer, finally disappearing. They were reduced to searching the thickets, and finding but one or two cows, and often none at all.

"Damn it," said Gil, "let's take what we have and go. We could spend the rest of the year beating the brush and not find a hundred more."

So they took the small bunch of cows they had found, and started back to join the rest of the herd. Gil took a quick tally of the final gather.

"By my count," he said, once the longhorns were again one herd, "we're short 175 head. Tomorrow morning we'll ride back to the Mendoza corrals for the horse herd. The following morning, at first light, we'll take to the trail. We're goin' home to Texas, to Bandera range."

★ ★ ★

"I feel some better," said Van at breakfast, "like maybe the devil ain't put a curse on this herd, after all. Seemed almighty quiet last night; wasn't even a coyote around."

"They were out there," said Gil. "Weren't they, Ramon?"

The little vaquero nodded at Gil, but when he looked at Van, he let his chin drop and emitted a faked snore. The predators had been there, he implied, but the Texan had slept through them. Everybody — even the Indians — had a laugh at Van's expense, and he laughed with them. It was the first evidence Gil had seen that these men had a sense of humor, the first time he'd ever heard them laugh. Laughter was good for a man, and Gil had a gut feeling there wouldn't be much of it on the long trail north. And it was just as well he didn't know how thoroughly justified that feeling was. When breakfast was done, he turned to Ramon.

"It's time to go for the Mendoza horses, Ramon. You, Pedro, Manuel, Estanzio, and Mariposa, saddle your horses. Everybody else will stay here with the longhorns. When I've had a word with Senora Mendoza, we'll ride."

As usual, there was no sign of Victoria. He wondered what in tarnation she had in the Conestoga, besides maybe a bed. He went around to the tailgate of the wagon and found the canvas pucker drawn tight. There remained a small aperture, but the interior seemed as dark as a cow's gullet. While he could see nothing, he

112

had no trouble hearing the snick as she eared back the hammer of the pistol.

"Put your head in here," she said coldly, "and I'll shoot you."

"Ma'am," said Gil, just as coldly, "if I was fool enough to be taken by you, I ought to be shot. We're goin' after the horses, and we'll be taking the trail at first light tomorrow."

7

JULY 5, 1843. On the trail north.

Gil approached Victoria Mendoza as she was harnessing the three teams of Conestogas to the cumbersome wagon. On the frontier it was unthinkable for a woman to do such work if there were a man available, but there were exceptions, and Victoria Mendoza was one of them. Once aware of his presence, she stopped what she was doing and faced him. He noticed she now carried a Colt tucked under her sash, beneath her short bolero. She said nothing, perhaps with yesterday's hard words fresh on her mind, waiting for him to speak. She had once accused him of bluntness, so he didn't beat around the bush.

"You said you could keep up with the herd, so I aim for you to stay ahead of it. The wagon will give the horse herd and the longhorns something to follow. When you're ready, move out."

He turned away without another word, pausing at the rope corral where the Mendoza horses had been gathered. Mariposa had given him a count of 194, predominantly blacks and grays. They were nothing short of spectacular, and in Texas they'd be worth more than every cow in Mexico. His intuition warning him, he turned. Mariposa and Estanzio were appraising the horse herd like proud parents. The Indians nodded. They seldom spoke to him, nor did

114

they now, but the white man and red men shared common ground. While their lives were so different the gap might never be completely bridged, for the moment they shared something words could never have expressed. Gil had plans for the Indian riders. He nodded to them, pointed to the horse herd and then to Victoria's wagon. Estanzio and Mariposa nodded their understanding. They were to take charge of the horses, the herd following the wagon. Van rode up, leading Gil's horse.

"Good idea," he said. "With the longhorns followin' the horse herd and the wagon, most of us can ride the flanks and the drag. Who's ridin' the point?"

"I am," said Gil. "I want you at the other end."

"Me? At drag? Why can't I ride point, while you take the drag?"

"Like you said," Gil grinned, "I'm the firstborn, so I have privileges. Besides, I'm trail boss."

"You're lookin' for trouble," said Van, seeing through the humor.

"I am," said Gil, "and it could come from ahead or behind. I have no idea what to expect, and I'll feel better with you at my back. I aim to stay ahead of the wagon, for several reasons."

"When trouble comes, you reckon it's goin' to involve Victoria and the wagon?"

"I don't know," said Gil, "but I have my suspicions. She's carrying a Colt under her sash. I don't question that, with what may be ahead of us, but I can't help wonderin' if it's because

115

she knows something that we don't."

"We'll be strung out for a long ways," said Van, "with a herd of horses and this many longhorns. Any hombres wantin' to cause us grief could hit us at one end, without the other bein' aware of it. Could be that's what they have in mind. If anything busts loose at drag, I'll fire warning shots."

"Make that a warning *shot*," said Gil. "We're not that flush with shells. Besides, we may be lined out so far, a shot can't be heard from one end to the other. It's a chance we'll have to take."

Although there were many horses, they had been gentled and trailed well. The two Indian riders had worked with so many of them, it was like a gathering of friends. Gil had counted on that, and it set his mind at ease, insofar as the horses were concerned. He was doubly thankful for the ease with which the horse herd took to the trail, because he feared the longhorns were going to more than make up the difference. When the drive was under way, with the flanks and drag covered, Gil rode ahead of the herd, past the horse herd, and caught up to the wagon. He rode past without speaking to Victoria. As he recalled, Matamoros was northeast of Durango, at the extreme southwestern tip of Coahuila County. Victoria had mentioned only Matamoros and Monterrey, so he had no idea what else lay ahead of them. While the poor map he had agreed with what Victoria had told him, he recalled the map of Ortega's had only the larger towns and villages. It showed only Durango County, and Gil had learned from Ramon that there was actually a village called Durango, not too many miles south of the Mendoza ranch. Why had Victoria Mendoza insisted on sending men to Zacatecas for supplies when Durango had been much closer? There was just a hell of a lot that didn't add up where Victoria Mendoza was concerned, and Gil decided that when he finally got the total, he wasn't going to like it.

Gil took out Ortega's map, now tattered and wrinkled, and studied it. Since Matamoros was a favorite rendezvous point for the Mexican army, they must veer far enough east to bypass the town. Even then, they had three hundred miles of hazardous trail before they could cross into Texas. Just getting past Matamoros wouldn't free them of the Mexican army, he thought glumly. They might meet soldiers retreating from border clashes, or be overtaken by fresh troops, marching northward out of Mexico City. They hadn't traveled more than four or five miles when Gil missed the distant rattle of the wagon. Looking back, he could scarcely see it, but he could tell it wasn't moving. Wheeling his horse, he trotted back to the wagon and found Victoria standing helplessly beside it. So much for her defiant vow that she could fix anything that happened to it. It wasn't difficult to spot the trouble. The huge left rear wheel had slid into what likely was a leaf-hidden hole left by a rotted stump. The wagon had tilted, raising the right rear wheel more than a foot off the ground. Victoria waited grimly, obviously prepared for a tongue lashing, but Gil wanted no more verbal fights with her.

"I'll get some help," he told her. "We'll have to get a pole under that wheel. Don't be pushin' the horses; leave 'em be until we lift the wheel."

She was furious because he wasn't, casting him a black look as he rode away. He recalled a stream a mile or so back. It would be a good place to halt the drive while they freed the disabled wagon. By the time he reached the creek, he could see the oncoming horse herd. He removed his hat with a downward sweep, the signal to halt. Leaving Mariposa and Estanzio to hold the horse herd at the creek, Gil rode back to meet the longhorns. They were fortunate, being so near water and graze. He looked at the sun, and decided they'd be lucky if they freed the wagon in time to travel any farther before sundown. Gil had ridden only a few hundred yards when the longhorns came into view. Again he swept off his hat, and Ramon kneed his horse into a trot, riding to meet him.

"*Carro*," said Gil.

That was sufficient. They were halting the drive because something was wrong with the wagon. Ramon understood. He raised his eyebrows and shrugged his shoulders, which might have meant anything. He wheeled his horse and rode back to the herd, waving his hat, calling the flank riders forward. When the horse herd and the longhorns had been settled along the shallow creek, Gil, Ramon, and Van rode ahead to free the bogged-down wagon.

"Rear wheel hit a stump hole, I reckon," said Gil. "With a good, strong pole, we can lift the wheel out, putting the other on the ground long enough for the horses to pull the wagon free."

"I hope her highness remembered to bring an ax," said Van. "I purely hate hackin' down trees with a Bowie knife."

"I'd as soon do that," said Gil, "as have another fight with her. She's expecting us to raise hell over this delay, and then she'll pounce on us like a gut-shot wolf. Let's just get the wagon out of the hole as quick as we can."

"*Noche pronto*," said Ramon.

"He's right," said Van. "It'll be dark or close to it by the time we get that prairie schooner back in business."

"I reckon we'll just make camp back there at the creek," said Gil, "and try to do better tomorrow. We haven't even made ten miles."

Reaching the tilted wagon, they dismounted.

"We'll need an ax," said Gil.

"In the toolbox, on the side of the wagon," Victoria said.

While there was an ax, it wasn't sharp. In fact, it hadn't been sharpened in a long time, if ever. They found a dead cedar, as big as a man's leg, and Van took first turn with the ax. After half a dozen blows, with barely a dent in the tree, he paused for breath.

"Here," he said, handing Gil the blunted ax. "When it comes my turn, I'll use the Bowie. It wasn't such a bad idea, compared to that ax."

They were successful in lifting the bogged wheel out of the hole, and in so doing lowered the other wheel to the ground. When Victoria popped the whip, the Conestogas leaned into their harness, and the wagon was free.

"Turn it around," said Gil, "and drive back to the creek. We'll go no farther today."

Gil divided the night into three watches, and they night-hawked in teams of four. In the darkest hour, before dawn, there was the chilling scream of a cougar. The horses nickered in fear, and didn't fully settle down until first light. Breakfast over, Gil and Van loaded the four packhorses. It was a morning ritual that nobody liked.

"What burns my carcass," said Van, "is that we got this big wagon rattlin' along, and we *still* have to unload and load these packhorses. What do you reckon she's got in that wagon, anyhow?"

"I don't know," said Gil, "and I don't care. Was I you, I wouldn't get too interested. I told you she's carryin' a Colt, and I don't think she'd mind shootin' either of us."

Victoria again took the lead. The longhorns had begun to settle down, to become trailwise. But there were still bunch-quitters, keeping the flank and drag riders busy. By noon a mass of thunderheads had gathered to the west, and there was faraway lightning.

"It's goin' to be another short day," said Van, "but we'd best be lookin' for a place to wait out that storm. I'm bettin' it ain't more'n two hours away."

It was a valid argument, and they barely found a place that offered a little protection. Water wasn't going to be a problem, so they stopped on the lee side of a hill, beneath an upthrust of rock. There was graze for the horses and cattle, but the animals showed little interest. It was a bad sign when horses and cattle became spooky just ahead of a storm. That meant thunder and lightning. Gil and Van Austin were used to the dry summers of South Texas, where summer storms were rare. So they weren't prepared for the fury that roared across the Sierra Madres, bringing thunder, lightning, wind, and rain. At the foot of the hill where they'd found shelter, the coulee had been dry. But in a matter of minutes it became a raging torrent, tossing tree stumps, logs, and debris before it. The thunder and lightning came closer.

"Come on," Gil shouted, "let's ride!"

Victoria had unharnessed her teams and was seeking to calm the big horses. Gil and the rest of the riders splashed across the flooded coulee at the bottom of the hill. The water was already belly deep on the horses. The longhorns and the horse herd had moved to the opposite side of the hill and begun to drift with the storm. Gil and half a dozen of the riders got ahead of the herd and started it milling. Estanzio and Mariposa were in the midst of the frightened horses, seeking to calm them. Thunder seemed to shake the earth. It began afar, rose to a crescendo, and finally rumbled away in the distance. Lightning speared the earth like great golden pitchforks. The longhorns began bawling their fear, until they could be heard above the crash of the thunder and the roar of the wind.

Gil and the riders circled the herd, but it was raining so hard, Gil couldn't identify the men nearest him. Just before a stampede, it seemed the cattle waited for something — a catalyst — that struck mutual terror into them all at the same instant. Gil held his breath, knowing the moment was coming. And there it was! On the ridge above them, lightning struck a huge, half-dead pine. The resinous old tree literally exploded, becoming a towering torch even the slashing rain couldn't extinguish. The herd was off and running, not sure what they were fleeing, but hell-bent on getting as far from it as they could. Worse, their terror had reached the horses, and they quickly joined the stampede. Gil rode hard, three other riders on his heels, as they tried to get ahead of the running herd. Just when it seemed the cause was lost, providence took a hand. A few hundred yards ahead of the stampeding herd, lightning set off a second fiery torch, the equal of the first. The leaders of the stampede found themselves running toward something more fearsome than that from which they fled. The lead cattle began to turn, and the stampeding herd doubled back on itself. Gil and his riders pressed their advantage. They rode along the northern slope, and as the herd began to turn, the riders forced the leaders into the belly-deep water that had flooded the arroyo. When the longhorns hit the water, they slowed, and when they emerged on the south slope, they were turned back the way they had come. Gil and three other riders crossed the newly flooded arroyo floor, pushing the longhorns back upstream, toward their original graze. The horse herd had followed the cattle, Estanzio and Mariposa keeping them bunched.

"Keep 'em moving!" shouted Gil.

The herd — horses and longhorns — were returned to the slope, across the flooded arroyo, from which they'd stampeded. The rain had slacked to a drizzle, and from far off the thunder was a faint grumble. At last the longhorns and the horses were grazing. Gil, Van, and Ramon rode around the herd, trying to take a tally. Estanzio and Mariposa were working with the horses.

"I can't see we've lost any," said Van. He looked at Ramon, and the vaquero shook his head.

"I reckon we got through this with a whole hide," said Gil. "I just hope we've done as well with the horses. Let's go see."

"No lose *caballo*," said Mariposa, shaking his head.

Gil sighed. It was a miracle, and God knew they needed one. But how many more would they need before they again saw Texas and their Bandera range? When they rode back to their camp, there were more surprises. Victoria had managed to hold her three Conestoga teams. She had also built a fire, and had hot coffee waiting.

"I got enough water in my boots to float a stern-wheeler," said Van. "Now that we got all these critters settled down to graze, why don't we just stay the night?"

"I reckon we might as well," said Gil. "Two

more hours and we'd have to bed down again. I'm gettin' me a feelin' this may become the damnedest trail drive in the history of the world. We ain't covered even twenty miles, and we've already had two broad-daylight stampedes."

"By the time we get to the border," said Van, "Texas and Mexico may have signed a peace treaty."

"Not with our luck," said Gil. "Maybe the day after we cross, but no sooner. We Austins never fill an inside straight. Remember Uncle Steve."

★ ★ ★

Again they night-hawked in teams of four, calming the horses and longhorns when distant cougars screamed. With hats, boots, and clothing again dry, and a good breakfast under their belts, they faced the new day in far better spirits. There were times when Victoria was cordial enough, and choosing such a time, Gil asked how far, leaving the Mendoza ranch, they must travel to reach Matamoros, Coahuila.

"Almost two hundred miles," she said. "Perhaps less, if you pass to the south of it."

"Three weeks," said Van, "if we can make ten miles a day."

But that seemed less and less likely. The storm of the day before had washed the sky a vivid blue and settled the dust, but two hours into the day's journey, there was another delay. Gil rode back to meet the oncoming herds. He had Estanzio and Mariposa halt the horse herd, and then rode on to meet the longhorns. Pedro Fagano and Vicente Gomez rode up from their flanking positions and began heading the herd. Gil waited until the tag end of the herd caught up, then he beckoned to Ramon and Van.

"What's wrong with the damn wagon this time?" Van asked irritably.

"Busted axle," said Gil. "Rear wheel slipped off a stone and came down hard on another."

"I've heard these wagons come equipped with a spare axle," said Van, "but if our luck's runnin' consistent, this wagon won't have one."

"You're dead right," said Gil, "and there's no wagon jack."

"One cancels out the other, then," said Van. "If there's no spare axle, then why would we need a wagon jack?"

"Because we'll have to lift that two-ton wagon *without* one," said Gil, "after we've made a new axle."

"This fool wagon's more trouble than the whole damn Mexican army."

The longhorns had settled down to graze, and the rest of the riders had ridden forward to see what was causing the delay.

"*Carro*," Ramon told them. "*Eje.*"

There was no mistaking their looks of disgust. Their tolerance for the wagon was wearing thin. It was one thing, riding for the *patrona*, working the range, but this was something entirely different. It seemed more the indulgence of a whim, and the big wagon appeared more and more unnecessary.

125

It was going to be a hell of a job, Gil decided, and they needed help. In Spanish and English, he conferred with Ramon. Among the vaqueros, wasn't there several who were handy with tools? There were.

"Manuel, Pedro," said Ramon, beckoning. Quickly he explained to Manuel Armijo and Pedro Fagano what Gil wanted. They nodded their understanding but said nothing. Gil thought they showed little enthusiasm for the task. He wheeled his horse and headed for the wagon, followed by Manuel, Pedro, Ramon, and Van. Victoria climbed down from the box as they dismounted.

"Here," she said, "I found a hatchet that may be sharper than the ax."

"A grubbin' hoe would be sharper than that ax," said Van ungraciously.

Gil nodded his thanks and walked around to the rear of the wagon. The others followed, and they all stood there looking morosely at the broken axle. It had given way near the hub, between the left rear wheel and the wagon box. Four heavy U bolts secured the axle to the Conestoga's chassis.

"This is purely goin' to get interestin'," said Van, "if she ain't got tools to take them bolts off."

"Try looking in the tool chest," said Victoria coldly, "if you think yourself capable of recognizing such a tool when you see it."

"Was I allowed to go through this rig," said Van, just as coldly, "then I'm right sure I could recognize a wagon jack. Do you aim to lift this

126

big bastard off the ground while we wrassle that axle loose?"

Her face flushed, Victoria turned away. Gil silenced Van with a hard look. He was no less frustrated than the rest of them, and they already had problems enough.

"We'll have to find some flat stones," said Gil, "and lift this thing high enough to build stone supports under each side of the wagon box. While the rest of you gather the stones, I'll cut us a tree to lift the wagon."

"It'd be quicker," said Van, "just to ride back and get the last one we cut. Kind of tools we got, it'll take half a day to cut another."

"You'd better hope not," said Gil. "I'm goin' to let you down a tree for the new axle."

Victoria had been right about one thing. The hatchet was sharper than the axe. Gil felled a tree and had a sturdy pole with which to lift the wagon before his unwilling helpers had found enough stones to place under the axle.

"No rocks close by," said Van, "except this big one she run over, that busted the axle."

The situation went from bad to worse. When they had enough stones to compensate for the missing wagon jack, they found that four men with one pole wasn't sufficient to lift the wagon.

"We lifted it out of the stump hole," said Van. "Just three of us."

"We lifted one corner of it," said Gil, "with the three teams pulling. The horses can't help us here; we'll have to raise the whole damn rear end. That means another pole, and some more strong backs."

Her mad worn off, Victoria returned. Gil turned to her.

"You'd as well unhitch the teams," he said. "We won't be going anywhere before sometime tomorrow."

"But there's no water here."

"Then we'll move on to the nearest water and good grass. You can ride one of your horses. We'll finish tomorrow what we're unable to do today."

"No," she said, "I won't leave the wagon."

"Suit yourself," said Gil. "There's cougars around. I won't spend the night in a dry camp, with no graze, for the sake of this damn wagon."

Gil didn't wait for her to explode. He turned to Ramon.

"Ramon, ride back to the herd and get three more men. Van, you stay with the wagon. The rest of us are goin' to cut another tree, for a second pole."

"Cut one about the right size for that new axle," said Van. "When we're done usin' it to lift the wagon, we can make the new axle from it."

"Brother," said Gil, in the first good humor he'd enjoyed all day, "there is hope for you, after all. Like Granny always said, we Austins are brighter than we look. While we're gone, take that big wrench and break the nuts loose on the U bolts holdin' the axle."

"We're leavin' the herd almighty short-handed," said Van.

"This will either work or it won't," said Gil,

"and it won't take that long, either way."

When Manuel, Pedro, and Gil returned with a second pole, Ramon, Juan Alamonte, Domingo Chavez, and Vicente Gomez were there.

"Now," said Gil, "we'll build a pile of these flat stones under each side of the wagon box. They'll have to be high enough that we'll only need to add one or two more to the pile once we lift the wagon. We need the wheels off the ground just far enough to remove them. Now we're ready to put the butt end of these poles under the rear of the wagon. With four of us to a pole, we'll lift the wagon just high enough to take the rear wheels off the ground. We'll need to hold it there only until another stone or two has been placed under each side of the wagon box."

"Makes sense," said Van, "but with all of us mannin' the pry poles, who's going to lay the extra stones to keep the wagon wheels off the ground?"

"The one person we have to thank for all this," said Gil. "Senora Mendoza, we need your help."

Victoria took her time getting there.

"It's going to take all of us to lift the wagon," Gil told her. "When we do, you'll need to put another stone or two on each of the piles we've built under the wagon box. Wedge them tight as you can; we must keep the rear wheels of the wagon off the ground."

She nodded, saying nothing. Gil took two of the largest stones, placing one before each of the front wheels, to prevent the wagon from rolling when the rear of it was lifted.

"Now," said Gil, "let's see if this is going to work. I'll take one pole, and Van, you get the other. The rest of you split up, half with me, half with Van."

The butt ends of the poles were placed on the ground beneath the wagon axle, one on the inside of each rear wheel. The men got in position, their shoulders under the poles, and when Gil gave the order, they put all their strength to the task. The big wagon rocked forward against the stones that blocked the front wheels, and slowly the rear of the Conestoga began to rise.

"That's far enough," Gil panted. "Let's see if we can hold it there until the extra stones are in place."

Quickly Victoria built up one side and then ran to the other. Gil was watching when she got to her feet.

"Now," he said, "let it down easy."

Slowly they let the wagon down, until its undercarriage rested on the two piles of stones. The extra ones Victoria had added kept the rear wheels of the wagon maybe three inches off the ground. It was enough.

"We have maybe enough time to pull the wheels and get that broken axle off before sundown," said Gil. "Let's get it done."

Van had already loosened the bolts securing the axle, and once the rear wheels were off the ground, removal of the broken axle wasn't difficult. Gil studied the axle, comparing it to the size of the heavy cedar from which he hoped to hew a replacement. Already the sun had dipped behind the Sierra Madres, and only a rosy glow remained.

"It'll be dark pretty soon," said Van. "No way we can finish this today."

"I think we can," said Gil. "In fact, I aim to." He turned to Ramon.

"Ramon, I'll need Van, Manuel, and Pedro here to help me. The rest of you ride back to the herd. It's been a while since we crossed a creek, so we're due one. Send Mariposa or Estanzio to scout ahead. If there's water close enough, drive the horse herd and the longhorns to it. If there is none, we'll stay where we are, in dry camp. We're goin' to replace this axle if we have to do it by firelight. I don't aim to start another day with this hanging over our heads."

Ramon rode back to the herd, taking Juan Alamonte, Domingo Chavez, and Vicente Gomez with him.

"We're going to need a small fire," said Gil. "Just enough to see what we're doing. Manuel, you and Pedro get us a fire going, while Van and me shape this new axle."

After cutting the cedar the right length, they did nothing more than shape the ends so that the hubs would fit and groove the wood in the right places to secure the U bolts. The rest of the "axle" still had the bark on. It was rough work, but it would do. They were pounding the wheels in place when Mariposa rode in from the north. He looked at Gil, shaking his head. There was no water near enough. After a hard day, they were stuck in a dry camp, without even coffee.

8

JULY 9, 1843. On the trail.

The entire outfit was up and about an hour before first light. There had been little sleep. The horses had been restless in their thirst, and the longhorns had refused to bed down. They had milled about, bawling their misery.

"This is my fault," said Gil. "I should have stuck to my first decision, trailed the stock to the nearest water and then fixed the wagon."

"Well," said Van, "next time — if there is one — we'll know how to handle it. I can't blame you for wantin' to stay with that wagon and be done with it. We'd already lost a day because of it, and I'd have hated to have it drag over until today. Soon as it's light enough, let's hit the trail."

"I aim to," said Gil. "We'll pass up breakfast, and eat when we reach water. Get the word to the riders, and I'll wake her majesty. I'm not of a mind to wait while she harnesses the teams."

Gil rapped on the wagon's tailgate with the butt of his Colt.

"What do you want?"

"I want you to harness your teams and be ready to move out in ten minutes."

He didn't wait for her response, if there was one. He didn't want to hear it. He found the outfit ready to ride. Van had saddled Gil's horse. Victoria took him at his word. She had harnessed her teams and moved out, even before the longhorns took the trail. Estanzio and Mariposa led the horse herd in pursuit of the wagon, while the other riders drove the restless longhorns into line.

"Every critter in the bunch is goin' in a trot," said Van. "They seem to know we're going to water."

"Thank God there's no wind," said Gil. "One little breeze with the smell of water, and we'd have a stampede like you've never seen."

Gil sent Estanzio ahead, and the Indian returned with the welcome news there was a creek not more than two hours away. But by the time they were within a mile or two of the water, the thirsty cattle sensed or smelled it, and there was no holding them. Gil and Van got ahead of the running herd, but there was no slowing or stopping them. The Texans had to ride for their lives. The Mendoza horses, seeing a solid wall of longhorns thundering toward them, yielded to their own panic, and the stampede was on. The horse herd quickly caught up to the wagon and split around it. The longhorns followed the same path, and it was all that prevented some of the animals being crippled or killed as they fought to reach the water at the same point. Instead they fanned out along the creek for a mile.

"Come on," shouted Gil, "we've got to get the horses out of there!"

The horses were in danger of being gored by the thirst-maddened longhorns. Mariposa and Estanzio were already hazing the horses out of the water. They and their mounts were in danger, because some of the longhorns hadn't yet reached the water and were fighting their way toward it. The animals would vent their rage on whoever or whatever stood in their way. The creek bank was congested with cattle, all fighting for water in the same limited area. Following Gil's lead, the riders doubled their lariats and started swatting longhorns. It had an effect. Those unable to reach the water were forced down the creek, where they could drink. Slowly the riders took control. Some of the horses had been raked with horns, but with some sulfur salve to protect them from infection and blow flies, they would heal. It was late afternoon before the last longhorn had drunk its fill and was content to graze.

"We're not going to risk another dry camp tonight," said Gil. "It's late enough in the day to just bed the herds down where they are. Startin' today, I aim to send Mariposa or Estanzio to scout ahead for at least a day's drive. They'll find the next water, of course, but they may be able to warn us of what may be ahead. Ramon, what do you think?"

"Is good," said Ramon. *"Bueno."* Many times, Gil had asked his opinion, and had taken his advice. The Texans had treated him — and all the riders — like men whose knowledge was respected, and not just as hired hands. Ramon spoke rapidly in Spanish to Mariposa and Estanzio, and they nodded their understanding.

"Estanzio go," said Ramon. "Mariposa *mañana.*"

There was still several hours of daylight, when Estanzio rode out. He could easily cover ten miles — a good day's drive — and return before dark. Gil was ashamed he hadn't begun this sensible practice from the first day on the trail. It was far better to bed down the herds near water, even if it meant losing part of a day. Pushing on, risking another dry camp, only invited a stampede such as they'd just experienced. Estanzio returned, reporting that he had found water within the next day's drive. But he had other news. Disturbing news.

"*Caballos*," he said. "*Soldados*." He held up both hands, the fingers spread. Then he dropped one hand. Fifteen mounted soldiers!

"Ramon," said Gil, "ask him how he knows they were *soldados*."

Ramon spoke rapidly, and Estanzio knelt down. With his finger he poked four holes in the soft ground, each at the corner of an imaginary square. Then he put the palms of his hands together, steepling his fingers.

"*Tienda*," he said.

The resourceful Indian had scouted the campsite, finding the small holes where tent pins had been driven into the ground. Who but soldiers — likely the officers — would use tents?

"Fifteen soldiers!" Van exclaimed. "What are they doing this far south?"

"I don't know," said Gil. "More important, where are they going?"

Gil turned to Estanzio and pointed north, south, east, and west. The Indian understood, and pointed to the east. The soldiers had ridden away to the east. Gil had one more question. The sun had set beyond the Sierra Madres, and Gil pointed to its afterglow. He raised one, two, and then three fingers. How many suns ago had the soldiers ridden away?

"*Uno*," said Estanzio, raising one finger.

"We don't know where they're going, or why," said Gil. "Starting tonight, we'll be more careful. Let's get supper out of the way, and douse the fire before dark."

They night-hawked as usual, in teams of four, but their concern went beyond the predators that might endanger the horses or cattle. They listened for sounds foreign to the night, such as the chink of a shod hoof against a stone, the creak of a saddle, or the jingle of a spur. But nothing disturbed the silence. The outfit had finished breakfast, and they waited for Victoria to lead out with the wagon. Estanzio and Mariposa were with the horse herd. All the riders were in position, except Van and Ramon. Gil had mounted, preparing to ride ahead of the wagon.

"Senora Mendoza!" said Ramon, pointing.

Victoria stood behind the wagon, waving her hat.

"Now what?" Van wondered aloud.

Then they saw the riders. There were four, and they paused for only a moment at the wagon. Apparently, they spoke to Victoria, and then rode on.

"Fan out," said Gil, "and be prepared for anything. I don't like the look of this. They're not soldiers, so they'll have to be outlaws or thieves."

The closer they came, the more ominous they appeared. They wore the high-crowned, wide-brimmed hats, but the rest of their garb was far fancier than a working vaquero could afford. Their breeches were skintight, with silver conchos down the outer seam of the leg. Their shirts were white, with ruffles, and their jackets were trimmed with gold braid. Their saddles were silver-mounted, with trapaderos. Each man carried a rifle in his saddle boot. They were all armed with pistols, their rigs low-slung, holsters thonged down just above the knee. They reined up a dozen yards away, and the lead rider spoke in English.

"I am Francisco Velasco," he said, "and these are my trusted lieutenants. We are scouts for the *milicia*, the army of General Santa Anna. May I ask what is the purpose of this *caravana*, and its destination?"

"This is the Mendoza outfit," said Gil, "and these horses and cattle are being driven north for use of the Mexican army."

"*Por Dios*," said Velasco, "such generosity. There are thousands of cows. Every *soldado* will have a *vaca* of his own. And what of the horses?"

The other three riders chuckled at their leader's humor. Gil said no more. He thought he knew what was coming.

"We have need of extra mounts," said Velasco, with a straight face. "You have many, and since they are for the use of the *milicia*, I think we

137

will take some of them with us. You may tell General Santa Anna you released them upon my order."

"We have no proof you are scouts for Santa Anna."

"You have my word," said Velasco, his good humor vanishing.

"And you have mine," said Gil. "Make a move toward those horses, a man of you, and you will die."

"It is you who will die," snarled Velasco. "You have made the big mistake, senor."

"You'll be making a bigger one," said Gil, "if you don't ride out of here. Pronto!"

Velasco wheeled his horse and rode away, his three companions following. They rode past Victoria's wagon without stopping.

"They're no more scouts for Santa Anna than we are," said Van. "Didn't seem to bother them that a pair of Tejanos are working for the Mendoza outfit."

"*Bandiojes*," said Ramon. "*Pistoleros.*"

"That's exactly what they are," said Gil. "Bandits and gunmen. They knew almighty well we wouldn't buy their story. They were here to size us up, to take our measure."

"*Noche*," said Ramon. "*Estampida.*"

"That's it, Ramon," said Gil. "Maybe not tonight, but *some* night soon they'll stampede the horses. Or try to."

"With a trail herd this big," said Van, "they know there has to be at least a dozen of us. We outnumber them three to one."

"Don't bet on it," said Gil. "These four

coyotes are part of the fifteen whose tracks Estanzio found yesterday. Two of the four who just rode out had bedrolls *and* canvas rolls behind their saddles. That's the tents that led Estanzio to believe they were soldiers. When they come after us, there'll be more of them. They'll bring the whole pack."

"*Por Dios,*" said Ramon. "*Veradero.*"

"If they're comin' to call," said Van, "the least we can do is arrange a welcome."

"Count on it," said Gil. "Startin' tonight, we're going to be ready for this bunch of coyotes. They're goin' to find themselves on the receiving end of a good old Texas ambush."

"Is good," said Ramon. "*Bueno.*"

"They won't come tonight," said Van. "There'll be a moon."

"Maybe not," said Gil, "and maybe they'll count on us thinkin' that way. So we can't gamble. We'll be ready."

"*Guardia?*" Ramon asked.

"Four night hawks until midnight," said Gil, "and eight from midnight to dawn. When we sleep, we won't shuck anything but our hats. See that all horses are saddled and picketed close by, but well away from the horse herd and the cattle. If everything goes to hell and there's a stampede, let every man have his mount close enough to grab the reins."

Victoria's curiosity got the best of her. She left the wagon where it was and returned on foot.

"Who were they and what did they want?" she asked.

"Thieves and killers, claiming to be scouts for

Santa Anna," said Gil. "They wanted horses. These four are part of a band of fifteen. Estanzio found their tracks yesterday. They may try to grab the horses by stampeding the herd. Don't picket your wagon teams at night. Hobble them, and keep them well away from the other horses."

Her face paled but she said no more. She turned away and returned to the wagon.

"Move 'em out!" shouted Gil, waving his hat.

They easily covered the distance to the creek Estanzio had reported the day before. It was the best day they'd had. Ramon sent Mariposa to scout ahead, so they'd know where the next water was.

"Mariposa *estar a la mirade pistoleros*," said Ramon.

"*Bueno*, Ramon," said Gil. "*Bueno*."

It had been a good move, sending Estanzio or Mariposa on a daily scouting mission. Now Ramon was making them more aware of the importance of reporting potential dangers. Such as the whereabouts of the band of thieves Gil expected to return. Mariposa returned, but without sighting the thieves or their trail. He had found water, but they must drive farther to reach it.

"Ramon," said Gil, "starting tonight, I want you to pick three riders and take the first watch. The rest of us will take it from midnight to dawn. That's when I expect trouble, and I want Van and me right on top of it."

"Pedro Fagano, Vicente Gomez, and Juan

140

Padillo," said Ramon.

It was significant that Ramon had not chosen Mariposa or Estanzio. As Gil had said, if there was trouble, it would most likely come in the dark, silent hours of the morning, when men slept the hardest and perceived the least. It was a time when the Indian skills of Mariposa and Estanzio would be most needed.

★ ★ ★

Ramon had nothing to report when they changed watches at midnight. It was a good camp, with plenty of water and graze. The horses and longhorns were silent. Because it was so peaceful, the night seemed to drag on forever. Gil had a breakfast fire going at first light.

"There'll be a longer drive ahead of us today," he said. "Let's eat and move out."

During the day's drive, they encountered no problems. But before they reached the creek where they would bed down for the night, Estanzio rode out. He would have farther to ride in his search for water. There was a cloud bank to the west. Beyond it, the sun had gone to rest early, leaving the Sierra Madres in shadow. There was a faraway rumble of thunder.

"Just what we need," said Van. "A storm, followed by a stampede."

"Perhaps *mañana*," said Ramon, shaking his head.

"Storm, or stampede?" Gil asked, with a grin. "Can't we just have one or the other?"

The first half of the night was peaceful. There

141

was no moon, and the big dipper showed it to be near two o'clock. Van leaned back in his saddle, one leg hooked around the horn.

"I realize you've never been wrong in your life, big brother, but this is goin' to be the first time. I don't believe they're comin'. I think — "

He got no farther. There was the patter of hoofs and the nicker of a frightened horse. They kicked their horses into a run, but they were already too late. The galloping horse had passed through the horse herd and was among the longhorns. There was no rider. The running horse trailed a lariat, dragging the hide of a freshly killed cougar. There was the cougar scent and the smell of blood, and it had the effect of touching flame to a keg of powder. If the Devil himself had taken a hand, the timing couldn't have been more diabolically perfect. The Mendoza horses surged to their feet in a nickering frenzy, just as the horse dragging the cougar hide galloped into the herd of longhorns. They were off and running, just in time for the horse herd to mingle with them. It wasn't a stampede, but an explosion, something out of a cowboy's nightmare. There was no pattern, no direction. The herds split seven ways from Sunday, and nothing would stop them till they ran out their fear. Slowly the riders came together in the aftermath of the disaster.

"My God," Van groaned, "we won't live enough years to round up all these brutes."

"I don't aim to hunt for a one of 'em," said Gil through gritted teeth, "until we round up

142

that bunch of yellowbellied coyotes responsible for this. And if they're hidin' behind Santa Anna, then maybe I'll end this scrap with Mexico myself!"

"They won't get much of a jump on us," said Van. "They can't round up horses in the dark."

They found the horse that had dragged the cougar hide. The unfortunate animal had been gored and then trampled. Mariposa and Estanzio rode up, followed by Bola and Juan Padillo. Gil's anger faded, and he became concerned for his riders.

"Sing out," he cried, "if you can hear me. Is any man afoot, or hurt?"

Every man answered when his name was called, and they came together, following the sound of his voice.

"Everybody roll in your blankets," said Gil, "and get what sleep you can. Be ready to ride at first light. Bring your lariats, your rifles, and all the shells that you have. The horses and cows will have to wait; we're goin' on a coyote hunt."

Gil rode to the Mendoza wagon. In the distance he could see the huge gray shapes of the Conestoga horses. Evidently she had taken his advice and had hobbled her teams. When he rode up, she was standing behind the wagon, only the pale oval of her face visible in the shadows.

"What has happened?" she asked.

"Stampede. A bad one. We'll be here awhile."

"How long?" she asked.

143

"A week, if we're lucky."

He said no more, nor did he wait for further response from her. Wheeling his horse, he rode back to see if there was anything left of their camp. Everything seemed in place. The packhorses were gone, of course, but they wouldn't be needed, he thought grimly, until that bunch of rustlers had been made to pay. His head on his saddle, unable to sleep, he waited impatiently for first light. Finally he got up, put on his hat, and started a breakfast fire. Van raised his eyebrows.

"I know it's still dark," said Gil, "but the hell with it. If a pilgrim sees this fire and wants trouble, he's come to the right place. When it's light enough, I aim to be on the trail of that bunch of thieving bastards."

Nobody had slept. They wolfed down bacon, flapjacks and coffee, knowing it might be their only meal until justice was done. Then, with Mariposa and Estanzio reading sign, they rode out.

"This ain't goin' to be easy," said Van. "The Mendoza herd is shod. How do we follow the tracks of the rustlers' horses? Which is which?"

"I'm leaving that to Estanzio and Mariposa," said Gil. "The way they all scattered, I doubt we'll find more than two or three running together. I'd say we'll ride in a widening circle until we cross a trail we can identify."

Suddenly, Estanzio and Mariposa reined up and dismounted, kneeling to study a particular track. Gil and Ramon dismounted, joining them. On the outside edge of the print in question, there was a clear impression of a bent nail.

"Not a Mendoza horse," said Gil.

Estanzio shook his head. The Indian riders had personally inspected the hoofs of the horses before leaving the ranch. While a bent nail might cause no harm, it was shoddy work, something neither Indian rider would have tolerated. They now had a hoofprint that could be readily identified among all the others. When they found this one rider, they would find at least some of the others. In good light, the sharp-eyed Indians could read sign at a trot. Occasionally they lost the trail, doubling back to the last identifiable print and taking a new direction. Mariposa reined up and swung out of the saddle to study another hoofprint. This one had a corner of the inside caulk broken off the shoe, leaving a track as distinct as that with the bent nail.

"This is some important information," said Gil. "We're trailing six horses, and two of them are the rustlers' mounts. That means this bunch has split up, working in twos and threes. We'll account for as many as we can, before the gang comes together again."

"We can just keep our distance," said Van, "and these two jaybirds will lead us to the others."

"Think, brother," said Gil. "You want to fight the whole gang at once, and maybe get some of us killed?"

"I reckon not," said Van, "but it'll take longer, trackin' them down two or three at a time."

"We'll take these two," said Gil, "and then

we'll worry about the others. Remember, we have Mariposa and Estanzio tracking for us, and these horses are like family to them."

Mariposa and Estanzio reined up for a moment, keening the wind like a pair of hunting wolves. There was a faint odor of dust in the air; their quarry was near. The Indians kicked their horses into a run, with the rest of the outfit following. They topped a ridge, and near the crest of the next one they saw the two riders they had been trailing. Each man had a pair of Mendoza blacks on lead ropes.

"Ride 'em down!" shouted Gil. "They'll have to free the horses, and when they do, some of you grab those lead ropes. The rest of us can grab these coyotes."

Their pursuers gaining, the fleeing riders dropped the lead ropes and ran for their lives. Mariposa, Estanzio, Domingo, and Pedro went after the freed Mendoza horses. Gil, Van, Ramon, and Bola were closing in on the rustlers. Gil and Van were in the lead, and shook out their lariats. Gil dropped his loop over one man's shoulders while Van roped the other. Ramon and Bola caught both horses. They would be needed. Gil and Van dismounted, Colts drawn, as the rustlers got to their feet. Ramon and Bola had returned with the two horses.

"Ramon, you and Bola take their guns," said Gil, "and then take some thongs and tie their hands behind their backs."

When the men had been securely bound, Gil and Van brought their horses.

"Mount up!" Gil said to the bound men.

But they were unable to mount, and had to be helped. There was plenty of scrub oak, head-high pine, and cedar, but they had to search for a tree substantial enough to suit their needs. Each condemned man had a thirteen-knot noose tied under his left ear. Gil looped the free end of one rope around his saddle horn, while Van did likewise with the other. Slowly, the riders progressed across the ridge, and near the foot of it found the tree they were seeking. Mariposa, Estanzio, Domingo, and Pedro had caught up to them, leading the Mendoza horses. Gil threw the loose end of his rope over an oak limb, and Van did the same. They then pulled the loose ends taut and tied them securely to the trunk of the oak. Then Gil spoke to the pair of rustlers.

"Any last words, hombres?"

One of the men cursed him in Spanish, but the other said nothing. They glared at their executioners, their dark eyes reflecting their hate. In a single motion Gil and Van each slapped one of the horses on the flank, and they leaped forward. Their former riders were left kicking the air, turning slowly. Mariposa and Estanzio had caught up the rustlers' horses. Gil and Van mounted and led out, the rest of the riders following. Nobody looked back.

"We'd better find a place to hide these horses," said Van. "If there was fifteen of these skunks, we've got a big day ahead of us. Six horses on lead ropes will slow us down."

"Good idea," said Gil. "That pair each had a rifle, and since I don't, I'm claiming one."

"Then I want the other," said Van. "Ramon,

147

their pistols are foreign-made. Any of our riders with a similar gun can use their shells. Search their saddlebags too, when you get the chance. If none of us has a gun that'll take their shells, then a couple of you take their pistols as extras."

They found a secluded area along a creek, and picketed the six horses where they could water and graze. From there, they rode in an ever-widening circle, as Mariposa and Estanzio sought another trail. When they found it, veering to the northeast, Mariposa and Estanzio reined up and dismounted. There were the tracks of more than fifty horses.

"That's a big piece of our herd," said Van, "and the way they're bunched, they're being driven."

The rest of them watched as Estanzio and Mariposa studied the tracks. They followed the trail on foot for a hundred yards, establishing the reliability of it, and then trotted back to their horses.

"*Bandidos*," said Mariposa. He extended five fingers and then two.

"Seven of them," said Gil. "This time we'll have a fight on our hands."

They had ridden less than an hour when they caught up to the lingering dust of the herd.

"Some of us could ride like hell," said Van, "circle around and get ahead of them."

"No," said Gil, "we don't split our forces. They can see our dust as well as we can see theirs. We'll stay on their trail, forcing them to take a stand. When they do, we'll try a flanking movement and maybe set up a cross fire."

"They know they can't escape by outrunning us," said Van. "I'm surprised they haven't set up an ambush."

"Greasewood and scrub oak don't offer much cover," said Gil. "Anyhow, we got a pair of hawk-eyed Indians reading sign. They'll let us know if somebody gets ideas and leaves the bunch."

But the country was becoming more broken. They crossed a ridge and trotted their horses down a slope that had eroded to bare rock and where nothing grew but an occasional yucca. At the foot of the slope was a dry, shallow arroyo, and beyond that, a steeper, more hazardous incline led to yet another ridge. Along its backbone ran a marching column of jagged stone upthrusts that looked like broken, uneven teeth. Mariposa and Estanzio reined up at the foot of the slope. A rifle slug whanged off a stone a few feet ahead of them. They were still out of range.

"Ramon," said Gil, "let's try flanking these *busardos* and getting a couple of our riders behind them. Send Mariposa down this arroyo to the south, while Estanzio follows it to the north. We don't know if it's one man up there with a rifle, or the whole bunch. Tell Mariposa and Estanzio to work around behind them, on the other side of that ridge. If it's just one bushwhacker, they can take him. If it's all of them, tell Mariposa and Estanzio to cut down on them. That'll give us a chance to get up this hill and hit 'em from this side."

149

The Indians quickly departed, while the rest of the riders waited.

"They'll expect us to try something like this," said Van. "They figure they got an ace in the hole, and I'm wondering what it is."

The answer came almost immediately. From the ridge behind them came the ominous crash of rifles. Lead kicked up dust all around them as they scrambled for cover in the shallow arroyo. Nickering in fear, their horses scattered. They were afoot, themselves caught in a deadly cross fire.

9

THE arroyo in which they had taken cover was wide and shallow. There wasn't enough depth to kneel or sit, so they ended up belly down on a flint-hard surface that was uncomfortably hot from the noon-high sun. Gil twisted himself around, but they were so strung out, he couldn't see all his men.

"Anybody hit?" he asked. There was no affirmative response.

"I think I busted both my knees," said Van, "when I took a dive into this ditch, and it ain't even enough cover for us to return their fire, without gettin' our ears shot off. Lucky for us it's just six more hours till dark."

"We won't last that long," said Gil. "We can't defend ourselves from here. All of you keep your heads down. It all depends on Estanzio and Mariposa. When they cut loose, that's our cue to hit that slope on the run. We'll top that· ridge with our guns smoking."

Gil twisted over on his back, and using a slender dead branch, lifted his hat into view. Rifles blasted immediately from both ridges. While his action may have seemed foolish and futile, it might serve them in two ways. It would further encourage his riders to make good use of the scant cover they had, until time to make their move. Also, the double fusillade was all the warning Mariposa and Estanzio

151

would need. They were now well aware that the rest of the rustlers were forted up on the opposite ridge, and that Gil and the Mendoza riders were caught in a cross fire. Not a breath of air stirred. The shallow ditch in which they concealed themselves had eroded down to bare rock, and Gil could feel the heat of it through his shirt. The sweat dripped off his nose, off his chin, and he sleeved it out of his eyes. The sun bore down with a vengeance, and they had no water. Their canteens had been thonged to their saddles, and their horses had gone God knew where.

"Them Injuns have been gone an almighty long time," said Van.

"They'll do it their way," said Gil. "When they cut loose, we'll charge this bunch at the top of the hill. Just don't let any grass grow under your feet. Those on the ridge behind us are in range, and when we make our move, we'll draw their fire. We've got to get out of their range and up that hill before this bunch ahead of us recovers from the surprise Estanzio and Mariposa will lay on 'em."

The first two shots came so close together, one seemed the echo of the other. Mariposa and Estanzio had arrived.

"Come on!" Gil shouted.

They were on their feet, zigzagging up the slope, and the fire from the ridge behind them was heavy. But the rustlers were shooting downhill, at rapidly diminishing targets. Firing continued from somewhere ahead of them, as Mariposa and Estanzio presented a new threat to the outlaws. Gil and Van had rifles now, and they topped the ridge shooting. The outfit had fanned out and every man was firing. Once their comrades had begun their attack, Estanzio and Mariposa had ceased firing, lest they hit some of their own men. Gil and the rest of the outfit gunned down five of the rustlers, while the last two disappeared in the scrub oak toward the bottom of the slope.

"Two of the bastards got away," said Van.

"No, they didn't," said Gil. "Estanzio and Mariposa are down there."

On the heels of his words, there were two quick shots from downslope. There was no further sound, no movement, until Mariposa and Estanzio trotted out of the scrub oak. Each man carried an extra rifle and pistol belt. Gil waved his Stetson at them. Then he walked to the crest of the ridge so he could see the opposite one, but there was no sign of the outlaws. Again he turned to the field of battle, and found his riders collecting pistols, shell belts, and rifles.

"That's nine of 'em," said Van, "includin' the two we strung up. The rest are hightailin' it, like the yellow coyotes they are. Are we goin' after them?"

"Not if they're making a genuine run for it," said Gil. "If they couldn't take us with fifteen men, I don't expect them to try again, with less than half that number."

"Velasco escaped," said Van, "unless he was one of the pair that Mariposa and Estanzio

153

gunned down. I'm bettin' we ain't seen the last of that skunk."

"You're likely right," said Gil, "but we'll have to deal with him when our trails cross again. With horses and long-horns scattered over half of Mexico, we're goin' to purely have our hands full for a while."

"*Caballos*," said Ramon.

Juan Padillo, Pedro Fagano, and Domingo Chavez had brought the seven horses belonging to the dead rustlers.

"Some of you take their horses," said Gil, "and go look for ours. While you're about it, see if you can locate the horses these thieves were taking."

"*Busardos* come," said Mariposa.

The big black birds had already begun to circle, waiting their time.

"Them damn buzzards," said Van. "They draw more attention than smoke signals. Too bad we can't bury this bunch of no-account varmints, so's the buzzards don't arouse too much curiosity."

"Forget that," said Gil. "Rocky as this ground is, you'd need blasting powder to crack the surface. We have our hands full, tracking down horses and longhorns."

"I *told* you Texas and Mexico would sign a peace treaty before we get to the border."

"You may be right," said Gil, "and I hope they do. God knows, we don't have anything else going for us. Let's ride."

They finished the day still missing sixty head of horses. Victoria was furious.

154

"You will find them!" she shouted. "Even one of them is worth more than every one of your miserable cows!"

"Maybe," said Gil calmly, "and we'll find them if we can. But we'll be looking for them while we gather longhorns. We start the cow hunt tomorrow."

★ ★ ★

July 23, 1843. Mexico City.

A hundred Mexican soldiers were about to depart for the long march north. There was instant pandemonium in the street when a crate fell from a cart and broke, loosing live chickens. The squawking, cackling birds ran in every direction, while the soldiers slapped their thighs and laughed at the spectacle. Patient burros bore hogskin bags of maguey sap — known as *agua miel* — which, when fermented, would become a volatile Mexican liquor called pulque.[1]

While the town square and portions of the capital city were festive, Mexico City had its dark side. Here, the streets were not cobblestone, but dirt. Dusty when dry, muddy when it rained. Here, the poor eked out only an existence, and hope was just one of the many things they lacked. Along these nondescript back streets were the cheap rooming houses, rundown cafés, dirt-floor

---

[1] The maguey is also known as the aloe or century plant.

155

bars, tamale vendors, brothels, and beggars. One such street was a dead end, and there crouched a forbidding building whose stone had weathered from gray to an appropriate macabre black. It was the infamous dungeon, a rat-and lice-infested hole where political prisoners and enemies of those in power lived. And died. Texans captured by Santa Anna's army were marched south, and those unfortunate enough to reach Mexico City alive were sent to the dungeon.

The prison was fully enclosed by an adobe wall a dozen feet high and a fourth of that thick. On the inside of these walls, to the height of a man, the adobe had been pocked by hundreds of rifle balls. It was mute testimony to the men who, for crimes real or fabricated, had been backed against the walls and shot to death. The nearest café — perhaps the worst of a bad lot — was the Cocodrillo.[1] It was half a block down a rutted street, a slab-sided, unpainted building with a rough bench under the roof overhang, which passed for a porch. The lone man who slouched on the bench seemed neither young nor old. He wore neither boots nor sandals, but deerskin moccasins. His hat tilted over his eyes, he appeared to sleep, to see nothing. But he saw everything. Solano waited. Inside the Cocodrillo a very fat Mexican woman had just hired a cook,

---

[1] Crocodile

156

and attempted to explain to the girl her many duties.

"*Puesta del sol, comida con guarda, calabozo. Comprender?*"

"*Comprender,*" said Angelina Ruiz. At sundown she would take supper to the guards at the dungeon.

★ ★ ★

July 25, 1843. On the trail.

Five days north of their near disastrous stampede and the fight with the Mexican horse thieves, Gil was still wary. He didn't believe they'd seen the last of Francisco Velasco and what remained of his gang. Gil talked to Ramon, and they continued with four riders until midnight, then doubled their force until dawn. Although Estanzio and Mariposa were part of the second watch, they spread their blankets near the horse herd and spent the first part of the night there. The hours before midnight was when trouble was least expected, but hardly a night passed when they didn't hear the distant cry of a cougar.

"No matter how far away they are," said Van, "the varmints purely make me nervous."

"You could say that for the horses too," said Gil, "but when you can hear 'em, that's when they're the least dangerous. Too bad the horses don't understand that. The times we don't hear 'em, I always wonder if it's because they're downwind, stalking the horses."

157

An hour before dark a storm blew in from the west. While there was wind and rain, there was no thunder or lightning. There wasn't even enough shelter to have a fire, so they had no coffee. The riders hunkered in the rain, eating cold biscuit and jerked beef.

"Nobody's sleepin' dry tonight," said Van, "except Senora Mendoza. Was this what she had in mind when she insisted on bringin' that big wagon?"

"Somehow, I doubt it," said Gil. "Anybody that ain't prepared to be rained, snowed, sleeted, and hailed on, purely don't belong on a trail drive."

They fully expected to spend a wet, miserable night, with little or no sleep. The rain ceased sometime after dark, but the heavy gray clouds remained. The night was so black, the moon and stars might not have existed. Adding further to the misery of that desolate night, a dense, clammy fog settled over the land.

"*Espectro noche*," said Estanzio. He nodded to Mariposa, and the two of them disappeared in the foggy night.

"Spirit night," said Gil. "Their old superstitions are gettin' to 'em. They'll likely spend the night with the horses."

"I kind of understand how they feel," said Van. "It's like the world just rolled over, and we're lost in the clouds. We've had five good days in a row, and I'm a mite uneasy. Hell's bells, I'm worse'n Granny Austin. When things kinda bottom out, I wonder why, I feel like . . . well, like there's somethin' out there that's just waitin' for us to stop and try to catch our breath."

While Gil didn't admit it, he felt a little uneasy. But he put it from his mind, telling himself they'd fallen prey to old Indian superstitions and myths. But later on he wouldn't be so sure. For that was the night the cougar came . . .

★ ★ ★

The horse herd grazed on the south side of the creek, while the longhorns had been bedded down on the north side. There was a light breeze — no more than an occasional breath of airs — from the northwest. A predator stalking the herds would come from the south, approaching its prey against the wind. Estanzio and Mariposa reached the first of the grazing horses. There Mariposa waited, while Estanzio trotted down the creek to the opposite side of the herd. Each would walk a horseshoe pattern around the grazing horses, but neither was ever far from that vulnerable south flank. Every few minutes they'd meet there, as they walked in opposite directions. They paused at every meeting, listening for any sound that seemed alien to the night. They had just parted when the attack came. The cougar sprang from the fog-shrouded darkness without warning, sinking its claws into Mariposa's back. The snarling cat on top of him, the Indian went belly down. His Bowie was on a leather thong, down his back, out of his reach. The nearest horse sounded an

159

alarm, nickering wildly, and the herd lit out across the creek.

It being early in the night, only four riders were circling the herds. With the terrified nicker from the horse, the rest of the outfit was in their saddles and riding. Even above the thunder of the stampede, Gil could hear the snarling and screeching of the cougar. He kicked his horse into a run toward the sound, his rifle ready. The clouds had parted and there was just enough light for him to witness the terrible struggle. The cougar had dug its claws into Mariposa's back and shoulders. Estanzio, being unable to shoot, had straddled the snarling cougar like a bucking bronc. The Indian had his left arm locked around the beast's neck, and had wrapped his legs around its lean flanks. In Estanzio's upraised right hand was his Bowie, as again and again he plunged it into the body of the cougar. With the big cat sandwiched between them, there was no way Gil could shoot without risking hitting Estanzio or Mariposa. But Estanzio's thrusts were taking a toll. The cougar seemed to pause in its struggle, and Estanzio took advantage, driving the big Bowie deep into the animal's throat. It was the beginning of the end. Estanzio let loose his death grip on the dying cougar, rolling free. He lay there panting, exhausted. Some of the other riders had arrived, and Gil hadn't even noticed.

"My God," said Van, in awe. "I've never seen anything like that in my life!"

There was no time for talk. With Van's help,

Gil dragged the cougar's lifeless body off and away from Mariposa.

"*Diablo felino*," said Estanzio. He drove his Bowie into the ground to clean it. He then knelt beside the silent Mariposa.

"I hope most of that blood's from the cougar," said Van.

Mariposa's shirt and jacket were slashed from shoulder to waist. Quickly Estanzio tore the material away, revealing the extent of the wounds. They were ugly and deep. The vicious teeth had torn into the shoulders and the back of the neck.

"We'll need hot water," said Gil, "and that means a fire. Damn the Mexican army, and anybody else that comes faunching around."

Mariposa groaned and tried to get up. Gil and Van knelt to help him, but the Indian spoke.

"*Reposo, entonces andar.*"

Gil looked at Estanzio, and the Indian nodded. Gil and Van backed away. Torn and bleeding though he was, Mariposa wished to gather his strength until he was able to walk. And walk he did. He fought his way to hands and knees, and they could hear his labored breathing. Three times he tried to rise to his feet, and three times he sank back to his knees. But the fourth attempt saw him upright, swaying uncertainly, but on his feet. The clouds had been swept away by a rising wind, and the starlight was sufficient for them to make their way back to their camp. Mariposa walked slowly but steadily. Gathering wood in the dark wasn't easy, but Van found a dead cedar and a rotted pine log, part of which was

161

resinous. Once there were some hot coals, Gil made a bed of them and put on a bucket of water to boil.

"Since we've got a fire anyway," said Van, "when you're done heatin' that water, I'm puttin' on the coffeepot. We could all use some hot coffee."

When the water was hot, Gil took an old undershirt that had once been Clay Duval's and ripped it in half. Mariposa sat before the fire, probably in pain, but saying nothing. Gil went to his saddlebag and got the tin of sulfur salve. He then pointed to Mariposa, to the bucket of steaming water, and held up the tin of salve. It was the same medicine they used to doctor horses and cows, and the Indian was familiar with it. For a while he said nothing, made no sign. Would Mariposa's pride lead him to refuse the little medical attention they had to offer? Estanzio said something to him, and Mariposa nodded his acceptance. When Gil had cleansed the bloody wounds, he applied the salve. It was all they could do.

★ ★ ★

Despite Gil's efforts, by dawn Mariposa had a fever. His wounds were swollen and festered. Estanzio spoke to Ramon, and the little vaquero turned to Gil.

"*Medicina*," said Ramon. "Estanzio find. Maguey *cacto. Bueno medicina*."

Gil nodded. He had heard of the healing qualities of the maguey. He knew something

162

must be done, or Mariposa would surely die from infection. Gil turned to Estanzio.

"*Medicina*," he said. "Maguey."

Estanzio nodded, mounted his horse and rode away.

"Well, Ramon," said Gil, "it's roundup time. Again."

"Nort'," said Ramon. "All cow, all *caballo*, nort'."

"That's a change," said Van. "The trail drive's headed north, and that's the way the stampede went."

"Don't get too excited," said Gil. "We'll still have to drag the longhorns out of the brush, and no telling where we'll find the horses. Mount up and let's ride. When Estanzio returns with his *medicina* plants, he can be the doctor."

But they weren't destined to get away so easily. Victoria Mendoza had left her wagon and was headed their way.

"Damn," said Van. "Granny Austin always said trouble comes in batches of three. First, Mariposa got chewed up, then all the horses and longhorns stampeded from here to yonder, and now Senora Mendoza is about to bare her fangs."

Nobody said anything. Most of the outfit still stood in awe of her volatile temper. They all had a pretty good idea as to why she was there, and she fully lived up to their expectations.

"I see," she said icily, "that you have again allowed the herds to run away. How many days will we lose this time?"

"Ma'am," said Gil just as icily, "we'll lose as

163

many days as it takes to find them. Mariposa was hurt last night, when a cougar jumped him. With a big cat that close, a thousand riders couldn't have prevented the herds from running."

With that, he mounted his horse and rode out. The rest of the outfit mounted and followed. But Victoria wasn't finished.

"Ramon," she shouted, "come here. All of you come here. I am ordering you!"

Not a man responded. They rode on as though they hadn't heard.

"*Borrico*,"[1] said Ramon, under his breath.

They had ridden north a dozen miles before they began finding bunches of grazing horses and longhorns. They were strung out along a deep, clear-running creek.

"Plenty of water and graze here," said Gil. "Van, rope a couple of the horses to carry the packs, and ride back to the old camp. Tell Victoria to get that wagon headed this way. Take a horse for Mariposa too."

"Mariposa may not be able to ride."

"Then he can ride in the wagon," said Gil. "Get going, or that blasted wagon won't get here before dark."

Van rode south, contemplating a possible clash with Victoria Mendoza. After her riders had ridden away in defiance, he had little doubt she'd be on the prod. He grinned to himself. Once they reached Texas, Senora Mendoza

---

[1] Stupid woman

might not *have* any riders. He half hoped
Mariposa wouldn't feel up to sitting a saddle,
so he could put the Indian in Victoria's wagon.
When he reached the old camp, Estanzio had
returned. Apparently he had found the healing
maguey and had applied a poultice to Mariposa's
wounds. Van dismounted. He pointed to the
packhorses, to the Mendoza wagon, and then
to the north. Estanzio nodded. Van then turned
to Mariposa, pointing to the Indian and to
the Mendoza wagon. Mariposa shook his head
violently.

"*Ninguno*," he said in disgust. "Squaw
carro! Ninguno squaw *carro!* Mariposa *caballo!
Ninguno* squaw *carro!*"

Van laughed. Having been mauled by the
cougar, unable to help himself, Mariposa's pride
had suffered mightily. Admitting that he was too
weak to fork a horse, and being forced to ride in
a squaw wagon, would be the ultimate disgrace.
Van rode on to the wagon. He'd as well get
her started. Victoria had seen him talking to
Estanzio and Mariposa and was waiting for him.

"We're moving camp to another creek north of
here," he said. "It's a good twelve miles. You'd
best get started."

He spoke quietly, not wishing to antagonize
her. She seemed not to take offense, but went
about harnessing her teams. Van crooked a leg
around his saddle horn and watched her. He felt
a little guilty, not helping her, but the memory
of her volatile temper overcame his guilt. When
she had the teams harnessed, he led out, and
she followed.

★ ★ ★

Being short three riders, Gil rode alone, allowing the rest of the outfit to work in two-man teams. They found nearly half the horse herd almost immediately, but the others would be more difficult. He came upon tracks of four horses, and they were headed north, as though they had some destination in mind. Gil followed, and the land became less broken, more wooded. Bees droned over his head. There would be a creek or river not too far distant, a likely haven for some of the missing horses and longhorns. Then, shocking in the solitude, came a cold, familiar voice.

"That is far enough, Tejano. You are covered."

Gil reined up, and his horse began cropping grass. It was a difficult situation, and he must buy some time. Gil spoke.

"You disappoint me, Velasco. Why didn't you just shoot me in the back?"

"*Por Dios*, it was a temptation, gringo, but I could not bring myself to do it. You took the time and trouble to hang two of my *amigos*, so how could I not do as much for you? Step down, senor, and move away from the horse. I have the ropes with which you hung my *amigos*. Alas, I regret I cannot hang you from the same tree, but one must make do. Now get off the horse, gringo, or I will shoot you out of the saddle."

10

GIL didn't know if he was covered only by Velasco, or by all the remaining outlaws. But it didn't matter; when the other man had the drop, one gun was enough. There was one thing he knew for a certainty: if he dismounted and surrendered his Colt, he was done. A few yards ahead, to his right, was a windblown pine. Its root mass was substantial, so there would be enough of a hole to offer some protection. Perhaps it was full of water, or worse, a haven for reptiles. But he preferred their company to that of the two-legged skunks gunning for him. He slapped the startled horse on the flank, and it bolted. Kicking free of the stirrups, he clung to the horse's neck with his left arm, his left boot hooked over the saddle. Three rifles cut down on him, and he heard the slugs whine close. From somewhere ahead a fourth rifle began blasting. One slug burned the flank of the black, while a second tagged the flying left stirrup. By then he was near enough to the uprooted pine, and he loosed his grip on the horse. He rolled with the fall, going feet first into the hole left by the fallen pine. To his relief, it was full of windblown leaves. He listened, but couldn't hear the galloping horse. He knew the animal had been nicked, but he didn't believe it was seriously hurt. If the rest of his outfit hadn't been near enough to hear the shots, the horse

167

was his only hope. The animal would return to their camp, and the empty saddle would be proof enough that he was in big trouble. But how long could he hold them off? He had only his Colt and the shells in his pistol belt, while the men stalking him were armed with rifles. It was an unpleasant fact quickly confirmed by Velasco.

"Enjoy the few moments you have gained, gringo. There are six of us, and we have rifles. The hole in which you hide will become your grave."

Gil said nothing. He had protection only as long as his adversaries fired from ground level. It was possible they might stand in their stirrups and angle some lead in at him. If that failed, they might step from their saddles into the lower branches of a tree and shoot at him from there. He must draw their fire, hopefully raising enough hell to attract the attention of his outfit.

"Velasco," he taunted, "you are no *malo hombre*, but a chicken-livered *bastardo*. You feed with the *busardos*, and your *madre* is a *mula*."

His tirade had the desired effect. One side of his hole was protected by the upraised root mass of the fallen pine. Velasco and his men took to shooting at the huge clump of roots, trying to ricochet lead from it. One such slug, mostly spent, burned a gash across the small of his back. Mostly they succeeded only in showering him with dust and dirt from the root cluster. It was a standoff that wouldn't last much longer. Most of the fire had come from the south and southwest. Once he had quit the horse, the rifleman to the north had joined the others. They covered him in a half circle, with the root mass of the pine to his back. To the west there was a clearing, and beyond that, some black oaks. They were well-limbed and leafy. While brush and scrub pine obscured the lower trunks and branches of the oaks, he could see the upper branches. Eventually he saw some of the leaves move, and knew his time was short, for there was no wind.

"Tejano," shouted Velasco, "it is your last chance. You will come out of that hole, or you will die in it."

"Then I will die in it, Velasco, you *asno*, you *perro*."

He scrunched down as far as he could, as the four riflemen in the oaks cut down on him. One slug snatched away his hat, a second burned across his shoulder, and a third tore a bloody furrow along his left thigh. They were well out of range of his Colt; without a rifle, he was at their mercy.

"Close, eh, gringo?" Velasco chuckled. "Shall we try once more?"

Gil said nothing. Dust mingled with the sweat that soaked his shirt and dripped off his chin. It was the last draw, and he had no hole card. He hunkered down as far as he could as the rifles roared. Having prepared himself for another devastating volley, it was a moment before he realized this fire wasn't directed at him. Lead clipped the leaves as Velasco's men were gunned out of the oaks. Gil leaped out of the hole and

169

ran to meet his outfit. He met Bola and Ramon loping their horses toward him.

"Shoot *busardos*," said the grinning Ramon, pointing to the oaks.

"Velasco," said Gil. "Did you get him?"

Ramon shook his head, pointing north. "Run like coyote."

"Not this time," said Gil. "Not fast enough, or far enough. Let me have your horse."

Without a word, Ramon dismounted, and Gil took the reins. He swung into the saddle and kicked the horse into a run. Ramon turned to the still-mounted Bola.

"Go," he said, pointing toward the hard-riding Gil.

Bola nodded, urging his own mount into a run. Soon his horse was neck-and-neck with Gil's. He raised his right hand, in which he held the bola, and Gil nodded. They rode on, already tasting the dust of Velasco's passing. Ramon's horse was lathered, and Gil realized the animal had been ridden hard as Ramon and the outfit had come to his rescue. But Velasco's mount would soon tire in the murderous July heat. They splashed into a creek that ran belly deep on their horses. Soon they were out of the wooded area, and there was greasewood-dotted prairie as far as they could see. At first there was only dust, but as they began to gain, they sighted their quarry. Velasco saw them and began quirting his weary horse.

"Let's move in," shouted Gil. "You bring down the horse, and I'll take care of Velasco."

As they drew nearer, Velasco twisted around

170

in his saddle and fired two shots from his pistol. This having no effect, he holstered the weapon and again took to quirting the horse. Bola urged his mount all the more, drawing ahead of Gil. When the gaucho judged himself close enough, he began swinging the three-headed bola like a lariat. Released, it went true, wrapping itself about the hind legs of Velasco's horse. The horse screamed and went down in a cloud of dust. Gil drew up and dismounted, waiting for the disheveled Velasco to get to his feet. They stood twenty yards apart, Gil's thumbs hooked in his pistol belt.

"Now, Senor Velasco," he said, "we'll see how tall an *hombre* you are in a fair fight. When you're of a mind to, pull your iron."

Bola had freed Velasco's horse, and led the exhausted animal away.

"You are the fool, gringo," said Velasco, with a nasty laugh. "I have killed many men. Not in all of Mexico is there one who is my equal."

He was fast. Almighty fast. But his first shot was high, snatching Gil's hat like invisible fingers. While the Texan's draw was a split second behind Velasco's, his action was deliberate, his aim true. The heavy slug caught Velasco high in the chest, between the lapels of his fancy braided jacket. Velasco blasted a second shot into the ground at his feet, then fell flat on his back in the dust.

"Maybe you were the fastest in all of Mexico," said Gil to the dead man, "but speed ain't worth a damn if you don't hit what you're shootin' at."

171

Bola collected Velasco's weapons and ammunition.

"*Gracias*," said Gil.

They mounted, and with Bola leading the extra horse, rode back to join the outfit. Ramon and the other riders had located the outlaws' picketed horses and had taken their weapons and ammunition.

"We're just a couple of hours from sundown," said Gil. "With all the shootin' goin' on, any horses or cows will have rattled their hocks out of here. We'd as well ride on back to camp and get a fresh start tomorrow. We'll have Van and Estanzio with us then."

"*Bueno dia*," said Ramon. "*Pistoleros muerto. Cezar vaca, caballo en paz.*" When Ramon was excited, he reverted totally to Spanish.

It *had* been a good day, Gil thought. They had rid themselves of the Velasco gang, but would they be allowed to hunt their horses and cows in peace? When they had again gathered the scattered herd and continued the drive north, every day would bring them closer to a confrontation with the Mexican army. He wished he had some idea as to the status of the conflict between Texas and Mexico.

A few minutes before dark, Victoria Mendoza drove the wagon into camp, accompanied by Van, Estanzio, and Mariposa. Gil wasn't surprised to find Mariposa in the saddle. The Indian wore no shirt, but rode with a blanket over his shoulders to protect his wounds from the sun. The three riders dismounted, Mariposa slowly, carefully.

172

"I think I insulted him," said Van, with a grin, "when I suggested he ride in the wagon. He'd have mounted that horse if it had killed him."

Mariposa rarely said anything. The little communication Gil had had with him had been through signs and a few Spanish words. He wanted to know how Mariposa felt, so he spoke to Ramon.

"Tell him I asked about him," said Gil.

Ramon spoke to Mariposa and then to Estanzio, who had learned some English. Estanzio surprised them all when he spoke directly to Gil.

"*Bueno*," said Mariposa. "Him tough like hell."

Gil told Van of their fight with Velasco's gang, while Ramon tried to explain it to Estanzio and Mariposa.

"*Bueno*," said Mariposa.

* * *

The following morning they were ready to ride at first light. Weak as he was, it took some doing to keep Mariposa out of the saddle.

"Chewed up and clawed as he is," said Van, "he still wants to ride. I reckon he'll make a good Texan. If we ever see Texas again."

"We'll get there," said Gil. "There's plenty of weapons and ammunition, thanks to Velasco's bunch bein' so well-armed. We picked up six more saddle horses and two packhorses."

"That's a hell of a pile of guns," said Van.

173

"We get the Mex army after us, we'll have some tall explainin' to do."

"We get the army on our tail," said Gil, "and we'll have some shootin' to do. We may need all those guns. I'd leave some of them, but they're Spanish, English, and French makes. That'd make some of the ammunition useless, and I can't see givin' that up."

"Why don't you turn on your Austin charm," said Van, "and sweet talk Senora Mendoza into haulin' all this extra firepower in the wagon?"

"No, thanks," said Gil. "I have bad feelings about that wagon. We'll take Velasco's canvas tents, wrap the extra weapons so they'll ride well, and use packhorses."

Their first day of searching produced 110 horses, and a thousand longhorns. Victoria Mendoza wasn't satisfied with so many horses still missing, but when she glared at Gil, he glared right back.

★ ★ ★

August 1, 1843. On the trail.

After five days they had gathered 4600 longhorns and 180 horses.

"That's it," said Gil. "We could beat the brush for a year and not find any more. We're movin' out in the morning at first light."

"Senora Mendoza will do a burn that'll make Hell look like a cook fire," said Van.

"So be it," said Gil. "No more horses, no more cows. Ramon?"

Ramon shook his head, and so did some of

174

the other riders. They had just finished eating, when Victoria Mendoza headed for their supper fire. They'd already seen her among the horses, so she knew. She didn't waste any words.

"Some of my horses are still missing."

"Fourteen," said Gil. "We're takin' the trail at first light."

"Do as you wish with your miserable cows," she snapped, "but I will remain here, with my vaqueros, until my horses are found."

"Victoria Mendoza," said Gil, exasperated, "don't be a damn fool. We've ridden for miles in every direction. You purely don't move stock through open country without losing some. That's the way it is on a trail drive. Now pull in your horns and be thankful you've only lost fourteen."

Furious, she said nothing more to Gil. Instead she turned to her riders, but found much of their humility had departed. Their eyes met hers, and she was shocked at what she saw.

"Ramon?" she said, pleading.

"No, senora," said Ramon. "No more *caballo*. Is finish."

Gil found himself feeling sorry for Victoria Mendoza. The fire had gone out of her, and she turned away quickly. She was hell on men, but Gil suspected there would be tears for the lost horses.

★ ★ ★

Gil was up before first light. The night had passed uneventfully. He was tempted to invite

175

Victoria Mendoza to eat with them, but thought better of it. He'd only get another tongue-lashing for his sympathy. Anyway, she ate only once a day, after they'd bedded down the herd for the night. Gil often wondered what Senor Mendoza had been like, how he had handled the fiery Victoria. She was beautiful in her own way, but so was the tawny cougar that had almost taken Mariposa's life.

"I don't see her makin' any moves to go with us," said Van.

"She'll go," said Gil. "All she has to do is harness the teams."

Gil hoped he was right. Suppose she took the bit in her teeth and defied him? Until they reached Texas soil, all the Mendoza horses were hers, even those the outfit rode. And he wanted some of those fine horses as much as he wanted the herd of longhorns. To his relief, Victoria harnessed the teams and led out ahead of the horse herd. Mariposa was again in the saddle, apparently healed. Since applying the sulfur salve, Gil hadn't seen the Indian's wounds. Estanzio had applied whatever medication he had concocted from the maguey plant. Mariposa was the most standoffish of the Indian trio. Estanzio had begun to communicate in English, but he had a ways to go. Solano had been the least distant of the three, and Gil wondered what had become of him and the enigmatic Angelina Ruiz.

Their first day's drive following the gather, they reached the clear, deep creek two or three miles north of the place Gil had been pinned down by the Velasco gang.

"Ramon," said Gil, "let's get back to our habit of scoutin' ahead for the next day's water."

"Mariposa go," said Ramon. "Him need ride."

Ramon had taken to speaking in English as best he could, and Gil noted with approval that some of the other riders had followed Ramon's lead. He couldn't help wondering if it was a further rebellion against the high-handed domination of Victoria Mendoza. These were proud men, and the Texans had treated them with respect. It was the stark contrast that was breaking Victoria Mendoza's hold on them. It was dark when Mariposa returned, an almost sure indication that tomorrow's drive would be a long one. Mariposa had some information, and it was going to be interesting to see how well the Indian could communicate. He'd been speaking through Ramon, and Gil suspected this was Ramon's way of breaking Mariposa's silence. He must learn to speak for himself.

Mariposa knelt and drew a line in the soft earth, and pointed to the nearby creek. Beyond that, parallel to it, he drew a second line. This time, instead of his finger, he used a stick, making a deep impression.

"Arroyo," he said.

"Water?" Gil asked, pointing to the creek.

Mariposa shook his head, scooped up some dust and let it dribble out of his hand. If the arroyo was dry, why had he made mention of it at all? But Mariposa had a reason. He stood up, raising his hands as high as he could.

"Arroyo deep," said Gil.

"Much deep," said Mariposa. He pointed to a tall, slender pine, then slowly raised his hands as high as he could.

"My God," said Van, "he's sayin' it's deeper than the height of that pine."

Mariposa nodded. He then knelt and drew a line from their present camp almost to the line representing the deep arroyo. But before the line that would be their trail reached the arroyo line, Mariposa made a sharp turn, paralleling the arroyo. After a distance, he drew their line of travel across that of the arroyo, turning them north again. Once he had crossed the line that was the deep arroyo, he drew a third line farther north. He pointed to it and then to the nearby creek.

"*Bueno*, Mariposa," said Gil. "*Bueno.*"

"*Manãna,*" said Ramon, "go, see."

"I reckon I'd better," said Gil. "This arroyo sounds like a dry canyon, two or three hundred feet deep. He's sayin' we'll have to drive around it, and that somewhere beyond is the next water. Long as it took him to ride there and back, we may have a twenty-mile drive ahead of us. The creek he's drawn may be ten miles the other side of this big ditch."

"I hope it is," said Van. "I'd not want to bed down these herds anywhere within runnin' distance of that canyon. Let a cougar scream a time or two, and every horse and cow we got would stampede. South, with our luck. Hell for leather, right over the edge of that canyon."

"That's something to think about and avoid,"

178

said Gil, "but Mariposa's found a way around it, so there's only a part of it deep enough to be a danger."

* * *

Gil rode out at first light. He wanted not only to see this hazard, but to determine how far away it was. If the terrain was rough, then the miserable wagon might slow them to the extent that they'd be unable to reach water before dark. That would trap them in a dry camp somewhere between the deep canyon and the water Mariposa had found. If that stampede Van had spoken of took place — for any reason — the herds just *might* run south. A thirsty herd, if the water ahead wasn't close enough for them to smell it, would stampede toward that behind them, which they remembered. Gil set his horse in a lope which he estimated would take him ten miles within an hour. Beyond that they'd be pushing their luck, with an average day's drive being only ten to twelve miles.

The "arroyo" Mariposa had reported turned out to be a canyon. A deep canyon, six or seven miles north of their last night's camp. That meant they must drive around this deep part, and then on to the next creek. Considering the time Mariposa had been gone, that could be another ten miles, or more. They would lose the time it took to drive around the deep part of the canyon, and more time as they veered west to take up their original route. He rode up to the canyon rim, and was astounded to find that it was four or five hundred feet deep! Not for just a short distance, but as far as he could see in either direction. The Indian hadn't exaggerated. In fact, with his limited speech and signs, he had understated the danger.

Gil turned his horse and started back, keeping an eye on the terrain as he went. He must decide where they would leave their original line of travel and turn to the east, paralleling the canyon. Having seen the obstacle, Van's fear of a southbound stampede didn't seem a bit out of reason. Two or three miles south of the canyon, he found some open country to the east, perhaps what Mariposa had in mind. He rode on, expecting to meet the wagon at any moment. When he did, it was jolting along on its own, the horse herd, the longhorns, and the riders nowhere in sight.

"Rein up," he told Victoria. "Something's wrong. There's no horses, no cows, and no riders in sight."

He rode on, kicking his horse into a run. He had ridden only a mile or two when he saw the riders. Van was in the lead, and behind him rode Esteban Valverde, his rifle virtually at Van's back. Behind Valverde rode the rest of the Mendoza outfit, including Estanzio and Mariposa. Following his eleven men, Gil counted fifteen riders, every man carrying a rifle. Gil reined up, waiting. A few yards from Gil, Van halted. Upon orders from Valverde, he spoke.

"They came from behind, Gil," he said bitterly. "They had our drag riders under the

180

gun, threatening to shoot them if the rest of us didn't surrender."

"Crude, but effective," said Valverde smugly. "Drop your pistol, Austin, and then your rifle."

Reluctantly, Gil did so.

"Now," said Valverde, "I will set your mind at ease. I have come for Senora Mendoza and the wagon. I want nothing more. My reasons are none of your affair. Suffice to say the senora owes me. I will not bore you with the sordid details. You will remain here, all of you, while I ride ahead. Any man attempting to follow will be shot out of the saddle, upon my orders. Once the senora and I have departed, my riders will detain all of you here for a time. Then you will be free to continue on your way, as long as it is north. Any man riding south, in pursuit, will be shot on sight."

With that, he rode around Gil, and was soon lost to distance.

"I feel like a damn fool," said Van, "but I wouldn't sacrifice even *one* of our riders for that wagon, and whatever's in it."

"Nor would I," said Gil.

Esteban Valverde reached the wagon and rode around it. He carried the rifle across his saddle, its muzzle pointed toward Victoria Mendoza.

"I have come to take you home, my dear. You *and* the wagon. There I will dismantle it at my leisure, and if what I am seeking is not somewhere within it, then I will have *you* to direct me to it."

"I will go nowhere with you!" Victoria shouted.

"Ah, but you will," he said, cocking the rifle. "You think I will not shoot? It is true, there was a time when I would have sooner shot myself, but that time — with many other things — is gone."

He dismounted, got his left foot on the hub, and climbed over the wide front wheel to the wagon box. In so doing, he allowed the muzzle of the rifle to shift, and Victoria grabbed it. She dragged the muzzle down, and it blasted a hole in the floor of the wagon box. He wrenched the rifle away, and she let go. From her waistband she snatched the Colt revolver. Valverde twisted her arm, and she fired by reflex. The slug tore into the flank of the offside wheel horse. The animal screamed in pain, and its panic quickly swept over the other horses. The teams bolted, the smell of fresh blood driving them on. Again the Colt roared, and the slug struck the second of the wheel-horse team. Valverde suddenly released Victoria's arm, and with all his strength, drove his right fist into her face. She went limp, slumping back on the seat. Valverde seized the loose reins.

But the reins might as well not have existed. The horses were beyond any command. Young pines and cedars were flattened as though they were weeds. They jounced over rocks, tore through thickets, and Esteban Valverde became afraid for his life. He fought the reins like a madman, but to no avail. The wagon remained upright only because of its enormous weight. Valverde fought down his fear. The horses couldn't run forever. Once they ran out their

182

fear, he would be safe. But time had run out. Fate had dealt Esteban Valverde his last card, and it was a loser. Faster they went, thundering toward the canyon rim, and a five hundred-foot drop to destruction . . .

11

THE Valverde men sat their horses in silence. Van's horse had begun cropping grass, and it had moved closer to Gil's. Van spoke softly.

"You reckon Senora Mendoza will just give in and go back with him?"

"No," said Gil. "They're both armed, and I look for hell to bust loose any minute."

It was a prophecy quickly fulfilled. The blast from the rifle was like a clap of thunder in the silence. Every man was shocked into immobility, and jolted out of it an instant later by the roar of a pistol and the agonized scream of a horse. The distant rattle of the wagon and a second blast from the pistol confirmed the reality of what had happened. The Valverde riders, fearing their *patrono* was in trouble, disobeyed the final order Valverde had given them. The riders split around Gil's outfit, galloping after the sound of the runaway wagon.

"There's nothing they can do," said Gil. "Nothing anybody can do. The wagon's headed for the canyon rim. All of you ride back and get your guns. No matter what's happened to Valverde, we still may have to fight this bunch."

Valverde's men rode hard, unsure as to what they could or ought to do, but feeling the need to do something. Three shots had been fired, but

184

only the first from Valverde's rifle. It was in their best interests to know if their *patrono* yet lived. They came within sight of the doomed wagon just in time to see it career over the canyon rim. The horses screamed in mortal terror, the piteous knell trailing away like a dying echo. The Valverde riders gritted their teeth, held their breath, and waited. The sound, when it came, was like the flat of the hand against a drumhead. Then there was nothing, causing the ensuing silence to seem all the more terrible.

"*Por Dios*," said one of the riders, crossing himself. "*Por Dios!*"

The Valverde riders turned their horses and rode slowly back the way they had come. One of them caught and led the saddled horse Esteban Valverde had ridden. As one, they reined up. Suddenly they were facing the guns of the men Valverde had left in their charge. Gil had his outfit strung out in a skirmish line, every man with his rifle at the ready. The Valverde riders were practical men. The *patrono* was gone, and his cause, whatever it had been, had died with him. Carefully they raised their hands, and the lead rider spoke.

"*Paz*," he said. "*En paz.*"[1]

"*Paz*," Gil repeated, and then with the muzzle of his rifle, he pointed south. No further order was needed or given. Gil's eyes met those of every Valverde rider, and each man nodded.

---

[1] Peace

185

Gil's skirmish line split, and the Valverde men rode through. Gil waited until the riders had ridden a hundred yards, and then he spoke.

"We'll follow them until they're well beyond the herds. I want to be damn sure this bunch don't try some final mischief, such as stampeding the cows and horses."

But the Valverde men rode past the herds and were soon lost among the greasewood and scrub oak thickets.

"We ought to go into that canyon," said Van, "and at least be . . . sure."

"I aim to," said Gil, "but we can't afford to delay the trail drive. We'll go on, turning east as planned, and where the canyon shallows down enough for the herds to cross, some of us will ride upcanyon and have a look. It won't be pleasant. I'll take two men with me."

Surprisingly, it was Mariposa who spoke.

"Estanzio go," said the Indian. "Estanzio and Mariposa. *Compasivo para caballos.*" He held his Bowie in his hand, its blade silver in the morning sun.

"Unless some of you object," said Gil, "Estanzio and Mariposa will go with me."

The other riders shook their heads. It would be a gruesome scene, at best, and no man envied the Indians the task that might await them. If any of the big gray horses still lived, they must be mercifully put out of their misery.

"Let's move out," said Gil. "Once we're far enough downcanyon to get the herds across, the rest of you will keep the drive going. Mariposa, Estanzio, and me will leave you there, and catch

186

up to you after we've had a look at what's left of the wagon. It's important that the drive keep moving, because we may still be a dozen miles away from water."

They reached the clearing that Gil had spotted earlier, and the horse herd was turned east. The longhorns, now accustomed to the horses ahead of them, followed. They traveled three miles before the terrain began to level, and Gil trotted his horse north, to the canyon. He turned east, following the rim until he could see flat country ahead. He rode back to the horse herd, waving his hat to Estanzio and Mariposa. They turned the lead horses north, toward the crossing that would put them on the other side of the dangerous canyon. When the last longhorn had crossed, and the horse herd was a mile or more beyond the canyon's north rim, Gil, Estanzio, and Mariposa turned the lead horses northwest. Gil then rode back to the flank and had a word with Van.

"I want you and Ramon with the horse herd while Estanzio and Mariposa are with me. Take the herds northwest maybe three miles, and then head them due north. That ought to put us back on our original course."

Van rode away to find Ramon, and Gil rode back to the horse herd. When Van and Ramon reached the point position, Gil nodded to Estanzio and Mariposa. They followed him back to the shallow end of the canyon. It was littered with debris, a sure sign of high water during heavy rain. The deeper they rode into the canyon, the higher the walls became, and the more oppressive seemed the silence.

"*Muerte*," said Estanzio.

Floating against the blue of the western sky were those inevitable black specks. Buzzards circled, waiting. Gil's horse snorted nervously, and he could feel the animal tremble. The very air held an aura of death. It seemed unnaturally hot, because there was no wind. The sun bore down on them with a vengeance, and Gil felt the sweat soaking the back of his shirt. The floor of the canyon was sandy, and nothing grew there. In places there was a clutter of rock and dunes of sand, evidence that there had been an occasional slide from the canyon rim. But for a few coyote and cougar tracks, there was no evidence that any living creature had ever visited the canyon. Half a mile ahead the canyon took a sharp turn, and somewhere beyond that — less than a mile, Gil believed — they'd find the remains of the wagon, its occupants, and the horses. He found himself hoping there were no survivors, lying there broken and bleeding, beyond help. When they rounded the bend in the canyon, the first thing they saw was a front wheel from the wagon. It had rolled, leaving a snake track in the sand, and come to rest leaning against the steep wall of the canyon. The three riders reined up. Ahead of them was the ominous sound of a falling stone. Dust hung in the still air, additional clouds rising as bits of sand and stone slid down from the canyon rim where the wagon had gone over. The dust settled, and a hundred yards ahead of them was a scene even more grisly than Gil had imagined. The three of them dismounted. They dared not take their horses any closer. The sandy canyon floor wasn't stable enough to hold a picket pin. Gil took the loose wagon wheel, laid it down flat, and they half-hitched their horses' reins to the spokes. There wasn't a blade of grass, not even a weed. Afoot, they started toward the wreckage, as more stones and sand slid from the rim. The wheelless wagon lay on its top, the front of it toward them. The wagon had struck first, and the unfortunate teams had been flung back across the wagon box, until the horses rested behind the smashed wagon. Suddenly, in the dead silence of the canyon, came the most hair-raising sound Gil had ever heard. It began as a nicker, trailing off to an agonized whimper. At least one of the horses still lived. Without a word, Estanzio and Mariposa took the lead, drawing their Bowies. Sick, Gil waited for them to finish what, in the name of mercy, must be done. Their unenviable task completed, the Indians knelt and cleaned the blades of their Bowies in the sand. Nodding to Gil, they returned to where the horses were tied. They wanted nothing more to do with the grisly, unnatural scene, and Gil didn't blame them. The rest was up to him, and he wanted to be done with it. Swarms of flies had already attacked the bodies of the horses. The wagon was two-thirds buried under the rock and sand it had torn loose from the canyon rim. At first he believed both of the unfortunate occupants of the wagon had been buried under the mass. Only the front of the wagon was visible. Then, from beneath the wagon box, he saw a slender arm and hand. He knelt, taking the hand, and the very feel of it told him what he had to know. He sought a pulse, and found none. Victoria Mendoza was dead.

Behind the smashed wagon, Gil found Esteban Valverde. One of the big horses lay on Valverde's lower body. He had fallen onto a stone outcropping and lay on his back. His face was a mask of crusted dried blood, and the stone beneath his head had been soaked with it. His arms were broken, the jagged ends of the bones having pierced the sleeves of his coat. There was no sign of life, and Gil turned away, sick. Then came a whisper of sound, ghostly in the silence, which chilled his blood.

"Austin . . . "

In an instant, Gil turned, his Colt in his hand. Esteban Valverde's eyes were clouded with approaching death, but they were open, pleading. Gil holstered his Colt, moving closer, as again Valverde spoke in a whisper.

"I . . . am paralyzed. Please . . . grant me . . . the mercy you've shown . . . the horses . . . "

His eyes closed and he said no more. Gil drew his Colt and shot Esteban Valverde through the head. Holstering the Colt, he turned quickly away. There was more dust, as bits of sand and rock slid down from the rim above. As Gil again made his way past what was left of the wagon, the sun struck fire from something among the rubble that littered the canyon floor. Gil retrieved the object and it was heavy in his hand. It was an ingot of pure silver, like many more that must have spilled from the smashed wagon box. It was ill-gotten treasure, and those who had lusted after it now lay dead in its midst. In disgust Gil dropped the ingot and walked away. When he reached the horses, Estanzio had loosed their reins from the wagon wheel. Quickly the three of them mounted and rode away.

As he rode, Gil tried to sort things out in his mind. What he had only suspected he now knew. Esteban Valverde had been a stuffy little man with a towering ego, and Victoria Mendoza had used him. Theirs had been an unlikely alliance, and there had been no romance, at least as far as Victoria had been concerned. Gil believed Valverde had murdered Senor Mendoza and hadn't received the compensation he had expected. It had all the earmarks of a double-cross. Whatever she had been, he found himself regretting he hadn't known Victoria under different circumstances. Not as she was, but as she might have been. Gil, Estanzio, and Mariposa quickly caught up to the trail drive, riding directly to point position, ahead of the horse herd. Ramon and Van waited, their eyes full of questions.

"Estanzio and Mariposa put two of the horses out of their misery," he told them. "The wagon's buried under sand and rock it tore from the rim."

"Before the day's done," said Van, "every buzzard in Mexico will be down there. With Victoria gone, we're in a far different position. As I see it, an almighty poor position."

"You're seein' it about right," said Gil. "Soon as we reach water and get these herds settled for the night, we got some hard decisions to make. This involves you, Ramon; we're going to need your help."

Ramon walked his horse closer, and Gil continued.

"We're no longer the Mendoza outfit, Ramon, but we're still going to Texas. You don't have to go with us — nor do any of the riders — unless you wish to. But you're a *bueno* outfit, and I'd like every man of you to return to Texas with us, as our riders. Now this is what I want you to do. Talk to the riders, tell them of my wish, and we'll speak of this again after we have reached water. *Comprender?*"

"*Comprender,*" said Ramon. "No more Mendoza. Who b'long *caballos?*"

It was a touchy question. They had 180 head of the finest horses in Mexico — maybe even the world — yet they had no legal claim to them. Gil sighed. It was a question to which every man in the outfit deserved an answer, and his response might determine whether or not these men remained with the trail drive. Deception was not the Austin way. He would tell them the truth. Win, lose, or draw.

"Ramon," he said, "Senora Mendoza promised us the horses we are riding, and a few for breeding stock, once we reached Texas. Now the Senora Mendoza is dead, unable to keep her promise. But what are we to do with these fine horses — these *bueno caballos* — if we do not take them with us? Do we turn them loose to fend for themselves among the cougars and wolves? Do we leave them to Santa Anna's army, to be shot down in border skirmishes?"

Ramon shook his head violently, sparks of anger in his dark eyes. Gil continued.

"Ramon, you and the other riders have a right to some of these horses. Van and I own many thousands of acres of land in Texas. Enough for a magnificent rancho. I'm offering every man of you a piece of that, a share of these fine horses, once we get them to Texas. It is a chance for each of you to become more than a beans-and-bacon vaquero. *Comprender?*"

"*Comprender*," said Ramon.

Enough had been said. Ramon turned his horse and made his way back to the plodding longhorns.

"That was some talk," said Van. "You even impressed me. Do you reckon they'll go for it?"

"I don't know," said Gil, "but as it stands, they're under no obligation to us. I'm countin' on their feelings for the horses to influence them. One way or another, these horses are doomed unless we get them out of Mexico. They'll be confiscated by the army, if nothing else. I'm countin' on these men to understand that."

The herds were trailing well, and Ramon was able to approach the riders individually. After a while Van rode up to the point. He grinned at Gil.

"If these boys don't throw in with us," he said, "it won't be Ramon's fault. He's doing his best."

"I thought he would," said Gil. "Without them, we don't have a prayer."

193

"I believe they'll stick," said Van, "but that solves only one of our problems. There's purely no way we'll ever get out of Mexico without havin' to explain ourselves to the Mex army. Nobody cares all that much about the longhorns, so we might get around them, but not the horses. More than one cowboy's bought himself a plot in boot hill because he had just one pony whose ownership was in doubt. Brother, we got a hundred and eighty of 'em, and my neck's already itching from the feel of that rope."

"We can still use the story Victoria came up with, until we reach Matamoros, Coahuila. I aim to go over it tonight with Ramon. From here on, when there's talking to do, especially to the army, Ramon will do it. Starting today, he'll be the segundo — the trail boss — in charge of the drive. He will be representing the Mendoza ranch."

"Smart," said Van, "up to a point, but when the Mex soldiers see our white skin and blue eyes, we'll be dead as last year's broom sedge."

"I aim to talk to Ramon about that too. Nothin' we can do about our Anglo eyes, except keep our distance. But there must be some way that we can change the color of our skin. If there's a plant or tree that'll do the trick, I'm countin' on Mariposa or Estanzio to know about it."

It was a long day's drive. After sundown they reached the creek Mariposa had found. They boiled their coffee and doused their supper fire before dark, in time for Gil to talk to the riders

194

before night-hawking began. Ramon opened the conversation without waiting for Gil.

"We go," he said. "Take *caballos*."

"*Bueno*," said Gil. "The toughest part will be gettin' past the soldiers. Here's what I want you to do, startin' now."

He quickly outlined his plan for Ramon to become trail boss and speak for the outfit. Then he asked for something — from tree or plant — that he and Van might use to darken their skin and light hair.

"*Mariana*," said Ramon. "When Estanzio ride."

Hearing his name, Estanzio looked at Ramon. In a few words Ramon told him he would be riding at first light to scout the next water. Along the way he was to gather what was needed to darken the skin and hair of the Tejanos. Estanzio nodded his understanding.

★ ★ ★

August 6, 1843. Somewhere south of Monterrey.

Estanzio rode out at dawn, seeking the nearest water. The rest of the outfit were saddling their horses. Van spoke.

"From what Victoria told us — assumin' that her figures are right — how far you reckon we are from Monterrey?"

"A hundred miles, maybe. More'n halfway, if her miles are right. We want to pass somewhere to the west of Monterrey, far enough that we don't attract any unwelcome attention from the outpost there. Since I'm not sure we can depend

195

on the accuracy of Ortega's hand-drawn map, I'm going to start ridin' twenty miles ahead of the drive each day. In our concern for dodging Monterrey and bands of soldiers on the move, we could stumble into other villages we don't know about. From here on, we'll need to know for sure what lies ahead; not just the next closest water."

"I can see the need for bypassing Monterrey and dodging soldiers," said Van, "but I think we're leaning too much on what Victoria Mendoza told us. She said the Mex soldiers march up the coast, turning west just to the east of Monterrey, and that purely makes no sense. Why wouldn't they just turn northwest at Tampico? It's got to be two hundred miles closer."

"Ramon says that's dry country, wet-weather streams, with little water."

"They could cross it at night," said Van. "If they're well-mounted, it wouldn't be a strain on men or horses. What I'm gettin' at, Gil, is the possibility that these Mex soldiers *could* turn northwest at Tampico, leavin' us in their line of march. Not a week from now, and a hundred miles north, but *right* now."

"That's another reason for me to ride twenty miles ahead of the drive every day. If the soldiers traveling north to Monterrey have been angling northwest out of Tampico, there'll be some sign. Startin' tomorrow, I'll be scouting far ahead. For water, and any sign of the Mex army."

Estanzio returned, having located the next water, and brought with him a quantity of reddish-brown bark. Nothing was said, but when they reached the creek and bedded down the herds, Estanzio built a fire. He filled one of the pots almost full of water and hung it over the fire. When it began to boil, he shredded the bark with his Bowie and added the slivers to the boiling water. He allowed the stuff to simmer, stirring it occasionally. Finally he set the pot off the fire and allowed the mixture to cool. Van dipped his finger in the liquid, then touched the finger to his tongue.

"My God," he exclaimed, spitting and gagging. "This stuff could poison a man."

"No drink," said Estanzio pityingly. "Shut mouth, shut eye."

Gil grinned. "Good advice. We'll rub it into our faces, necks, ears, hands, arms, and hair. Then, if you like, you can drink what's left."

The vaqueros chuckled at Van's sheepish grin. While Estanzio and Mariposa didn't laugh or smile, a twinkle in their dark eyes suggested they appreciated the cowboy humor.

"Peel off your shirt," said Gil, "and I'll paint you with this stuff. Then you can do the same for me."

Gil dipped out a handful of the potent liquid and rubbed it into Van's sandy hair. The effect was amazing. Next, Gil did the ears and the neck, saving the face until last.

"Now," he said, "shut yer eyes, and shut yer mouth — for a change."

When he was done, it was still light enough for Van to see his Mejicano reflection in the creek.

"My God," he said, "I won't have to worry about bein' shot by the Mex army. If we ever get to the border, the Texans will fill me full of lead."

"We'll just have to get close enough for them to see the blue of our eyes," said Gil. "There's still your arms and hands to be done, but you can do them yourself. Look at my hands."

He held them up, and they were the hands of a Mexican vaquero.

"I'll get started on you," said Van, "and do the parts you can't reach. Then we can both do arms and hands."

The transformation was remarkable. But for their blue eyes, they might have been born Mexican.

"Estanzio," said Gil, "*gracias.*"

Estanzio and Mariposa were uncomfortable with praise. Theirs was a world where one did what needed doing and expected no commendation. Estanzio nodded.

"By God," said Van enthusiastically, "I'm startin' to believe we actually can pull this off. If I just don't forget and talk like a Tejano, or get close enough for 'em to see my eyes."

"Shut mouth, shut eye," said Estanzio.

"That Injun's goin' to be almighty hard to live with," said Van, "when he learns some more English."

★ ★ ★

Gil rode out at first light the following morning. He had begun to suspect the poor map they had,

198

showing only the larger towns, might well be deceiving them. There might be lesser villages ahead, each with an *alcalde* eager to gain favor with the Mexican army. He didn't believe the Mexican people would be a danger. But this trail drive, with the magnificent Mendoza horses and the thousands of long-horns, was a thing of such magnitude that it would be remembered and spoken of. He was more convinced than ever that his riding far ahead of the drive was the only insurance they had against their stumbling onto some unexpected village or isolated cabin. He had ridden what he judged to be twelve miles when he found a suitable stream to bed down the herds at the end of the day's drive. If he rode another ten miles, he would have a knowledge of the trail two days ahead. When he decided he had ridden far enough, and was about to turn back, he saw a thin tendril of smoke against the blue of the sky. It was what he expected and feared. Gil rode on, determined to discover the source of the smoke.

Gil reined up at the edge of a clearing. There was a chimney, but the smoke he had seen didn't curl from it. The lonely looking mud-and-stick chimney was all that remained of a cabin. It had burned, and the spiral of smoke came from an ember that had not yet died. There was brush between him and the site, so he could see little else. Then his eyes drifted to a poorly constructed log barn, some distance from the house. He could see the shake roof, but only parts of the log walls through the trees and bushes. It never paid to ride in blind, so he circled around, coming in with the barn between him and the burned cabin. He dismounted, leaving his horse behind the barn, and started around the crude building. By the time he reached the corner, he knew this was no accidental fire. A few yards from where he stood was the bloated body of a mule. It had been shot through the head.

Cautiously, Gil followed the path from the barn to the smoldering ruins of the cabin. Once he was able to see the yard, he froze, sucking in his breath. It was a scene of wanton, brutal murder. The man's hands were still bound behind him, and he'd been shot in the head. So had the woman. Both had been stripped, and mutilated with knives. It was a thing so heinous, so totally depraved, it would have made a Comanche envious. But he knew that it wasn't the work of Indians, when he found the tracks in the sandy yard. Every horse was shod, and from the nighttime tracks left by crawling things, he decided the atrocity had taken place in the late evening of the day before, probably after sundown. That accounted for the buzzards not having arrived, but they were on the way. He could see them wheeling around against the blue of the sky. Somehow he would have to bury these unfortunate people; they had been degraded enough. He wondered if they even owned a pick or shovel. He had started for the barn when his horse nickered. It was a frightened nicker, and Gil drew his Colt as he ran.

Whoever had disturbed the horse would have heard him coming, and when he rounded the corner of the barn, he was prepared to fire. He had expected maybe an Indian, a thieving Mexican, or even a soldier, but not the little bundle of fury that charged him. The thin little girl was maybe seven or eight, and stark naked! There was hate in her eyes, and a three-tined pitchfork in her hands.

12

HER small face a mask of hatred, she ran at Gil with every intention of driving the fork into his belly! Barely in time, he sidestepped the thrust and grabbed the handle of the pitchfork. But she was stronger than she looked, and boiling over with hate, so it wasn't easy wresting the deadly tool from her grasp. When he finally did, he flung it away, only to have her fly at him again, her fingers splayed out like the bared claws of a bobcat. He caught her by the arms, and she kicked him in the belly with a bare foot. He seized both her wrists in his left hand, holding her at arm's length while he fumbled at his belt for a piggin string. She kicked him in the face, but he kept his grip, turning her around so that her back was to him. Again he reached for a piggin string, and feeling a bit guilty, managed to bind her wrists. For lack of a better way, he got her on the ground belly down, straddling her while he bound her ankles. That done, he rolled her on her back, and she spat in his face.

"*Soldado bastardo!*" she shrieked. "*Soldado perra!*"

She thrashed about like a hog-tied longhorn, calling him names in Spanish at such a rapid rate, he couldn't understand most of them. She had called him a soldier, one possible clue as to who had been responsible for what had happened at this isolated little cabin. Finally she began to tire, as he had known she must, until her struggling ceased. Her eyes met his, and he saw no fear in them; she had been subdued, but that was all.

"*Ninguno*," he said. "*Ninguno soldado*." He pointed to her eyes, and then to his own. To his surprise, she spoke.

"*Quien es?*"

"*Tejano,*" he said.

She only looked confused, and he realized his words didn't fit what she was seeing. His face and hands were as brown as her own. He unbuttoned the front of his shirt far enough for her to see his white skin.

"Tejano," he repeated. "*Nombre?*"

"Rosa," she said.

Could he trust her enough to loose her bonds? He put his finger on the knot in the rawhide that bound her feet. Then he let his eyes meet hers.

"*Paz?*" he asked. "Rosa, Tejano, *en paz?*"

"*Paz,*" she said.

First he freed her ankles, massaging them. Then he loosed her hands and massaged her wrists. Now that he had made peace with the little catamount, the easy part was over. He must bury the dead — obviously her parents — and he wondered if she knew of their deaths. More important, had she accepted them? Had she been hiding in the barn all this time? He sighed. He must begin somewhere.

"*Habla?*" he asked. "*Soldados ayer?*"

Cat-quick, she rolled out of his reach. She was

on her feet and gone before he could so much as move. He followed, realizing she was headed for the cabin, or what remained of it. So terrible had been the tragedy, she had put it from her mind, unable to come to grips with it. When he had spoken of the coming of the soldiers, the stark reality of it had come rushing back. She had halted a few yards from the mutilated bodies, a skinny brown waif in the hot August sun. A lump rose in Gil's throat, and he could have wept for her.

"Rosa," he said.

She turned to him, tears streaming, and the last barrier fell. She became just a little girl with more grief than her small shoulders could bear. She ran to him, and he knelt to receive her.

"*Padre*," she sobbed. "*Madre*."

She threw her arms around him, and he held her close. When there were no more tears, she lifted her eyes until they met his. Never in his life had he been so touched.

"*Desnudo*," she said. She seemed embarrassed by her nakedness, and he thought there was a flush in her cheeks. He led her back to the barn, to his horse. From his saddle-bag he took one of Clay Duval's flannel shirts. He slipped it on her, and it reached her ankles. The sleeves swallowed her hands. He buttoned the shirt, rolled up the sleeves, and stepped back to look at her. There was so much sadness in her, she was unable to smile, but her eyes told him he had earned her trust.

"*Pala?*" he asked, pointing toward the barn.

She said nothing, but turned toward the barn,

and he followed her into it. She led him to a crude tack room where a few tools were kept. The old spade's original handle was long gone. It had been replaced with an oak limb, with the bark still on. It would have to do.

"*Padre, Madre,*" he said simply, holding up the spade.

She knew. Tears made fresh tracks down her dusty cheeks. She needed something to occupy her while he dug the graves.

"*Tener hambre?*" he asked.

She nodded, and from his saddlebag he took some jerked beef and hardtack. He sat her down, her back against the barn wall, and left his canteen with her. Then he took the spade, and on the slope beyond the burned cabin, began the task that decency demanded. Thankfully, the soil showed evidence of recent rain, and while it was hot work, the chore didn't take as long as he had expected. It was a crude burial, without even a blanket in which to wrap the bodies, but better than being left at the mercy of buzzards and coyotes. He filled the graves and mounded the dirt. He wished he had a Bible, but he didn't. Since he couldn't read the word over them, he recited the Twenty-Third Psalm, which was the only one he remembered in its entirety. Returning to the yard, he took the time to further study the tracks he had seen earlier. He followed them to a grassless area the riders had crossed as they had ridden away. There were tracks of fourteen horses, all of them shod. The trail led east, but something Van had said bothered him. If the men were soldiers — likely returning to Mexico City — it meant they had left Monterrey and were traveling southeast, toward Tampico. That meant the line of march given them by Victoria Mendoza was all wrong. That meant the trail drive was in immediate danger of encountering Mexican soldiers going *to* or *from* Monterrey!

Rosa still sat with her back to the log wall of the barn, and in the hot August sun had fallen asleep. What in heaven's name was he going to do with a child — a female at that — on a trail drive? Lead might fly at any time. But what choice did he have? If she had kin, this was no time to go looking for them; his very life was in peril as long as he remained in Mexico. Rosa would have to go with them, and at some better time and place he would decide what to do about her. He gently awakened the sleeping child, and with her in the saddle in front of him, he rode out. It would take some time, but he decided to follow those tracks that led east. At least for a while. He circled around so that Rosa wouldn't have to see the new-made graves, and picked up the trail a mile east of the burned cabin. Slowly but surely the trail veered to the southeast, confirming his suspicions. He turned, riding west until he judged he had traveled three miles, and then headed due south. He urged his horse into a fast gallop, feeling the need to return quickly to the outfit.

★ ★ ★

Van Austin was uneasy. Despite himself, he kept looking to the southwest, where a veritable cloud of buzzards swirled above that distant canyon of death. You'd think the varmints had some kind of signal, and that their families and friends from around the world had flown in for the occasion. Van had begun to wonder what was keeping Gil. It seemed he'd been gone long enough to ride to Matamoros, Coahuila. The herd was moving well, so Van trotted his horse to point position and rode beside Ramon.

"Senor Gil," said Ramon, "long time."

"Too long," said Van. Ramon said no more, but he didn't need to. Clearly, he too was concerned with the length of time Gil had been gone. Van was about to return to his own position when they saw the riders coming from the northeast.

"*Soldados*," said Ramon.

"Comin' from Monterrey," said Van. "Ramon, you know what to say. You are the trail boss, responsible for delivering these horses and longhorns to the Mexican army, at Matamoros. Whatever they say or do, insist on taking the trail drive on to the next water. Whatever you do, don't let 'em provoke you into a fight. We can't afford for these *soldados* to see me up close, so I'll ride back to the drag. I'll warn the rest of the riders to follow your lead. Once I've got the trail drive and its dust between me and these *soldados*, I'll circle around, ride north, and find Gil. Take the herds on to the next water and bed them down for the night. If these *soldados* get suspicious and maybe decide to hang around, don't look for me and Gil until after dark. We'll work our way back and then decide what to do."

Ramon eventually counted fourteen riders. The lead man began waving his hat, the signal to stop the drive, but Ramon kept it moving. Van needed time to warn the other riders, to reach the drag, and to get away without being seen. Finally the column of soldiers turned due west, crossing the path of the trail drive. Ramon could ignore them no longer; he swept off his hat, signaling a stop. He rode forward, and the Mexican officer advanced to meet him, his captain's insignia flashing in the westering sun. Ramon slumped in his saddle, his sombrero tilted over his eyes. The captain looked upon him with contempt, and when he spoke, it was in English.

"I am Captain Miguel Salazar. What is the purpose of this *caravana*, and where is it bound?"

Ramon kept his silence, apparently thinking. Or sleeping. It was a total lack of respect, and Captain Salazar was furious.

"Look at me, peasant, while I am speaking to you!"

Slowly, Ramon lifted his hunched shoulders and lazily tilted the sombrero back on his head. "No *comprender*," he said.

Irritated, Salazar repeated the question in Spanish. Ramon told him the prepared story, insisting that they must reach water before dark. The *vacas* and *caballos* had been long without water.

"You lie," snapped Salazar. "Santa Anna has been deposed, and runs like the dog he is!" He then pointed to the cloud of buzzards circling above the distant canyon and, his eyes boring into Ramon's, he spoke.

"*Busardos*," he said. "Millions of *busardos*. So much death demands that it be investigated. You come this way; perhaps you know the cause?"

"*Vaca, caballo sediento*," said Ramon.

"Ah," said Salazar sarcastically, "so noble a cause must not be delayed. For your safety, I think we will accompany you to Matamoros, Coahuila. I wish to assure myself that these *vacas* and *caballos* Santa Anna has so generously provided are received by the Mexican army. Already you are near water; drive on. What attracts the *busardos* can wait. The dead do not wander."

Ramon nodded. One way or another, there was going to be trouble. He waved his hat to the flank riders, and they passed the signal along. When it reached the drag riders, the longhorns slowly lurched into motion. The horse herd moved out under the direction of Estanzio and Mariposa. Ramon was relieved when Salazar led his column of soldiers into position a hundred yards ahead of the horse herd. The captain didn't wish to eat dust. Ramon walked his horse back to the flank, sending Juan Padillo ahead to ride point. Reaching the drag, Ramon sent Domingo Chavez to replace Juan at flank. He then turned his anxious eyes to the south, where trail dust hung in the air like yellow clouds. Desperately, Ramon wished to talk to the Texans before they bedded down the herds. But he could see no riders; only an empty plain, and the dust of their passing . . .

★ ★ ★

Van rode hard, unsure as to how perilous a situation they faced. He crossed the creek where the herds would bed down for the night, and three or four miles beyond, he met Gil. His eyes went wide at the sight of Rosa, but his questions must wait. Quickly he told Gil of the arrival of the soldiers.

"Much as I hate to admit it," said Gil, "you were right. This bunch is evidently on their way south, and for sure they aren't going through Monterrey to the coast. They rode southeast, and that means we're in the path of all soldiers approaching Monterrey or leaving it."

"I'm wonderin' if this bunch wasn't on their way to have a look at that canyon," said Van. "Must be a million buzzards, and you can see 'em for miles. Now, where'd you get the little lady?"

"Found her hidin' in a barn," said Gil. "Some sneaking, murdering soldados killed her mama and daddy. Mutilated them with knives so bad, it would've turned a Comanche's stomach. Rosa, here, says it was soldiers. I trailed 'em a ways. Far enough to learn there's fourteen of the bastards, and it has to be the same bunch that discovered our trail drive."

"I told Ramon we might not ride in until after

210

dark, if these jaybirds decide to hang around. We can't have 'em looking too close at us. I'd say the drive wasn't more than a couple of miles away from water, when we got stopped. By the time we get back, Ramon will have the herds bedded down. These Mex soldiers may be suspicious, but they won't have any reason to keep an eye on our riders. Yet. Maybe we can circle around and ride in from the south. We can picket our horses, and when it's dark, move in with our outfit. We need to know what we're up against."

"*Quien es?*" Rosa asked, pointing at Van.

"*Hermano,*" said Gil.

They rode far enough to the west so that when they turned south, the smell of their dust or the sound of the horses wouldn't announce their coming. They crossed the creek, and when they had ridden three miles to the south of it, rode to the east until they reached the still-dusty path the trail drive had taken.

"The cover kind of thins out up ahead," said Van. "We'd best rein up a mile or so from camp. You and Rosa stay with the horses, while I mosey in and talk to Ramon. I warned him to back away from any trouble with them."

"If they're still there," said Gil, "with intentions of staying awhile, there's going to be trouble. If they'd kill and rob a dirt-poor peasant, what wouldn't they do for some of the Mendoza horses? I aim to take these varmints by surprise, and kill two birds with one stone. We'll rid ourselves of them and their threat to the trail drive, and we'll make them pay for the

211

two poor souls they murdered. Tell Ramon to keep our riders away from the soldiers. Tell him these men are killers, and that we have proof of it. Once you've talked to Ramon, you and me are going in close enough to accuse these bastards of murdering Rosa's mama and daddy."

"That'll blow the lid off."

"I aim for it to," said Gil. "A guilty man won't talk; he'll go for his iron. Tell Ramon to keep our riders out of our line of fire, and ready to cut loose when we open the ball."

Van moved out at dusky dark. The wind, what there was, was out of the northwest. Gil could smell smoke; that meant a cook fire. They would do well to time their approach and arrive during supper. He took a blanket from his roll, draped it over Rosa's shoulders, and sat her down with her back against a pine. He knelt beside her, searching for words that would keep her there until he and the outfit had completed their deadly task.

"Rosa," he said, "*esperar con caballos. Tejano volver pronto.*"

For a moment she said nothing, and he thought she was asleep. But her hand found his in the dark. "*Si,*" she said.

Van returned as quietly as he had departed.

"That bunch is gathered around a fire big enough to roast a longhorn," said Van, "and they're passing around a bottle. I couldn't get that close, but Ramon says they're all armed with pistols and saddle guns. The tall dog in the brass collar is Captain Salazar, and when Ramon told his story, the captain lost all interest

212

in that horde of buzzards that's been botherin' me. Salazar told Ramon that Santa Anna's been kicked out. He called Ramon a liar, and aims for his company of soldiers to follow the trail drive on to Matamoros, Coahuila. Just to be sure it arrives safely."

"Well, that tears it," said Gil. "Let's be done with it." He touched Rosa's blanketed head to reassure her, and they departed. He hoped the presence of the two saddled horses would inspire confidence in the girl, that she wouldn't feel abandoned and come looking for him.

"Salazar's bunch is on the other side of the creek from our riders," said Van. "Ramon played the Mex peasant, discouraging any mixing."

Gil could see the unnecessarily large fire long before they were within pistol range. It was foolish for men to sit and stare into the fire; it destroyed their night vision, blinding them to an attacking enemy. Perhaps it was because the soldiers felt superior to the Mexican vaqueros and saw no danger in them. After all, their enemy was the foolish Tejanos who raided villages along the border.

"Whoa," said Gil in a whisper, halting. "If there's a shoot-out, we'll end up with horses and longhorns scattered from here to Tampico."

"I don't think so," Van whispered back. "Ramon's way ahead of us. He intentionally moved the herds up the creek as far as he could, because he's disturbed by Salazar and his men. The herds might run, but it's a chance we'll have to take."

They moved on, coming out a hundred yards

up the creek from the noisy soldiers. Gil and Van moved down the south bank of the creek, using brush for cover. The brush began to thin out, but they were well within pistol range. While Gil could see nobody else on their side of the creek, there was a brief glow from a cigarette somewhere beyond the limits of his night vision. His outfit was there, and they were ready. Gil took a deep breath and flung the challenge in their faces.

"Salazar, we have evidence that you and your men are killers. We have a witness. I'm ordering you to surrender, or suffer the consequences."

The effect was instantaneous. Every man went for his gun, some of them falling to the ground and rolling away from the fire. Gil and Van dropped to their knees, providing lesser targets, as slugs whipped the air over their heads. But the surprise had been total, the cowboys ready, and their fire deadly. Gil saw Salazar take three slugs, each of them puffing the dust from his fancy coat.

"*Matar soldado bastardos!*" said Rosa.

Gil grabbed the child and pulled her down beside him. It was a miracle she hadn't been hit. He was sorely tempted, in the midst of a gunfight, to pause long enough to spank her. But the fight was over. The scene across the creek was total destruction. Gil's riders trotted in out of the night, their pistols still in their hands.

"*Bueno*, Ramon," said Gil. "*Bueno*."

From somewhere up the creek, a cow bawled.

"Uh-oh," said Van, "we took the first hand,

but we're about to lose the second one."

"No *estampeda*," said Ramon. "Juan, Manuel, Domingo, and Pedro *pacificar vaca, caballo.*"

"Ramon," said Gil, astonished, "I could kiss you for sending riders to calm the herd, but I ought to scalp you for leavin' the rest of us to face that bunch of killers, outnumbered two to one."

"*Ventaja*," said Ramon.

"Sorry, big brother," said Van, "but he's right. We had a hell of an edge, includin' the element of surprise, and shootin' from the dark. Ramon, you're a *muy bueno segundo.*"

"Sorry, Ramon," said Gil. "I shot from the hip. That was a fine piece of work. Where's Rosa?"

Vicente Gomez, Juan Padillo, Estanzio, Mariposa, and Bola had crossed the creek and by the light of the fire were searching the dead soldiers and taking their guns. Juan Padillo had taken two pistols off the body of the captain and was going through Salazar's pockets. Rosa looked on with grim approval. "*Matar soldado bastardo*," she said.

"You bloodthirsty little *vagabundo*," said Gil. Juan Padillo laughed.

Gil took Rosa back across the creek; he wanted Ramon, with his superb command of Spanish, to talk to her. Ramon quickly established a friendship, speaking to the child in Spanish. Then he turned to Gil.

"Salazar, the *capitán*, ordered the killing," said Ramon.

In searching the dead Salazar, Juan Padillo

215

had found something that he thought important. He crossed the creek and in the poor light from the fire dangled a small gold locket by a thin golden chain.

"*Madre!*" cried Rosa, reaching for the locket. "*Madre!*"

Padillo gave her the locket, and she sank to her knees, sobbing over it.

"If there was ever any doubt," said Gil, "that wipes it clean. We'd best get started; there's a full night's work ahead of us."

13

"RAMON," said Gil, "we have a hard night ahead of us. You're able to talk to Rosa much better than I can; get some blankets, make Rosa a bed, and convince her it's bedtime. She's had some hard experience for one so young. Make a place for her near the herds, so the night riders can keep an eye on her. Tell her the horses and cows are ours, and that our riders will be close by. Tonight we'll night-hawk in three watches, four riders at a time. There's an almighty lot to be done before anybody sleeps."

Ramon had an earnest conversation with Rosa, and she didn't want to go with him. She protested in Spanish, ran to Gil, and it was he who finally persuaded her to go with Ramon.

"Congratulations," Van chuckled, "you're a daddy. You sure picked one hell of a time and place for it to happen. Ramon can talk to her just like I'm talkin' to you, but it's an ugly old Tejano she listens to."

"Whatever respect she has for me," said Gil, "I earned it. She tried to run a pitchfork through my gut. God knows, we have problems enough, but I couldn't just ride away and leave her there."

"Not a man of us would have," said Van. "Besides, I don't know what she could do that

217

would drop us in a deeper bog hole than we're in already."

Estanzio, Mariposa, and Bola came splashing across the creek, laden with weapons taken from Salazar and his men.

"I purely don't see how we can take any more guns with us," said Van. "I'd bet every last one of these is a foreign make."

"More'n likely you're right," said Gil, "and we do have to draw the line somewhere. Any of our riders having similar weapons can likely use the extra ammunition, but we'll have to dispose of the weapons. But that's just part of it; we must also conceal the saddles *and* the bodies."

"That means some serious digging," said Van. "You got any notion as to what we'll use for tools?"

"Soldiers on the move carry field packs," said Gil, "like that bunch that grabbed us right after we crossed into Mexico. On the outside of those packs, they carried short-handled spades, for entrenching. Go over there and check out some of those packs. By then, Ramon should have returned, and we'll decide how we're going to conceal all these things that could put us before a Mex firing squad."

Ramon came down the far bank of the creek, crossing to join them.

"Thanks, Ramon," said Gil. "You sure she ain't followin' you?"

"*Parte querida, parte diablo,*" said Ramon, with a laugh.

"While we're hidin' the bodies and belongings of these dead *soldados,*" said Van, "let's not

218

overlook their horses. If we just turn 'em loose, I'd bet they'll drift back to Monterrey, and with our luck, they're all wearin' Mexican brands."

"We'll have to add them to our herd and take them with us," said Gil. "Anytime we meet up with a company of soldiers between here and the border, I doubt it'll make any difference. We already have so damn many problems, so much to explain, what's a few horses with Mexican brands?"

They found six of the soldiers had carried the shorthandled entrenching spades as part of their field packs.

"There's eight of us," said Gil, "so the two men not involved in the burying can look for places to dispose of extra weapons, saddles, and packs. Make the holes deep enough, in case some scavengers show up with diggin' on their minds. But don't mound the dirt; pack it tight, level it, and cover each place with leaves and brush."

"There'll be a moon in a while," said Van, "so I reckon there'll be light enough for the digging. But we'll need to hide the rest of this gear in whatever woods and brush we can find. All we'll accomplish is getting ourselves clawed ragged on briars, thorns, and limbs. That part's going to have to wait for first light."

"Likely you're right," said Gil. "Let's move our camp farther up the creek, nearer the herds; it'll take some doing to cover the sign we've left here already. Ramon, tell the boys across the creek to leave those packs for now; let's get the hard part behind us. When you made

Rosa's bed, did you tell the night riders what happened and what's to be done?"

"Si," said Ramon. "Rosa want *soldado caballo*, but no like *soldado* rig. She ride bareback."

"What he's sayin'," Van laughed, "is that he promised Rosa one of the soldier horses to get her to sleep."

"Why didn't I think of that?" said Gil. "That's all we've got a blessed plenty of, is horses, saddles, and cows. This is going to be a hard night; let's get started."

Ramon crossed the creek. When he returned, he brought with him their five riders and the short-handled *soldado* tools they needed for digging. The full moon had risen above the distant horizon, further illuminating the ghastly scene across the creek. With a sigh of resignation, they listened while Gil told them what must be done.

★ ★ ★

August 10, 1843. Mexico City.

Antonio Mendez enjoyed his work. The ring of keys he carried on his belt gave him a sense of power. Each day at sundown he became God, in the sense that he controlled the lives of all the unfortunates within the stone depths of the infamous dungeon. While the pay was a pittance, there were certain benefits. For some reason nobody had ever explained to him — perhaps it was the poor pay — the night guard at the dungeon was brought his supper each day at sundown. While the Cocodrillo was a poor excuse for a café, the food wasn't bad, and there was always plenty of it. But the food, its quality or the lack of it, didn't matter. What excited him was the *querida* who brought it! She was a dark-haired beauty, a good ten years younger than he, but he had begun to charm her. What else could it be? She had taken such an interest in him, she wished to be shown through the forbidding stone corridors of the prison that was in his charge. Ah, it was time for her to arrive! He must unlock three massive iron gates to reach the courtyard, and a fourth that was the only entrance through the adobe wall surrounding the dungeon. She waited at the fourth gate, and by the rules was not allowed to proceed any farther. But who was going to know? Once he locked the gates behind her, they were safe, and she was his for as long as he could entice her to stay.

"Ah, Angelina," he said, flashing her what he considered his most captivating smile.

She returned his smile, following him through the gate. She carried a cloth-covered tray and an earthen jug of hot coffee to which she often added something more potent. When at last they were in the inner sanctum and all the gates had been locked, she placed the tray and the earthen jug on his battered desk.

"Eat," she urged, "before it is cold."

"Ah," he said, as eloquently as he could, "I would much prefer to feast my eyes on you."

"You can do that while you eat," she said. "I'll be here. Remember, you said you'd show

221

me the prison today."

"I remember," he said, his ardor somewhat dampened, "but it is far too enormous for a single visit. Perhaps just some of it today?"

"Then take me through the halls where the gringo dogs are kept, the border ruffians captured by our glorious General Santa Anna."

He sighed. It was the part of the prison he liked the least. Those "gringo dogs" she spoke of had been there for months, many of them in chains, yet they still glared at him in grim, fire-eyed defiance. They seemed to know something he did not, and it never failed to unnerve him.

"If that is what you wish to see," he said, "I will escort you."

He led her down winding stone stairs to the basement, where there was never any sun, never a breath of fresh air. There were two long rows of barred cells, with a stone-floored corridor between them. They walked slowly, their footsteps producing a ghostly echo. There were four lamps; one at each end of the corridor, and two more midway, one on each side. The caged men stared at Angelina as though they couldn't believe their eyes. Their beards and hair were long and unkempt, their only garment ragged trousers. Antonio tried to walk faster, to end the tour as quickly as possible, but Angelina lagged behind. At first she didn't recognize Clay Duval, and if he recognized her, he gave no immediate sign. Like the others, he had a beard and shaggy, matted hair. He looked at her with empty, expressionless eyes, and Angelina wondered if they'd broken his mind. But no! He waited until Antonio had turned away and Angelina was about to. Then the dirty, bearded derelict closed one eye in a slow wink.

"Now," said Antonio, when they had reached the end of the corridor, "are you satisfied?"

"Yes," said Angelina.

They started back down the long corridor toward the stone steps. Clay's cell was near the middle of the corridor, with one of the guttering bracket lamps on a stone abutment outside his cell. There were ridges in the floor where the stones joined, and it was over one of these that Angelina appeared to stumble. She fell to her hands and knees just inches from the barred door of Clay Duval's cell. Concerned, Antonio sought to help her to her feet, and she gave him her right hand. In her left, against the stone floor, she clutched a thin piece of paper, folded many times into a tiny square. When she got to her feet, the bit of paper remained there. The concerned Antonio's eyes missed it, but the ever vigilant ones of Clay Duval did not.

★ ★ ★

August 8, 1843. On the trail, south of Monterrey.

"Before we move out," said Gil the next morning, "let's go over this area one more time. There must be no evidence of what happened here last night."

"We meet any more Mex soldiers," said Van, "I hope we don't have to gun them all down. It

223

gets a mite tiresome, bein' on the trail all day and then diggin' holes all night."

"We won't have to do it again," said Gil. "We had an edge last night, and we were lucky. Did you check the Mex horses for brands?"

"All branded," said Van, "but all different. Likely each man's personal mount. I just hope we're long gone from Mexico before somebody stumbles on all them guns and saddles we've tried to hide."

Ramon brought up a bay horse, and Rosa straddled it bareback as though she belonged there. She wore a pair of old vaquero breeches from which a good part of the legs had been cut away. Far too loose at the waist, they had been drawn tight with a red sash and made to fit. Her short jacket was also too large, but her eyes sparkled with pride. Ramon returned to Gil his shirt, which Rosa had been wearing.

"Better for ride *caballo*," said Ramon.

"How do you know she can ride?" Van asked, with a grin.

"*Mulo*," said Rosa indignantly. "*Mulo*."

"Move 'em out, Ramon, when you're ready," Gil said. "I aim to ride far ahead, like I did yesterday, and see what's out there."

Gil rode north. He had begun to notice a change in the country as they traveled. The region was more arid, with oak and cedar more dominant. There were other hardwoods, new to him, that he had learned were mahogany and ebony. It fitted a pattern he'd begun to notice, insofar as Mexico's streams were concerned. They were invariably shallow. Not once since this trail drive had begun had they forded a stream deep enough to present a problem. In less arid regions it was no problem; frequent rains kept creek — and riverbanks full. But in this northern country, where rain was less frequent, a shallow stream might dry up to sun-cracked, stone-hard mud before the next rain.

Gil estimated he had ridden fifteen miles when he came to a creek. Or what was sometimes a creek, for it was dry, not a hint of moisture in the sun-cracked mud. It was shallow, like the others, and there was an accumulation of debris along the banks to suggest an occasional overflow. It could flood during heavy rain and be dry a few days later. He feared that might be the case with many of the streams ahead. He rode another ten miles without finding water. Worried, he continued, and by his calculation, he had ridden more than thirty miles before he finally reached a creek in which there was water. It too was on its way to becoming a dry bed, unless there was rain. The water was shallow, no more than hock deep, but it would be enough. If they could reach it. His horse was thirsty, wanting to get to the water, but he rested the animal until it could safely drink. Then he mounted and rode south, the bearer of bad news. They were facing a fifteen-mile drive this day, with a dry camp at the end of it, and a second fifteen-mile drive tomorrow before reaching water. Up to now they had been fortunate, and Ramon wouldn't be pushing the herd, but that would change when Gil delivered his unwelcome news. The miles they failed to cover today would only seem longer and far more difficult tomorrow. When Gil met the drive, he judged they were still less than halfway to the first dry creek he had discovered. Ramon rode ahead to meet him.

"Dry camp, Ramon, and a good fifteen miles from there to the next water."

"*Malo*," said Ramon. "*Muy malo*."

The horse herd was trailing well, so Mariposa and Estanzio rode forward. Gil shook his head to their unasked question. They shook their heads and turned back to their positions. They didn't have to be told to step up the pace of the drive. Gil rode on past the horse herd and around the plodding longhorns. What had begun as a normal day was about to change.

"Dry camp tonight," Gil yelled to the nearest flank rider. Those on the other side couldn't hear him, but he would get to them after he spoke to the drag riders. Van was at drag, along with Bola, Domingo, and Pedro.

"Dry camp tonight," Gil told them. "We'll have to make fifteen miles today, and at least fifteen tomorrow."

"It purely ain't possible," said Van.

"We're going to have to *make* it possible," said Gil. "The farther north I rode, the drier the land became. There may be more dry camps. We'll push on tonight until it's too dark to go farther. Won't matter where we bed 'em down if there's no water. And they won't graze if they're thirsty."

"Then we'd better night-hawk six of us at a time, in two watches," said Van.

"Yes," said Gil, "and when it's your turn to

sleep, don't even take off your hat. Leave your horses saddled and picketed close by. In a dry camp, always expect trouble. Then if it comes, and you're ready, you'll have some small chance of dealing with it."

They moved on. Two hours before sundown the sun slipped behind a cloud bank far to the west. The backbone of the Sierra Madres stood stark against the splash of red on the western horizon.

"*Illuvia*," said Ramon. Then he thought of the English word. "Rain."

"Maybe," said Gil, "but when?"

Ramon shrugged his shoulders. Even if it came tonight, it might fall short of them, ending somewhere west of the Sierras. It was almost too dark to see when they reached the first dry creek, the fifteen-mile point Gil had established. The horses and cattle surged into and across the dry bed. They knew it was a creek bed, and they sensed a cruel trick had been played on them. Finding there was no water, the thirsty longhorns began bawling in frustration.

"Keep 'em moving," Gil shouted. "Keep 'em bunched, and move 'em away."

Since there was no water, the horses and longhorns had to be moved beyond any suggestion of it. They had to forget the dry creek they had just crossed. The riders drove the thirsty, restless animals half a mile north and tried to bed them down. They managed it with the horses, but the longhorns milled about, stretching their necks toward the south,

227

bawling like lost souls viewing the pits of Hell. Six of the riders immediately began circling the longhorns, lest their rebelliousness spread to the horses. But the cattle wouldn't graze, nor would they bed down.

"If there was a moon," said Gil, "I'd take them on. They'd be no worse off on the trail, and we'd be that much nearer water."

"Mayhap it come to us," said Ramon.

The cloud bank to the west had lost its red. The absence of the setting sun had left the clouds a dirty gray, and they seemed closer. Even as they watched, golden tongues of lightning flicked from the heavens. The wind was out of the north, rising.

"I hope you're right," said Gil, "but it may not get here in time to be of any help to us. If the wind shifts to the west — or even the northwest — then God help us. Once this bunch gets the scent of water, even if it's rain and fifty miles away, they'll rattle their hocks out of here. Every cowboy in Mexico couldn't hold them."

In less than an hour the lightning had moved markedly closer, and was accompanied by a distant rumble of thunder.

"No rest for any of us tonight, *amigos*," said Gil. "Might as well catch up fresh horses and all of us take to the saddle. We may not get any of the rain, but we're goin' to get the thunder and lightning, and it won't take much to light the fuse. All that longhorn powder keg is waitin' for is a spark."

But the spark wasn't necessary. The wind continued to rise, shifting to the northwest, and with it came the torturous scent of distant rain. The mournful lowing of the longhorns became a mad frenzy. As one, they turned their noses west and thundered into the night, seeking the water the treacherous wind promised. The horse herd was caught up in the hysteria, and there was no heading them. Some of the riders managed to get ahead of the stampede and then had to ride for their lives to avoid being trampled. The riders could only rein up, listening, as the stampede rumbled on. What was the use in galloping their horses after a herd that couldn't possibly be headed? They were unfamiliar with the land, and in darkness a horse and rider might pitch headlong into a hidden arroyo. So they listened helplessly as the thunder of the stampede was lost in that of the approaching storm. The bitter irony of it struck them, along with the first few drops of rain. Within minutes they were drenched with torrents of it. In less than an hour the once dry creek bed was a raging torrent. The thunder and lightning began to diminish, but the rain did not.

"You were right, Ramon," said Gil. "The water came to us. Too bad the herd couldn't understand that."

"We got one thing in our favor," said Van. "Thirsty as they were, they won't run any farther than they have to, gettin' to water. Even a fool cow's got sense enough to stop and drink from a puddle."

"Is so," said Ramon.

"I wouldn't bet any money on it," said Gil in disgust.

"Where's Rosa?" Van asked.

"Come," said Ramon. "I find."

Gil had forgotten all about Rosa. He and Van followed Ramon to a little rise that had some shelving rock midway up the slope. Partly sheltered by the rock, huddled under a square of canvas, was Rosa.

"Good place for her," said Gil. "Ramon, tell her to stay there the rest of the night. Otherwise, she'll end up wet and muddy, like the rest of us."

They spent a perfectly miserable night, not wanting to roll into wet blankets, too uncertain of their location to risk a fire. At first light Van found a standing dead cedar, hacked off some limbs with a Bowie, and started a small fire.

"I won't balk at jerked beef for breakfast," he said, "but I'm flat goin' to have me some strong hot coffee to go with it."

"That's a sentiment I can share," said Gil. "While I make the coffee, why don't you ride out far enough to catch a horse for Rosa? She can't stay here alone while we beat the bushes for longhorns and horses."

Van rode out, taking Juan Padillo and Vicente Gomez with him. They were all restless, knowing the hard task that lay ahead, wanting to get on with it. When Juan, Vicente, and Van returned, they each led two of the runaway horses. And they had some good news.

"When the rain started," said Van, "it looks like most of the horses dropped out of the stampede, and they won't be hard to find. But with that, our luck runs out. Them fool cows was runnin' like they aimed to drink out of the Pacific and was three days late for the appointment. Only varmints in the world that can run through water hock deep, dyin' of thirst."

"That's why we couldn't head them last night," said Gil. "They were so crazy for water, they'd have trampled us and our horses if we had been in their way. I expect it'll take some hard ridin' to round 'em up, but since they ran west, we shouldn't have to dodge soldiers."

Van's prediction regarding the horses was accurate. Once the rain had begun and there was enough runoff, the horses had stopped to drink. Then, their thirst satisfied, they had begun to graze. But the riders covered half a dozen miles before they began finding longhorns. The farther west they rode, the more mountainous the country became. The slopes were thick with oak, ebony, cedar, and other hardwoods. But they made an alarming discovery. But for the accumulation from last night's rain, there was little water.

"*Norte*," said Ramon, "Chihuahua *desierto*."

"I'd expect the desert to be dry," said Gil, "but this isn't desert. Even after a good rain — like last night — the sun will suck up the water pronto. If we spend too much time here, we'll still be stuck with a herd of thirsty cows. That next creek — fifteen miles north of where the stampede started — was mighty low. Right now we're more than twenty miles from it, and if we take too long, it may be dry by the time we get there."

Gil trotted his horse alongside Rosa's, and she had a half smile for him. She was a sight in her dusty, solid black, too-big vaquero clothes, but he had to admit she'd have been a disgrace, riding astraddle clothed only in his old shirt. He noted with approval that she handled her horse well. Her mule riding had taught her something. Reaching a shallow stream — little more than the runoff from a spring — they stopped to rest and water their horses. Suddenly Ramon came up with something that none of them had thought of.

"*Soldado caballos*. No find."

It was a sobering thought. While they had located and bunched most of the horse herd, they had not come across one of the horses belonging to Captain Salazar and his men. Van put it into words.

"They lit a shuck for home, wherever that is. I'd bet a double-eagle against a plugged peso they're on their way to some soldier camp, somewhere between us and the border."

"Wherever they show up," said Gil, "if they all pile in together — or within a day or two — somebody may decide to backtrack them."

"There's been rain since we planted that bunch of Mex killers," said Van. "At least they can't be tracked back to where the shoot-out took place."

"No," said Gil, "but if the army decides to investigate, they'll come straight to us. Even if they can't tie us back to their missing *amigos*, we've still got more to explain than we could handle in three lifetimes."

232

"Find cow," said Ramon. "Find cow pronto, vamoose."

It proved easier said than done. After two days of dawn-to-dusk riding, they had gathered only 2500 of the missing longhorns.

"This purely don't fit the pattern of a stampede," said Van. "Half the herd won't run themselves out, while the rest keep going."

"No," said Gil, "we're overlooking something. We can't waste any more time chasing our own tails. Mariposa, Estanzio?"

The Indian vaqueros were very much aware of the problem, for thirty of their prized Mendoza horses were still missing. Using Spanish, limited English, signs, and occasional help from Ramon, Gil told them what he wished them to do. It was then almost noon of the third day of their search.

"We'll wait here," said Gil, when Mariposa and Estanzio had ridden out. "They'll ride in an ever-widening circle from the place where we found most of the longhorns. Trouble is, we've been goin' at this as usual, following the path of the stampede until the brutes wear themselves out. If they've all run the same distance, then it makes sense that they'll all be out of wind about the same time. That bein' the case, they should all eventually be grazing in the same general area. But that hasn't happened here. Why are we missing half of our herd of longhorns and thirty head of horses?"

"*Banditos*," said Ramon. "Border *banditos*."

Gil had heard of them. They were the Mexican equivalent of the Texas frontier's Comancheros.

These men — actually outlaws — thought of themselves as "soldiers of fortune," and were of many nationalities. There were half-breeds, Mexicans, Spaniards, Americans, and God knew who else. They holed up in the wilds of Mexico, and were virtually unmolested. There were several reasons. First, there was hundreds of miles of inadequately patrolled border. Neither Texas or Mexico seemed capable of protecting it all simultaneously. Second, the Comancheros seemed a minor irritation compared to the other difficulties between Tejano and Mejicano. Texas law and order depended on the Texas Rangers — organized in 1835 — and Sam Houston's Republic of Texas volunteers. In Mexico it was the militia, whose effectiveness depended upon who had control of it. So while Tejano and Mejicano fought one another along the border, the Comancheros busied themselves stealing from both sides. Horses and cattle rustled in Mexico were sold to unscrupulous traders across the border. Horses and cattle stolen in Texas were disposed of in Mexico.

"We may be too late," said Van. "If we're up against rustlers, they could have a two-day start, on their way to the border."

"We don't *know* that's who we're dealing with," said Gil. "Ramon thinks so, and it fits our situation following the stampede. We'll wait for Mariposa and Estanzio to report. If we've been robbed, we'll catch up to them."

"*Banditos!*" said Rosa. "*Matar!*"

The hours dragged. The sun was less than two hours high when Mariposa and Estanzio

234

returned. They dismounted, and Estanzio got right to the point.

"Find *caballo*, find cow," he said.

"Where?" Gil asked.

"Arroyo," said Estanzio. "*Hombres* take."

"Many?" Gil asked.

Estanzio held up his hands, fingers spread. Then he shrugged his shoulders. They had accounted for ten men, but perhaps there were more. He didn't know.

"*Volver?*" Gil asked. "Take us there?"

Estanzio nodded, pointing to the westering sun. Darkness wasn't that far away.

"*Plenilunio*," said Gil, pointing to the horizon where the full moon would appear.

Estanzio nodded his understanding, quickly followed by Mariposa. Their dark eyes were bright with anticipation. They had come to appreciate the ways of these Tejanos. They killed those who needed killing, quickly and without mercy. Nobody understood that better than an Indian. At moonrise they would ride to the outlaw camp and reclaim what was theirs. The men who had taken their horses and cows would die.

14

WITH Mariposa and Estanzio leading the way, they rode out under a full moon. There was no wind. Nothing disturbed the silence except the sound of their passing and the occasional distant cry of a coyote. Slowly, almost imperceptibly, the unseen trail the Indian riders followed led to the northwest. They traveled at a walk, lest some sound betray their coming. In the still of the night, an iron-shod hoof against stone might be heard for half a mile. Insignificant sounds, such as the creak of a saddle, seemed inordinately loud in the night. As he rode, Gil considered their options. He had no definite plan. He knew only that there were at least ten of the outlaws and that they were holed up in a canyon. Such a hideout would have been chosen with an eye for defense, its secondary purpose being that it offered a convenient enclosure for rustled cattle and horses. Gil believed their only safe approach would be at night, even if they must wait until first light to make their move.

Estanzio, in the lead, raised his hand. The Indian vaqueros dismounted, signal enough for the rest of the outfit to do likewise. There was no talk, and none necessary. Somewhere ahead, there was the peaceful murmur of a creek. Estanzio and Mariposa took a few steps forward and paused. Gil and any he should

236

choose to accompany him were to follow. Gil touched Ramon's arm, then raised his hand in silent command to the rest of the outfit. He and Ramon followed Estanzio and Mariposa. Gil had decisions to make, but first he must know what the situation demanded. Then he would decide if they should make their move tonight or if they should wait until dawn. The creek they followed was an excellent water source, and he was expecting to find the outlaw camp well-fortified. Even before Estanzio raised his hand, Gil had picked up the faint odor of tobacco smoke. There was at least one sentry, and he had given away his presence in the most obvious manner. Gil and Ramon waited, as Mariposa and Estanzio faded into the shadowy darkness beneath the trees that overhung the creek. Stars winked silver against the purple velvet sky, and Gil judged by the big dipper that midnight wasn't more than an hour away. He suspected the watch would change then. With Mariposa and Estanzio out there in the night, armed with deadly, silent Bowie knives, they might lessen the odds before the gang knew of their presence. Estanzio suddenly appeared, motioning for Gil and Ramon to advance. They climbed through a rail fence and followed Estanzio to the sentry position, a hundred yards into the canyon. Pale moonlight reflected off the barrel of a rifle that leaned against an upthrust of rock upon which the sentry had sat. Estanzio passed the blade of the Bowie under his chin in a simulated slash far more eloquent than words. Then he pointed toward the north end of the canyon.

"Mariposa go," he said. "Him wait, we come."

Gil raised his hand, palm out. It was a sign for Estanzio to remain where he was. Gil and Ramon then made their way out of the canyon and returned to where the rest of the outfit waited.

"Two sentries," Gil told them quietly. "One at each end of the canyon. Estanzio disposed of this one, and Mariposa's gone after the other. I look for them to change watches at midnight. I aim to have Estanzio and Mariposa waiting for these new sentries. That'll take four of the gang out of the fight before it begins."

"It'll begin," said Van, "when them first two sentries don't go back to camp."

"Maybe," said Gil, "but there's a chance the rest of them will be sleeping. You're right, we could end up settling this in the dark, but to better the odds, I'll risk it. We're going to conceal ourselves in the canyon now, as near the camp as we can. Once these relief men leave the camp, Estanzio and Mariposa will take them out of the fight, just as they did the first two. Even if the rest of the gang is wide-awake, we should be able to move in and get the drop before we're discovered. Juan, you stay with the horses, and Rosa, you stay here with him. Hog-tie her, Juan, if she gets too ornery."

For Rosa's benefit, Juan repeated Gil's instructions in Spanish. Gil led out, the others following single file. Reaching the place where the first sentry had been hidden, they found they didn't have to go to Mariposa. He had returned, having discovered something Gil needed to know.

"*Cabana*," said Mariposa quietly. "*Bandito cabana.*"

So the outlaws were holed up in a cabin! That changed the picture completely. While they could still ambush the relief sentries, those within the cabin would fight. What of the sentry at the other end of the canyon?

"*Centinela?*" Gil asked in a whisper.

"*Muerto,*" said Mariposa.

Two men were out of it, and perhaps they could take two more without endangering themselves. Gil wanted a look at that cabin. He wanted to know where and how it stood in relation to the canyon walls, and whether or not there was more than one way into and out of it. He took Van, Ramon, Estanzio, and Mariposa with him. The canyon seemed full of cattle and horses. They walked more than a mile before they finally saw the gray hulk of the cabin. Gil could see grazing horses and cattle far beyond the cabin, so the canyon probably wasn't a blind one. The cabin crouched against the east wall of the canyon. Why had it been built at this particular place? Gil thought he knew. Every rat hole had some means of escape. They might surround the cabin, only to have the outlaws appear on the canyon rim with rifles. Many an ambush had been reversed, becoming a death trap for the instigators because they had overlooked or ignored just one important factor. Van was having similar thoughts. The others crept close to hear, when he began to whisper.

"They're bound to have some way in and out of there, besides that front door. Even if we set the place afire, we could lose 'em."

"I know," whispered Gil. "Once we pick off the relief sentries, we need some means of getting the others out of that cabin, where we can get to them."

"Cougar come," said Ramon, "*banditos* come. Save horse, save cow."

"That'd bring 'em out barefooted and in their long johns," said Van, "but where's the cougar? You know of one that'll trot through here, squall a time or two, and then vamoose?"

"Mariposa," Ramon chuckled quietly.

"Him speak like cougar," Estanzio added. "Scare hell from out *hombre*, horse, cow."

"Mariposa," said Gil, "in a little while, you're goin' to be a cougar. First, let's take out these two sentries that'll be goin' to take over for the pair that's been permanently relieved. Mariposa, you and Estanzio are our *cuchillo hombres*.[1] The rest of us will stay with the horses. When you've taken care of these new sentries, one of you come and get us. Then we'll all surround the cabin, and Mariposa can sing to these *banditos* in his best cougar voice."

Mariposa and Estanzio faded into the night. Gil, Van, and Ramon then returned to the south end of the canyon, joined the rest of their waiting riders, and they all made their way back to the

---

[1] Knifemen

240

horses. The next move belonged to the Indian vaqueros.

Within the canyon, the door of the outlaw cabin swung open on leather hinges. A pair of shadows emerged, buttoning their shirts and stomping their feet into their boots.

"This is some hell of a bother," grumbled one of the men, "gettin' up in the middle of the night, listenin' to cows an' hosses chompin' grass till daylight. All the months we been here, we ain't seen a soul."

"Don't bitch to me, Frenchy," said a second voice. "This is Quade's idea, an' he's got his reasons. Them two thousand longhorns an' that bunch of blooded hosses ain't mavericks. They're a big chunk of somebody's stampeded herd. Quade aims to be damn sure they all been give up fer lost 'fore we move 'em out."

"Tonio, you're near 'bout as slow as Quade, sometimes. We could of took the trail two days ago, run these critters over the border, an' had the gold in our pockets, without nobody bein' the wiser."

"Frenchy, that's why Quade's the boss an' you ain't. Quade reckons the outfit that lost them hosses an' cows ain't about to give up that easy. If they come lookin' fer us here, we're dug in solid. But what happens if they could of come after us on the open range, with all these hosses an' cows on our hands? Men on good hosses can cover five times more ground than a trail herd. Them riders would of trailed us, laid an ambush, an' purely shot the hell out of us. Keep yer yap shut an' listen to Quade, an'

241

you'll live a mite longer. You want the north end er the south end?"

"North," said Frenchy. "Ain't got as far to walk."

"Lazy, no-account bastard," muttered Tonio under his breath.

The full moon hung low on the horizon; soon it would be gone. The unwary outlaws made their way to opposite ends of the lonely canyon, unafraid of the lengthening shadows about them. They didn't know, nor would they ever know that two of those elusive shadows were armed with Bowie knives . . .

★ ★ ★

When Estanzio came for them, Gil again left Juan Padillo with the horses, and with a final admonition to keep a tight rein on Rosa. Once inside the canyon, Estanzio led them to where Mariposa waited. It was a final opportunity for them to talk before they closed in on the outlaw cabin.

"Before we go any farther," said Van, "something's botherin' me. When Mariposa lets go with his cougar scream, we're goin' to have to cut loose on whoever steps out that door. Estanzio and Mariposa counted ten of these owlhoots. Four of 'em are out of the game, leavin' six. When Mariposa throws the cougar scare into 'em, they may not all come boilin' out in a bunch. Six rifles can't kill a cougar any deader than one rifle. I reckoned this was a good idea at first, but if we only draw a couple of 'em out of that cabin, our shooting will warn the others. Shootin' from cover, they can stand us off till Hell freezes, or sneak out a back door we don't know about. If a couple of 'em managed to get out and up on that rim with rifles, they could make it hot for us."

"We won't risk that," said Gil, "because we'll have a couple of our men on that rim, above the cabin. Estanzio, you and Mariposa get your horses, take your rifles, and ride to that rim above the cabin. When the two of you are ready, Mariposa can do his cougar cry from there. Even if all six of 'em come out the door, there's still nine of us, and we'll have surprise on our side. Mariposa, you and Estanzio watch close. I'd gamble there's a back door to that cabin, and some of these coyotes may run for it. You'll be able to see us in the canyon. If you reach the rim before we're ready, wait for us. After that, it's time for Mariposa's solo."

Estanzio and Mariposa faded into the shadows, and Gil continued.

"We'll spread out, facing the cabin. Nobody fires until I do. We'll get within range, but no closer. After the first round of firing, hold your positions. If they don't all come out that door pronto, we'll have to depend on Estanzio and Mariposa catching them as they sneak out somewhere on the rim. Now let's take our positions and be done with this."

Again they crept down the canyon until they were within a few yards of the darkened cabin. Gil led them along the west wall until they were fanned out, forty yards from the cabin door. Gil thought he detected movement on the rim, and within seconds there came a hair-raising screech that would have been the envy of every cougar in Mexico. Even before it died away, there was the frightened nickering of horses and the terrified bawling of cattle. Then there was the thud of hoofs, as the animals fled to the farthest ends of the canyon. Suddenly the cabin door swung open and two men stepped out carrying rifles. A third followed, and the trio stood there uncertainly, as though hoping the menace had departed on its own. Since there had been no shooting, Mariposa let loose a second bloodcurdling squall which seemed to come from everywhere and nowhere.

"Damn it," bawled a voice from the cabin, "he's on the rim! Move out there where you can see to shoot!"

When the three moved away from the door, a fourth and fifth man emerged. Gil dropped the fifth man and Van the fourth, and there was a simultaneous thunder of rifles as the rest of the riders began firing. In seconds, five men were down, and the firing ceased. The silence that prevailed seemed all the more intense. Gil broke it with a challenge.

"You in the cabin," he shouted, "you're surrounded."

There was no response, and he expected none. It had been a warning to Estanzio and Mariposa that they hadn't been able to account for all the outlaws. Van had moved up beside Gil.

"Cover me," he said, "and I'll move in from the side of the cabin, make my way to the door and kick it open. I ain't of a mind to stand here until daylight. With the door open, we can throw enough lead in there to be sure it's empty."

"That sixth man may be inside," said Gil, "just waitin' for such a move. There may be gaps between the logs, and you could be gunned down from what you think is a blind side."

Then, as though in answer to his objection, there was a distant rifle shot. It came from somewhere beyond the canyon rim.

"There's the sixth man," said Van. "I'm goin' to kick in that door and end this standoff. I'll move in from the side, and if that door *should* move, pour some lead through it."

Gil didn't doubt the cabin was empty. The bodies of five men lay before it, and like Van, he believed the shot they'd just heard accounted for the sixth outlaw. But still he was uneasy, as that old premonition dug its claws into him. Van approached the cabin from the north side, and Gil kept his eyes on the closed door. Van reached the hinged side of the door, kicked it as hard as he could, and it slammed against the inside wall. But there was a spark of life in one of the outlaws sprawled before the cabin. Partially through caution, partially from weakness, he eased his pistol free. In the still of the night the cocking of the weapon seemed inordinately loud. It was the most unmistakable sound a frontiersman ever heard, and as Van turned, his Colt was in his hand. There was a roar, and a tongue of flame seemed to leap from the ground. The slug drove Van against the cabin wall, and he hung there, barely conscious. Somewhere, rifles roared, but to him they seemed muffled and far away. He slid to a sitting position, his back to the cabin wall, and the next thing he knew, Gil was beside him.

"You're right . . . more . . . than you're . . . wrong," he mumbled.

Ramon and the rest of the riders surged into the cabin. With the aid of a sulfur match, Ramon found candles on a shelf, and lighted two of them. Vicente Gomez helped Gil bring Van into the cabin. Wooden bunks had been built along the walls, with only thin straw ticks over bare wood. They lifted Van onto one of the bunks, and even in the poor light from a guttering candle, they could see the blood soaking the front of Van's shirt. Gil held his breath as he unbuttoned the shirt, praying the slug hadn't pierced a lung or some other vital organ. He sighed with relief when he found the wound was high, just under the left collarbone. Unless the lead had struck a bone and been deflected elsewhere, there would be an exit wound. Having similar thoughts, Ramon brought one of the candles closer. They lifted Van enough to strip off the shirt, and with Ramon holding the candle, they found the exit wound above the shoulder blade. At least it was clean, with no lead to be dug out, but it was serious none the less.

"No *bueno*," said Ramon, "no *malo*."

It was one of those things that could go either way. Many a man on the frontier had received a superficial wound, only to die from infection. There was the sound of approaching horses, as

Estanzio and Mariposa returned. Gil looked up and found the Indian vaqueros watching silently from the doorway. Estanzio raised one finger. The outlaw gang was finished. Gil had known they were a resourceful outfit, but this night they outdid themselves. The cabin had a fireplace, and already there was a fire going. Hanging above it, suspended from an iron rail, was a cast-iron pot that had been filled with water. Ramon had sent Estanzio and Mariposa to help Juan Padillo bring in the horses. Soon Rosa was there, wishing to help, but not knowing quite how. The riders were searching the outlaw cabin.

"I need some whiskey," said Gil. "Enough so that I can pour some of it into this wound and the rest down him when the fever comes."

Their search unearthed all manner of things, including some stick candy, but no whiskey. They found a tin of sulfur salve for the doctoring of livestock, but that was all. Gil cleansed the wound with hot water and applied some of the salve, knowing it wouldn't be enough. Fever would come, and with it, killer infection.

"Ramon," said Gil in desperation, "I need something to cauterize this wound, to prevent infection, to fight the fever when it comes."

"Maguey *cacto*," said Ramon. "Much *alcoholico*. Make pulque."

"I need some of this cactus *medicina*," said Gil. "Where and how do we get it?"

"Juan Padillo find," said Ramon.

"I'll go with him at first light," said Gil. "There is much to do. Choose two riders to

247

stay here with Van and Rosa, then you take the others and ride back to where we left the rest of our horses and cows. Drive them here, so that all of our stock is gathered in this canyon. We'll be here until Van's able to ride."

"*Comprender*," said Ramon. "I find and tell."

Gil saw him speaking earnestly to Juan Padillo. Juan was less talkative than Estanzio and Mariposa, and Gil wondered why Ramon had chosen him. Van had begun breathing hard, and Gil chafed at the delay. He had heard of the potent maguey liquor called pulque, but the sap had to ferment for a day and a night. Granny Austin had called the maguey a "century plant," because it bloomed only once in its lifetime. The rising sap produced the bloom, and only a maguey about to bloom could be "milked." Evidently, Juan Padillo knew how to draw the sap and where to find the plants. Gil was still uneasy. Allowing time for the maguey sap to ferment, he was still twenty-four hours away from being able to help Van. By then there would be a raging fever. Rosa came over to the bunk and stood looking at the restless Van.

"*Malo?*" she asked.

"*Malo*," said Gil.

"*Triste*," she said. "*Muy triste*. He *bueno hombre*."

Her eyes were somber. She *was* sorry.

"*Gracias*," said Gil. "At dawn, I go with Juan Padillo for *medicina*."

"Whiskey," she said. She had begun picking up some English.

"*Si,*" said Gil. "While Juan and me are gone, you look after Van for me."

He pointed away, then to her, and finally to Van.

"*Comprender,*" she said, pleased. She flashed him that half smile, still a little sad, but the remembered sorrow had begun to fade from her eyes.

★ ★ ★

They felt safe enough in the seclusion of the canyon to have a breakfast fire before first light. There had been some provisions in the outlaw cabin, including coffee beans, bacon, dried apples, and several kinds of dried beans. While waiting for first light, some of the riders had begun going through the confiscated weapons and ammunition. There were three Colt revolvers, with a supply of ammunition. They'd found an iron skillet, and Rosa was on her knees before the fire, frying bacon. Van had spent the night in fitful sleep, and seemed to have some fever. It would rise as the day wore on, and Gil feared it would be rampant before they could concoct the medicine to combat it. With the first gray light of dawn, he looked at Juan Padillo, and the vaquero nodded. One of the useful items they had found was a large old army canteen with a stopper. Gil had cleaned it up, and into it would go the maguey sap. As he and Juan rode out, Ramon and the riders he had chosen to go with him were saddling up. Juan Alamonte and Pedro Fagano would remain at the cabin with Van and Rosa. Gil and Juan left the canyon at the south end and continued on down the winding creek. Juan seemed to know exactly where he was going, and Gil followed in silence. He desperately wanted some idea as to how long this trip might take. When they had been on the trail an hour, they reined up to rest the horses.

"*Muchos cacto?*" Gil asked, holding up the canteen he hoped to fill.

"*Uno,*" said Juan, holding up one finger.

They rode over mostly stone-studded slopes where there was little moisture and the hoofs of their horses kicked up dust. It was the kind of land on which most cacti native to Mexico seemed to thrive. As far as Gil knew, he'd never seen the maguey, and when they found one, he was astounded at the size of the thing. He had seen a ripe pineapple once, and this big maguey reminded him of the foliage at the stem end of that pineapple. The leaves were thick and broad at the base, tapering off to sharp points, and flared up like a mass of green flames. The farthest tips were over their heads. Juan raised his hand, and Gil remained in the saddle while the vaquero dismounted. He parted the broad leaves of the maguey until he was able to reach the base of the plant from which the bloom would rise. He backed away, shaking his head, mounted his horse, and they rode on. Gil lost count of the many plants Juan inspected and rejected. He believed they were a good thirty miles south of the canyon when Juan eventually found what he was seeking. This maguey was as large or larger than the one they'd first found, the difference being that this one had formed a large bud near its base. Left on its own, the plant would raise a stalk with a bloom at the top. With his Bowie, Juan carefully cut around the outside of the bud. Then he pulled the bud loose, like taking the cork from a bottle, leaving a natural bowl. Even as he watched, Gil could see the sap seeping into the hollow of the stalk.

"What happens to the maguey after we take the sap?" Gil asked. Without thinking, he had spoken in English. To his surprise, Juan answered him in English.

"Him die," said Juan. "Sap make stalk, stalk make bloom. No sap, no stalk, no bloom."

Gil thought it took the bowl almost an hour to fill. Juan went to his horse, and from the saddlebag took a bone spoon. Gil handed him the canteen. Carefully Juan spooned the sap into the canteen until the maguey's bowl was empty. They waited while more sap collected. The August sun bore down unmercifully. Sweat dripped off Gil's chin and soaked the armpits of his shirt. Juan waited with the patience and determination of an Indian, saying nothing. Six times the bowl filled, and Juan patiently spooned the liquid into the canteen. After that only a little sap collected. The flow had ceased.

"Him dead," said Juan. He handed Gil the canteen. "More?" he asked.

Gil tilted the canteen until he could see the liquid. One more time would have filled it. He weighed the odds. They were far from the canyon, and might search until dark without finding another maguey about to bloom.

"We'll go with this," he said. "*Gracias, amigo.*"

Juan nodded, and they mounted up and rode out. Juan set a faster pace, knowing the job wasn't finished. The sap still must ferment to be of any use. Gil only hoped there would be enough. He caught Juan's eye and tilted the canteen, as though drinking.

"Much?" he asked.

"Little," said Juan, shaking his head. "Pulque strong. Much kill."

Gil had heard old-timers in St. Louis speak of the stuff, claiming it was at least 140 proof. He trusted Juan's judgment. He would be very careful. They reached the canyon two hours before sundown, to find that Ramon and his riders hadn't yet returned with the rest of the herd. Van tossed restlessly, talking out of his head. Rosa had found some rags, was soaking them in cold water and applying them to his face. There was no wind, and the sun had dropped to just the right level to beam all its August heat against the cabin and the canyon wall. Gil went outside, wondering where Ramon and the rest of the riders were. The sun had dropped below the west wall of the canyon when they heard a horseman coming, riding hard. Gil was out the door and waiting when Vicente Gomez reined up on his lathered horse.

"Cougar kill cow," he said, "herd scattered. Find some *caballos*, some *vacas*. Find others *mañana*, mebbe."

15

IT was bad news. After a cougar kill, the terrified horses and longhorns might run for miles. Gil knew he needed to be with Ramon and the outfit as they sought to gather the scattered herds, but he dared not leave Van until the fever broke. He couldn't help having doubts as to the medicinal benefits of the fermented maguey sap. All he knew of the powers of the stuff was what he had read and the little he had heard. Once the medicine was ready, he wanted to administer it himself. Lest he be tempted to use the mixture before it was ready, he decided Juan Padillo would say when the sap had fermented to maximum potency. Vicente awaited his response. Gil spoke.

"Vicente, catch up a fresh horse. Ramon left Manuel and Pedro here with Van, but I'm sending them back with you. I must stay here until there is some change in Van's condition, and I'm keeping Juan Padillo with me. I know Ramon needs us all, but there'll be nine of you, and that will have to be enough. Tell Ramon to continue the search until sundown tomorrow. The following day, he should drive the horses and cows he has gathered to this canyon. Left untended, a cougar scream could stampede them all again. Once the new gather is safe here in the canyon, we can always ride back and continue the search. *Comprender?*"

"*Comprender*," said Vicente. He unsaddled his tired horse and caught up another. Gil found Manuel and Pedro, and they went to saddle their own horses. It would be well past dark before the three vaqueros reached Ramon's camp. Gil and Juan Padillo watched the trio ride away. Before they reached the south end of the canyon, they were lost in purple shadow. Gil walked to the cabin to see if Van's condition had changed for the better, knowing it had not. He found the tireless Rosa still soaking rags in cold water and applying them to Van's forehead, face, and neck.

"Rosa," he said, his hand on her shoulder, "take a rest."

"No tired," she said. He was amazed at how rapidly she learned. But he thought he knew why she kept herself occupied, however trivial the task. Not only had she lost her parents, she evidently had witnessed their torture and murder. The horrifying scene had burned itself into her mind, and she was keeping it at bay the only way she knew how. She often fell prey to it at night, and wept in her sleep. Every man in the outfit had begun listening for the start of her nightmares, responding with a reassuring hand, calming her. She paused, pointing to the candle on the table.

"Candle," said Gil.

She repeated it after him until she got it right. It had become a game. She would pick up or point to something, and he would name it for her in English. At first the Spanish-speaking riders had been amused, but as her English

254

improved, they became envious. It had sparked a desire within them to better their own English. After all, were they not on their way to a country where familiarity with the language would be beneficial? Rosa's sudden intake of breath startled Gil. Van had opened his eyes, and to their surprise, he spoke.

"Pretty senorita," he mumbled. "Have I died and gone to Heaven?"

"Not yet," said Gil, moving his stool closer to the bunk. "Juan Padillo milked a maguey plant. The sap has to set overnight until it ferments. Then it should have enough alcohol in it to kill any infection. After that, you get a strong dose of what's left, to sweat the fever out of you. How do you feel?"

"Dry," said Van. "Like I been ventilated and everything leaked out."

Rosa had one of the canteens ready, tilting it so he could drink. When he had satisfied his thirst, Gil put a hand on his flushed face, and finally his throat.

"Still not too much fever," said Gil. "You have Rosa to thank for that. She's spent the day keeping cool wet cloth on your face."

But Van's eyes had closed and he said no more. Rosa looked at Gil, concern in her eyes.

"Rosa, what you're doing is a help," said Gil. "Just go ahead, and when you get tired, I'll give you a rest. While you're doing that, Juan and me will get some supper started."

Gil, Juan, and Rosa ate flapjacks, beans, and bacon. Then they took turns until midnight, fighting Van's fever with cold compresses. But despite their efforts, his temperature began to rise. Once more he opened his eyes, but they were empty of recognition. His speech became rambling, incoherent mumbling.

"*Medicina*," said Juan. "Pulque fix."

"When?" Gil asked. "How long? Do we have to wait a day and a night — a full twenty-four hours?"

"Mebbe," said Juan. "Mebbe no. Taste pulque."

They had finished collecting the maguey sap about two o'clock the previous afternoon. If the stuff had to ferment a full twenty-four hours, then they'd be waiting until afternoon of the approaching day. By dawn, Van had a raging fever. Juan tasted the fermenting pulque.

"T'ree hour, mebbe," he said.

During the night, a cool wind had risen. Gil had used that as an excuse for Rosa to get some sleep, opening the door so that the restless Van might benefit. Now, as the sun rose with promise of another hot day, Rosa again began applying the rags soaked in cold water. But the fever didn't relinquish its hold. They were an hour shy of noon when Juan Padillo pronounced the pulque potent enough for use. Gil used it sparingly, pouring some of it into the wound. He then made a cloth pad for front and back, soaking them in the powerful liquid. With Juan's help, he forced Van to drink a little of what remained. Neither of the Austins were drinking men, and Van reacted violently. He lay there gasping for breath, his eyes open to mere slits.

"What — is that?" he wheezed.

"Pulque," said Gil. "Considerably better than hundred proof, I reckon. I've doused your wound with it, but you'll have to sweat out that fever. So while you're able to understand me, I want you to down a slug of this stuff. I can't afford to dribble it into you while you're out of your head, because we don't have enough of it to waste any. Here, drink."

Van took a long pull on the canteen, swallowed, and almost suffocated before he could take a breath.

"My — God!" he finally whispered. "If I ever get shot again, leave me be. I'll take my chances with the lead."

"You got a pretty good dose," Gil said. "If your fever drops and you start to sweat, I'll spare you the rest of it. But if I don't see some sweat pretty soon, then you'll get some more. It's all we can do for you."

"You could just shoot me again." He shuddered, closed his eyes, and Gil stoppered the canteen. Juan Padillo and Rosa had witnessed the ordeal.

"*Malo* whiskey," said Rosa.

"Pulque," Juan said, with a grin. "Whiskey no more so branch water."

"Van will say amen to that," Gil said. "Powerful as this stuff is, maybe what he's downed will be enough. He's likely to have a headache that'll hurt worse than bein' shot."

An hour before sundown, Van began to sweat. Gil again used the pulque to saturate the pads

257

that covered the entrance and exit wounds. Rosa came in.

"Vaqueros come," she said. "*Caballos, vacas* come."

Had Ramon and the rest of the outfit finished the gather so soon? They had not; he could see the frustration in their faces as they reined up before the cabin.

"Fi' hun'red *vaca*, twenny-fi' *caballo*, no find," said Ramon. "Storm come, *estampeda*, mayhap."

Gil looked to the west, and the sun had set behind a cloud bank, coloring it a glorious mix of pink and red. They still were short both horses and longhorns, but if thunder and lightning was on the way, they very well might have also lost the horses and cows they'd managed to gather. Ramon had made the right decision, returning early with what he had.

"*Bueno*, Ramon," Gil said.

It *was* a good move, securing the stock they already had, well ahead of the impending storm. But there was a negative side Gil didn't mention. He didn't need to; Ramon was well aware of it. The storm would wipe out all tracks, lessening their chances of recovering the rest of the missing stock. But Ramon wasn't finished; there was yet a chance.

"Estanzio and Mariposa stay," he said. "Find *caballo*, find *vaca*. Then come."

Despite the grim report, Gil chuckled. The Indian vaqueros refused to give up their prized horses so easily. If they could be found, Mariposa and Estanzio would find them, waiting out the storm and riding until they again picked up the trail. Lagging behind, Bola rode in, leading a skittish horse that bore the carcass of a freshly killed deer. Its throat had been cut, and Gil didn't have to wonder how Bola had accomplished such a feat. The storm struck just before midnight. Howling wind swept through the canyon, driving blinding sheets of rain before it. The creek soon overflowed its banks. Whoever had built the cabin had not only built it sturdy, but had laid its foundation on stone, raising it several feet above the canyon floor. Thunder was a continuous drumroll of sound. Jagged tongues of lightning — blue, green, gold — licked into the canyon. Horses and longhorns huddled fearfully against the canyon walls, too frightened to run if there'd been anywhere *to* run. The awesome spectacle seemed to come from everywhere, leaving no escape. The riders grinned as Rosa crawled into her bunk and covered her head with a blanket. If the world was about to end, she didn't want to see it. At the height of the storm, Van awoke.

"My God," he groaned, "it's hot in here. With all the fire and brimstone outside, I was afraid I'd cashed in and the Devil was about to slap his brand on me."

"Later, maybe," Gil said, "but not tonight. Are you hungry?"

"I don't know. Right now, I just want water. Gallons of it. I'm dry as a tumbleweed."

"More pulque?" Juan Padillo questioned cheerfully.

"Come near me with that," Van threatened,

"and when I get my hands on a gun, I'll shoot you."

★ ★ ★

Estanzio and Mariposa found the trail they were seeking just before dark. There would be no moon, and a storm was building somewhere west of the Sierra Madres. They could do no more until dawn; they found a bluff facing east, its overhang sufficient to shelter them from the impending storm. Come the morning, there would be no tracks to follow, but they would ride until they caught up with the trail that must eventually appear in the aftermath of the storm. The old trail, until darkness had stolen it from them, had been due north. Once the storm had passed, they had little choice but to continue riding north until they either struck a new trail or concluded the herds had stampeded before the storm. All the missing Mendoza horses had been mares, which left Estanzio and Mariposa with but one conclusion. The northbound trail they had discovered just before dark had confirmed their suspicions. The tracks had been a mix of shod and unshod horses, with tracks of a single unshod animal trailing the herd. It had taken the vaqueros some time to sort it all out, for the trail had been totally eclipsed in places by cow tracks. Mariposa and Estanzio squatted in the dark, chewing jerked beef.

"*Salvaje* stallion steal Mendoza mares," said Estanzio. "Them go with unshod *salvaje* herd. *Vacas* follow *caballos.*"

"*Si*," said Mariposa.

They were agreed the Mendoza mares had become part of a wild horse herd, trailed by a domineering stallion. The remnant of the longhorn herd, being accustomed to trailing the horse herd, had followed. Unchecked, the horse herd would soon leave the longhorns behind, and they could be recovered without difficulty. But the wild stallion might take them on a run when they went after his newly acquired mares. Mariposa and Estanzio hadn't been all that concerned about the missing cows, but now that they knew where the animals were, Ramon should be told. Estanzio spoke.

"*Mañana*, find track. Trail *caballo*, trail *vaca*. I tell Ramon, we follow. Ramon take *vaca*, us trail *caballo*."

Before going after the horses, they had an obligation to the outfit to see that the longhorns were recovered. Their chase might take many days, ending with them having to shoot the troublesome stallion. Estanzio waited until the storm blew itself out. He then mounted his horse and headed for the distant canyon.

★ ★ ★

The vivid lightning had given way to darkness, the thunder was only a distant rumble, and the wind had died to a whisper. The patter of rain on the shake roof of the cabin was pleasant. Gil knelt before the fire, a venison steak broiling at the end of a long stick. Once Van had satisfied his thirst, he was hungry.

"Rider come," said Ramon.

Juan Padillo put out the candle and they waited, their hands on the butts of their pistols. Without the lightning, the night was pitch-black. Standing to one side of the door, Ramon cracked it enough to see out.

"Is Estanzio," he said.

Quickly Estanzio told them of the wild horse herd, of the stallion's stealing their mares, and of the trailing remnant of the herd of longhorns.

"None of this surprises me," said Gil, "except those fool cows trailing along after a wild horse herd. Estanzio, how many wild *caballos*, how many Mendoza?"

"*Salvaje*," said Estanzio, raising his hands twice, fingers spread. "Same Mendoza, but fi' more."

"That's bad news," said Van. "If that stallion's got only twenty in his bunch, he ain't goin' to give up them twenty-five new mares without a fight."

"Him dead," said Estanzio, "him no fight."

For a while nobody spoke. It was an extreme measure, a thing none of them liked to think about, but time was their enemy. They were on a trail drive, fraught with uncertainty and danger. Gil broke the silence.

"Five days," he said. "It'll be that long before Van's able to ride. You have until then to convince this *salvaje caballo* to give up our mares."

"I'll be able to . . . " Van began, and paused. Estanzio knew they must recover the Mendoza

262

mares, but he didn't want to shoot the gallant stallion.

"I'll be able to ride by then, I reckon," Van said.

"Estanzio," said Gil, "take Bola with you; this might be more difficult than you think."

"Get cow?" Ramon asked.

"Take three men with you," said Gil, "and go with Estanzio. While he, Mariposa, and Bola catch up to this band of horses, take your men and turn that bunch of longhorns back this way."

"I take Vicente, Pedro, and Manuel," said Ramon.

"Those outlaws had horses and cows in this canyon when we got here," said Van. "Are we claimin' them?"

"That's what we're going to decide in the next few days," said Gil. "We'll have trouble enough gettin' across the border, without having stolen stock in our herd. Any horse or cow in this canyon that's wearin' a brand goes free. They can find their way home, or just wander forever, as long as they can't be tied to us."

Estanzio and Bola rode out at first light, followed by Ramon, Vicente, Pedro, and Manuel. Juan Padillo, Juan Alamonte, and Domingo Chavez remained in the canyon.

"The four of us," said Gil, "are going to tally the horses and cows that were in this canyon when we took over. The horses won't be a problem, but longhorns look pretty much alike. While we're about it, we'll count them all. Just keep track of any that's wearin' brands.

We'll back them out of the total, and know how many we've gained. Don't worry with cropped ears; we can get around that. Do all of you have a pencil?"

Each man dug in his pocket for his stub of pencil. Many a rider who couldn't read or write knew his numbers and could copy brands. Gil handed each man two blank pages he'd torn out of a tablet.

"Don't bother copying brands," said Gil. "If a cow or horse is branded, I don't care *what* the brand is. When we're done, we'll compare tallies and see where we stand."

★ ★ ★

By the time Estanzio and his riders reached the bluff where the Indian vaqueros had waited out the storm, Mariposa was gone. His trail was plain, leading due north, and they followed it at a gallop. The first evidence of the longhorns they found was a profusion of tracks in a scrub oak thicket, where the herd apparently had taken refuge from the storm. As a result of the heavy rain, every gulley — most of them normally dry — was bank-full. The riders had covered only a few miles when they began seeing grazing longhorns. They rode on, intending to get beyond the farthest ones, gathering the rest as they drove south. Estanzio and Bola continued north, leaving Ramon and his riders to gather the errant longhorns. Estanzio looked at the ground only occasionally. There would be no tracks of the wild horse herd until they were beyond the path of last night's storm. Mariposa's trail continued north. He was gambling the horse herd hadn't turned either east or west before or during the storm. If they didn't soon sight the herd or find tracks, they'd have to assume the herd had stampeded, probably to the east, the wind at their backs. Then they must spend tedious hours riding a widening circle, until they struck a new trail, tracks left after the storm's passing. If Mariposa didn't soon see some evidence the wild horse herd had continued north, he would begin to circle, seeking to cut the new trail. He was leaving a plain trail, knowing that if he began his circle to the east, Estanzio would circle west. The wet weather streams became less frequent, until finally they were beyond the swath of last night's storm. Estanzio and Bola rode down a grassy slope, and in the sand at the bottom was the trail they sought. Estanzio read the tracks, and from the strides of the horses, it seemed they had simply run off and left the trailing longhorns. Estanzio decided the horses, frightened by the thunder and lightning, had stampeded, seeking only to escape the storm. Wherever they were, they would be tired. Once Mariposa sighted the grazing herd, he would not move alone. They found him waiting at the foot of a ridge, his nearby horse cropping grass. Estanzio and Bola reined up.

"*Salvaje caballos.*" Mariposa pointed toward the crest of the ridge.

"We take Mendoza *caballo*," said Estanzio. "No take *salvaje caballo. En tiempo.*"

Mariposa mounted his horse and the three of them rode to the top of the ridge. There was no hope of keeping their presence a secret. They would first try to ride down the herd, to cut out their mares. Failing in that, they'd have to dispose of the stallion. One way or another. The stallion, a big gray, saw them coming. He began nipping the flanks of his charges, nickering his impatience with their slow response. The Mendoza mares were farthest away, the wild bunch between them and the pursuing riders. Leaving Bola at the rear, Estanzio and Mariposa flanked the herd on opposite sides, seeking to drive a wedge between the mares and the wild horses. But the big gray stallion had expected that. He was everywhere, biting and nickering. Before Estanzio and Mariposa could split the herd, the stallion bunched them, driving the wild horses among the Mendoza mares. He was immediately on the heels of the stragglers, forcing them into a gallop. In turn, they crowded the front ranks, until the entire herd was in a mad gallop. Bola reined up, waiting for Estanzio and Mariposa to join him. This was new to him; he would follow their lead. Estanzio handed him a yard-long length of strong rope.

"We catch," said Estanzio. "Hobble hind legs."

Bola nodded. They'd never catch their mares as long as the stallion was free to control them. The trio kicked their horses into a gallop. The stallion could travel no faster than the herd, and the riders soon caught up. Mariposa and Estanzio took the lead, building their loops, riding straight for the big gray stallion. Mariposa's loop went true, snaring the animal's head, while Estanzio's underhand toss caught the hind legs. His nicker a mix of fear and anger, the stallion went down in a cloud of dust. Each rider backed his horse away from the stallion, taking up the slack in his catch rope. Bola was out of his saddle in an instant, securing one end of the rope to each of the stallion's hind legs. He could stand and take short steps, but he couldn't spread his hind legs enough to rear. The stallion exploded, floundering like a hooked fish, snapping at the empty air like a mad dog. The riders backed away, allowing the horse to exhaust itself enough for them to loose their lariats and flip them free. That accomplished, the trio galloped away after the horse herd.

Without the big stallion nipping at them, the herd had begun to graze. Before they were close enough to alarm the horses, Mariposa and Estanzio separated, again flanking the herd. Bola continued to advance. Without the stallion there to alarm them, the Mendoza horses didn't fear the riders. But the wild horses ran nickering away. Their fear was contagious, but the Mendoza mares hadn't moved quickly enough. Mariposa and Estanzio were between them and the retreating wild horse herd. There were twenty-six mares, and without the stallion's influence, they surrendered meekly. Once the three riders had their recovered herd bunched, they took a wide half circle around the hobbled stallion. The big gray horse was on his feet, but he made no move toward them, nor did he nicker after the departing mares. Before they rode out of sight, Estanzio paused and looked back. Like a big gray statue, the stallion stood looking after them. Estanzio rode on. Had it been another time, another place, he thought, it might have ended differently.

The stallion lay down and began chewing at the rope that hobbled his hind legs. Eventually he would free himself, but it would take him several hours, and by then the mares would be well out of his reach. When finally the last strand of rope parted, the big gray horse got to his feet and shook himself. For a moment he stood looking south, the direction his departing mares had gone. Slowly, he set out on the trail of his old herd . . .

16

THE tally finished, Gil compared their individual counts.

"Twenty extra horses," said Gil, "and three hundred longhorns. No brand on any of the cows, so they're as much ours as anybody's. But the horses all have brands. Mexican brands. I'm not sure some of them aren't the army horses we took from Salazar that later got away from us in a stampede. I'd say these horses would have been taken across the border and sold, and if we got caught with 'em, it would be evidence enough to stretch our necks on the spot. We'll leave the branded horses where they are."

In the late afternoon, Ramon and his riders drove the missing longhorns into the canyon. There were 504.

"*Caballos?*" Gil asked.

"*Mañana,* mebbe," said Ramon. "Bola, Estanzio, and Mariposa find."

"No use in us waitin' any longer," said Van. "I'll be plenty able to ride by tomorrow. When they get here with the mares, let's take the trail again. What day is it, anyhow?"

"August fifteenth," said Gil, consulting his notebook. "We'll plan on moving out the day after Ramon and his riders return with the rest of the horses. Ramon, from those outlaw saddles, help Rosa choose one for herself."

As Ramon had predicted, Bola, Estanzio, and Mariposa arrived the next morning just before noon, with the Mendoza mares.

"That's it," said Gil. "Unless somethin' changes my mind between now and then, we'll move out at first light."

Following a hurried breakfast, they cut out the branded horses that were to be left in the canyon, hazing them toward the north end. Their own horses and the longhorns were driven toward the south end of the canyon, with four riders to hold them there. Gil and the rest of the outfit loaded the packhorses. Rosa had found a big iron skillet in the outlaw cabin. It had been a blessing in the frying of bacon and venison steaks, and a necessity in the making of flapjacks. She brought out the skillet, lest it be forgotten.

"Take," she said.

Ready, they rode away from the lonely cabin, toward the south end of the canyon. Rosa fell behind. Gil dropped back and found her twisted around in the saddle for a last look at the cabin.

"Leave bunk," she said wistfully. In the short time they had been there, she had already begun to think of it as home.

"When we get to Texas," said Gil, "you'll have a bunk of your own, and you won't be leavin' it behind."

The herds, well-watered and grazed, moved out readily. Once they were all clear of the canyon, Gil roped the posts and pulled down the fence.

"The rest of you ride on," he said. "I'm goin' back and stampede those Mex-branded horses from here to yonder. If I don't, they'll follow us."

They rode east, eventually back-trailing along the path the stampede had taken. Reaching the once-dry creek from which the stampede had begun, they found the stream now had water. Following it to the point where they had been forced into dry camp, they headed the drive due north.

"From my scouting before the stampede," said Gil, "we know there's water within a day's drive north, but we need to know what lies beyond that. I'll begin scouting ahead again tomorrow."

"You'd better have Estanzio boil us another pot of that Mex color," said Van. "We're startin' to look like gringos again."

August 16, 1843. On the trail.

While Gil hadn't said so, these daily rides had become more than just a quest for water and graze. He had begun to suspect that the Mexican government had established a third outpost even farther to the east. A camp he didn't know existed, a camp from which Captain Salazar and his company had departed. Salazar and his men had been too far eastward to have just left Monterrey, and Matamoros, Coahuila was out of the question. Gil decided he lacked some vital information, that there likely was no way their trail drive could reach the border without encountering Mexican soldiers. A third outpost made sense; there was entirely too much border to be secured by outposts at Monterrey and Matamoros, Coahuila. But if he knew the third camp's location and they avoided soldiers on the march between camps, they still might slip between this third outpost and the one at Monterrey. Scouting far ahead, he could probably prevent their blundering into a camp unexpectedly, but he couldn't protect the drive against discovery by soldiers on the move. His scouting two days ahead of the drive might in itself prove their undoing. The trail ahead — which had seemed safe enough two days ago — might be alive with Mexican soldiers by the time the trail drive progressed that far. And once the drive was discovered, they were trapped. There was no way they could outrun or outmaneuver the soldiers. They would be caught just as surely as Salazar's small company had caught them. While they had shot their way out of Salazar's clutches, that wouldn't be possible against a larger force. The tables would turn, with Gil and his riders being gunned down. The trail drive would be entirely dependent on how convincing a story Ramon could tell, and the more Gil thought of that story, the less confidence he had in it. He had no idea what might happen when they were called on by Mexican authorities to explain the purpose of the trail drive and its destination. He could only scout ahead, hoping they might somehow slip between the soldier encampments without being spotted by soldiers on the move.

Suddenly Gil's horse shied and reared. In an instant Gil had his Colt drawn and cocked. The horse was looking off to Gil's right, where Gil could see little except scrub oak and brush. He listened for a while, and hearing nothing, rode on. Gil was uneasy, but would have been even more so if he'd turned back without knowing what had startled the horse. He had ridden less than a mile when again the horse shied, dodging the loop intended for it. But Gil wasn't so lucky, being at a disadvantage when the horse reared. There was the hiss of a lariat, and a second loop pinned his arms, jerking him out of the saddle. The frightened horse galloped away. Gil fought the rope, trying to reach his Colt, but there were three of them with sticks and clubs. Keeping his head down to protect his eyes, he fought back. He buried the heel of his boot in somebody's groin, and there was a satisfying cry of agony. But he soon became blinded by his own blood, and dizzy from the rain of blows to his head. It was a fight he couldn't win. They would beat him till they broke his bones or crushed his skull. He ceased his struggle and went limp, as though unconscious. The blows ceased. Rolling him over, they bound his hands behind him. Then, as they were about to tie his ankles, they discovered his white skin.

"Gringo!" shouted one of his attackers. "*Soldados* pay!"

He didn't understand the rest of their excited jabbering, but he did catch the words *mañana*, Meoqui, and Monterrey.

Gil thought he remembered seeing Meoqui

on their crude map. It was to the west of Monterrey, and would account for Captain Salazar's company being farther west than they had any right to be. Apparently intending to rob him and take his horse, his captors now planned to take him either to Monterrey or Meoqui, claiming the Mexican government's bounty on fugitive gringos. He lay still, listening, trying to make sense of their rapid-fire Spanish. Finally he heard the creak of wheels and the plodding of a horse or mule. One of them took his arms, another his ankles, and they dropped him flat on his back in the bed of the vehicle. Once they got under way, through his slitted eyes he could see the slatted sides of a two-wheeled cart, and the backside of the mule hitched to it. One of his captors walked beside the mule. He couldn't see the others, but he could hear them. He was unable to fully open his eyes because of the dried blood, but he could see the sun wasn't yet noon high. He hoped they hadn't caught his horse. The empty saddle would be all the message Van and the riders would need. If he was to escape, it would have to be tonight; tomorrow they would take him to the nearest army outpost.

★ ★ ★

Ramon was riding ahead of the horse herd, and it was he who first saw the riderless horse. Catching the lathered animal, he led it back toward the oncoming herd of longhorns. Van and Juan Padillo rode ahead to meet Ramon. There were no questions asked, and none

274

needed. A riderless horse told its own story. Its rider was dead, or in deep trouble.

"Ramon," said Van, "I'll take Juan Padillo and Estanzio with me. If it's more than we can handle, one of us will come for help. If you reach the next water before you hear from us, go ahead and bed down for the night. Keep your guns handy and every man on his guard. Once we find Gil, we may have to wait for dark to make our move. One way or another, you'll hear from us before dawn."

Van unsaddled Gil's tired horse and caught up a fresh one. Estanzio took the lead, followed by Juan Padillo and Van, leading the extra horse. Once the trio reached the place Gil had been dragged from the saddle and beaten, Estanzio had no trouble reading sign. They rode east, trailing the mule-drawn cart, and as soon as they crossed a sandy bottom, Estanzio found the tracks of Gil's three captors.

"No *soldado*," said Estanzio. "*Mejicano pelado*."

"*Ladrons*," said Juan Padillo.

"If they're robbers," said Van, "why didn't they take the horse?"

"Him 'fraid," said Estanzio. "Loop miss, him run."

"They took Gil with them," said Van. "That means they have plans for him. We may not have much time."

"*Soldados* pay for Tejano," said Juan Padillo.

Van didn't doubt the correctness of that judgment. They must find and free Gil before he was sold to Mexican soldiers for the bounty.

275

Even now one of his captors might be on a fast horse, bound for the nearest outpost.

★ ★ ★

Gil had a thumping headache, and if there was a place on him that did not hurt, he didn't know where it was. It seemed hours before the old cart creaked to a stop. His eyes were so crusted with dried blood, he could see just enough to tell it was still daylight. If his horse had returned to the trail drive, there was still a chance he might be found. Somebody let down the slatted tailgate of the cart, took him by the ankles, and dragged him out. He stiffened his neck to prevent his already throbbing head from being slammed against the ground. Once he was out of the cart, two of the men carried him into a cabin. Through slitted eyes he could see the log walls, but once inside he could distinguish nothing in the dim interior. They dumped him unceremoniously on the floor, on his back, his hands still bound uncomfortably behind him. Then a door closed, and all he could hear was the muffled sound of voices. His lips were bloody and swollen, he had bitten his tongue, and his thirst was all but unbearable. Despite his bruised and bloodied condition, he slept, awakened by the cramping of his upper arms and the pain in his bound wrists. He turned his head as far as he could, trying to study his surroundings. The room had no windows, but a thin beam of sunlight leaked through one wall. It had to be a west wall, the bit of light creeping in

276

where the elements had stripped away the mud chinking between the logs. It wasn't much, but at least he would know when it got dark. Only then could he hope for rescue.

★ ★ ★

Estanzio stepped up the pace. While they likely wouldn't be able to help Gil until after dark, they must find where he was being held, and under what circumstances. The wind was out of the northeast, and with less than an hour of daylight left, they smelled wood smoke. Estanzio raised his hand in silent signal, halting his companions. The three of them dismounted, and Estanzio passed his reins to Juan. He would scout ahead on foot. He was gone only a few minutes. When he returned, he pointed to the westering sun.

"We wait," he said. "*Cabaña.*"

Estanzio had said little, and what he had not said was significant. Gil was being held in a cabin. Estanzio hadn't observed any of the men who were Gil's captors, so it must be assumed they were in the cabin. There was little they could do until darkness made it possible for them to approach the cabin without being seen.

"Leave *caballo* here," said Estanzio.

He led them to the edge of a clearing where they could see the cabin from concealing brush. What had once been a lean-to had fallen to ruin, and the place looked to have long been abandoned. It had bothered Van that Gil's abductors might be poverty-stricken

Mexican farmers, seeking a windfall from the government. Now it seemed probable that the trio were thieves who had set out to rob Gil, had discovered his identity, and had chosen the abandoned cabin to hole up for the night. But for the promised bounty, taking Gil captive made no sense. Had it been only nine months since they had left Texas? To Van Austin, it seemed a lifetime ago. The killing had begun with the Mexican captain, Hernandez Ortega, and it seemed that each incident begat another. It seemed that in every bend of the trail it was shoot or be shot, that they must gun men down like dogs, or suffer the same fate themselves. With their enormous herd of longhorns and the blooded Mendoza horses, they had a fortune on the hoof, yet they were fugitives, with a price on their heads. Van had grown weary of the killing, and with each passing day, he wondered if the end of it would come with their own deaths.

"*Tiempo*," said Estanzio.

It was time for them to go and do what they must to free Gil. Once the sun dropped behind the Sierras, it was a matter of minutes until the purple shadow took possession of the land. Van saw no barn, no shelter of any kind, and he wondered what had become of the mule and cart. The three of them circled through the covering underbrush and came in behind the cabin. There seemed no way inside. What passed for a back door didn't look very promising. They discovered the place had no windows, had never had any. In the front and on each side there were shutters. When the weather permitted, they were

278

opened. When closed — and they were closed now — they were latched from the inside. The wind had died; smoke drifted lazily from the chimney.

"No way we can bust in there," said Van, "without taking a chance on bein' cut down with a hail of lead. Or they might just shoot Gil."

"No go in," said Estanzio. "Them come out." Before they could respond, he was gone, swallowed by the gathering darkness.

Van and Juan waited, suspecting what Estanzio had in mind, and when he returned, he confirmed it. He had his lariat and two big clumps of grass he'd pulled up by the roots. He circled around the cabin to the end where the chimney was. Juan Padillo and Van moved to within a few yards of the front door and drew their pistols. Estanzio built his loop and dropped it deftly over the chimney. Quickly he tied two piggin strings together, tied each end to a clump of the grass, and hung the pair of them around his neck. Aided by the lariat, he "walked" up the chimney until he could grasp the top edge of it. From there he pulled himself onto the roof. Once he had stuffed the two big clumps of grass into the narrow maw of the chimney, he loosed his lariat, crept down the roof to its lowest point, and dropped to the ground. By the time he joined Juan and Van near the front of the cabin, his handiwork had begun to pay off. The front door slammed open and the trio stumbled out, coughing, wheezing, and cursing. Van put a slug into the wall beside the door, and it got their immediate attention.

"You're covered," shouted Van.

One man threw himself toward the cabin's open door, and Juan Padillo's shot cut him down. The other two broke for the corner of the cabin and the shadow it afforded. There was no help for it; Van and Estanzio fired together, and it was over. Estanzio dragged the dead man out of the cabin door and went to check on the other two, while Van and Juan headed into the cabin to find Gil. The only light they had was from the fire. The cabin had but three rooms, only one of which had a door, and it was closed. Van kicked it open, and in the poor light from the fire, his first look at Gil was a shock.

"I hope you're in better shape than you look, big brother."

Gil said nothing. His throat was dry as a saddle blanket, and his tongue felt like an oversized hunk of wood. Being totally numb, his arms and legs no longer hurt. Van rolled him over and slashed the bonds on his wrists, while Juan Padillo freed his ankles. With the door open, smoke had fogged up the room. Van took Gil's shoulders, Juan Padillo his feet, and they carried him out into the cool of the night. Stretching him out on the ground, they began massaging his wrists and ankles. But at the sound of approaching horses, they were on their feet, pistols drawn. Then they relaxed. Estanzio rode his horse and led the other three. Dismounting, he took his canteen from his saddle, unstoppered it, and knelt beside Gil. He took a little of the water but had trouble getting it down. Finally he was able to drink deeply, and then he spoke.

"Never . . . been so dry . . . in my life."

"When you feel up to it," said Van, "you'd better walk around some."

"I heard shootin'," said Gil. "All of them?"

"Yeah," said Van, "and they might not have been armed. I feel kinda bad about it."

"I don't," said Gil. "They purely beat the hell out of me. If you kill a man with a club, he couldn't be deader if he'd been shot. They aimed to sell me to the Mex army for the bounty."

"For thieves," said Van, "they didn't have much savvy. They hauled you here in a cart, leavin' a trail Granny Austin could have followed without her spectacles."

"They didn't expect to be followed," said Gil. "I couldn't understand much of what they said, but I picked up one piece of information. While they were talking of selling me to the soldiers, I heard them speak of Monterrey and Meoqui. That means there's a third outpost at Meoqui, somewhere northwest of us. That's why Captain Salazar and his company found the isolated cabin where Rosa lived, and why they were far enough west to run into us. They had left Meoqui, riding southeast. By scouting ahead, we can avoid the outposts themselves, but not the soldiers on the move. If Salazar was bein' honest with us, if Santa Anna's no longer in power, then our story about takin' these horses and cows to him purely won't work. And we don't know who's taking his place."

"Anybody but a pair of damn mule-stubborn Tejanos that still believe in Santa Claus," said

Van, "would just surrender and be done with it. If you can ride, we need to move out. I told Ramon some of us would get word to him before he takes the trail in the morning."

"I can ride," said Gil, "but before we go, drag those three hombres into the cabin. We've left a trail of buzzards all the way from Durango County."

Gil clenched his teeth, stifling a groan as he swung into the saddle. Leaving the lonely cabin and its macabre secret behind, they rode west. But suddenly the silence was broken by the plaintive braying of a mule.

"He may be tied where he can't graze or reach water," said Gil. "Let's find him and take him with us. We can always use a good pack mule."

"You got more feelin' for a mule than for them three hombres we shot," Van chided.

"The mule didn't beat me half to death and then try to sell me to the Mex army," said Gil.

From the darkness came a sound neither of the Texans had ever heard before. Estanzio had understood Gil's words, and laughed.

★ ★ ★

August 20, 1843. Mexico City.

Angelina was late, and Antonio Mendez had allowed his impatience to get the better of him. As he paced the stone floor of the infamous dungeon, the sound of his footsteps seemed inordinately loud in the quiet. He wasn't

282

concerned about his supper; he could satisfy his belly anytime. He had another appetite, far more fierce, and he believed this night he might take the edge off it. Since he had shown her those squalid cells on the lower floor of the prison, Angelina seemed more taken with him than ever. She had begun staying with him longer than usual, and he sensed this was building up to an experience such as he had never before encountered. He'd taken to changing his uniform daily, and for the tenth time in as many minutes he finger-combed his dark hair straight back, smoothing it around his ears. He took the lamp from his desk, turned the flame as low as he could, and placed it on a stand near the door. He might have need of the desktop, and he cleared it with that in mind. Finally he sat behind the desk, where he could see out the open front door, through the series of gates.

A cart passed, drawn by two mud-spattered black horses, a *pelado* walking beside them. The horses had been intentionally muddied, lest they be taken for more than just a working team. Solano had carefully muddied the Winged M brand that each bore on its left hip, while he had attired himself as a nondescript peon. His high-crowned sombrero had a wide, flopped-down brim, as though it had been rained on once too often. It virtually hid his face. He turned the team down the dusty road that ran alongside the prison's high west wall. He halted the team, sat down with his back against the adobe wall, and tilted the sombrero over his eyes. But not so much that he couldn't see the Cocodrillo café up the street. He watched Angelina come out, walk up the street, and he lost sight of her as she crossed to the prison gate.

"Ah," said Antonio, as he unlocked the outer gate, "come in, come in."

His heart pounded so fiercely, he feared she could hear it. When she was about to place his supper tray on the old battered desk, he took the tray from her and placed it on the leather seat of his swivel chair.

"There is more room for us," he said playfully.

She said nothing. She leaned against the desk, flashing him a smile that he interpreted as an invitation. He leaned there beside her, boldly putting his arm around her shoulders. She wore a voluminous ankle-length dress, but it had a row of buttons down the back. His fingers found the first one. The buttons, and then the sash. She did nothing to discourage him as he fumbled with the first button. He was mentally cursing himself for his clumsiness, when the first button let go. He moved on to the second, then the third, until he reached the last one. His confidence rose to new heights as he felt bare skin. She wore nothing under the dress! He slipped his hand down her back, and reaching the bow in her sash, he tugged it loose. Cautiously he moved his eager hand below her waist. Suddenly she leaned forward, raising the hem of her skirt. He froze.

"I am letting my garters down," she said.

He had no idea what she was talking about, and when she straightened up, he set about slipping the dress off her shoulders and the sleeves off her arms. But that wasn't what she wanted. She had her right hand behind her, but with her left one she reached down and took the hem of the skirt, raising it high. Antonio Mendez caught his breath. He forgot about removing the dress. He lifted her until she sat on the edge of the desk, and then swiveled her around, stretching her out lengthwise. He fumbled himself out of his uniform trousers, banged his bare knee smartly against the corner of the desk, and straddled her. Her arms went around him, and he never saw the steel dagger she clutched in her right hand. Once, twice, three times, she drove it into his back. When she humped him off of her, he rolled off the desk and fell facedown on the stone floor.

Angelina put her dress in order, then took Antonio's discarded trousers and removed the key ring from his belt. She had purposely been late, so that it would be dark before she made her move. She went to the lamp and turned up the flame, lest its dimness arouse suspicion. Then, the ring of keys in her hand, she ran for the stone stairs that led to the basement cell block. The men stared at her like silent, bearded specters, as she ran down the stone corridor to Clay Duval's cell. She said nothing, nor did he. Gripping the iron bars, he watched as she tried key after key. She was down to three untried ones, her heart in her throat, when the lock finally clicked open. Clay Duval swung the barred door back and stepped out.

"Give me the keys," he said.

"You're going to free the others?"

"I am," he said, taking the ring of keys. "I'd be a poor excuse for a human being if I didn't."

"Then let me have some of them," she said, "and I'll help. I'm scared, and I want us to get out of here."

"No," he said, "these are keys for the entire prison. There's maybe a dozen men down here; it won't take us that long. I'll do it."

"God bless you, ma'am," said the first man, stumbling from his cell. He looked at Angelina as though she'd descended from heaven, wearing wings.

There were similar expressions from the others. Once they were out of their cells, Clay had some advice for them.

"That's all we can do for you, pardners; you're on your own. Go as far north tonight as you can. Hide by day, travel at night. Get yourselves some Mex duds, if you have to rob a clothesline. *Vaya con Dios*."

They all took the stone steps two at a time. Angelina took the keys and, with trembling hands, unlocked the gates that led to freedom. She and Clay waited until the rest of the men had vanished into the night. Then, as they exited each gate, they locked it behind them. Once outside, they kept within the shadow of the outer wall until they reached the cart where Solano waited. The Indian got to his feet and without a word took the Texan's hand. From the cart, Angelina took peon clothes for herself and for Clay.

"Here," she told him, "get into these, and

286

then get in the cart, under the straw."

"What are you goin' to do with the keys?" he asked.

"I'll take them with me. I hope this is the only set they have."

17

GIL, Van, Estanzio, and Juan Padillo reached camp without incident. Gil was bloody, battered, and bruised, but he dared not start a fire. His need for hot water was overshadowed by the possibility that a fire would attract unwelcome attention. He slept poorly, and was up before first light.

"I wasn't sure you'd be able to get up without help," Van said.

"I wasn't all that sure of it, myself," said Gil. "Soon as it's light enough for a fire, I'll heat some water and at least wash off the dirt and blood."

"Estanzio's ready to boil us another pot of that Mex color," said Van, "but I reckon we ought to wait a day or two, until you've had a chance to heal. That stuff in an open wound might poison you."

Gil dug out Ortega's now tattered map, seeking to find Meoqui. Ramon had been told of the possibility of a third military outpost, and had joined Gil and Van for a look at the map. Finally they found Meoqui a few miles south of Chihuahua.

"If Monterrey is two hundred miles west of Matamoros, Tamaulipas," said Van, "this Meoqui has to be more than three hundred miles northwest of Monterrey."

"That's a good guess," said Gil. "Now that

puts us in the position of having to squeeze between Meoqui and Monterrey, without alarming either outpost."

"Mayhap we can," said Ramon. "Is far between."

"I'm not as concerned with the location of the outposts," said Gil, "as I am troop movement between them. Soldiers on their way to or from Meoqui could stumble on to us at any time, or we could ride right into them."

"Border *soldados* too," said Ramon.

"True," said Gil. "Soldiers on their way to or from Meoqui are only part of our problem. Those who have been fighting along the border must eventually return to Meoqui or Monterrey. Even if we're able to slip past both outposts, there may still be soldiers between us and the border."

"From here to the border," said Van, "we'll be in constant danger of encountering soldiers, but I'm ready to have a go at it. I purely don't like having an ax hangin' over my head, never knowin' when it's gonna split my skull."

Gil's big pot of water had begun to boil, so he peeled off his shirt, and with some of the rags Rosa had used on Van, began soothing his hurts. His upper arms and shoulders were a mass of purple bruises, and from the way it felt, his back didn't look any better. His face and head had taken the worst punishment, and as he washed away the dried blood, some of the cuts began to bleed again. Without a word, Rosa took some of the rags, soaked them in the hot water, and began cleansing the cuts and bruises on his back and shoulders. When breakfast was over, the riders began saddling their horses, preparing to take the trail. Gil's sore muscles screamed in silent protest when he hoisted the saddle. Van was watching.

"Sorry we don't have a wagon for you to ride." He grinned.

"I might be tempted to take advantage of it," said Gil. "I feel like I've been pawed by a grizzly. That bunch jumped me before I found water for tonight, so if I'm going to scout ahead for today and tomorrow, I've got some ridin' to do."

Ramon pointed the drive north, and Gil rode out ahead of it. When he reached the place he'd been roped out of his saddle, he was only three or four miles from where they'd bedded down the herds the night before. Reining up, his eyes searched the sky to the east, where stood a lonely cabin with its three dead men. This time there were no telltale buzzards. He didn't know what he expected to see, and when he saw nothing, he rode on. Before he found water, he had ridden almost fifteen miles. It was a shallow stream, but it got deeper as he rode toward the source. It was the runoff from a spring, and he rode westward, along the south bank. Eventually he reached a surprisingly large pool at the foot of a rock outcropping. He reined up, viewing the deep, clear water with a frontiersman's appreciation. But when his eyes roamed to the far side of the pool, he caught his breath. He saw the partially burned embers of a recent fire. Gil rode up a low ridge, circled the spring, and came down on the other side of the pool. He left his horse far enough away so as not to spoil any tracks. Even from where he stood, he could smell the damp ashes from the dousing of the fire. The previous visitors hadn't been gone that long. He easily found tracks of a dozen shod horses, where they had approached the spring from the northwest, and where they had departed, toward the south-east.

If the riders continued in the direction they were headed, they would pass to the north of the trail drive. He followed the tracks to the point where he had first reached the stream, and they continued southeast. He turned north and rode on. They would have water tonight, but he wanted to stay two days ahead of the drive. Once he was certain there was water for the herds, he could concern himself with other things. Such as dodging the Mexican army.

★ ★ ★

August 21, 1843. Mexico City.

Carlos Arista arrived at the dungeon to assume his duties for the day, and found the gates locked with nobody to let him in. It wasn't the first time, and he cursed Antonio Mendez for a fool. How many times had Antonio partaken of pulque, forcing Carlos to awaken him from a stupor? Carlos had shouted until he was hoarse, without result. He was tempted to just return home, allowing Antonio Mendez to awake if and when he chose, but he dared not. Antonio, *bastardo* that he was, would claim that Carlos Arista had not shown up for work. Each of

291

Antonio's bouts with the bottle was worse than the last, and Carlos vowed this was going to be the end of it. Since this was a military prison, authorities at the presidential palace would become involved. Since Santa Anna's ouster, there was a new prison director, and Carlos was afraid of him. He was the kind who might behead the bearer of bad news. Carlos did not know how to report the problem to the military; besides, the presidential palace was four miles distant. Suddenly he saw a way out. He hurried to the home of Hidalgo Gonzales, the *alcalde*.

"You suspect Antonio Mendez is sleeping off a drunk," said Gonzales, "and you wish *me* to summon the prison director to awaken him?"

"I do not know that he sleeps," said Carlos desperately. "I do not know what is the matter with him. I wish only to do my job, without trouble from the new presidente and the *milicia*."

Gonzales sighed. How well he understood. The city's officials had, at best, a shaky alliance with the liberals who had wrested control of the government from Santa Anna. Suppose there *was* something wrong at that miserable dungeon, and he, the *alcalde*, did not report it?

"Let us try once more," said Gonzales. "If we are still unable to arouse this Antonio Mendez, then I will call on the prison director."

Carlos was waiting nervously before the gates of the dungeon when the new prison director arrived. Santo de Alimosa glared at Carlos Arista in disbelief. Finally he spoke.

"There is but one set of keys?"

"*Si*," said Carlos. "Antonio Mendez has them. If there are others, perhaps General Santa Anna . . . "

His voice trailed off, as he realized what he had almost said. Just the mention of the ex-dictator's name could put some thoughtless wretch before a firing squad. But the new prison director was lost deep in his own gloomy thoughts. For an insane moment he wondered if the diabolical Santa Anna had somehow brought this calamity upon him. Everybody — perhaps even his comrades within the new regime — would be laughing at him, for now he must suffer the embarrassment of breaking into his own prison! *Por Dios*, he vowed he would make an example of this *pelado*, this Antonio Mendez. If not the firing squad, then perhaps a public whipping . . .

★ ★ ★

Many miles north of Mexico City, a peasant-garbed Solano walked beside the cart, while a poorly dressed Angelina rode within it. In this first gray light of dawn, Solano was seeking a sanctuary where they might conceal themselves during the daylight hours. They traveled north, toward Tampico. When they reached a shallow stream that angled away toward the gulf, Solano turned his team westward. The stream bed deepened into an arroyo. Gangling Clay Duval was climbing out of the hay-filled cart even before it stopped moving. He wore peasant

293

clothing, a flop-brimmed hat, and Indian moccasins.

"I don't aim to sound ungrateful," he said, "but this is the worst damn ride I ever took. I need a critter I can wrap my legs around, even if it's a Missouri jack without a saddle."

"Better cart than *juzgado*," said Solano.

The Indian didn't waste words. Angelina laughed. The cart had been her idea, and they'd had little money, even for that. Solano was more than justified, for he had hated Mexico City.

"*Amigo*," said Clay, with a chuckle, "you purely know how to humble a man. If I had to crawl to Texas on my hands and knees, I'd be better off today than I was yesterday."

They had just the bare essentials. Even if they'd dared risk a fire, there was no need for one. Hardtack and jerked beef never spoiled, as long as it was kept dry, but there was no improving it. Once they had finished their meager meal, Solano stretched out on the shaded bank of the stream, tipped his sombrero over his eyes, and slept.

"I brought a razor," said Angelina, "so I can cut your hair. I can rid you of the beard too, but it'll have to be without soap, and in cold water."

"I'd sacrifice some hide to have my face feel clean again," said Clay. He removed the rough peon shirt.

First she cut his hair, trimming it close above the ears and in the back. But the months-long beard wasn't easily conquered. When she had finished, he splashed cold water on his face, washing away the blood from the many cuts. Despite his discomfort, she laughed.

"I feel like I been in a knife fight," he said, "and everybody had a knife except me."

Nothing disturbed the solitude except the chatter of birds, and the munch-munch-munch of the picketed horses cropping grass.

"Now," he said, "soap or not, I aim to find a place in this branch where the water's deep enough to wash off this prison stink."

She followed.

"I aim to get jaybird naked," he added. "You still want to come along?"

"Haven't I earned the right?"

"I reckon you have," he said.

★ ★ ★

After leaving the spring, Gil rode another twenty miles before finding suitable water. It was almost a two-day drive, and he had visions of another dry camp. He had ridden a hundred yards north of the creek when he made an alarming discovery. A large party of riders had come this way, riding northwest. The horses were shod, and the tracks appeared day old. But there was something more. At first he thought they were wagon tracks, changing his mind when he could account for only two wheels. A two-wheeled cart? If these had been soldiers — and he was virtually sure they had been — they'd use pack mules or horses. The terrain was far too rugged for cart or wagon. Whatever the thing was, it had been heavily loaded, for the wheels

295

had cut deep tracks. The wheels were set close together, the rims wider than those of Victoria Mendoza's Conestoga. Suddenly, like twin bolts of lightning, it hit him. These were the tracks of a carriage-mounted, horse-drawn cannon, and this almost had to be the route the Mexican soldiers were taking to the farthest outpost at Meoqui!

But what of the tracks he had found near the spring, twenty miles south? Those soldiers had been on their way to Monterrey or Mexico City, he decided, and their line of march could vary a few miles. But this trail over which the cannon had been drawn *had* to be the most direct route to the outpost at Meoqui. Nobody in his right mind, pulling an ungainly field piece over rough terrain, would travel more miles than he had to. Gil followed the tracks for a mile and soon found the proof he sought. There were many older tracks underlying the most recent ones. He rested his horse until it was safe for the animal to drink, and then he rode south in a slow gallop, bearing the bad news. Gil met the herd halfway to the spring where they would bed down for the night. Ramon and Van rode ahead to meet him, and listened grimly as he told them what lay ahead.

"The next couple of days, then," said Van, "will either see us past the outposts at Monterrey and Meoqui, or in the hands of the Mex army."

"That's how it stacks up," said Gil, "but don't spend all your time just worryin' about that. Once we leave that spring runoff, it's a good twenty miles to the next water. Even if we push 'em hard, the last half a dozen miles we'll be risking a stampede every foot of the way. They'll be dry, ornery, and one whiff of that creek will have 'em on the run."

"At least they'll be headed north," said Van, "and that's the way we want 'em to go."

"Dust," said Ramon, shaking his head. "*Soldados* see dust, mebbe hear *estampeda*."

"He's dead right," said Gil, "but even if that fails to draw them to us, we'll still be directly in their line of march while we try to gather the stampeded herd. One way or another, if we lose 'em and they scatter along that creek, I look for trouble. Soon as we bed down for the night, I'll warn the other riders."

★ ★ ★

August 22, 1843. On the trail north.

Gil was awake long before dawn. Rosa was rolled in her blankets next to him. Last night, while he had explained the possibility of a clash with Mexican soldiers, he had seen the fear in Rosa's eyes. She hadn't forgotten, and when she had spread her blankets next to his, he knew why. Now, as he looked at her in the dim starlight, she sat up.

"*Soldados*," she said softly. "*Soldados* come. *Soldados* kill."

"Rosa," he said.

She crept over next to him. Fully dressed, except for his boots, he tucked his blanket around her. Soon she slept. He suspected she'd

297

slept as poorly as he had, and he sat there longer than he'd intended, because he hated to awaken her. Ramon sought out Gil at first light. He knew the day's drive would be a killer.

"Mebbe we go now," said Ramon. "Not eat."

"No," said Gil, "we're going to eat a hot meal and enjoy hot coffee, because we may be until after dark getting to the next water. Eat while you can; we may be in a cold camp tonight."

When they moved out, Estanzio and Mariposa pushed the horse herd harder than usual. It would be hardest on the longhorn cows, the cow's stride being shorter than that of a bull. Gil had seen to it that most of the cows had been moved to the front of the herd. If they lagged, they risked being hooked from the rear by the impatient bulls and steers. Gil soon decided it was a tactic he'd never use again, if they ever made it to water. Some of the cows, tired of having their rumps and flanks raked with horns, decided to solve the problem by simply quitting the herd. It kept the flank riders sweating, as one cow after another made a run for it. Not being too smart to begin with, cows never seemed to learn do from don't. The same ones kept quitting the herd, and had to be forced back into it.

"My God," Van groaned, "this is worse than first day on the trail with a new herd."

Gil had to agree. By noon he doubted they had traveled even ten miles. He had made a costly mistake, so he sought Ramon's help, and they set about correcting it. They reversed the order, moving the longer-strided bulls and steers to the front, and the cows to the rear.

"Estanzio and Mariposa will continue to drive the horse herd," said Gil. "Ramon will take one flank, and Juan Padillo the other. The rest of us will eat dust at drag. Keep the cows bunched and moving. Double your lariats and dust their backsides."

There was immediate improvement. The cows escaped the bite of the lariats by staying bunched and keeping up with the leaders. That ended the epidemic of bunch-quitting. The August sun bore down, and the dusty flanks of the longhorns darkened with sweat. So did the dusty shirts of the riders. Far beyond the Sierra Madres the sky was being painted a dusky rose by the westering sun. The wind had been out of the northwest all day. Gil caught Ramon's eye and pointed to the west. Ramon shook his head. At least there would be no storm, with the promise of water brought by a deceitful wind.

"Now what?" Gil wondered. He was riding drag, and the flank riders had signaled a stop. Before he reached the point, Gil could see what had caused the delay. Estanzio was riding toward the herd, his rifle at the ready. Before him walked a pair of terrified Mexicans, one of them leading a mule. The mule's load had been diamond-hitched over a pack saddle. Ramon rode behind Estanzio, and it was Ramon who spoke.

"*Hombres* go to Monterrey," he said.

Estanzio had reined up, and his captives stood there looking for the world like what they probably were — a pair of dirt-poor farmers on their way to town to trade the little they had for food. Gil rode past Estanzio and spoke to Ramon.

"I know it's bad news, Ramon, but there's no help for it. Tell Estanzio to let them go."

Ramon walked his horse alongside Estanzio's and spoke in Spanish. The Indian, saying nothing, eased his rifle off cock and slid it into the boot. Ramon spoke to the Mexicans, and their relief was pathetically obvious. Departing in haste, they were almost dragging the mule. Van had arrived in time to see them leave. Before he could ask, Gil answered his question.

"They're going to Monterrey."

"So are we," said Van, "once they've spilled their guts to the soldiers. I don't often disagree with you, big brother, but I'd have hog-tied that pair, took 'em with us, and let 'em go at the border."

"Just one more thing you'd have to explain to the soldiers," said Gil. "Everybody to your positions. Ramon, move 'em out."

The sun slid behind the Sierra Madres, and even with no wind, it seemed mercifully cooler. Gil judged they had traveled fifteen miles; three quarters of the way to water. First he spoke to Ramon, then made his way along the strung-out herd to the rest of the riders. Rather than risk a dry camp, they would push on. There was no trouble with the horse herd, but the longhorns grew restless. They were tired, they were thirsty, and while they weren't all that smart, they knew day from night. It was time to drink, to graze, to rest.

"Keep them bunched," Gil shouted. "Keep them moving."

Some of the herd, especially those near the drag, tried to turn back. Strong in their memory was the water and good graze of the night before. Even without the moisture-laden wind, they were becoming hard to handle. Gil rode ahead, catching up to the horse herd.

"Estanzio," he said, "you and Mariposa take *caballos* to water. Let them drink, then take them to graze."

Estanzio nodded. Once the longhorns scented water, they were likely to gore anything or anybody in their way. While the longhorn herd was limited to the shorter stride of the cows, the horses had no such restriction. They could reach the water, drink, and be safely grazing before the longhorns arrived. The cattle might stampede toward the water and scatter from hell to breakfast, but at least they wouldn't take the horse herd with them. Once the sun was down, darkness seemed to descend on them immediately. There would be a moon later, but that was no help now. It was the first time they had trailed the herd after dark, and the longhorns seemed confused. Even as they plodded along, they began bawling their weariness, frustration, and thirst. At first only a few protested, but like coyotes, the others joined in until there was a bovine chorus such as none of the riders had ever heard.

"My God," said Van, "the way sound travels

at night, the Mex soldiers in Monterrey will know we're here, without them Mex farmers sayin' a word."

The melancholy chorus continued, seeming to swell in volume. They were three hours past sundown when the leaders thought they smelled water somewhere ahead. Gil and Ramon tried in vain to slow them, but finally had to ride for their lives to avoid being trampled. The riders followed in the wake of the stampede. There was no hurry now.

"At least they won't be scattered over half of Mexico," said Van. "We'll find 'em somewhere along the creek."

"Yes," said Gil, "but however long it takes to gather them, that's time we don't have. We're right in the line of march for soldiers going to or from Meoqui. If that's not enough, by tomorrow evening that pair of farmers will have reached Monterrey. It'll be a miracle if we get through without being spotted by soldiers from Monterrey or Meoqui."

★ ★ ★

August 23, 1843. South of Tampico.

Solano rode out in the dim starlight. Before they resumed their journey, he would scout ahead. The farther north they traveled, the greater the danger, and the more of a hindrance the cart became. It was presently concealed in a coulee where Clay Duval and Angelina awaited his return. They were in need of a horse and saddle, and when the opportunity presented itself, Solano would have both. It was part of his purpose in riding out ahead of each night's departure. The wind was from the north, and before he had ridden far, he smelled smoke. Picketing his horse, he continued on foot. *Soldados* always built a fire big enough to roast a *vaca*, he thought, and this bunch was no exception. He counted twelve of them. Circling their camp until he found where the horses were picketed, he sought one whom he could reach without alarming the others. He approached a black, muttering his "horse talk" just loud enough for the horse to hear. It was a friendly, comforting sound the horse found familiar, and once Solano had the animal safely away from the camp, he returned. Quickly he examined the saddles by feel, choosing one that was not military, one that had a rifle in the boot. He pulled picket pins on the rest of the horses, took the saddle, and faded into the night. Circling the camp, he retrieved his own horse and rode back to the coulee where Clay and Angelina waited. Solano swung out of the saddle and passed the reins to the Texan.

"Leave cart," said Solano. "Go, pronto."

Angelina's saddle was still in the cart. Solano quickly saddled the third horse, and Angelina mounted. When they rode out, Solano led them far wide of the soldier camp. Once they were a mile north of it, Solano passed his reins to Clay.

"Hold," he said. "Cougar come."

With that, he was gone. When he was within three hundred yards of the soldier camp, he

303

loosed the eerie, spine-chilling cry of a cougar. The horses lit out south, some of them tearing right through the camp itself. Victim to a flying hoof, one soldier cried out in pain. Others cursed, and one emptied his pistol into the night. Solano returned to where Angelina and Clay waited. Without a word he took the reins from Clay, mounted his horse and led out.

★ ★ ★

August 24, 1843. Mexico City.

General Paradez, having defeated Santa Anna, was furious. Expecting a hero's welcome, he had returned to Mexico City to find the town laughing at him and his newly appointed liberal administration. Not only had they been forced to break into their own prison, they had found their jailer dead, and every gringo in the prison had been freed. Poor Antonio Mendez — found dead and half naked — had been disgraced, and his family had disappeared. General Paradez himself had gone to the Cocodrillo café to question the old Mexican woman who owned it. He had accomplished little, except to scare her out of her wits. She knew nothing about the girl, except her first name — Angelina — had no idea where she was from or where she might have gone. General Paradez pounced on one of his hapless aides.

"I will depart for Matamoros, Tamaulipas at dawn," he said. "I will take a hundred soldiers with me."

"But my general," the aide stammered, "we

do not have a hundred soldiers!"

"*Por Dios!*" bawled Paradez. "Then I will take as many as we have."

Using the little information that he had, Paradez issued an arrest order on the girl he knew only as Angelina, charging her with the murder of Antonio Mendez. There was a reward of five thousand pesos. Dead or alive.

★ ★ ★

When Gil and the rest of the outfit reached the creek, they found it full of longhorns. Many of them, having drunk their fill, grazed along the banks. Estanzio and Mariposa splashed their horses across the creek. They had wisely driven the horse herd to the other side, grazing them well beyond the stream.

"Nothing more we can do tonight," said Gil. "Come first light, we'll gather them as quickly as we can and move out. No fires tonight. The usual watch, but when you sleep, don't get too comfortable. Since we don't know what to expect, we'll have to be ready for anything."

★ ★ ★

Gil was up at first light. There were bunches of longhorns grazing along both banks of the creek. He doubted the gather would take long. Still, it would lessen the daylight hours they would need to reach the next water.

"Ramon," said Gil, "I'm going to take my usual ride, because we need to know what's

305

ahead. Water especially. They don't seem too scattered, so I reckon you can gather them quickly. Move out as soon as you can."

Gil didn't feel comfortable leaving them to do the gather without him, but he was concerned, not only about water and graze for tonight, but how near they might be to Monterrey. He had ridden less than ten miles when he came upon something that was a total surprise. It was a small lake, the result of some unseen source, and it didn't look to have ever been dry. It was an ideal campsite, and there was evidence of old fires. Soldiers perhaps, but they would have to take that chance. Even with the time it took to gather the longhorns, the trail drive could easily reach this water before dark. With that assurance, he rode on. He still must find water for tomorrow, and that old premonition that warned him of impending trouble began to stir.

18

"IS good," said Ramon as they brought the last bunch of cows into the newly gathered herd.

"We lucked out on that one," said Van. "Now let's get 'em on the trail. We don't know how many miles we are from the next water."

Watered and grazed, the herds trailed well. Van watched Bola ride off up the creek they were leaving. He was leading an extra horse.

"Hunt deer," said Ramon.

It was a welcome change from a diet of bacon and beans. Van had come to appreciate Bola's unique talent. It was especially useful in country where a rifle shot might bring an enemy on the run. When Bola eventually caught up to them, the led horse bore the carcass of a deer. The sun was still more than an hour high when they reached the lake Gil had discovered.

"That's it for today," Van said. "We don't know how far we are from the next water, but there's no hope of reaching it before sundown."

"Mebbe far," said Ramon. "Gil not come back."

"We're always havin' to track him down and keep him from gettin' his ears shot off," said Van. "Maybe I'd better ride out a ways and see if he's in trouble."

Gil was having problems, but nothing he

couldn't handle. After leaving the lake, he had ridden almost ten miles without finding water for the next day's drive. Suddenly his horse put its left foot into an unseen hole. Gil dismounted, examined the leg, and found the skin broken. When he led the horse a few steps, it limped.

"Well, old son," he said, "if you can walk, I'll walk with you."

Walk they did, the black favoring the sore leg. It was the horse Solano had chosen for him, and Gil wouldn't have taken a thousand dollars for it. When the sun had set, purple shadows crept over the land, and the only sound was the sigh of the wind and the sleepy chirp of birds. Man and horse plodded on.

★ ★ ★

In his concern for Gil, Van almost didn't see the soldiers in time to avoid having them see him. He was only minutes from camp, and the trail drive was only minutes from discovery. The soldiers rode in columns of two, and while he had been unable to see them all, he believed there were twenty or more. There was no way to avoid discovery; the dreaded time was upon them. All he could do for Ramon and the outfit was give them a few minutes' warning. He turned his horse, and when he was far enough ahead of the soldiers, he urged the animal into a gallop. He rode in at twilight; it would be dark within minutes.

"Soldiers," he told them, "ridin' in from the northwest."

"Many?" Ramon asked.

"Too many," Van said. "I couldn't see 'em all, without them seein' me. There's got to be twenty or more. Change your story a little, Ramon. Don't mention Santa Anna. Just say this is the Mendoza outfit, and the horses and cows are for use by the Mexican army. The trail drive is on its way to Matamoros, Tamaulipas. That has to be the larger of the two outposts."

Van hated to pile all the responsibility on Ramon, but it was their only hope. He must remain in the shadows, lest his blue eyes give him away. If this bunch of Mex soldiers decided to stay the night, they were finished, for his and Gil's identity was a secret he doubted could stand the light of day. But a more immediate worry was Gil himself. If he was in trouble, he was on his own, for they couldn't help him. When the soldiers rode in, it was even worse than Van had suspected. Including the officer in charge, there were forty-three men! The officer bore an alarming resemblance to Captain Ortega, fat and arrogance included. He halted his columns and walked his horse to within a few yards of where Ramon, Juan Padillo, and Estanzio waited. While he couldn't see the multitude of longhorns, it was impossible for him not to be aware of their presence for there was a distant lowing and clacking of horns. The officer spoke in English.

"I am Major Gomez Farias," he said. "Perhaps you will explain who you are, where you are going, and the purpose of your journey."

"No *comprender*," said Ramon. He must

convince the officer they were but poor vaqueros, following the orders of their *patrono*.

Farias repeated the order in Spanish, and Ramon answered in Spanish, speaking slowly. Once Ramon had told his prepared story, he said no more. Major Farias stroked one end of his curled moustache, pondering. When he spoke, he confirmed Van's fears and suspicions.

"I have heard of the Mendoza horses. I, myself, am poorly mounted, and so are my men. You have horses for the *milicia*, no? *Por Dios*, we *are* the *milicia*, and we shall have some of these Mendoza horses before they are taken by others."

Ramon, still speaking in his slow *peon* Spanish, explained that the caballos must be delivered to the commander of the *milicia* at Matamoros, Tamaulipas. It was by order of the *patrono*.

"Such loyalty is to be commended," said Farias. "We shall escort you to Matamoros, and there take our pick of these fine horses you are taking to the *milicia*."

There it was! Van sighed in the darkness. Farias gave the order to dismount, and they were surrounded by Mexican soldiers. Within minutes there was a roaring fire. Ramon gritted his teeth as the soldiers began helping themselves from the trail drive's packs. There were shouts as they discovered the deer Bola had brought in. Van jumped when someone touched his shoulder.

"Big trouble," said Gil from the darkness. "Where's Rosa? The way she feels about soldiers, God knows what she's likely to say or do."

"I don't know," said Van. "Between wondering where you were and how we're gonna get out of this, I haven't even thought of her. But what can she say or do to make things worse than they are already?"

He soon found out. There was a screech from Rosa, and in the outburst that followed, the mildest term she had for the soldiers was "murdering dogs." One of the soldiers flung Rosa to the ground before the fire. They'd ripped off her too-big vaquero pants, their intentions obvious. Gil and Van were fighting their way through the soldiers, trying to reach her, but Rosa took things into her own hands. Seizing the cool end of a flaming ember from the fire, she drove the flaming end of it into the groin of the soldier who had attacked her. The man screamed, and one of his comrades knocked Rosa to the ground. Ramon's fist smashed him on the chin and he dropped like an axed steer. Half a dozen of them piled on Ramon as Gil and Van moved in, bashing heads with the heavy barrels of their Colts. But their cause was lost. But for the four riders watching the herd, the entire outfit went down under odds of five-to-one. Quickly they were beaten into submission, but the worst was yet to come. Gil and Van no longer wore shirts, but tattered rags that did nothing to conceal their white skin. Major Farias hadn't taken part in the fray, nor had he attempted to stop it. Now he stood looking down at the bruised and bloody Texans. He then turned to an equally bruised and bloody Ramon.

"Ah," said Farias, with an evil laugh, "I can see that you are truly surprised to find that two of your riders are fugitive gringos with prices on their heads."

Ramon said nothing.

"Since you have deceived me in this one important matter," Farias continued, "I find myself doubting what you have told me. There is but one thing of which I am sure. I have in my hands two gringos whose heads are each worth a thousand pesos. You say that you are taking horses and cows to Matamoros, Tamaulipas for use by the *milicia*. Very well, I shall permit you to do so, and to be sure that you do, I will leave enough soldiers so that you do not change your mind."

He gave an order in Spanish, and one of the soldiers brought Rosa to him. She had been securely wrapped in a blanket, only her head visible. Again Farias turned to Ramon.

"Yours?" he asked, pointing to Rosa. Ramon shook his head.

"Ah," said Farias, "you have told me what I wish to know, although the truth is not in you. When I depart for Matamoros, Tamaulipas with the *gringos*, I will also take with me your child. When you have delivered the horses and cows to the *milicia*, General Paradez will decide what is to become of you. If he is merciful and does not have you executed, perhaps this young *felino* will be returned to you . . . ."

He gave an order, and the soldiers stripped every rider of his pistol. Gil and Van were hustled to their feet and their hands were

312

bound behind them. Again Farias spoke to Ramon.

"Go to the riders who are watching the horses and cows. Take riders to replace them, and bring these armed riders to me. They will surrender their weapons, if they are to live. See that they do not resist."

When Ramon rode out, four of the soldiers mounted and followed. Farias gave another order, and the soldiers began taking rifles from the vaqueros' saddle boots. Their backs against opposite sides of an oak, Gil and Van were roped securely to the tree. They had no idea what Farias had done with Rosa. Strong on their minds was the thought that the Mexican officer had done nothing when his soldiers had assaulted the girl. Once Ramon returned with the riders who had been left with the herd, the soldiers seemed to lose interest in him. Ramon came to the tree where Gil and Van were tied.

"Ramon," said Gil, "Talk to Rosa if you can. Tell her to do and say nothing, that she's going with Van and me. Remember, once we reach Matamoros, Tamaulipas, we're less than thirty miles from the border. This General Paradez must be the man who's replacing Santa Anna, and I expect we'll be held there at Matamoros, Tamaulipas until he arrives. Pretend you're beaten, but look for a chance to get your guns and break loose from these soldiers. With any luck, Farias won't leave many, and that'll lessen the odds. If there's any way, Van and I will find some means of escape and join you before you reach Matamoros, Tamaulipas. *Vaya con Dios*, pardner."

"We fight," said Ramon.

Both men had spoken with a confidence they didn't feel. From somewhere in the darkness came the eerie, quavering cry of a screech owl. Ozark legend said that the screech owl was a harbinger of death, that soon after its warning, someone would die. Gil and Van had heard Granny Austin speak of it as though it were fact, and as they listened to the laughter of the soldiers, it seemed less a superstition and more a reality.

★ ★ ★

Gil and Van spent a miserable night bound to the tree. Their bonds were removed at dawn so they could eat. Farias designated fourteen soldiers to remain with the trail drive, to escort it to Matamoros, Tamaulipas. Major Farias and the rest of the soldiers would depart immediately, taking Gil, Van, and Rosa with them.

"That Mex varmint can't wait to get us to Matamoros, Tamaulipas," said Van. "He's bucking for more rank, and he aims to buy it with our blood."

"We're not dead yet," said Gil. "We escaped once; let's set our minds to doing it a second time. Like I told Ramon, Matamoros is maybe thirty miles south of the border. This may not be the best way, but it's one way of gettin' our herds close enough to drive them into Texas.

All we have to do is break loose, stay alive, and take over the trail drive when it reaches Matamoros."

"This Farias is a trashy bastard," said Van. "He really believes Rosa is Ramon's kid, so he's taking her to keep a noose around Ramon's neck until the trail drive reaches Matamoros, Tamaulipas."

"It'll be hard on Rosa," said Gil, but she'll be safer as a hostage. She had nothing to fear from our outfit, but left here in a camp with soldiers in control, that could change. That ruckus last night wasn't Rosa's fault. One of them was about to take advantage of her, and she reacted the only way she knew how. She's young, but she's had a hard life, and she's not dumb. She knew we were outnumbered, and I just don't believe she would have blown up like that if she hadn't been forced to."

Farias gave an order, and the men who would ride with him to Matamoros began saddling their horses. Ramon and Juan Padillo had saddled horses for Gil and Van, while one of the soldiers saddled a mount for Rosa. Their hands bound behind their backs, Gil and Van had to be helped into their saddles. Once there, their ankles were bound together by a rope passed under the horses' belly. Finally, they each had a rope looped about their necks, with the other end dallied around a soldier's saddle horn. While Rosa wasn't bound, her horse was on a lead rope, the other end secured to a soldier's saddle horn. She again wore the old trousers Ramon had cut down to fit her, and when they lifted her into the saddle, she wept so long and loud, Farias shouted her to silence. Farias led the way. Behind him rode Gil, Van, and Rosa, followed by the three soldiers who held lead ropes. The remainder of the soldiers Farias elected to ride with him followed. As Farias and his soldiers took them away, Rosa buried her face on her horse's neck and wept. Ramon, Juan Padillo, Estanzio, Mariposa, and the rest of the outfit looked on in silence. They couldn't speak, but Gil's heart leaped when he saw their eyes. There was anger, reassurance, and a grim determination that said there would come a day of reckoning. This wasn't over!

While Gil and Van were bound securely during the day, their bonds were removed at night. While it was a relief, and made sleep possible, there was no possibility of escape. They were watched constantly by two armed guards, and the sentries were changed three times during the night. When the guards became bored, they talked freely in Spanish, and it was through them that Gil and Van learned they would not go immediately to Matamoros, Tamaulipas, but would stop in Monterrey for one night.

"Farias aims to show us off," said Gil. "He wants to crow some, show the rest of this Mex army what a big man he is."

It was exactly what Farias had in mind. Once they reached Monterrey, they were led through the village, then turned around and led back. The soldiers already in Monterrey seemed to be walking wounded. Most of them wore bandages on arms or legs, or limped when they walked.

As it turned out, the outpost at Monterrey had a small stockade for prisoners. It was crude; heavy logs had been set deep in the ground, their sharpened upper ends well above a man's head. There was just one way in or out, and that was through a massive log gate in the stockade wall. Before the gate stood a soldier with a rifle. Gil and Van were pushed inside, and the gate closed behind them. The shelter inside was no more than three log walls with a shake roof. The entire front was open, like a chicken coop. The floor was dirt, and the only accommodation was a bench along the back wall. One man sat on it, hunched down as though asleep. His left leg was bandaged from knee to ankle. His Texas boots stood on the ground and his hat lay on the bench beside him. He sat up, stretching his arms and legs, yawning like a sleepy cat. Van was the first to recover from his surprise.

"Long John Coons, what'n hell are you doing here?"

"Jus' come fer a visit," drawled Long John, "an' liked it so much, I stayed."

"We left you to watch our Bandera range," said Gil. "With you here, who's doing that?"

"Ain't got no idee," said Long John, "onless it's some of them that lives there, which I doubt. The most unneighborly sonsabitches that ever come down a wagon road. When ye git back — if ye do — I expect that bunch of lobos will be whinin' their heads off."

"So you got the neighbors on the prod," said Van, "and they told you to vamoose."

"Like hell!" said Long John hotly. "I go when

317

I'm ready, an' I was ready. We laid up at yer diggings till the grub run out, and fer a spell a'ter that. Fin'ly we kilt what we reckoned was one of yer cows, an' some slanch-eyed old bastard says we's rustlers. Says that cow's his, an' somebody's goin' t' pay. So I reckon ye'll be hearin' from him. We din't want t' cause ye no trouble, so we moved out an' moved on."

"We left three of you at the ranch," said Gil. "Where are your friends?"

"Dead," said Long John. "I was comin' t' that. Some gents rode in that I knowed back in Shreveport. They was on their way south, aimin' t' loot some Mex tows acrost th' border. Since we was plumb outta grub, and yer neighbors was so damn onfriendly, we throwed in with 'em. Me, Shorty, an' Banjo. It was thirteen of us, an' I reckon that number was some onlucky. First town we hit, they purely set our tail feathers afire. They burnt down four of us right off. The rest of us lit out fer the Texas side o' the river, an' run plumb into a passel o' Mex soldiers. Ever'body got shot t' doll rags, 'cept me, an' here I am."

"How long have you been here?" Van asked.

"Nine days," said Long John. "I talk some Mex, an' understand some. I been hearin' 'em talk about takin' me t' Matamoros, Tamaulipas. I reckon it's a right smart of a ride, an' they been waitin' fer some more poor bastards they could send along wi' me. Look like they got some, don't it?"

"Matamoros, Tamaulipas is just the start of the trail to Mexico City," said Gil. "If you get

318

there alive, there's a military prison waiting."

"Then we're dead pelicans, either way," said Long John. "Jus' takes a mite longer in the *juzgado*."

"Matamoros, Tamaulipas is less than thirty miles from the border," said Van. "We've got a herd of horses and a herd of longhorn cows on the way there."

"By God," said Long John admiringly, "ye young Texas roosters is purely got sand in yer craws! I'd gut-shoot a man that said different. They ain't been a meaner stacked deck since the Alamo, but jus' gimme a chancet, and I'll buy chips in whatever long-shot game ye got in mind."

★ ★ ★

August 26, 1843. On the trail north.

Difficult as it was, Ramon went about pulling the outfit together. He got no help from the soldiers. They were there to be sure the trail drive continued to Matamoros, Tamaulipas. Ramon knew that prisoners taken there were then taken south, along the coast, to Mexico City. Since he no longer had to worry about the military post at Monterrey, Ramon slowly but surely turned the drive to the east. It would be a longer drive, and eventually they would reach Matamoros. But Ramon expected Gil and Van to be taken south, and if the trail drive approached Matamoros from the south, there must be a meeting. Ramon had spoken to the riders, and they had rallied around him.

Estanzio and Mariposa still had their concealed Bowies, cautioned by Ramon to wait until the right moment. When the time came, the *soldado* sentries could be quickly eliminated. But Ramon remembered what Gil Austin had said. Matamoros was near the border. As long as the *soldados* rode with the trail drive, Ramon need not fear the army. He would use the *soldados* to get the herds as near the border as he could. From there they might have to fight their way across, but *por Dios*, they had a chance!

★ ★ ★

Clay, Angelina, and Solano continued to hide by day and travel at night. When Clay had examined the big black horse in daylight, he was delighted. It bore a Winged M on its left flank. Even in the dark Solano knew his horses. Clay had begun to lose his prison pallor, and without the shaggy hair and long beard, he would have been difficult to identify as a former resident of Mexico City's dungeon. Angelina had found him quiet, and there were times when she spoke to him that he seemed not to hear. Finally she had left him alone. He would have to come to her. They circled far around Tampico, passing to the west of it. Before first light, Solano found them a secluded coulee where they could spend the daylight hours. Solano devoted his day to sleeping. Or appearing to. Only once since his escape had Clay spoken of Gil and Van Austin. Angelina had told him of their arrival, of their plans for the trail drive, which was all she knew.

320

Clay had said so little to her, it startled her when he spoke.

"Why did you come lookin' for me, taking the chances you took?"

"I do not know," she said. "Perhaps I thought you were worth saving. I saw Victoria throw herself at you, try to use you, and saw you refuse. I believed then — as I do now — that if a woman were worthy, if you wanted her for herself alone, all the devils in Hell couldn't stop you from having her."

"That's exactly how it is," he said. "A man don't like bein' crowded."

"Have I ever crowded you?"

"No, ma'am," he said, a twinkle in his eyes. "Solano's a man to ride the river with, but he couldn't have busted me out of that Mex jail without you. That took courage, girl, and more. I got a serious question to ask you, if we get back to Texas alive."

"I'll have a serious answer for you," she said, "and we *will* get to Texas alive."

He took both her hands in his and their eyes met in silent understanding.

19

AUGUST 28, 1843. On the trail to Matamoros, Tamaulipas.

Sergeant Aguilla had been left in charge of the soldiers who had stayed with the trail drive. Besides Aguilla, only four of the soldiers were veterans. The rest were conscripts who were friendly to Ramon and his vaqueros when Aguilla wasn't hounding them. However remote, Ramon saw the friendliness of these soldiers as a chance to further reduce the odds against the outfit. He did not wish to reach Matamoros too soon. It was the Mexican stronghold for the border war, a rallying point for soldiers arriving from or departing to Mexico City. Besides, there might be soldiers at Matamoros on their way to or from Monterrey or Meoqui, as well. Too many soldiers! Ramon believed that if Gil and Van were awaiting an opportunity to escape, it wouldn't come until they had been taken from Matamoros, and were en route to Mexico City. Ramon reasoned that if he gradually turned the trail drive eastward, approaching Matamoros from the south, they might meet the soldiers taking Gil and Van to Mexico City. Of course, there was a disturbing factor that might make all Ramon's planning meaningless: General Paradez might just have the Texans executed at Matamoros. But Ramon didn't think so. Like Santa Anna, Paradez would want to flaunt his captives, to impress his superiors in Mexico City. Ramon tried to think of a means of slowing the trail drive. The Austins must have time to reach Matamoros, to be taken from the soldier stronghold, while he and the outfit awaited them to the south. Ironically, Sergeant Aguilla himself caused the needed delay. Their third day on the trail with Aguilla in charge, Ramon approached the sergeant.

"Senor, we must send a rider ahead of the drive to scout for water. The *caballos* and *vacas* must have water each day."

"No," said Sergeant Aguilla. "None of you are permitted to leave. It is an order."

"Then send one of your soldiers," Ramon pleaded. "We must find water."

"There was water yesterday," said Aguilla, "and water the day before, no?"

"*Si*," said Ramon resignedly.

"Then why," responded the arrogant Aguilla, "should there not be water today? Enough of your whining, *borrica*."

Ramon said no more, but when sundown came, there was no water. Despite Aguilla's objections, Ramon pushed the herds as hard as he dared, hoping they might yet reach water. But darkness forced them into a dry camp, and it was a situation the herds refused to accept. The longhorns wouldn't bed down, and their disgruntled bawling became an ominous dirge. Sergeant Aguilla behaved like a petulant child, demanding that the riders quiet the thirsty cattle. Ramon and his men remained in their saddles, not attempting to satisfy Aguilla's foolish demands, but to avoid being left afoot when the stampede began. The day had been hot and oppressive, but when the moon rose, so did the wind. While it was just a gentle breeze from the south, it became as much a catalyst as a bolt of lightning during a storm. Whether the south wind actually brought the smell of some distant stream, or just revived the memory of last night's deep-running creek, it was enough. Sergeant Aguilla's roar of rage became a cry of fear as the long-horns, followed by the horse herd, came thundering toward the soldier camp. Men ran for their lives, falling behind rocks and climbing trees. The madness was contagious, and every soldier's horse was caught up in the stampede. Their saddles, packs, blankets, and anything else in the path of the thundering herd suffered mightily. Ramon and his riders, knowing the futility of it, hadn't tried to head the stampede. When the dust began to settle, and Sergeant Aguilla climbed down from a tree in which he had taken refuge, he found Ramon and the riders had followed the herd. Come the dawn, or whenever Aguilla and his men chose to follow, they would be walking. It had been a devastating stampede, and might require days to gather the scattered herds, but Ramon Alcaraz wore a satisfied grin. He welcomed the delay, and *por Dios*, the walk would be good for the arrogant Sergeant Aguilla!

★ ★ ★

August 29, 1843. North of Tampico.

Clay, Angelina, and Solano had just unsaddled their horses after riding most of the night. Without the cart slowing them down, a night's travel not only covered many miles, it lessened their chance of discovery. Clay and Angelina had reached and passed a crucial milestone in their relationship, and both were aware of it. Secure in the knowledge that he wanted her, that she had a place in his life, Angelina brought up a subject she knew he was reluctant to talk about.

"Gil and Van Austin came to Mexico because you asked them to," she said. "When I freed you from prison, after I told you they had come, I expected you to go immediately to the Mendoza ranch. To go looking for them."

For a while he said nothing, and she feared that he wasn't going to, that she had hurt his pride. When he finally responded, it was with a query of his own.

"If I had done that — gone looking for them — would you have gone with me, knowing the risk you were taking?"

"Yes," she said, "I would have gone with you."

"I thought so," he said, with a half smile, "and that's one of the reasons I didn't go. Right now, I'd bet the Mexican government would pay more for your head than for Sam Houston's. Whatever I owed Gil and Van, it was too late to worry about. I owed you my life. How could I better repay you than by savin' yours? How else could I do that, except by gettin' you out of Mexico?"

He had said exactly the wrong thing; he saw it

325

in her eyes. In a single sentence he had reduced their relationship to his fulfilling an obligation. Irritated by his clumsiness, his poor choice of words, he took her by the shoulders and forced her to look into his eyes.

"Damn it, girl, I didn't mean that like it sounded. I didn't mean I'm only takin' you with me because you broke me out of the *juzgado*. I meant that it was too late to help Gil and Van, and that if I tried, I might lose *you*, without ever findin' them. They're the grandest pards a man ever had, but if it was you or them, they'd be goners. Can't you see that?"

"Yes," she said, and the light was back in her dark eyes. "This feeling is new to me, and for a moment, I was afraid . . ."

"God knows, you have plenty to be afraid of, until we cross the border, but losin' me ain't any of it. What I said about throwin' Gil and Van to the wolves for your sake was only to show how strong I feel for you. Like I told you, Gil and Van Austin are pards to ride the river with. They done their best to talk me out of comin' here, horses or not, but we Duvals are the kind that thinks we can whip our weight in bobcats. Mule stubborn as I am, I'd sooner be throwed and stomped every day for the rest of my life than have Gil and Van throw their lives away, tryin' to save mine. This is a long speech for a feller that ain't very good at it, but since I committed myself to you, I want you to know I ain't the coldhearted bastard I sometimes may seem. When we get to Texas, if Gil and Van ain't there, then I reckon I'll know why. It's a thing that'll haunt me the rest of my life."

It was a side of Clay Duval she didn't know existed. She was touched by his sincerity and humility. She thought of the days, weeks, and months he had spent in a Mexican prison, accompanied only by the belief that he had led his friends to their deaths. She wiped her eyes on the sleeve of her peon camisa before she spoke. Then she took him by the shoulders, as he had taken her.

"Gil and Van Austin are strong men, Clay. Within a day after their arrival, I knew why you had sent for them. I left before the drive began, so I cannot be certain, but I believe if anyone could succeed, they will. As Victoria tried to intimidate you, so did she attempt to intimidate them, and again she failed. She went so far as to tell them she was carrying your child."

Despite herself, Angelina had wondered if there had been a shred of truth in that, if Victoria had indeed gotten herself in that condition. It would have been a difficult hold for Clay to have broken. She looked at him, but he couldn't look at her. His face crimsoned, the color creeping down to his shirt collar. Hard as she tried not to, she laughed, and was immediately sorry. Finally he spoke.

"You didn't believe that . . . did you?"

"Of course not, even before she admitted it was a lie. Gil Austin called her a liar, said there was no child, and accused her of using that to get a hold on you. Not only did she admit to the lie, but cursed you for a perfect gentleman. Are you?"

"Mostly," he said, with a half grin, "but that might change once we get to Texas and don't have the Mex army gunnin' for us."

"I'll take that for a promise," she said, "and hold you to it."

★ ★ ★

Ramon and his men rode south to the creek where they had bedded down the herds the night before. They didn't doubt they'd find their horses and cows somewhere along that creek, and while they could do nothing in the darkness, they would be ready at first light. But Ramon had an even better reason for following the stampede. The foolish *soldados* were afoot. Had he and his riders remained, the arrogant Sergeant Aguilla would have simply taken *their* horses, leaving him and his men afoot. Now the sergeant and his *soldados* would have no choice; they would have to walk a good twelve miles to reach the creek. Ramon grinned in the darkness. Perhaps the *estupido soldado* sergeant would learn something.

Reaching the creek, Ramon and his riders rolled in their blankets and slept. As dawn approached, so did the weary Sergeant Aguilla and his soldiers. Ramon hadn't bothered with a fire, since their packhorses had stampeded and all their supplies were a dozen miles away. Once they caught some horses to carry the packs, he would send for their supplies. In the gray first light, Ramon saw the soldiers coming. They stumbled along in a ragged line, making no attempt at formation. Ramon readied himself for Sergeant Aguilla's anger, but Aguilla didn't have the strength. Not only was he exhausted, he was dry. Along with the rest of the soldiers, Aguilla headed for the creek. They all fell on their bellies, hung their heads over the low bank and satisfied their raging thirst. Ramon approached Aguilla.

"Senor," he said, "I must send riders with packhorses to bring our supplies. We have no food."

Ramon expected Aguilla to object, since the sergeant had refused his request to scout ahead for water. But Aguilla did not; he kept his silence, lifting his hand in dismissal. Ramon sent Pedro Fagano and Vicente Gomez to rope a pair of horses to carry the packs. The other riders hadn't even saddled their horses, a thing that soon attracted Sergeant Aguilla's attention. He got to his feet, scowling at Ramon.

"The sun shines," he said, "and you do nothing. Why do you not gather these animals for the trail?"

"Because we are hungry," said Ramon shortly. "We have had no food since yesterday at dawn. We will do nothing until we have eaten."

It was something even the stubborn Aguilla couldn't deny, for he and his men were also weak from hunger. They had been about to prepare supper when the stampede had destroyed their camp. Still, they might have eaten from Ramon's supplies, had Sergeant Aguilla not allowed his anger to get the best of him. Furious, his only thought was to get his hands on the vaqueros who had ridden away, leaving him afoot. Gathering his men, he had ordered an immediate march southward, in pursuit of the riders. As his anger had cooled, he had regretted his hasty decision, for they had not a drop of water among them. Every man's canteen had been thonged to his saddle, and while their saddles had survived to some extent, their canteens had not. How was he, Sergeant Aguilla, to explain the destruction of their equipment to Major Farias, when their assignment had been so simple? Why hadn't the sergeant been *told* those foolish *vacas* would run away when they had no water? *Por Dios*, he *had* been told! Recalling Ramon's plea that he be allowed to scout ahead for water, he became furious all over again. This vaquero, this *pelado*, had made a fool of him, but he would pay, Sergeant Aguilla vowed. Sometime before they reached Matamoros, he would pay.

Before they had much-needed food and hot coffee, the sun was more than two hours high. Once they had eaten, Sergeant Aguilla — almost civil — asked Ramon to have the riders round up the soldiers' horses. Once the animals had been found, Aguilla detailed seven of his men to return to last night's campsite. There they would recover saddles and anything else that might have survived the stampede. Each man must ride bareback, leading an extra horse, and there were complaints from those chosen to go. Ramon noticed all seven men were the conscripts. Sergeant Aguilla played favorites; when the time was right, it might be used against him. Ramon and the riders spent the rest of the day gathering the horses, and come sundown, some of the herd was still missing.

★ ★ ★

Gil and Van looked at the unappetizing supper that had been left inside the stockade gate. They had three bowls of watery stew, tortillas, a jug of cold coffee, a trio of pewter cups, and three wooden spoons.

"Better eat," said Long John. "This is some improvement over the usual. I reckon they're puttin' on a special feed in yer honor."

"If this is better than usual," said Van, "I'm glad we didn't get here any sooner."

They finished it all, even the weak, cold coffee. Long John piled the empty bowls, cups, the jug, and the spoons by the stockade gate.

"You're mighty accommodatin'," said Van. "Make 'em come in after that stuff. Might be a chance to bust out."

"You reckon I didn't think o' that?" said Long John. "They don't come in. They's two *hombres*; one t' git the dishes, an' one with a rifle. The gent with the rifle tells ye to bring the stuff near the gate, put it down, an' back away. I reckoned I'd make a run fer it betwixt here an' Matamoros. But from in here, fergit it."

At first glance Gil and Van had seen nothing within the three-sided shelter except the bench along the back wall. But once their eyes had become accustomed to the poor light, they saw some thin, dirty straw ticks on the dirt floor

331

beneath the bench. Gil nudged them with the toe of his boot.

"Less'n ye got a tough hide," said Long John, "I'd leave them mats alone. Full o' fleas an' other varmints, all of which bites. Sleep on the dirt floor an' make the bastards come lookin' fer ye."

The three captives stretched out on the hard floor, using their boots for a pillow. Despite the primitive conditions, they slept, to be awakened well before first light by the opening of the stockade gate.

"Breakfast," said Long John, when the gate had closed. "Means we gon' be leavin' here. They ain't never fed this early afore."

"From hearin' 'em talk," said Van, "you got any idea how far we are from Matamoros?"

"I'd figger it at two hundred mile," said Long John. "Heard one of 'em say I wasn't worth a three-day ride."

"Your luck just ran out," said Gil, "because this Major Farias that grabbed us is in a hurry to show us off. I have a strong suspicion that the coyote takin' Santa Anna's place is already at Matamoros, or on his way."

"Damn," Long John swore, "we might not git sent t' Mexico City."

"I reckon you'll be disappointed," said Van.

"Disappointed an' dead," said Long John. "You rather they'd back ye agin th' wall at Matamoros an' fill ye full o' lead, er throw ye in that prison in Mexico City?"

"Either way," said Van, "your trail comes to an end. The dungeon just takes longer."

"My trail ain't come to no end," said Long John, "till I'm stone dead, planted, an' the devil's dabbed his loop on me. They ain't a *juzgado* in the world what can't be broke out of, if'n a man's hell bent on it."

"Glad you feel that way," said Gil, with a grim chuckle. "They give us a choice of bein' shot at Matamoros or bein' thrown in prison, then I reckon I'd agree. I choose the prison."

It was macabre humor, and Long John said no more. Gil hoped he hadn't got on the bad side of the Cajun; he didn't need any more enemies.

★ ★ ★

"I do not know for sure the distance from Mexico City to Matamoros," said Angelina. "While I worked at the café near the prison, I heard some of the soldiers speak of the journey. If what they said is to be believed, it is almost six hundred miles."

"We must have covered half of that," said Clay Duval. "When we're within a day's ride of Matamoros, we'll circle it to the northwest and cross the border into Texas."

"Texas," said Solano. "No *soldados*, no fight?"

So seldom did the Indian speak, he had taken them by surprise. Clay laughed.

"No *soldados*," he said, "but plenty fight. There's horse thieves, cow thieves, claim jumpers, gun throwers, gamblers, and Comanches."

"Go," said Solano, pleased. "Fight."

"In Mexico," said Angelina, "we have only the *milicia* to fear. When we have crossed the border, we will have to fight the whole world."

Clay laughed. "Maybe, but not all at the same time. Besides, we'll have help. Texas has an army. We beat hell out of Santa Anna at San Jacinto. Then there's the Texas Rangers. Just last year, they had a bloody battle with the Comanches in Bandera Pass."[1]

"There may yet be war between your country and Mexico," said Angelina. "Besides all those others, we may still have to fight the Mexican army."

"There'll be war," said Clay, "before there's lasting peace.[2] Have you changed your mind about goin' to Texas?"

"No," she said, "it is your country, and it will become my country. If we must fight, then we

---

[1] In 1842, a company of forty Texas Rangers, commanded by Captain John Coffee (Jack) Hays, was ambushed in Bandera Pass by more than a hundred Comanches. Most of the fighting was hand-to-hand, with Bowie knives. The Comanche chief was killed. Five Rangers died and six were wounded.

[2] The first skirmish of the war with Mexico occurred on April 24, 1846. During the course of the war, Mexican soldiers captured Monterey and San Francisco, California. Peace finally came with the signing of the Treaty of Guadalupe, Hidalgo, February 2, 1848.

will fight. In war or in peace, I shall be there beside you."

"*Bueno*," he said. "It's frontier now, but one day the fighting will be done, and the stars and stripes of the United States will fly over Texas from the Red River to the Rio Grande."[1]

"You make it sound so glorious," she laughed, "how could I not wish to become a part of it?"

* * *

Ramon and the riders took their time with the gather. When Sergeant Aguilla swore at him because of the delay, Ramon stood up to him.

"Senor," said Ramon coldly, "it is you who has made this gather necessary. Each night the *caballos* and *vacas* are without water, you are inviting the *estampeda*."

Sergeant Aguilla was a man not accustomed to making mistakes, or taking the blame for them when he did. He glared at Ramon for a long moment before he spoke.

"There is truth in what you say," he grudgingly admitted. "Hereafter, you will be permitted to send a rider ahead to find water, but see that you reach it before the night. I will not tolerate another delay such as this."

Some of Ramon's riders and several of

---

[1] Texas was admitted to the Union on December 29, 1845.

Aguilla's men had come close enough to hear the concession, and they grinned openly at Aguilla. He silently cursed them for laughing at him, and himself for having given them a reason. These vaqueros knew what they were doing, he decided, and lest he continue making an *asno* of himself, he would have to allow them freedom to do their work.

★ ★ ★

September 2, 1843. On the trail.

The third day of their gather, Ramon made a decision. They were still missing sixteen of the Mendoza horses. Most of them were from that bunch of mares they had rescued from the wild stallion, and Ramon had no intention of losing them again. Taking Estanzio with him, he followed the creek to the east. It didn't make sense that the rest of the horse herd had stopped at the creek while these wandering few had gone on. But apparently they had. Estanzio led out, following their tracks eastward along the creek. After three or four miles the trail veered off to the southeast, becoming more southerly as it progressed. At that point the horses had started to run. Estanzio reined up and dismounted, Ramon following. The cougar tracks were faint but distinct, overlying the tracks of the fleeing horses.

"Him scare horse," said Estanzio. "Then him follow."

It began to make sense. The mares had grazed along the creek, had drifted away from the rest of

336

the herd, and had been frightened by the cougar. They mounted their horses, and Estanzio led out at a gallop. They were three days behind; unless the mares had literally outrun the big cat, the damage had already been done.

★ ★ ★

August 31, 1843. North of Tampico.

Solano rode out an hour before good dark, for he had some tracking to do. Last night, somewhere to the north, he had heard a cougar squall. He wanted some assurance they wouldn't encounter the beast in the dark, that it wouldn't end up stalking their horses. At the same time, he hoped he wouldn't have to shoot it. In the evening quiet, the sound of a shot would carry for miles. On the very heels of that thought came the eerie, womanlike scream of the cougar. Solano's horse reared, nickering, and he had to force the trembling animal ahead. Somewhere another horse nickered its fear. Then, like an echo, there was a second, a third, and a fourth. The cougar was stalking a horse herd!

Solano reined up on the crest of a ridge, his eyes on the valley below. Even in the fading light, he could see several of the horses. They had paused midway of the valley, looking fearfully back the way they had come. Solano tied his horse securely, took his rifle from the boot, and started down the hill on the run. These horses were not behaving like wild ones, and Solano quickly decided they were not. There should have been a stallion, bringing up the rear, facing the danger. There was none. A few minutes more and it would be too dark to see. Or to shoot accurately. There was a rustling of leaves and underbrush, and Solano froze. Fifty yards ahead, to his left, was a huge uprooted oak. Supported by the root mass, the horizontal trunk of the tree rested well above the surrounding brush. Suddenly the cougar sprang to the trunk of the fallen tree, seeking to locate the fleeing horses. In the failing light it was Solano's best and only chance. The big cat spotted him just as the Indian fired. With a screech, the cougar reared on its hind legs and toppled backward off the log. Solano waited, but there was no sound.

It was a bad situation. A wounded cougar was the most dangerous of all. If he went close enough to be sure of his kill, the cat might yet be alive, with strength enough to tear him apart. But he dared not wait. Solano ran to the very top of the fallen tree, climbed to the trunk and crept down it. The upended root mass kept the trunk high enough so it was unlikely the wounded cougar could reach him. It was barely light enough for him to see the tawny hide of the animal. He had shot the big cat through the head. It was a perfect shot, considering the poor light, and he swelled with pride. For a moment he forgot the horses, but only for a moment. He trotted back up the ridge, slid his rifle into the boot and swung into the saddle. It was dark, but he was going to find those horses the cougar had been stalking. He rode down the ridge and turned his horse along the valley in the direction the horses had gone. When his horse nickered, two others answered.

Solano rode on, and as he neared them, he began talking his guttural horse talk. While it said nothing, it meant much. Out of the darkness a big black nuzzled him familiarly. When he dismounted, more of the horses came to him. While it was too dark for him to see their brands, he suddenly knew what he was going to find come the dawn. Quickly he ran his hands over the flanks of several of the horses. His heart leaped when his fingers traced the familiar lines of the Winged M brand!

Solano was reluctant to leave, and the Mendoza mares clearly didn't want him to. But they would have to wait while he carried this important information to Clay Duval. This was part of the Mendoza herd, in sufficient numbers that they would never have been abandoned. Unless the trail drive's riders — including Clay Duval's Tejano friends — were dead.

20

SEPTEMBER 3, 1843, Monterrey, Mexico. Long John had been right. By first light the three captives had been led out and prepared for the journey to Matamoros. Their hands were bound behind their backs, and once they were mounted, their ankles were tied together by a rope passed under the horse's belly. This time there were no ropes around their necks, but soldiers still led their horses. Only once did Gil have a chance to speak to Rosa, and she didn't respond. Her eyes were red and swollen, and she looked not to have slept at all. Another officer was riding with them, having been with the force at Monterrey. More and more it looked as though some high-level meeting was about to take place at Matamoros. When they eventually stopped for the night, three soldiers were detailed to guard the prisoners.

"Fergit what I said 'bout makin' a run fer it on the trail t' Matamoros," said Long John glumly.

"Same treatment we got all the way to Monterrey," said Gil. "All we got to look forward to is that ride to Mexico City."

"You reckon we got a chance, then," said Long John, "betwixt there an' Matamoros?"

"A chance," said Gil. "Nothing more."

"*Silencio*," said one of the guards. He and

his two companions came closer, and the conversation was finished for the night.

★ ★ ★

Depending on his horse talk to calm them, Solano quickly tallied the horses. He counted sixteen. While a few might have strayed, this seemed more the remnant of a stampede. Stalked by the cougar, this bunch had become lost. Could they be part of the trail drive the Tejanos had planned? Reluctant as he was to leave the newly discovered Mendoza horses, Solano mounted and rode south. Clay and Angelina would be waiting. He realized he was returning much later than usual, but if he knew Clay Duval, their journey was about to be delayed. *Soldados* or not, come first light they would be back-trailing the Mendoza horses. He rode in to find Angelina and Clay with their horses saddled, impatiently waiting for him.

"We heard the shot," said Clay.

"Cougar," said Solano. "Him hunt horse. Mendoza horse. Many."

"They must be part of the trail drive," said Angelina.

"I don't see how," said Clay. "They're too far east. Victoria told me the soldiers from Mexico City travel right up the coast to Matamoros. Why in tarnation would Gil and Van bring the drive this far east? When they turn north, they'll be headed straight for Matamoros."

"Back-trail horse," said Solano.

"I aim to," said Clay. "We can't do it in the dark, but we can start at first light. Solano, take us to these horses."

Angelina had never seen Clay so excited. Although they couldn't back-trail the horses until dawn, Clay Duval couldn't wait to assure himself they were really there. Solano led out, and they followed. The horses had moved on down the valley until they had reached the runoff from a spring. There they grazed, and Clay Duval went from one to the other, greeting them like long-lost friends. Once it was light enough to see, they counted sixteen of the magnificent horses, every one bearing a Winged M brand on its left hip.

"Let's ride," said Clay.

Solano led out at a gallop. The horses had left a broad trail they could follow with ease. When Solano reined up, Clay and Angelina reined up beside him.

"Wait," said Solano, and he rode on.

"He's one smart Injun," said Clay. "Mendoza horses or not, he aims to see we don't ride hell-bent for election into trouble."

Solano saw the two riders in time to avoid being seen by them. Waiting until they were well past, he fell in behind them. When he was near enough, he spoke.

"*Buenos dias, hombres.*"

Startled, Ramon and Estanzio turned, their hands falling away from the butts of their pistols when they recognized Solano. Quickly they rode toward him. Ramon offered his hand, and Solano took it. Estanzio, in a rare burst of enthusiasm, offered his hand. Gravely, Solano took it.

"Find horse," said Solano. "Kill cougar. Follow horse tracks. Come."

Solano wasted no time. For some reason he had yet to learn, the trail drive not only had not left Mexico, but seemed to have strayed dangerously off course. It involved Clay Duval's Tejano friends; if they were not already dead, they soon might be. There was much talking to be done. In time Solano would know the dangers they faced and what must be done to overcome them, but the most immediate need was for Ramon and Clay to talk. There were glad cries of recognition from Clay and Angelina when Ramon and Estanzio reined up. Leaning out of her saddle, Angelina caught the startled Estanzio around the neck, and the Indian actually blushed.

"Come on," said Clay, "and let's ride back to the horses. There's a spring. We got some talking to do, and I reckon we'll be a while."

Reaching the spring, they dismounted and picketed their horses.

"Ramon," said Clay, "you do the talking. Tell it all, includin' why the trail drive's so far east it's practically in the lap of the Mex army. This ain't even close to the route I planned."

Ramon began by explaining they were *already* in the hands of the Mexican army, and that their southerly approach to Matamoros was a last-ditch effort to free Gil and Van.

"Ramon," said Clay, "that took guts. It's a smart move, maybe the only way, but you and

343

your riders are risking your lives for a pair of Tejanos."

"We Tejano outfit," said Ramon. "No more Mendoza."

"Victoria?" Angelina asked. "She is . . . "

"Dead, senorita," said Ramon. As gently as he could, he explained what had happened.

"Oh, damn her," said Angelina, through tears, "for involving herself with Esteban Valverde, and damn him for being the rotten little weasel that he was!"

When Angelina had recovered from the shocking news, Ramon continued. He planned to use the presence of the *soldados* to get the trail drive near Matamoros, and then dispose of his military escort for the run across the border.

"That's as good a plan as anybody could come up with," said Clay, "but it could stand some improving. First, we must know when the soldiers leave Matamoros with Gil and Van, and then we need to know how many soldiers we're up against. Once they're within a few miles of the trail drive, then we need to rid ourselves of Sergeant Aguilla and his men. Then we ride north, taking that southbound bunch by surprise, freeing Gil and Van. That done, we'll drive the herds all night, north toward the border. We'll stampede 'em hell for leather, right through Matamoros if we have to."

"Is good," said Ramon.

"Except for one thing," said Angelina. "Ramon and his men have a soldier escort. None of them can ride north, watching for soldiers heading south with Gil and Van."

"No," said Clay, "but we can. It'll be up to us to tell Ramon when to eliminate his soldiers, when to move north to join us."

"I ride ahead each day," said Ramon. "Look for water."

"*Bueno*," said Clay. "The day we are to make our move, we will meet you somewhere ahead of the drive. After dark, Solano and me will join you. We will then do away with your soldiers however we must, and ride north to free Gil and Van. Remember — when you're scouting for water, I'll be somewhere ahead of you. Tell the rest of the riders what we've planned. Tonight, we'll ride around the drive and travel north. We'll learn as much as we can about the situation at Matamoros. Maybe we can find out how many soldiers will be going to Mexico City."

"I could take a job in a café," said Angelina, "and listen to the soldiers talk."

Clay only looked at her, but the look in his eyes surpassed anything he might have said. Her mischievous smile faded.

★ ★ ★

"I never been so damn tired o' layin' on my back in my life," Long John grumbled.

"You talk their lingo," said Van. "Ask our guards to back us up to the trunk of a tree. Beats layin' all night with rocks and gravel diggin' into the back of your skull."

Long John made his request, and to his surprise the guards complied. Actually, they

345

were backed up against the lightning-blasted stump of a tree, but it stood a dozen feet high and was sturdy. They dozed. At first light, before breakfast, the pompous Major Farias, accompanied by another officer, came to view the captives. Farias said something, and the men laughed. When they turned away, Long John spat in their direction.

"God," said Long John piously, "I ain't a religious man, ain't a prayin' man, but some'eres down the road, jus' gimme my Bowie and a minute with them Mex buzzards."

Their second day on the trail was no better or worse than the first. What hurt Gil more than their predicament was Rosa's puffy eyes and thin face. The child had been thin as a fence rail when he had first brought her to camp, and he had enjoyed watching her cheeks fill out. Now she looked gaunt as a half-starved lobo wolf. He didn't believe they were denying her food; she just wasn't eating. He tried to think of some means of escape, but his mind was blank. There seemed no way. Even if he, Van, and Long John somehow broke loose, there was Rosa. What would become of her? If he left her there, her thin face and sad eyes would haunt him as long as he lived. He believed she was being kept in the officers' tent at night. Farias had believed she was Ramon's child, and perhaps Ramon would be allowed to take her. But once the trail drive reached Matamoros, Gil feared that Ramon and the rest of the riders might also be sent to prison in Mexico City. Worse, they might be executed at Matamoros.

★ ★ ★

September 5, 1843. Matamoros, Tamaulipas. Military outpost.

The village of Matamoros was somewhere north of the military outpost. While there was no stockade, the post had some order about it and was much more impressive than the facility at Monterrey had been. There was a long, low log building that included an orderly room, the commanding officer's office and his living quarters. Next to that was a log building with iron-barred windows, which housed prisoners until they could be sent to Mexico City. Next to the guardhouse was a long, low barracks for soldiers recuperating from wounds, bound for Mexico City or en route to the outposts at Monterrey or Meoqui. A fourth building beyond the barracks provided quarters for officers.

Gil, Van, and Long John were taken immediately to the guardhouse. It had a corridor down the middle, with four cells along each side. There were iron bars from floor to ceiling, heavy iron-barred doors, and in each cell near the ceiling, a small barred window. The window was so small, even without the bars, a man couldn't have gotten his head through. Each cell was large enough for four men, and the three captives were locked in the first one on the right. The rest of the cells were empty. From the one tiny barred window, they had a view of the soldiers' barracks. There were low wooden benches along three sides of the cell. The benches were wide enough to sit on or sleep

347

on, but there wasn't even a flea-infested straw tick. In one corner of the cell was a slop jar that had been used often but emptied seldom.

"Will ye look at that," said Long John in disgust. "They's room enough fer 'em t' slide the grub under the door. How they 'spect a man to bust outta here?"

"We won't be busting out of here," said Van, "unless you got a keg of black powder in your pocket."

Gil stretched out on one of the broad benches, his hat over his face. He was weary of Long John's bitching about things that couldn't be helped, and Van's humorous responses. He dozed, awakening when somebody shoved their supper under the barred door. There was stew and tortillas, with one small improvement. The coffee was still warm. They ate quickly before total darkness engulfed them. There was but a single lamp in the building, near the front door, and the flame guttered low.

Gil slept on the bench along the back wall, beneath the little barred window. Far into the night, he sat up. Something had awakened him. He sat there for a moment trying to recall the sound. Finally he decided it had been a dream, or his desperate imagination, and lay down. No sooner had he put it out of his mind than he heard it again. It was soft, metallic, insistent. Somebody was tapping on the iron bars that secured the window! Quietly Gil got up, noiseless in his bare feet, and stood on the bench.

"Who are you?" he asked softly.

"Solano," came the whispered response.

"Solano," Gil whispered excitedly, "how . . . what . . . ?"

"Leave *juzgado*," Solano whispered. "Be ready. We come. Solano, Ramon, Estanzio, Senor Clay. Here talking paper."

Gil took the piece of paper between the bars. Standing on tiptoe, he managed to look out the small window, but there was nobody in the starlit night. Solano was gone. Quietly he slipped down to a sitting position on the bench. But for the folded paper in his hand, it all might have been a dream, and he couldn't even read it until dawn. For the first time, his heart swelled with hope. Clay Duval was alive, ramrodding the outfit, with Ramon, Solano, Estanzio, Mariposa, and all the others siding him! He felt like shouting. He slept no more, waiting for the first gray light of dawn to creep into the cell. Finally, by standing on the bench, there was light enough from the small window to read the message. Clay had written:

Pards, Solano will watch for them to take you south. When time is right, we will eliminate soldiers with trail drive. Then we'll free you.

There was no signature, but none was needed.

Van sat up, rubbing his eyes. "Why are you standin' up there?" he asked.

"Reading a note from Clay Duval," said Gil calmly. "Solano brought it last night."

349

"What?" Van shouted.

"Quiet, damn it," hissed Gil.

Long John Coons was awake, looking at them owl-eyed.

"Here," said Gil. "Read it for yourself. You too, Long John."

They read it again and again. Long John was the first to speak.

"I cussed you gents right smart after ye was gone six months, leavin' me with no grub an' at the mercy o' yer bastard neighbors. Reckon I was a mite hasty. I'll make it up to ye. Oncet we git out, I'll go back an' gut-shoot them that makes it hard on ye."

"You do any shootin' on our behalf," said Gil, "save it for the time we make our break, and help us fight our way across the border."

★ ★ ★

Clay, Angelina, and Solano had ridden wide of the trail drive, and had found a secluded stream a few miles south of the outpost at Matamoros. They set up camp, and Solano rode north. He watched the soldier caravan ride in from the west, and observed Gil, Van, and an unidentified third man being taken to the guardhouse. Then he rode back to camp and reported to Clay Duval. Clay had written a message, and far in the night, when the *soldados* slept, Solano had delivered it. The following morning, Clay rode south and met Ramon as he scouted ahead of the trail drive for water.

"One day," said Ramon, "mebbe two, *caballos, vacas* be ready."

"Stay where you are as long as you can," Clay cautioned. "I want them well away from Matamoros before we make our move."

"There be many," said Ramon. "We kill?"

"No," said Clay, "I have a better idea. We'll allow them a day's ride from Matamoros, and then we'll move in after dark. Solano, Estanzio, and Mariposa can silence their sentries. You, me, and maybe a couple of the others will grab the officer in charge. With a gun to his head, we'll disarm the rest of them. Then we'll give the lot of 'em a dose of what they've been givin' Gil and Van. We'll tie their hands behind their backs, put them in their saddles, and take 'em south about fifty miles. We'll let 'em loose, but we'll bring their horses back with us. Afoot, they'll be a week gettin' back to Matamoros. By then we'll be in Texas."

"Is good," said Ramon. "Many *soldados* conscripts. No want to fight."

★ ★ ★

September 7, 1843. South of Matamoros, Tamaulipas.

Ramon had delayed the trail drive as long as he could. It was the third day since Gil and Van had arrived at Matamoros. It bothered Ramon that Gil and Van might be held at Matamoros until the trail drive reached the military outpost. That would effectively destroy all their plans.

351

Instead of facing a smaller detail of soldiers taking Gil and Van to Mexico City, they would be up against every soldier at Matamoros.

★ ★ ★

General Paradez had left Mexico City with twenty-four men, a far cry from the number he had requested. He needed a show of force, something to add luster to what he perceived as his tarnished reputation. He had deposed that idiot Santa Anna just in time to lose every captive Tejano from Mexico City's prison. But alas, had he not compensated for that? Before his mounted soldiers stumbled no less than ten of the Tejano dogs who had been released from the prison. His soldiers had captured them as they sought to reach the border, and he had no choice except to march them on to the outpost at Matamoros. But their capture was a mixed blessing. Exhausted and afoot, they had slowed him down.

Now, Paradez was headed for a showdown with Major Farias, and he didn't relish the prospect. Farias and his men had been in the field for months, and it was past time for them to return to Mexico City. The trouble was, Paradez had needed forty-three men to fully relieve Farias and his men, and he had only twenty-four unwilling conscripts. That meant eighteen of Farias's men would be stuck at Matamoros or Monterrey for months. Worse, Paradez had no officer to replace Farias, and carried orders forcing the major to remain in the field with the new recruits. Even after so long a journey, Paradez decided he would remain at Matamoros only one night. It would be all he could stomach of that pompous *asno*, Major Farias. He was bad enough anytime, but give him a legitimate complaint, and he would be unbearable.

★ ★ ★

Clay Duval wasn't the kind to sit and wait. While Solano kept close to Matamoros, Clay and Angelina often rode eastward. Clay believed it was time for more soldiers to be arriving from Mexico City.

"A company of soldiers ridin' north," said Clay, "ought to give us some idea as to how many soldiers will be returning to Mexico City. When new recruits are sent into the field, I figure an equal number of men will be sent home. I look for them to take Gil and Van with them."

It seemed the Mexican army was fulfilling Clay's prediction when Clay and Angelina observed General Paradez and his twenty-four soldiers riding north. But their elation was short-lived, for stumbling along ahead of the soldiers were no less than ten ragged, exhausted captives!

"My God," groaned Clay, "the Mex bastards caught 'em."

"Maybe it's . . . maybe they're not the same ones we set free," said Angelina.

"It's them," said Clay grimly. "They were

353

caught too far north to have this bunch of soldiers turn around and take them back to Mexico City. This means they'll likely be sent back with the next soldiers ridin' south."

"Then we shall free them a second time," said Angelina angrily, "and this time, they'll cross the border with us."

"They will," said Clay, "and every man with his gun smoking. We'll make good use of those *soldado* rifles and pistols. Right now, even with those men afoot, they ain't more'n two or three days out of Matamoros. Maybe four days from now, I expect Solano to ride in and tell us the journey to Mexico City is under way."

★ ★ ★

September 8, 1843. South of Matamoros, Tamaulipas.

It was time to move out. Ramon was unable to justify delaying the trail drive any longer. He had managed to waste an extra day, and had spent most of it listening to Sergeant Aguilla's complaints and threats. The drive had been moving northeasterly, but Ramon had cautioned Estanzio and Mariposa to watch for a well-defined trail from the south. Tracks of *soldado* horses traveling north meant it was time for the trail drive to turn north toward Matamoros. Sergeant Aguilla was riding with Ramon ahead of the plodding longhorns when Estanzio rode back to meet them.

"*Soldado* horses," said Estanzio. "North."

"How many day old?" Ramon asked.

354

"*Uno*," said Estanzio.

"*Hombre*," said Sergeant Aguilla, "I wish to see these tracks."

Aguilla followed Estanzio until the trail drive's horse herd blended its tracks with those of the northbound soldier horses. Sergeant Aguilla back-trailed the soldier horses for a few hundred yards, reading the tracks. A pair of Aguilla's veteran soldiers had followed. Aguilla turned to them, pointing to the tracks.

"Twenty-five of them," said Aguilla sourly, "and forty-three of us. Some of us will not be returning to Mexico City for a while."

His two comrades looked at him, trying to decide if he was joking. They looked at the tracks again, and decided he was not. They began cursing long and loud. Sergeant Aguilla laughed.

★ ★ ★

Gil, Van, and Long John viewed their breakfast without enthusiasm. It consisted of corn mush and cold coffee.

"It ain't easy downin' this slop," said Long John, "now that they's hope fer us bustin' loose."

"One small problem," said Gil. "We don't know how long we'll be stuck here until they take us south. You could get mighty lank after a couple of weeks."

"One other small problem," said Van. "When they take us south, Rosa won't be going with us."

355

"That won't make any difference," said Gil, "because we'll be coming back this way once we're free. I'll find her if I have to level every damn building on this side of the Rio."

"Mighty strong sentiments," said Long John, "fer a kid that ain't even yourn."

"Until somebody puts in a stronger claim," said Gil, "Rosa's mine."

"Fer thirty-five year," said Long John, "I ain't cared a damn fer nobody's hide but my own."

It was a callous thing to say. While the Texans said nothing, viewing Long John with disgust, they never forgot what he had said. Fate had a way of playing cruel tricks on a man, and before Long John Coons's trail came to an end, he would remember and bitterly regret those words.[1]

★ ★ ★

Major Gomez Farias had been at Matamoros less than twenty-four hours, and already Captain Felix Diaz was sick of him. Diaz, the post commander, had become skeptical of Farias's strange story about the Matamoros-bound trail drive. *Por Dios*, after Santa Anna's extravagance, Mexico could scarcely pay its soldiers the pittance they were promised. How then were they to pay for the thousands of horses and cows Farias had said were coming?

---

[1] Trail Drive Series #5. *The California Trail.*

"A week, now," said Diaz, "since you encountered this strange trail drive. Do you not wonder why we have seen nothing of this *caravana* and the soldiers you left behind?"

Major Farias slumped down in his chair and said nothing. While he outranked Diaz, the post commander was within his rights in questioning the whereabouts of a full third of Farias's men. While Diaz made no accusations, his skepticism was obvious. Farias believed he was leading up to something, and Diaz proceeded to confirm his suspicion.

"Major Farias," said Diaz, "General Paradez himself will soon arrive with soldiers to replace you and your company. For your sake, may your missing soldiers and this — ah, trail drive — reach Matamoros first."

"Madre mio!" shouted Farias, leaping to his feet. "If they do not arrive tomorrow, I will personally go after them!"

But time and luck had run out for Farias. General Paradez and his soldiers arrived the following morning.

21

SEPTEMBER 11, 1843. Military outpost at Matamoros, Mexico.

Gil stood on the bench so that he could see out the small barred window. While he could see little but the soldiers' barracks, that seemed to be the scene of all the commotion. Most of the soldiers — Major Farias's men — were outside. There were a few cheers, but mostly grumbling and cursing.

"They ain't enough room fer us all t' see out," said Long John. "What's all the fuss about?"

Before Gil could reply, the outside door to the guard-house swung open and one of their former guards entered with a ring of keys. He opened the iron-barred doors of three of the cells on the opposite side of the corridor. Into the guardhouse, prodded by soldiers, came ten dirty, ragged, bearded men. Their feet were bare, and some of them left bloody footprints on the stone floor. Four of the captives were herded into the first open cell, and the soldier with the keys locked the heavy barred door behind them. The second four prisoners were locked in the adjoining cell, and some of them immediately collapsed on the floor. The ninth man went into the third cell, but the tenth — and last — was unable to go any farther. He fell on his knees before the door. The soldier with the keys kicked him into the cell and then locked the door. The four soldiers then departed, the man with the keys going out last. Long John, Van, and Gil stood at the barred door of their cell looking at the unfortunates in the cells across the aisle. Gil wanted to question them, but they looked incapable of talking, more dead than alive.

"Can't be more'n a hour," said Long John, "till they fetch us some kinda slop fer dinner. Them boys looks like they ain't et sincet the Alamo."

One of the men in the cell directly across from them took hold of the bars and pulled himself to a sitting position on the stone floor. When he spoke, his voice was raspy, and there were times when it failed him completely.

"Fed us . . . ever' other day," he mumbled. "Nothin' for . . . the last two days."

"You're close to feeding time here," said Gil. "It ain't like San Antone, but it's considerably better than nothing."

"Lord God!" cried the newcomer, "if I could just see Texas again — any part of it — I'd feel . . . like Moses lookin' at the promised land."

He lay back on the stone floor, exhausted. Several of the other captives had revived, and one of them took up where his comrade had left off. He was a bit stronger, and answered some of the questions Gil was dying to ask.

"We was part of the Mier expedition," he said. "If you ain't heared of it, I'm most ashamed to tell. Two hunnert and sixty of us damn fools went acrost the river and challenged three thousand Mex soldiers to a shootin' match. We was forced to surrender, them of us that wasn't shot all t' hell. While we was bein' took to Mexico City, we busted loose. But we was afoot, in strange country, an' without grub. They caught us agin, and this time there wasn't no way we could git loose. We was took to Mexico City and stuck in a stinkin' hole they call the dungeon. When it looked like we'd be there at least till the resurrection, this purty young gal shows up. This Mex jailer was shinin' up to her, but she wasn't carin' about him. He couldn't see it, but the rest of us could. This lady was there lookin' for her man, an' she found him. Nex' time we see her, she's alone, 'cept for that big beautiful ring of keys in her hand. She done her part, God bless her, but we couldn't do ours. Twenty-five of them Mex bastards was on the way here, an' they caught us just this side of Tampico."

Gil and Van looked at one another. They knew who the angel of mercy had been, and the man she'd gone looking for.

"Only twenty-five soldiers?" Gil asked. "I was expecting more."

"God knows," said the newcomer, "that's enough. I'd as soon they just shoot me as t' drag me back to that miserable dungeon."

"Speak fer yo'sef," said Long John.

"If they take you back," said Gil, "I expect we'll be going with you."

He shot Van and Long John a warning look. While these men were fellow Texans, Gil didn't really know them. When the time came, they could all make their bid for freedom, but he wasn't yet ready to divulge their secret. The guards brought their dinner, and poor as it was, the newly arrived captives fell to like it was a feast. When they had eaten, they slept.

"I reckon I see what Clay's got in mind," said Van. "Now that these soldiers are here from Mexico City, some of them that brought us in will be ridin' south."

"Yes," said Gil, "and that's why I thought there'd be more than the twenty-five that just rode in. Remember, Farias had forty-two men. He left fourteen of them with the trail drive, and the trail drive hasn't shown up. If I was the Mex officer over Farias, I'm damned if I'd allow him or any of his men to rotate until those fourteen men with the trail drive are accounted for."

"If Clay's plan works," said Van, "we know the soldiers with the trail drive won't be showin' up. Now if what you're sayin' is true, that means the rest of this bunch — some of 'em, anyway — will be back-trailin' Farias, if only to account for the missing soldiers."

"Much as I hope I'm wrong," said Gil, "it's what I expect, and it's going to complicate our plans. With the twenty-eight men Farias has, and the twenty-five that rode in today, that's fifty-three. I doubt they'll send more than a dozen men to look for the trail drive and the missing soldiers. That means we'll still be locked in here, and this outpost will have more than forty men to defend it."

"Damn," said Long John in disgust, "that means, 'sted o' yer boys havin' fourteen o' them Mex bastards t' git shut of, they'll likely have twicet that many."

"Clay Duval is equal to that," said Gil. "The problem is, unless some of these soldiers are sent back to Mexico City and take us with them, we'll be stuck here behind bars. By now, Clay knows there's twenty-five soldiers just in from Mexico City. Now if Solano reports a group of soldiers ridin' away without us, Clay will have a good idea what's wrong. He won't know when — or if — we're to be taken to Mexico City, and he'll have no choice except to break us out of here."

★ ★ ★

General Paradez was not one to postpone an unpleasant duty. The moment Paradez and his twenty-four recruits had ridden in, Major Farias and his men had known what was coming. Paradez, once he had eaten and rested, met with Felix Diaz, captain and post commander. Diaz shook his head when told that eighteen men could not be rotated. That fitted in with the doubts he'd been having about this enormous trail drive Farias insisted was bound for the post at Matamoros. When they were so short of soldiers, why did they need more horses, and enough cows to feed all of Mexico? Captain Diaz told Paradez what he knew, stressing the fact that fourteen of Farias's men were unaccounted for.

"What I wish to know," said Diaz, "is who authorized this trail drive, and how are we to pay for these many cows and horses? You *know* we are unable to pay our soldiers. There is but

362

one man capable of such extravagance in the very face of bankruptcy."

"Santa Anna," said General Paradez, and he uttered the name as though it were an obscenity. Throwing lavish parties for any reason or for no reason at all, Santa Anna had squandered millions.

"That brings us to Major Farias," said Diaz, and Paradez knew what he meant. Farias, while not a friend of the deposed Santa Anna, was part of the old regime. Since Farias had been in the field, at Meoqui, Paradez had been unable to get rid of him. Even now, with the shortage of men, the best Paradez had been able to do was extend Farias's tour of duty at one of these distant outposts, where he had no influence. General Paradez was elated. When he returned to Mexico City, he would see that this obvious incompetence did not go unnoticed. He might yet rid himself of Farias.

"I think," said Paradez, "I will interrogate some of the men from Major Farias's command. Then I will see Farias."

The party in question sat hunched on a chair before a window in the officers' barracks. Farias wasn't surprised when an orderly came to the enlisted men's barracks and departed with four of his men. Farias cursed. So Paradez knew of the still-missing soldiers and of the trail drive. It was the ultimate insult, Paradez taking the word of common soldiers over his own. By the time Paradez finally requested his presence in the post commander's office, Farias was seething. Closing the door behind him, he saluted and stood there wordlessly.

"At ease, Major," said Paradez. "You may sit, if you wish."

Farias continued to stand, his hands clenched behind his back.

"I understand," said General Paradez, "that somewhere to the southwest of Monterrey, you allegedly encountered a trail drive consisting of a herd of horses and several thousand longhorn cows. You were told this *caravana* was bound for this military outpost. You brought two gringo prisoners with you, claiming to have taken them from among the trail drive's riders. You then left fourteen of your men with the trail drive. After more than a week, you are still missing a third of your command, and there is no trail drive in sight. This *misterio* does not alarm you?"

"My general, I was about to ride out to seek the cause of the delay," said Farias.

"That will not be necessary," said Paradez. "In the morning, I will ride until I find this trail drive, if it exists. I wish to know who authorized the delivery of this livestock."

Furious, Farias turned, and his hand was on the door handle when his superior spoke.

"Major Farias," said Paradez, "I have not dismissed you."

Farias struggled to gain control of himself before he again faced the hated General Paradez. His teeth clenched, Farias glared at Paradez, waiting.

"I am sure you are aware," said Paradez, "that only twenty-four recruits rode in with me. That

364

means eighteen of your men cannot be rotated. You will remain as the officer in charge, and the men I have chosen to leave with you are those with the least time in grade. You are dismissed, Major."

★ ★ ★

September 12, 1843. South of Matamoros, Tamaulipas.

Clay and Angelina rode east, positioning themselves on a rise where they could see a great distance to the north.

"It is much too soon for them to return south," said Angelina, "but I am concerned that the trail drive is getting so close to Matamoros."

"I reckon it's time to be concerned," said Clay. "We're cuttin' it mighty thin. If a band of soldiers don't ride out by tomorrow, takin' the prisoners south, we'll have to get with Ramon and stop the drive again."

"What of the soldiers riding with it?"

"When I say 'stop the drive,' I mean we'll have to get rid of those soldiers," said Clay.

"I liked your plan, taking them far to the south and leaving them afoot," said Angelina, "but how can we do that until the soldiers leave for Mexico City? We cannot get to the prisoners until they are taken from the jail and marched south."

Clay was already considering the possibility that nobody would return to Mexico City until the trail drive reached the outpost at Matamoros. If a high-ranking officer was in

365

charge of the newly arrived soldiers, would he not solve the mystery of the trail drive and the missing soldiers before he departed? It was two hours before sundown when Clay got his answer. Solano rode in, and the information he brought forced a change of plans.

"*Soldado* ride," said Solano, spreading his fingers on both hands. "*Uno oro chaqueta*, some come." He pointed south.

The worst had happened. Ten soldiers were riding south, including the "gold coat" — the officer — who had arrived the day before.

"It is as I feared," said Angelina. "They seek the trail drive and its soldier escort. We cannot wait for them to take the captives south, for tomorrow they will reach the herd and all will be lost."

"No," said Clay, "they'll reach the herd tonight, but not in the way they're expecting to. Come dark, we're takin' these *soldados* on a long ride south. This new bunch, and their *amigos* with the trail drive. Solano," he said, pointing north, "find the *soldado* camp and return here. Then we will ride south and meet the trail drive."

Solano nodded and rode out. Angelina looked at Clay, and he saw the doubt in her eyes.

"There's no other way," he said. "Once it's dark, one of the night hawks can send Ramon to us, and we'll plan our attack. When the soldiers with the trail herd have settled down for the night, we'll take them without firing a shot. We'll let the Injuns take out the sentries, and then we'll all go after what's left. We'll hog-tie the lot of them, leave some guards, and go after that new bunch Solano's going to locate for us."

"Then you intend to take them all south and leave them afoot."

"It's that," said Clay, "or shoot them in cold blood. Ramon says some of them are conscripts who won't resist, who don't wish to fight. Call me a fool, but I won't gun a man down in his sleep. Not if there's another way."

"I do not question what you are about to do," she said. "With the help of Ramon and his riders, I do not doubt that you can capture these soldiers. What I do not understand is how we are to rescue Gil and Van without them — or some of us — being killed."

"Once we have these soldiers out of the way, we can take the trail drive on to Matamoros. From there we may have to make it up as we go along. Once this bunch of soldiers is hog-tied, I aim for Ramon and some of the riders to take them as far south as they can by first light. While that's being done, Solano and me will have a look at that soldier outpost. If we got to bust Gil and Van out of that calaboose, then I need a look at it, to get some idea as to how it can be done."

"Tomorrow, then?" she asked.

"Tomorrow night," said Clay. "There had to be some soldiers at this post before that bunch brought in Gil and Van. There's fourteen with the herd, and another ten a few miles north of here. Even without the soldiers we're about to be rid of, we could still be facing at least forty when we go after this outpost at Matamoros. We need some advantage, an edge, and that's what Solano and me will be looking for."

"Am I to . . . ride with you?"

"Most of the way," said Clay, "but not into the outpost. We'll have to go in afoot, and I want you to stay with the horses."

★ ★ ★

When the newly arrived captives had eaten, they fell into an exhausted sleep. Gil again got up on the bench, so that he could look out the tiny window. He was unable to see the officers' quarters, because the enlisted mens' barracks stood in the way. But when Major Farias went to the post commander's office, he had to come around the enlisted mens' barracks and pass in front of the guardhouse. Gil watched Farias as he came and, a few minutes later, as he returned.

"Either tell me what's so almighty interestin'," said Van, "or let me look for a while."

"I reckon our *amigo*, Major Farias, has just caught hell," said Gil. "He left his barracks, was gone a few minutes, and now he's goin' back to his barracks. He looks like he's been throwed and stomped."

"Don't get too happy over Farias gettin' his tail feathers set afire," said Van. "It could mean this new officer that just come in aims to have a look at the trail drive. If that's so, it means we don't get out of here as slick as Clay's got it planned. Maybe we don't get out at all."

"Nobody's going to march these poor devils anywhere for a while," said Gil. "They're all dead on their feet."

"It was you," said Long John, looking at Van, "that was bullyraggin' me about havin' a keg o' black powder on me. That might be 'zactly what it'll take t' bust us outa this *juzgado*."

Gil didn't hear Van's response, if there was one. After drawing nothing but deuces, Long John might have unknowingly grabbed an ace. An idea began to take shape in Gil's mind. A farfetched idea that depended heavily on Clay Duval, and that little keg of black powder Ramon might still have . . .

★ ★ ★

September 12, 1843. The military outpost near Matamoros, Tamaulipas.

The area between the guardhouse and the enlisted men's barracks was for assembly, and so Gil got his first look at the newly arrived General Paradez. Nine soldiers waited, their horses saddled and ready. When Paradez rode in from the officers' quarters, the waiting men scrambled to their feet.

"At ease," said Paradez, returning their salutes. "Column of twos. Prepare to mount."

When Paradez gave the order to mount, the nine men swung into their saddles. A sergeant rode beside Paradez, the rest of the soldiers following. Gil eased himself down to a sitting position on the bench. He didn't wait for the question he knew was coming.

"The officer that rode in yesterday is ridin' out," said Gil, "taking nine soldiers with him."

"He aims to find our trail drive," said Van, "before returning to Mexico City."

"Looks that way," said Gil. "I don't know where else he could be going."

"Now whar's that leavin' us?" Long John wanted to know.

"Right here in the *juzgado*," said Gil, "until we hear from Clay."

"Ye got an almighty lot o' confidence in that hombre," said Long John.

"I know what he can and will do," said Gil. "By dark he'll know we're going to have to change our plans. Before dawn he or Solano will be here to talk to us."

★ ★ ★

When they were within a mile of the bedded-down longhorns, Solano reined up and dismounted. Clay and Angelina followed. Solano passed his reins to Clay, and without a word vanished into the night.

"He found the other camp so quickly," said Angelina, "they must be very close."

"That's why we're making our move tonight," said Clay. "Tomorrow they would have run right into the trail drive."

Solano returned, a silent shadow in the starlight. He touched Clay's arm, and Clay leaned close to Angelina.

"Wait," he said.

Clay followed Solano to where Ramon waited,

370

near the bedded-down longhorns. Clay could hear talking and laughing among the soldiers.

"*Soldados* no sleep," said Ramon.

"Too early," said Clay, "and we'll have to wait. It's pistol or rifle butts. No shooting. How many sentries do the *soldados* usually have?"

"Two, t'ree," said Ramon. "No more."

"Go, Ramon," said Clay, "before you're missed. Solano and me will wait here until you return. Once we know where the sentries are, and the rest of them are asleep, we'll make our move. Be sure and tell the men no shooting. Our aim is to knock this bunch senseless, just long enough to hog-tie them. Then, a few miles up the trail, we'll have to do the same thing all over again."

Clay and Solano waited. It was taking so long, Clay almost went back to reassure Angelina. But he had told her to wait, and wait she would, however long it might be. It was a good two hours before the camp settled down, and even Clay had begun to begrudge the time. Every minute it took to subdue these soldiers and those to the north lessened the distance they'd be able to take these men before turning them loose afoot. When Ramon returned, he had with him Estanzio and Mariposa.

"No *guardia*," said Ramon. "Estanzio and Mariposa take."

The four night hawks had been watching for Ramon. They dismounted. For this they would gladly leave the herd for a while. To a man, they were fed up with the domination of the soldiers. Led by Ramon, they silently made their way to the sleeping camp. Joined by their three waiting comrades, they were a dozen strong. There were twelve sleeping soldiers, and the task was finished quickly. Every soldier was bound hand and foot.

"Now," said Clay, "strip them of every weapon and all ammunition. Take their rifles from their saddle boots, and any ammunition you find in their packs or saddlebags."

The first of the bound soldiers to regain his senses was Sergeant Aguilla. He bellowed like a fresh-cut bull, and when he ran out of obscenities, he started over.

"Ramon," said Clay, "shut him up."

Ramon took a yard-long strip from a soldier's saddle blanket and proceeded to accomplish what he had yearned to do since the abusive Sergeant Aguilla had forced himself upon them.

"Ramon," said Clay, "I'll need five men to ride with Solano and me. When I send them back to you, they'll have ten more *soldados*, all hog-tied just like Aguilla and his men. Solano and me will ride on to Matamoros, but we'll be back here before dawn. Once you have these ten *soldados* I'll be sending you, add them to the bunch you already got. Mount the lot of them, tie them up, take them south at least fifty miles. Turn them loose, but bring their horses and saddles back with you."

"We do," said Ramon. "Take Estanzio, Mariposa, Manuel, Pedro, and Bola. *Vaya con Dios, amigo.*"

Clay and Solano led out, followed by the five riders Ramon had chosen.

"I have been frightened out of my wits," said Angelina when they stopped for her. "You were gone so long, and I could hear nothing, except someone cursing."

Clay laughed. "Sergeant Aguilla. Ramon had the honor of tying a piece of saddle blanket across his big mouth."

Solano, knowing the location of the soldier camp, took the lead. When he reined up and dismounted, the others followed. Silently, he chose Mariposa and Estanzio to accompany him, and the three faded into the darkness. By the Big Dipper, Clay decided it was close to midnight. The Indian trio returned as silently as they had departed.

"*Uno guardia,*" said Solano softly, but he extended three fingers in the starlight. They had disposed of three men, leaving seven.

Mariposa, Estanzio, and Solano led the way, followed by Clay, Manuel, Bola, and Pedro. They moved swiftly and soon had their captives bound hand and foot. They had been stripped of weapons and ammunition, and the spoils were heaped on a blanket.

"Bola," said Clay, "distribute the weapons and ammunition among you. We will need some or all of it. The five of you get these *soldados* back to Ramon as quickly as you can."

They had to release the feet of the soldiers so they could mount. Once in the saddle, their ankles were tied together by a rope passed under the bellies of the horses. The soldier with the gold braid on his coat — the officer — suddenly spoke in careful English.

"You, senor, the gringo. Do you not know who I am?"

"I know you're not that coyote, Santa Anna," said Clay, "or you'd have got more than a pistol butt alongside your head. I'd have gut-shot you."

"I am General Paradez, and for this atrocity I will see that you rot in prison."

"General," said Clay grimly, "I've been to your prison once, and there ain't enough soldiers in Mexico to put me there again. When I'm done, it may be *you* that'll rot in your stinking dungeon."

Once the ten captives were mounted and their ankles roped together, Clay, Solano, and Angelina watched Ramon's five riders depart, each with two of the soldier horses on lead ropes.

"The easy part's over," said Clay. "Now we ride to that soldier outpost at Matamoros and try to figure some way to free our *amigos*."

"Last night," said Angelina, "I did not truly believe you could do this. I still do not know how you will free your friends and get us all to Texas alive, but of this one thing I am sure: if there is a way, Clay Duval, you will find it."

"*Querida*," said Clay, "this time tomorrow night we'll be on our way to Texas. I ain't exactly sure how, but by the Almighty, we're going!"

22

GIL was awake until past midnight, expecting Clay or Solano. Finally he slumped down on the bench and slept. But when the signal came, so soft it might have been imagination, he was instantly awake.

"Here," whispered Gil, mounting the bench.

"Tomorrow night, pard," said Clay softly.

"Soldiers?" Gil asked.

"We hog-tied that bunch with the trail drive," said Clay, "and the ten that rode out yesterday. By dawn they'll be halfway to Tampico, afoot. Who's in there with you?"

"Van and Long John Coons," said Gil. "The ten men they threw in here yesterday are in bad shape. Can we take them with us?"

"I aim to," said Clay. "Was Angelina and me that freed 'em from the dungeon. We'll have horses and guns for them. Trouble is, gettin' the lot of you out of there won't be easy. I'd say there's maybe forty soldiers still here, but we can divert their attention from you long enough to bust you out. I still got to figure how I'm goin' to do that."

"No sentries here?" Gil asked.

"None," said Clay. "They're almighty sure of this place. I won't have a chance to see this *juzgado* in daylight; are there any weak points that you can see?"

"Nothing weak about it," said Gil. "Vulnerable

maybe, but only the outside walls and the roof, and you'd have to blast them away."

"I've used black powder," said Clay, "but we got none."

"Maybe we have," said Gil. "Before we set out with the trail drive, Ramon sent to Zacatecas for supplies. There was no ammunition available, but we got a keg of black powder. Maybe Ramon still has it."

"We could burn all our powder," said Clay, "and not put a dent in these log walls. A charge under each corner of the roof will bring it down, but there'll be some risk. Except for the bars dividin' the cells, there won't be a thing to keep it from comin' down on your heads."

"It's a risk we'll have to take," said Gil. "If we know when the blow's coming, we can back up against the outside walls, and it shouldn't fall directly on us. It's the only chance we have. We never see the keys to these cells. They slide the grub under the barred doors. If Ramon has the powder, set the charges and blow the roof."

"I'll talk to Ramon," said Clay. "I'll set the charges, and right on the heels of the blast there'll be men here with horses and guns. Just don't stop to rest while you're fightin' your way through the rubble. I can buy you a little time, but not much."

"With the soldiers' barracks just beyond the assembly ground, I wasn't expecting much," said Gil. "Soldiers will be all over us before the smoke clears."

"I reckon they won't," said Clay, "when there'll be five thousand hard-running longhorns between us and them, followed by a horse herd. Right on the heels of that, some of our riders will be throwin' some lead. It'll be a hard drive, gettin' the herds here in time, but whatever happens, I'll be here tomorrow at midnight."

Then he was gone.

"I couldn't hear Clay's side of that," said Van from the darkness.

"Me neither," said Long John.

Quietly as possible, Gil explained the situation to them. Suddenly a sleepy voice spoke from one of the cells across the corridor.

"What is it? What's goin' on over there?"

"Pardner," said Gil quietly, "we'll talk to you tomorrow. For now, get what sleep you can. You're going to need it."

★ ★ ★

Clay and Solano returned on foot to where Angelina waited with the horses. The three of them mounted and rode south, and when they were well away from the military outpost, Angelina had a question.

"You have decided how to free them?"

"Maybe," said Clay, and explained Gil's proposed use of the black powder.

"If Ramon still has it," said Angelina. "And if he does not?"

"We've reached a bend in the trail where we can't see that far ahead," said Clay. "When I talk to Ramon, we'll go from there. Black powder, or the lack of it, ain't our only problem. The trail drive's two days south, and it's got to be ready to invade that soldier camp tomorrow night."

"Ramon and his riders will not sleep tonight," said Angelina, "and they must ride all day tomorrow and tomorrow night."

"It's going to be hell on us all," said Clay, "but there's no help for it. We dared not take the trail drive any closer until we eliminated those soldiers already with it and those comin' to look for it."

"I cannot forget the words of General Paradez," said Angelina. "If Santa Anna was cold and cruel, then so much more so is this man. How is such a cruel exchange to help the poor people of Mexico?"

"I doubt Paradez is goin' to be around long enough to be a problem," said Clay. "Bastard that he is, Santa Anna's still the craftiest one of the bunch. By the time the United States gets around to a war with Mexico, they won't have to fight General Paradez. When war comes, we'll be fightin' that bastard Santa Anna."[1]

They reached the herds two hours before dawn, finding only Manuel Armijo and Domingo Chavez there. As Clay had feared, Ramon and his men had gotten too late a start for the

---

[1] General Paradez was a good soldier, but a heavy drinker, and by no means the political equal of Santa Anna. In 1846 Santa Anna's liberal friends forced Paradez out of office, reinstating Santa Anna as president as well as commander-in-chief of Mexico's armies.

distance they had to travel and then return. They were leading horses both ways, and it was a good two hours into the new day before Ramon and the riders returned.

"Go mebbe forty mile," said Ramon. "No more."

"That was a good decision, Ramon," said Clay. "It was all the time you could spare, and it'll have to do. With this bunch afoot and unarmed, we'll be dead or in Texas long before they can trouble us."

Clay then explained what must be done and the little time they had in which to do it. When he mentioned the black powder, Ramon's eyes lighted.

"Is here," said Ramon. "Is not open."

He dug into their supplies and brought it out, wrapped in a slicker. It came from the factory in tin flasks or kegs, fine-grained for pistols, coarser-grained for rifles and heavier pieces. It was highly volatile, and when it let go, there was white smoke, and plenty of it. Clay hefted the keg. There ought to be plenty to suit their purpose. If there was not, the cause was lost.

★ ★ ★

September 13, 1843. South of Matamoros, Tamaulipas.

General Paradez soon transferred his hatred from Clay Duval to his own Sergeant Aguilla. If they ever reached a military outpost, the best Aguilla could expect would be a court-martial. If Paradez had his way, the *estupido* sergeant would be backed against a wall and shot. Paradez and his men had been left their canteens, and so they had water, but Aguilla's men had none. They quickly made it plain to Paradez that their canteens had been lost due to the ignorance and negligence of Sergeant Aguilla. All of Aguilla's men lagged behind, and as soon as they reached decent cover, eight of them deserted. Paradez said nothing, but the black looks he directed at Aguilla said much. Before the miserable day was over, Sergeant Aguilla wished he had deserted with his conscripts.

★ ★ ★

Following their corn mush and cold coffee breakfast, Gil decided it was time to tell their ten recently arrived companions of the proposed escape. The men listened in silence.

"There's a possibility," Gil concluded, "that we'll get hurt when the roof comes down, but there's no other way."

"I'd as soon die in the blast," said one of the men, "as go back to that hole in Mexico City."

"Damn right," the others agreed.

"We'll know when it's coming," said Gil, "and we can back up against the outside log walls. That should offer us some protection. Way we're all separated by bars, the whole roof's got to go for all of us to get out. Once we're free, there'll be horses and guns. I look for us to have to shoot our way across the border."

"For that privilege," said one, "I'll thank God every day for the rest of my life."

There was a chorus of amens, and they settled down to wait for the night and the anticipated escape. For some reason they were unable to determine and never discovered, the arrogant Major Gomez Farias came into the guardhouse in the late afternoon. He was accompanied by a soldier who let him in the front door, and his escort waited there with the keys. Apparently Farias wasn't trusted with them. He stalked down the corridor, ignoring the latest arrivals, pausing before the cell in which Gil, Van, and Long John waited. The three captives ignored him, and Farias left without a word. The soldier with the keys followed, locking the door.

"What was *that* all about?" Long John wondered aloud.

"Who knows?" said Gil. "Maybe he's wondering if capturing a pair of Tejanos is going to compensate for losing fourteen soldiers."

"If we're his hole card," said Van, "that's all the more reason for us to bust out."

★ ★ ★

Clay and Angelina rode with the longhorns, while Solano joined Estanzio and Mariposa. Upon orders from Clay, they were pushing the horse herd so hard that the longhorns were having trouble keeping the pace. The drag riders had their work cut out for them. The cows, with a shorter stride, constantly fell behind. Clay was there, popping dusty flanks

381

with a doubled lariat.

"Let's keep 'em bunched," he shouted.

Although the twenty-four mounts taken from the soldiers trailed with the horse herd, the animals wore their saddles. Each saddle had a rifle in the boot, and most of them had a gun rig with holstered pistol thonged to the saddle horn.

"First water we come to," Clay had told Ramon, "we'll let 'em graze and drink an hour or two. As I recollect, we'll reach a good creek in the early afternoon. We want them to drink long and deep; I doubt they'll water or graze again until they're on the other side of the Rio Grande."

The sun was still two hours high when they reached the water Clay had in mind. The riders ate their evening meal, allowing the horses and longhorns to water and graze. The cattle didn't want to take the trail again at sundown, and the riders had to force them along. Some of the flank and drag bunch decided to quit the herd and return to the good water and graze. But the riders headed them. Bawling their objection, they ran to catch up to their less troublesome companions.

"No like trail in night," said Ramon.

"Just this once," said Clay, "they'll make an exception, if we have to swat their behinds every step of the way to Matamoros."

And that was pretty much what they had to do. By star-light and light of the rising moon, they should have made good time, but the longhorns became ornery. Heavy dew made the grass especially inviting. Once the cattle concluded they weren't going to bed down for the night, they slowed, trying to feed on the dew-drenched grass. They fell farther and farther behind the horse herd.

"Damn," groaned Clay, "Paradez and his soldiers will reach Matamoros afoot ahead of these fool cows."

"We have come far," said Angelina.

"Not far enough," said Clay. "We're still maybe fifteen miles away, and that's a good day's drive, even when the herd's trailin' decent."

"I know you promised midnight," said Angelina, "but as long as we move in the darkness, we can still take them by surprise. Can't we?"

"Yeah," said Clay, "if it's still dark when we finally get there. It's maybe two hours away from midnight; if we can't make our move by four o'clock, we're done."

"We get there," said Ramon. "You ride, tell Senor Gil."

"Go," said Angelina. "You promised them you would be there at midnight. Do not destroy their hope. Tell them we are coming. I will remain with the herd."

To her surprise, Clay Duval leaned over and kissed her cheek. Then without a word he rode out, heading north. In his saddlebags he carried four equal charges of black powder, each securely bound in half a woolen saddle blanket. Each charge had a woolen "fuse" that would be consumed quickly, but two were much longer. These he would set first, allowing him to get to the second pair, and hopefully they would all let go together. He wished he could go ahead and set the charges, but he dared not. The night air with its heavy dew might foul the powder.

Clay reached the outpost well before the appointed time, and left his horse at a great enough distance that it wouldn't attract or be attracted by horses somewhere on the outpost. He paused while he was still far from the cluster of log structures, looking and listening. The only light was a dim glow from the front window of the post commander's living quarters. While it was unusual for such an outpost to have no sentries, it was in his favor. Let them feel secure; it made them all the more vulnerable. This night their carelessness was going to cost them. He took the same route Solano had taken, going around and well beyond the log building that housed the commanding officer.

This roundabout approach led him to the guardhouse from the rear, keeping him within its shadow. He then moved around the log structure against the wall, allowing the roof overhang to drop its shadow over him. Even to one standing behind a darkened window of the soldiers' barracks and looking across the assembly ground, he was virtually invisible. Some of the outside chinking had weathered away, allowing him a foothold between some of the logs. With one foot in place, he used the other to boost himself off the ground, catching one of the bars with his hand. He could hang there as long as he had to, in the shadow of the roof overhang.

"Clay?" Gil's cautious voice inquired.

Before he could respond, a shot, like a clap of thunder, shattered the stillness of the night. The slug struck the wall just inches from Clay's head, and he dropped to the ground only seconds before a second and third lead slug slammed into the wall beneath the barred window. Still within the shadow of the overhang, Clay moved swiftly back the way he had come. By the time he reached the rear of the guardhouse, there was an excited babble of voices from beyond the assembly ground. The moon had been shrouded by a mass of clouds. A half-grown oak near one rear corner of the guardhouse was strong enough to suit Clay's purpose. He shimmied up the tree to the guardhouse roof, thankful for the moccasins Solano had provided in Mexico City. Once on the roof, he crept along it until he was near the front of the building. He then crawled to the very peak of the roof, and lying on his belly, hung his head over the ridge. Three men were crossing the assembly ground, one of them carrying a lighted lantern.

"That old fool Major Farias," said one of the men, but not loud enough that Farias might hear.

"*Si*," said a companion. "He is an old woman, firing at shadows. I wish there be no track, that the *capitán* might see him for the *borrico* that he is."

As they drew near the log building, Clay could no longer see them. But he could hear them and their fiendish laughter.

"Is no track," said one. "*Espectro!*"

That drew others, and Clay could see them in the dim starlight, coming across the assembly ground. One of the late arrivals was Major Farias himself. Clay didn't know him, but one of the soldiers said his name, and it silenced the others.

"The *linterna*, please," said Farias. "Return to your quarters at once."

It wasn't a request, but a command, and again some of the soldiers came into Clay's view as they retreated to the assembly ground. Farias had taken their lantern.

"*El capitán* comes," somebody hissed. The post commander had arrived.

"*Por Dios*, Major Farias, is this your idea of a joke, firing your weapon in the deep of the night?"

"It is no joke, Captain Diaz. I saw something — somebody — near this window of the guardhouse."

"It is well you have brought the light," said Diaz. "We will look for tracks."

There was a long silence. Captain Diaz broke it.

"Major Farias, first you see a trail drive that has vanished, taking a third of your command with it. Now you are firing at *espectros* that leave no tracks."

"There was a man!" shouted Farias.

One of the soldiers who still loitered on the assembly ground laughed.

"To your quarters!" shouted Diaz. "If you are *perdido carneros* with so little to do, I will inspect your quarters at dawn. Go and prepare!"

The Diaz wrath was sufficient, and they departed.

"Major Farias," snapped Diaz, "there are no tracks. As post commander, I am ordering you to return to your quarters. Major, if you again fire at some figment of your imagination, I swear by the blessed virgin I will confiscate your weapon!"

Major Farias, still carrying the lighted lantern, made his way across the assembly ground and passed beyond the soldiers' barracks. Clay breathed easier. Captain Diaz was going to be disturbed again before the dawn, and the next time he would have a firsthand look at those elusive longhorns that kept haunting Major Farias.

Inside the guardhouse there was total silence until Long John spoke.

"Damn it," he said dejectedly, "thar goes our rescue."

"I don't think so," said Gil. "You heard what went on out there. They found no tracks, so they'll be more secure than ever, convinced it's just old Farias seein' things. But we'll have to wait until they settle down. Long as it's dark, we can still make our move, still take 'em by surprise."

It seemed hours before Gil again heard the awaited signal. Quickly he climbed up on the bench.

"Solano's moccasins." Clay chuckled quietly. "I may never wear boots again."

Quickly he told Gil about the keg of powder and the problem with getting the herd there in time.

"I'll have Solano scatter their horses," said Clay. "When you hear the stampede comin', get ready for the blast. We'll have the horses somewhere behind this jail. They'll be back a ways, because of the blast, hobbled with slip knots, close enough for you to reach 'em quick. Mount up and fall in behind the stampede; I aim to run 'em all the way across the border. The horse herd will follow the longhorns, and some of our riders will be on their tails, keepin' 'em bunched. This is it, *amigo*. I'm ridin' back to the herd. You'll hear us coming. Be ready."

Clay circled back to his horse. A second lamp burned in another window of the log structure that was the post commander's office and living quarters. From there, if anybody chose to look, they could see the saddled horses and riders that would be stationed in the clearing behind the guard-house. Even hobbled, it wouldn't be easy holding the horses with a stampede thundering past on two sides. And if that wasn't enough, within seconds the roof would be blown off the guardhouse!

★ ★ ★

In the guardhouse, nobody slept. For a while, after the sound of the shots, their spirits had sagged. Then had come the exchange between Captain Diaz and Major Farias. Every prisoner had known enough Spanish to understand and appreciate the conversation between the Mexican officers. Not only had the shots missed, their "target" had left no tracks! Based on what Clay

388

had told him, Gil had some final advice for his companions.

"The horses will be right behind this building, hobbled so they can't run. Once the roof blows, don't waste any time. If any man gets trapped and needs help, sing out. Once you're free, hit the saddle and follow the stampede. No firing, unless you have to defend yourselves. Save all your ammunition for the border. There'll be close to five thousand longhorn cows coming through here on the run. Once you're in the saddle, try to catch up to the herd. If we can keep the longhorns bunched, and the horse herd right on their heels, we can run down anything or anybody standing between us and the border. This is our chance, our only chance, for freedom. Come morning, I aim to watch the sun rise from the other side of the Rio Grande!"

★ ★ ★

Clay pushed his horse, anxious to reach the trail drive. He knew he'd been gone long enough for them to suspect there had been trouble. This was their last hand in a high stakes game, and they had to fill an inside straight. Clay met Solano riding well ahead of the horse herd. The Indian was not one to worry, taking things as they came, and Clay suspected Angelina had likely sent Solano to look for him. It bothered him some, her wielding so much influence over Solano, but how could he complain? Had it not been for their unlikely alliance, he might still be in a Mexican prison. Not too far behind Solano, he met Angelina.

"I had begun to worry," she said.

"There was a ruckus," said Clay, "and I had to keep out of sight for a while, before I could talk to Gil. They're ready, waitin' for us. Before I go to set the charges, we'll spend a little time decidin' what each of us is to do. Once all this begins, it'll move like a prairie fire. We'll have to stay ahead of it, or some of us won't live to see Texas."

"I will not hide from the danger," she said. "Tell me what I must do, but do not try to protect me. If I am worthy of your Texas frontier, then I must fight for it. I will do what must be done, and I can shoot."

"I don't doubt that for a minute," he said, "and you're going to have as much a part in this as any of us. Soon as we can get with Ramon, we'll make some definite plans."

They reached the longhorn herd, to find it trailing well, although it was still considerably behind the horse herd. When they met Ramon, Clay, Solano, and Angelina turned their horses so that they rode with him ahead of the herd.

"*Amigos*," said Clay, "we got some serious talkin' to do. Ramon, when I blow the roof off that guardhouse, I want you, Angelina, Solano, Estanzio, and Mariposa there with the horses. We'll need thirteen horses for the men we're goin' to set free. Add to that one horse for each of us, and there'll be a total of nineteen. I aim to hobble the horses, so they can't break loose and join the stampede, but when the roof blows, you'll have your hands full trying to calm them. All of you may be in some danger, because the area behind the guardhouse is wide open and less than a hundred yards from the commanding officer's quarters. You'll have some protection during the stampede, because the herd should split and pass on each side of the guardhouse, one leg of it passing between you and the commanding officer's place. But we'll have only a few minutes until the worst of the stampede is past, and that may not be enough time to free the men from the guardhouse. Some of them may still be trapped if the roof fails to break up. Have your lariats ready, and pull down some walls if you have to. If the stampede passes before we're done, we may have to shoot our way out. So if the stampede moves too fast, or we move too slow, we may have forty men from the soldiers' barracks throwin' lead at us. We must make every minute count; if we don't, this could be hell with the lid off, and some of us will die. *Comprender*, Ramon? Solano?"

"*Comprender*," they said, in one voice.

"Solano," said Clay, "I want you to ride ahead and remain with the horse herd. Explain to Estanzio and Mariposa what I have just told you. When you reach the valley just south of the *soldado* camp, hold the horse herd there. Once we arrive with the longhorns, both herds will be held there until we're ready for them to run. *Comprender?*"

"*Comprender*," said Solano. He rode quickly away.

"I'll take your place with the herd, Ramon,"

said Clay. "I want you to talk to the rest of the riders, tell them what I've told you. Be sure they understand. Every rider not actually involved in freeing the men from the guardhouse is to pursue the herd, keeping the horses and longhorns bunched and moving. Tell them to hold their fire unless forced to defend themselves. I aim to scatter those *soldado* horses from here to yonder, but something *could* go wrong, and we'll need all our ammunition at the border. *Comprender?*"

"*Comprender*," said Ramon, and he rode away in the darkness.

Angelina kneed her horse close to Clay's, and when she reached for his hand, she found it seeking her own. When she spoke there was anxiety in her voice.

"Now that the time nears, I am afraid. Not for myself, but for those who are placing their lives in our hands. Perhaps the darkness and the stampede will separate us, but I will pray that in the new light of the dawn, we will again be together in Texas. *Vaya con Dios*."

The Big Dipper said it was nearing two o'clock in the morning. The trail drive was two hours south of the Matamoros outpost, and it was but one hour until Clay Duval would ride ahead to set the charges. Finally, in that darkest hour before the dawn, there would be no turning back. With hearts in their throats and guns in their hands, behind a thundering herd, they would make their bid for freedom!

23

AFTER the humiliating ultimatum from Captain Diaz, Major Farias returned to his quarters, but only until the post settled down. Farias then took his pistol and his rifle and crept into the night. From the day he had encountered that cursed trail drive, it seemed that *El Diablo* himself had taken a personal interest in the life of Major Gomez Farias. He *had* seen a man beneath that barred guardhouse window, and so bold a man might return. All the proof that Farias had, insofar as that elusive trail drive was concerned, was the pair of Tejanos he had taken prisoner. He vowed they would not be stolen from him, if he had to patrol this wretched outpost himself, until General Paradez returned. Still, he must not incur the further wrath of Captain Diaz, lest this entire affair be presented to General Paradez in an unfavorable light. Farias knew he needed some vantage point from which he could see most of the area without exposing himself. This outpost, he decided, had been laid out by a pulque-sodden *pelado*. It was strung out in a line, with the horse barn and corral at the eastern end. The only structure from which he might see any distance was the log barn, with its hay-filled loft. To his dismay, he found that while he could see the officers' quarters and the enlisted men's barracks, he was able to see only the front of the guardhouse. Beyond that, the commanding officer's quarters was only a pair of lighted lamps in the darkness. By four o'clock the moon would have set and the world would become as black as the inside of a chimney. But his anger toward the righteous Captain Diaz had not abated, and as long as he could see, he would wait.

★ ★ ★

A few minutes before three o'clock, Clay Duval left the longhorn herd and rode north. Reaching the little valley he had mentioned to Solano, he found the horse herd already there, waiting. The three Indian riders rode out to meet him.

"Solano," said Clay, "the horses behind the guardhouse will be hobbled, so we can hold them. I need you somewhere else. You know where the *soldado* horse corral is, and I want you there before our herd starts to run. When you hear the *estampeda* coming, pull down the corral fence and scatter the *soldado* horses. Then quickly ride within rifle range of the *soldado casas*. When the *estampeda* comes, the *soldados* will come runnin' out. Throw some lead among them, drive 'em back inside, if you can. If they return your fire, back off and ride out of range. When the *estampeda* has passed, ride away to the west and circle in behind the guardhouse. We may still be there, needin' your help with the prisoners. If we're gone, hightail it and catch up to the herd. While you're waitin' for Ramon and the longhorn herd, the three of you get the saddled horses ready for the men

394

in the guardhouse. See that every saddle boot has a rifle, and that a belt rig with a pistol is thonged to every saddle horn. Be sure, Solano, that you tell Ramon you're going to scatter the *soldado* horses. *Comprender?*"

"*Comprender*," said Solano.

"Mariposa," said Clay, "you and Estanzio will go with Ramon and Angelina, taking the thirteen saddled horses. Ramon knows the best way to get them in behind the guardhouse, well away from the blast. Once there, hobble the hind legs of every *caballo*, including your own. Use slipknots, so that when the roof's blown off the jail we can all run for it. *Comprender?*"

"*Comprender*," said the pair, in one voice.

"*Amigos*," said Clay, extending his hand. One by one they took it. Clay then rode north, and was soon lost in the darkness.

Clay looked up at the darkening sky. By the time he reached the outpost, the moon would have set, lessening the danger of his being seen. His mind raced as he tried to think of something vital he might have overlooked. The stampeding herd would come between the soldier barracks and the guardhouse, offering them a few minutes' protection from the soldiers. Solano scattering the soldiers' horses would leave them afoot, unable to pursue the stampede and lessening chances of a fight at the border. What bothered him — the one factor over which he had no control — was the blowing of the roof. It was a clumsy, unpredictable, and dangerous plan, but they had no other. He sighed and rode on.

He rode in from the west, and at first saw only the one lamp's glow in the post commander's quarters. Drawing nearer, he saw a second glow, not as bright, and realized it was bleeding through a partially open door. There was a second lamp in the parlor, which faced the guardhouse. He rode in behind the building, passed to the rear of it, and reined up in the area behind the guardhouse where they would have to hold the extra horses. From his saddlebag he took a yard-long length of rope, knotting one end of it to each of his horse's hind legs. The horse could take only short, stilted steps, and could not spread its hind legs enough to rear. Clay took the saddlebags with their blanket-wrapped powder charges and set out afoot for the rear of the guardhouse. The stars had already begun to dim, and the Big Dipper told him he had only a few minutes. He hung the saddlebags around his neck and again climbed the young oak at the back corner of the guardhouse. He would set the last charge here before leaving the roof. Staying well below the roof's peaked ridge, he crept to the front corner, facing the post commander's quarters. Lying on his belly, he leaned over the edge of the roof, jamming one of his blanket-wrapped charges under the corner of the eave. From there he crept to the ridge of the A-frame roof. He paused, listening. He must place two of the charges on the side of the building next to the assembly ground, and beyond that, the soldiers' barracks. Taking a deep breath, he crept down the roof to the other front corner. Lying on his belly, head over the edge, he placed his second charge. Slowly he moved along the roof to the rear corner and placed a third charge. He sighed with relief when he crossed the roof's ridge and descended to the back corner at which he would place the fourth and last charge. Finished, he stepped into the oak and made his way to the ground. He dug into his saddlebags again, seeking the little oilskin pouch Ramon had given him. In it was a block of yellow-headed, phosphorous matches, and a rough, dry, flat stone upon which to strike them. They must be struck quickly and properly. Repeated attempts usually popped the heads off, making them useless.

Clay returned to his hobbled horse, the packet of matches in his hand. He was as jittery as a squirrel in a treeful of bobcats. He wondered how much time Ramon had allowed himself to get the horses here before the rest of the riders would get the stampede under way. These would not be the Mendoza horses, but those taken from the soldiers. Why risk having their hard-won blooded animals wounded or killed in a gunfight? These soldiers would be afoot, but just across the assembly ground, well within rifle range. Once the stampede was out of the way, the soldiers could cut loose with a hail of lead. They'd be lucky, Clay thought grimly, if horses were *all* that died there behind the guardhouse. Just when he was ready to give the whole thing up for a lost cause, Ramon, Angelina, Estanzio, and Mariposa rode in with the extra horses on lead ropes. Ramon led four, and each of the others led three.

"Mariposa," said Clay, "you and Estanzio slipknot hobble your horses. Ramon, you and Angelina stay mounted, and keep your lariats ready. We may need your horses to pull down some walls. I want all of you with the horses until the roof blows. I'll stay afoot, because I may have to help somebody out of the rubble once the roof is down. Now let's hobble these extra horses. Hind legs with slipknots. We don't have much time."

Suddenly, from somewhere beyond the soldiers' barracks, there were two quick shots.

"Solano!" cried Angelina. "Solano's in trouble!"

"If he is," said Clay, "we're *all* in trouble."

"*Estampeda* come!" said Ramon.

Sounding far away, yet distinct, Clay heard it. He ran, knowing every second was crucial. Reaching the corner of the guardhouse where he had set the fourth charge, Clay popped a match into flame. His trailing wool "fuse" caught readily. Each makeshift "fuse" had been doubled, doubled again, and then doubled a third time, lest they burn too rapidly. He ran to the next corner, lighted the trailing fuse to the first charge, then rounded the front of the guardhouse to the other side. His makeshift fuses to the second and third charges were only half the length of the two he had already lighted. Once the last two were burning, he ran toward the hobbled horses. Already, as a result of the shots, there was a babble of voices and excited shouts from across the assembly ground. But all other sound was lost as the first and fourth powder charges blew. It was good timing, one blast seeming the echo of the other. The leading longhorns were already pounding across the assembly ground. The leaders tried to turn, but had nowhere to go except straight ahead. Then, on the side of the guardhouse nearest the stampede, just seconds apart, the second and third powder charges blew. The longhorns thundered on, those nearest the blast hooking their front-running companions in their eagerness to escape this earthly hellfire. Shakes from the roof fell like rain, and clouds of white smoke hung in the darkness like pale fog. Clay stumbled to his feet and started for the wreckage. Ramon and Angelina, mounted, were right behind him. The ten captive Texans brought in by General Paradez had been fortunate. On their side of the jail, the first two blasts had gone off simultaneously. The roof had buckled in the middle, toppling the wall, allowing the captives to scramble out unhurt. They ran to the waiting horses. Gil, Van, and Long John hadn't been so fortunate. Their wall had held, and although the roof lay flat, it still effectively trapped them in their cell.

"Ropes!" cried Clay.

From their saddles, at opposite ends of the log wall, Ramon and Angelina looped their lariats around log ends. Lead began thudding into the logs as three rifles cut loose beyond the assembly ground. Ramon and Angelina backed their horses away from the wall, dragging it down with a crash. Without the support of the wall, the collapsed roof broke up. Seconds before it fell in a pile of rubble, Long John, Van, and Gil scrambled out. With both walls of the guardhouse down, a rifle opened up from the commanding officer's quarters. There was fire coming from both sides, but it was still too dark for accurate shooting. First light was just minutes away, and the stampede was gone. A few longhorns loped across the assembly ground, heading back the way they had come, bawling like lost souls.

"To the horses!" shouted Clay.

The ten liberated Texans had already set off at a gallop, following the remnant of the stampede. When they reached the horses, Mariposa and Estanzio had them ready.

"*Amigos*," said Clay, "they left just three or four men here. That means we'll have to fight our way across the border. I tried to avoid that, by sendin' Solano to scatter their horses, but he didn't make it. You heard the shots. I'll just have to take my chances at the border, but I'm goin' after Solano. Who wants to go with me?"

Angelina kneed her horse over next to Clay's. Mariposa, Estanzio, and Ramon followed.

"I'd go with you," said Gil, "but I have unfinished business here. Ride back this way, and we'll head for the border together. Van, I'll need you to watch my back; I'm going after Rosa."

"Do I gotta ride t' the border an' git shot by m'sef," Long John asked, "er can I wait an' go with the outfit?"

"Stick with Van," said Gil. "You're welcome to get shot at the border with the rest of us. For right now, you and Van find yourselves some kind of cover where you can see that commanding officer's house. I'll take my chances with whoever's in the house, but I'll be in full view of those Mex sharpshooters over there in the barracks. It's been dark, and they haven't really had anything to shoot at. That's about to change."

Van and Long John took cover behind the blown-out wall and its resulting rubble, which faced the commanding officer's quarters. Gil left his horse far behind the ruins of the guardhouse and ran for the log structure where he believed he would find Rosa. Almost immediately someone in the cabin cut loose with a rifle. Gil zigzagged on, while somewhere behind him, Long John or Van, began pouring lead through the front windows. The firing from the cabin ceased, and Gil leaped to the long porch that spanned the length of the front of the building. The few soldiers left behind had discovered where Van and Long John had taken cover and, with good light, had begun firing in earnest. Gil, with his back against the wall, moved up beside the shattered window. There was a heavy curtain, and he could see nothing. Suddenly, flames shot to the top of the window, devouring the curtain. The place was afire! Drawing his pistol, Gil kicked the door as hard as he could. Unlocked, it slammed back against the inside wall. A man lay facedown on the floor, and he wore the gold-braided coat of a Mexican army officer. His hand still clutched the muzzle of his rifle. Some of the lead directed at the man on the floor had struck the lamp, spewing oil onto a heavily upholstered chair and onto the rug that covered most of the floor. Already, flames feeding on the heavy rug had eaten their way a third of the distance across the room. This was a parlor, with a fireplace at one end and a closed door at the other. Gil kicked open the second door, revealing a sparsely furnished bedroom. Nobody was there, and he could see no other door leading out of the room.

"Rosa," he shouted. "Rosa!"

But he heard nothing except the continuing rattle of distant gunfire and the ominous sound of the growing inferno behind him.

★ ★ ★

Clay led out, and the five riders rode north until they were half a mile beyond the soldiers' barracks and the officers' quarters. From there they rode east until they could see the distant horse barn with its adjoining corral.

"Solano *caballo*," said Ramon, pointing.

Beyond the corral stood a lone horse with reins trailing. It was mute testimony to the faithfulness of the horses Solano had gentled that the animal hadn't allowed itself to be caught by one of the soldiers. Estanzio rode to catch the horse, and his companions continued on toward the barn. Warily, they circled it, and found Solano just beyond, a few yards from the now empty horse corral. Solano lay on his back, his unfired rifle beside him. He had been shot twice; once in the left shoulder, and again in his left side, dangerously low. Blood had pooled a rusty brown in the sand beside him. Angelina caught her breath and bit her lip. Clay was out of his saddle in an instant, seeking a pulse. At first he found none. Finally he pressed his fingers into the flesh beneath Solano's chin, searching until he found the big artery.

"He's alive," said Clay. "Shuck out some extra blankets. We'll have to tie him on his horse."

"It is a risk to move him," said Angelina. "From the ride, he may die."

"We try an' doctor him here," said Clay, "and we'll *all* die. These Mex soldiers ain't known for their compassion. We're taking him with us; it's the only chance he has."

They wrapped Solano in blankets and bound him, belly down, across his saddle. Nobody hated it any more than Clay Duval, but they might have to do some hard riding, and there simply was no other way to keep the wounded Solano in the saddle. They mounted up and rode out in silence, Clay leading Solano's horse. They rode back the way they had come, still hearing the distant rattle of gunfire, an indication that Gil, Van, and Long John were still there.

"*El casa*," cried Ramon. "It burns!"

While flames hadn't yet broken through the front of the cabin, smoke had, boiling out the broken window and through the open door.

"Let's ride," said Clay. "With Gil's luck, he's in there!"

★ ★ ★

403

Frantically, Gil looked for another door. Half of one wall, floor to ceiling, was draped with a blanket. Why? Gil caught the bottom edge of the blanket and ripped it away, revealing the door he sought. He tried the handle, and while there was no lock, it apparently was barred on the inside.

"Rosa," he shouted. "Rosa, are you there?"

She tried to answer him, but her cry was choked off. Somebody was with her, restraining her! He threw his shoulder to the door, and it didn't give in the slightest. It was seasoned oak, and after half a dozen attempts, all he had gained was a sore shoulder. The flames behind him began to crackle, and clouds of smoke stung his eyes. He searched desperately for something heavy enough to break down the door. Turning back to the smoke-filled parlor, he found the floor — thanks to the heavy rug — totally engulfed in flames. He ran through them, feeling the heat through the thin soles of his boots, until he reached the fireplace. There was a slender iron poker, and he rejected it as useless. Logs had been laid in preparation for a fire, and it was on the way. He grabbed one of the cedar logs from the fireplace, but it was short, light, and useless. He threw the rest of the logs out onto the burning floor and grabbed one of the heavy andirons. They were "bull heads," with the familiar head atop each of the tall uprights. While it was an awkward object, it was iron, heavy enough to suit his purpose.

Again he ran through the fire, feeling it singe his eyebrows and hair. Grasping the ponderous andiron by the upright, just beneath the bull's head, he swung it like an ax against the stubborn door. Despite the solidness of the door, he felt something give. After a second blow, he could see a crack between the door's edge and the jamb. The door itself hadn't budged, but he was tearing loose one end of the bar and whatever secured it. When one of his blows sent the door suddenly crashing against the wall, catching him off balance, all that saved him was the heavy andiron he hefted for another blow. Rosa cried out as a pistol roared and lead sang off the andiron, ripping into the ceiling. Grasping the pistol was the biggest Mexican woman Gil had ever seen. She could have taken the horns of a bull and thrown the animal, without it having a chance. In a single motion he slammed the heavy andiron down on her moccasined feet, then grabbed the wrist of the hand that held the pistol. He forced the muzzle of the pistol toward the ceiling, and again the weapon roared. Fisting her free hand, she slugged Gil just below his left ear, and he almost blacked out. But he clung to her arm, and slowly but surely, forced her to drop the pistol. Before it hit the floor, she had a dagger in her left hand. Gil wasn't expecting that, and when she made a pass at him, the tip of the blade slashed the front of his shirt.

Gil caught the wrist of the hand wielding the knife, and a new struggle began. She brought up a vicious knee, and Gil twisted just enough, quickly enough, to spare his groin. But there was one element neither of them had counted on.

A pistol roared, and Gil's bull-strong antagonist stiffened. Gil backed away. Her fingers went limp, she dropped the dagger, and fell facedown. On the floor sat Rosa, clutching the smoking pistol in both her small hands.

"*El Diablo bruja*," said Rosa.

Dropping the pistol, she sprang to her feet and ran to Gil. He caught her up and stepped out the door, only to encounter an inferno of flames. He turned back to the room they'd just left, but there was no exit, not even a window.

"Rosa," he cried, "there must be a kitchen. Where?"

She pointed to what seemed a solid wall at the other end of the first bedroom. He found the outline of a cleverly concealed door, but how in tarnation did it open? He kicked it hard, but it held. Gil put Rosa down and turned back to the other room, where the andiron lay. Taking his hold again, he swung the thing against the concealed door. Something moved on the other side, and he struck another blow with the andiron. Two more battering blows with the andiron snapped the lock. There was the kitchen, with its barred back door, but before he reached it, the entire back wall came down! Part of the roof came with it, and Gil moved away with Rosa just in time. When the dust cleared, Gil and Rosa stepped out into the sunlit morning. Van and Long John were coiling their lariats, and Ramon led Gil's horse.

"We was gettin' a mite concerned about you," said Van, grinning.

"You should be," said Gil. "That's the second

damn roof that's fell on me in an hour."

"Hit the saddle and let's ride," said Van. "Clay and the others are up the trail a ways, waitin' for us. Swing wide of the guardhouse; the hombres with rifles tried to get me and Long John in a cross fire, but a couple of 'em run headlong into Clay, Ramon, and the others. That's two we won't have to fight at the border."

They rode west of the burning building until they were well away from the outpost. Then they turned northeasterly until they reached the path the stampede had taken. There they turned north, toward the border.

★ ★ ★

A few miles to the south, General Paradez and fifteen weary soldiers had stopped to rest. The cool of the night had departed. They looked longingly toward the north, in the forlorn hope that wish might become reality, that somehow the long miles ahead might diminish. Paradez at first thought his eyes deceived him. It could not be smoke; it was only morning vapor the sun would soon burn away.

"*Fuego*," said one of the soldiers, pointing. "*Humo*."

They marched on, and when the sun rose, the smoke to the north of them was even more obvious against the blue of the sky. The rising column seemed suspiciously near the outpost toward which they traveled. While the soldiers were curious, they looked at General Paradez

407

and the grim set of his jaw, and wisely kept their silence.

★ ★ ★

Clay and his riders reined up when they reached the path the stampede had taken.

"It's been long enough," said Clay, "for them to be ahead of us."

"If we are to cross the border safely," said Angelina, "we must do it together. Perhaps they face difficulty of which we are unaware."

"Is so," said Ramon.

"Let's go, then," said Clay. "If they need us, we'll be there, and if they don't, we'll meet 'em headed this way."

Clay cut his eyes to the horse he led, which bore the critically wounded Solano. They had lost their edge — surprise and darkness — and God knew what awaited them at the border. Suddenly, two rifle-bearing soldiers darted out of the woods ahead. Too late, they discovered the riders bearing down on them. Clay drew and fired, with Ramon a second behind.

"That means our *amigos* are still there," said Clay. "That pair of coyotes aimed to sneak around and do some back-shooting. Ramon, ride in and let 'em know we're here. If you need us, fire a shot and we'll come a-running."

There were no more unexpected soldiers and no warning shot from Ramon. Clay heaved a sigh of relief when Gil, Van, and Long John rode into view. When the trio reined up, Clay grinned at Gil and the bright-eyed, disheveled

Rosa. Ramon was amused; he knew what was coming.

"Amigo," said Clay, "she's a beauty, but she's a mite young for you."

"Give her another fifteen years," said Gil. "I'll wait. Solano is — "

"Alive," said Clay, "but hard hit. If we don't soon take care of his wounds, he won't last the night."

"All the more reason for us to cross the border pronto," said Gil, "whatever it takes."

"I expect it'll take a fight," said Clay. "That's why there was only three or four soldiers throwin' lead at us. We had darkness on our side, and they couldn't see to shoot, so they left just enough rifles behind to slow us down. Now we'll have the whole damn bunch waitin' for us at the border, and us in broad daylight."

"It wasn't Solano's fault they cut him down before he could scatter the horses," said Van.

"I know that," said Clay. "It could have happened to any man; it's just one of those things we couldn't allow for. It was the best way, though, just stampedin' the herd across the Rio, with us ridin' behind. Now we got no herd to ride behind."

"Don't be too sure of that," said Gil. "Matamoros is thirty miles south of the border, and the outpost is south of Matamoros. You couldn't keep a stampede going for thirty miles if the world was on fire."

"You may be right," said Clay. "Ramon, who did you leave in charge of the herd?"

"Juan Padillo," said Ramon. "He got cow

savvy. No leave *amigos*."

"Let's ride, then," said Clay. "Maybe we can put some new life into that stampede."

They hadn't ridden far when they met Juan Padillo. He was leading the mule that had belonged to the trio of Mexicans who had waylaid Gil.

"*Estampeda* leave him," said Juan. "He cry, raise hell."

"*Mulo!*" cried Rosa. "Want *mulo!*"

"Juan," said Gil, "we've just found a need for him. You can have him, Rosa, but you'll have to wait for a saddle and bridle."

"No need," said Rosa happily, "for *bueno mulo*."

"Juan," said Clay, "you didn't ride back to bring a lost mule. Where's the herd?"

"*Caballo* tired," said Juan, "*vaca* tired. No run. Find arroyo, they wait. *Soldados* want fight, they wait."

"Well, by the Almighty," said Clay, "I ain't one to disappoint a man that's spoilin' for a fight. Let's ride!"

24

THE arroyo to which Juan Padillo led them was at least ten miles south of the border. The sanctuary was not a box canyon, but it had water and graze. And a sentry! Everybody — especially Gil and Van — was surprised to find on duty one of the ragged, bearded Texans that General Paradez had recaptured near Tampico.

"*Dos guardias*," said Juan Padillo. There would be a second sentry at the north end of the canyon.

Despite their precarious situation, they felt better. With twenty-four riders, they had a chance, and only the critically wounded Solano dampened Clay's spirits. He feared that his friend would never see Texas, that Solano would be left in a lonely grave somewhere south of the Rio Grande. Gil and Van Austin shared his concern.

"Clay," said Gil, "let's see what we can do for Solano. Ramon still has half a canteen of the pulque we made when Van was shot. We can at least boil some water, cleanse the wounds, and pour some of this cactus poison into them. Then before we move out, we can bind some pulque-soaked pads over the wounds. It might mean the difference between him living and dying."

"You're right," said Clay. "Those Mex

411

soldiers know we're here, and if they decide to come after us, they won't have to follow our smoke."

"They won't bother us here," said Gil, "unless we stay the night. Come dark, the advantage is all theirs. They could put men on both walls of this canyon, and with no danger to themselves, cut us down in a cross fire. They know we have to cross the border, and they aim to be there waiting for us."

"I'll start a fire and boil the water," said Angelina.

"I purely don't believe those Mex soldiers are all that organized," said Gil. "They don't even have an officer in charge, unless it's Major Farias. I found Diaz, their commanding officer, dead in his cabin, and the almighty General Paradez is somewhere to the south, nursing blistered feet."

That drew a laugh, even from Mariposa and Estanzio.

"When old Paradez gets back to that outpost," laughed Clay, "he'll *still* be afoot. We got all his horses, and the corral is empty."

"I ain't never had hoss stealin' agin me," said Long John.

"Don't let it bother you," said Van. "They got enough on us to back us against a wall and have us shot a dozen times, without ever-gettin' to the horse stealing."

"Ye shore know how t' comfort a man," said Long John.

By the time Angelina had the water hot, Clay and Gil had Solano off his horse and his wounds bared. The Indian still clung to life.

"At least there are exit wounds," said Gil. "It's hell on a man when you have to dig into his wounds with a Bowie, searchin' for the lead."

"Yeah," said Clay, "and when it don't come out clean, there's a chance it struck a rib and was deflected into some vital organs."

"For this I am thankful," said Angelina, "but he still could die from the wound in his side."

"Woman," said Clay in mock anger, "it ain't proper for you to be lookin' at a pore hombre that's out of his head and out of his britches."

"He is my friend," said Angelina, "in or out of his britches. Now if you will allow me, I will cleanse and tend his wounds."

Rarely did anybody get Clay Duval's goat, and if the girl hadn't been dead serious, Gil and Van would have laughed. Western men had a habit of laughing in the face of any calamity, even death. If Angelina Ruiz were to become a Texan in every sense of the word, she was going to have to develop a tolerance for cowboy humor.

"Ma'am," said Clay, with a grin, "I never seen a woman that couldn't outdoctor a man, when it come to fixin' wounds. You just patch ol' Solano up like you think it oughta be done."

Angelina did, pouring the pulque into the open wounds and then covering them with pads soaked in the fiery liquor.

"If he can survive that poison poured into his open wounds," said Van, "he ain't got a thing to worry about."

When Angelina had finished dressing Solano's wounds, Clay and Van again wrapped him in

413

blankets. Amazingly, the Indian still had no sign of fever, and his pulse was stronger.

"He will live," said Angelina.

"We already have a fire," said Gil. "Let's have ourselves a decent meal before we make our run for the border. Anything but corn mush."

Ramon and Juan Padillo had been rough-tallying the longhorns, while Mariposa and Estanzio had tallied the horses. The result was far better than any of them had expected.

"We have two hundred horses," said Gil. "Twenty-five are soldier horses, and the rest are Mendoza. And we still have at least forty-four hundred longhorns."

"*Uno mulo*," said Rosa.

They laughed, and it was good that they were able to, thought Gil. This time tomorrow, some of them might be dead. They enjoyed their meal and put out the fire. Long John asked the question that was on all their minds.

"The Injun's been patched up, we know how many hosses an' cows they is, and we et. Now when air we goin' t' Texas?"

"When we do," said Van, "let's get the herd closer to the border before they run."

"That stampede was my idea," said Clay, "and although it didn't reach the border, we needed a diversion. Without it, you'd be stuck in a Mex prison till Gabriel blows his horn."

"We're well aware of that," said Gil. "You did what you had to do. We ought to be thankful the stampede didn't reach the border, because we weren't there to follow it across. Before we make any more moves, why don't we scout the border and see what's ahead of us? Unless somebody's got a better plan, I'll take Mariposa and Estanzio, and we'll find out what we're up against."

"It's got to be done," said Clay. "Just don't let 'em see you, or it'll tip our hand. They'll know we're gettin' ready to run. I'd like them to think we aim to stay the night, that maybe we'll make our play just before the dawn tomorrow. Let 'em think they have time to come here in the dark and pick us off in a cross fire."

"While we move as near the border as we can," said Gil, "and make our move after sundown."

"That's it," said Clay. "They know we're going to run, but they don't know when. That's all the advantage we have, so let's play on it."

"It's our best shot," said Gil. "If we can get the herds close enough to the border without being discovered, this time we *can* take the drive on across. Then we'll ride behind them, burnin' some powder if we have to. If we can stall until after dark, like Clay says, so much the better."

They were all in agreement. Two hours before noon, Gil, Mariposa, and Estanzio rode out. Bearing in mind Clay's caution about not being seen, Gil allowed Mariposa and Estanzio to take the lead. When they bid him wait, he waited, holding the horses while the pair scouted on foot. They moved as silently as shadows, startling him when they suddenly reappeared. Finally, only Estanzio returned.

"Leave *caballo*," he said. "More *soldado* come."

415

Gil tied the horses and followed Estanzio. The soldiers, he decided, had set up their camp maybe three miles away from the border. Mariposa and Estanzio had slipped dangerously near, viewing the activity from a slope that offered no cover other than scraggly greasewood. It was an exceptional point of observation, the cover being so poor that nobody but a pair of Indians would have dared risk it. Then Gil saw the soldiers Estanzio had spoken of. They rode in from the northwest in a column of twos, and Gil counted thirty-two. One of them was an officer whose rank he was unable to determine from so great a distance. Estanzio caught Gil's eye with a silent question. Gil nodded, pointing to the distant columns of arriving soldiers. He must remain long enough to determine what these new arrivals might do. If theirs had been a long ride, if they needed food and rest, they might do exactly as Clay had predicted, and wait for darkness. These men would swell the Mexican forces to more than sixty.

Gil heard the officer give the order to dismount, then heard him dismiss the men. They immediately began unsaddling their horses. It was a good sign. Finally, Gil saw the newly arrived officer conferring with none other than Major Gomez Farias. Again Estanzio caught Gil's eye, and Gil nodded. He followed Mariposa and Estanzio back to the horses, and they mounted. Kicking their horses into a slow gallop, they soon reached the canyon, where Gil made a quick report, followed by a recommendation.

"Thirty-two more soldiers have arrived," said Gil. "Either from border patrol or from Meoqui. We're outnumbered almost three to one, and with the numbers on their side, they'll believe they can take us anytime they feel like it."

"So they'll hold off and hit us after dark," said Van.

"We can't count on that," said Clay.

"No," said Gil, "we can't. This canyon makes a fine holding pen, but if we're caught here in a cross fire — day or night — it'll be the Alamo all over again. I believe we ought to have Mariposa and Estanzio watch that Mex camp until sundown. If they break camp and show any signs of comin' after us before dark, we need to know. We dare not get trapped in this canyon with the Mex soldiers on the rims."

"I'll go along with that all the way," said Clay. "If these soldiers make no move before dark, we'll know they aim to come after us tonight, or lay for us near the border. So unless they make some move between now and sundown, we'll wait until it's good dark, and hit 'em with another stampede. This time we'll be right on the heels of it, our guns ready."

It was a plan satisfactory to each of them, better than anything they'd had up to now. Mariposa and Estanzio rode out to begin their vigil, with the next six hours perhaps to determine the fate of them all. Clay and Van took the opportunity to talk to some of the bedraggled Texans who had made the break with Gil, Van, and Long John. Gil knelt beside the blanketed Solano, touching the Indian's

417

forehead. While there was no sweat, there was no fever either. Suddenly Solano blinked his eyes, and they met Gil's.

"*Fracaso*," said Solano.

"No," said Gil, "you're not a failure, Solano. We're near the border, we have the herds together, and we're still going to Texas. You will live to go with us, *amigo*."

Solano had closed his eyes and said no more. Gil was unaware Angelina stood behind him until she spoke.

"He believes he failed. That will hurt him more than his wounds."

Gil got to his feet and turned to face her.

"I reckon it will," he said, "but this whole thing seemed near impossible, even if everything had gone right. Luck's been with us; I just hope it holds a little while longer."

"Thank you for your kindness to Solano," she said. "It is because of you that we took the risk of seeing to his wounds this morning. You are a strong man, Gil Austin. I am proud you are a friend to Clay and to Solano. It is my wish that you will become a friend to me."

She turned away and he watched her go. She was an enigma, in her own way as strong as any of them, and living proof of what Gil had long believed. Clay Duval was the luckiest man alive.

They all watched the westering sun, each hoping they wouldn't see Mariposa or Estanzio until purple shadows marked the coming of the night. By the hour their chances improved, and miraculously, so did Solano. The early attention to his wounds, his being bundled in blankets, and the potent, highly alcoholic pulque, had made a difference. He had developed no fever.

"I know it ain't possible," said Clay, "but I just wish he was able to stay in his saddle instead of bein' tied belly down across it. His wounds will break loose and bleed again."

They began breaking camp an hour before sundown. When Mariposa and Estanzio returned, they would be ready to move out. The horse herd had been bunched at the south end of the canyon. The longhorns would lead the drive, and eventually the stampede. They put off tying Solano across his saddle until the last minute. Then Mariposa and Estanzio rode in, and it was time to move out.

"No ride belly down," said Solano. His pride had suffered enough; he was drawing the line. His eyes were wide open and he still had no fever.

"He's got sand," said Long John. "Let'm straddle the hoss like a man. Can't hurt him no worse'n bein' roped across the saddle."

"That's gospel," said Van, "if he don't fall."

"No fall," said Solano. "No fall."

Clay and Gil released him from the blankets in which he'd been wrapped. Solano rolled over and hoisted himself to his knees. Angelina tried to get to him, to help him, but Clay held her back. Solano had to do it himself. Taking hold of the offside stirrup, he tried to get to his feet. Three times he tried, and three times he failed. But on the fourth attempt he made it. For a while he only stood there, and when he could

419

delay no longer, he then managed to get his right foot in the offside stirrup. Then, with his right hand gripping the horn, he tried to mount. Time after time he tried and failed. Any man there would have helped him, but they knew better. It was a struggle that only Solano could win. His bronze face paled and beads of sweat dripped off his chin. Finally, still lacking the strength, but making up the difference in raw nerve, he cleared the horse's rump with his left leg. Gripping the horn with his right hand, he settled himself in the saddle. He sat there breathing hard, sweating harder, but there was an unmistakable look of triumph in his dark eyes.

"Let's move 'em out!" shouted Gil.

The longhorns had grazed all day and had drunk their fill. Again they were taking the trail in the twilight, but it no longer seemed strange to them. Gil, Clay, and Ramon led the herd. Even as the horse herd brought up the rear of the drive, Mariposa and Estanzio remained with it. Solano rode with them, ramrod straight in the saddle, whatever the cost. At his request, he had his own rifle in the boot. Because of his wound, Clay had refused to allow him to buckle on his gun rig and pistol.

"We're maybe ten miles from the border," said Gil, "so that means we're seven miles south of the soldier camp. When we're close enough to start the stampede, Mariposa and Estanzio will bring the horses on up near the longhorns. Then Mariposa will sing his cougar song, and if we know what's good for us, we'll get out from in front of this herd."

"I like this," said Clay, "runnin' a stampede right through that soldier camp. They'll be so almighty busy dodgin' them horns and hooves, they won't think of grabbin' a gun."

"I hope that's how it is," said Gil. "There's still more of them, and if we stop to fight, some of us will die. Shoot only if you're forced to. We're not out to see how many Mex soldiers we can kill. All we want is to cross that border into Texas."

It was important that the longhorns be kept bunched, since they would lead the stampede. Gil had placed most of the riders directly behind the longhorn herd, because that was where they'd be the most needed. Following the cougar cry, the horse herd wouldn't need any prodding. Gil had Rosa behind the horse herd with the Indian riders, because that's where he would be. Once the stampede was under way, the drag — behind the horse herd — would become the most vulnerable position. A soldier getting his hands on a gun was unlikely to even get a shot, except at the drag riders. Once the herd began to run, Gil, Clay, and Ramon would ride out of its path and fall back. The three of them would be with the drag, behind the horse herd, before the stampede hit the soldier camp. There, the three of them could keep an eye on Rosa, as well as the wounded Solano. Once the stampede crossed the Rio Grande, without considering Solano, there would be five riders to discourage pursuit.

Van and Long John were ahead of the horse

herd, directly behind the longhorns. If the longhorns were kept running hard, they would wreak enough havoc among the soldiers that the horse herd — and the riders following — should pass unmolested. If it all worked according to plan, they ought to cross the border without losing a rider. Clay had insisted that Angelina remain with Van and Long John, between the horse herd and the longhorns. It was already dark, too early for the moon, and the stars seemed dim and far away.

"We're close," said Gil. "Get ready for the cougar."

He kicked his horse into a gallop, followed by Ramon and Clay. They must distance themselves from the longhorn leaders, so that they had time to ride free of the stampeding herd. Gil had forgotten just how real, how devastating, Mariposa's cougar squall was. When it came, even with him expecting it, cold chills galloped up his spine. The lead steers, bawling in terror, lit out like the devil himself was two jumps behind, snorting fire and brimstone. Gil, Clay, and Ramon rode beyond the running herd, and it fanned out into a horned, hooved avalanche half a mile wide. Right behind it came the horse herd. Gil, Clay, and Ramon fell in behind the last horses. Rosa rode her 'bueno mulo' alongside Solano's horse, as Gil had told her to. While the riders watched Rosa, they could also watch Solano without his being aware of it. Gil, Clay, and Ramon dropped back to join Mariposa and Estanzio, putting Solano and Rosa safely between them and the horse herd. The cougar scream fresh in their memories, the horses galloped madly, seeking to escape.

* * *

Major Juan Davila and his thirty-one men had been on border patrol for a month, and had been on their way to the Matamoros outpost when they encountered Major Gomez Farias and his thirty-five soldiers. Farias had explained the situation facing them, and had found Major Davila more amused than sympathetic.

"*Infierno*," said Davila, "since you have been unable to capture or kill these few gringos, we will help you. But not today, not tonight. We have ridden more than three hundred miles, and we are weary. What is the hurry? We are between the gringos and the border, no? We shall take them at our leisure, when we have rested."

Farias had said nothing, but he was furious. Must he do everything? Only his watchfulness, his rifle, had prevented their horses being stampeded. He had organized the pursuit, getting his men to the border ahead of the fleeing gringos and their herds. Once it was dark, without endangering himself or his men, he had planned to ambush the gringos. He had vowed that he would yet, with or without the help of Davila and his soldiers. But when he approached his own men, they refused to follow him! Were they not as good as Major Davila and his men? They too would wait until the dawn. Taking his rifle, Farias left the camp, walking toward the south. He felt restless, frustrated, and wished to be alone. When he first became aware of the alien sound, it might have been the far off roar of an approaching storm. But it was a sound Farias had heard before, and he knew what it was. By the Blessed Virgin, the gringo herd was running, getting closer, even as he listened!

Farias ran, knowing he could never reach the camp ahead of the thundering herd. The wind had changed, coming from the south, and when he looked back, dust stung his eyes. Farias ran on, and when he again looked fearfully behind him, he could see them coming. They were a black, moving mass, seeming to stretch from one horizon to the other! Farias could not outrun them, and when he came to an upthrust clump of rocks, he dropped gratefully behind them. He fired in the air, trying to warn the doomed camp, doubting they were aware of the oncoming wave of destruction. Finally, somewhere ahead, he heard a few scattered shots and shouts. But their pitiful attempts to turn the stampede were in vain, and it thundered on, their shots, shouts, and screams only adding to the momentum. Somewhere there would be gringo riders, and Farias cocked his rifle. The longhorns had passed, and he was surrounded by horses. Suddenly there were riders, and he fired. But his shot was returned, and the slug slammed into his throat. Time stopped, and he fell on his face, his life spilling into the sand . . .

★ ★ ★

When the lead sang past Gil's head, he drew and fired at the muzzle flash, and the rifle spoke no more. His horse shied away from scattered, still-glowing embers that had been a fire, and from the battered, ugly things that had once been men. In the dim starlight, Gil could see trampled saddles, blankets, and pieces of clothing. The horse herd had begun to tire and to slow, its terror subsiding. Mariposa loosed another cougar cry, and the drag riders had to gallop their horses to keep up. The longhorns had begun to lag, but the cougar seemed in hot pursuit, driving new life into their pounding hooves. The lead steers hit the Rio Grande on the run.

"Hieeeyah!" shouted Van Austin. "Hieeeyah! Run you longhorn bastards, run! We're on the Bandera Trail, ridin' home!"

Gil and Clay raised a shout of their own when their horses splashed into the shallow river that was the border between Mexico and the Republic of Texas. When the herds again slowed, Gil and Clay popped some flanks with doubled lariats. They wanted none of the herd wandering back across the river during the night, or even close to it. The Mexicans might be furious enough to seek revenge. The longhorns were tired and more than ready to call it a night. Clay, Gil, and Ramon galloped their horses ahead of the leaders and started them milling. Angelina and the riders who had followed the longhorn stampede rode up, followed by Rosa on her mule. The Indian trio had remained with the horse herd.

"We're home," said Gil. "If anybody's hurt, sing out." They were silent.

"I am going to ride back and see about Solano," said Angelina.

"I'll go with you," said Clay.

"We gonna stay here fer the night," Long John asked, "er push on?"

"There'll be a poor moon," said Gil, "and it'll rise late. Besides, the horses and longhorns are give out, so we'll stay here until first light. I don't want these horses and cows even close to the Rio Grande, so we'll need some night hawks. I'll take charge of the first watch, and Ramon, you take the second. We'll change the watch at two o'clock. Ramon will need three riders, and I'll need three. Volunteers accepted."

"I'll take first watch," said Van.

"Reckon I will too," said Long John.

"Me," cried Rosa. "I no sleepy."

Ramon got his volunteers for the second watch, and when Clay and Angelina returned, they had a favorable report on Solano. The Indian seemed no worse for the ride, and still had no fever. Mariposa, Estanzio, and Solano bedded down near the horse herd, and there wasn't a sound out of the longhorns. Circling the herd on her mule, Rosa wore them all out with excited chatter.

"I ain't never seen it so quiet," said Long John, "but fer the kid."

"Enjoy it while you can," said Gil. "Texas has its share of rustlers and renegade Indians."

"After all them Mex soldiers," said Long John, "I could damn near make friends wi'

426

the rustlers an' renegade Injuns. But not yer bastard neighbors. I ain't gon' be s'prised at nothin' they done whilst ye was gone."

"You run out on us, Long John," said Van as ominously as he could. "We get home and fine the place burnt to the ground, what do you aim to do about it?"

"Gut-shoot them that done it," said Long John, dead serious, "er git me a *cuchillo* an' whack off some pieces o' their carcass they'd purely hate t' lose."

"Which pieces?" Rosa asked, becoming interested.

"Rosa," said Gil, "this does not concern you."

"Do so!" said Rosa. "He *malo bastardo Tejano. Bueno hombre.*"

Van and Long John slapped their thighs and howled with laughter.

"Pappy," said Van, when he could speak, "you purely got your work cut out for you!"

"Smart little senorita," said Long John, flattered by Rosa's unflattering appraisal. "Jus' gimme a chancet, an' I'll take on them renegade Injuns, rustlers, an' yer bastard neighbors t' boot."

Come the dawn, they were in for a surprise. Their stampede had picked up another thirty head of horses.

"If we'd stayed a mite longer," Van crowed, "every soldier in Mexico would of been afoot."

"Thank God we were able to quit the game while we were ahead," said Gil. "With the Austin luck, if we'd stayed longer, we'd have been backed against a wall, shot dead, and left for buzzard bait. I hope I can go the rest of my life without seeing a Mexican soldier."

"*Soldado bastardos*," said Rosa. "Kill, feed to *busardos*."

"Amen," said Long John reverently. "Girl, if ye was two er three year older, I'd grab ye an' run off t' Californy."

25

SEPTEMBER 15, 1843. The Republic of Texas, south of San Antonio.

Gil rose at first light, but he had something he wished to do before the drive took the trail north to the Bandera range. He waited until breakfast was done before he spoke.

"You gents that busted out of the prison in Mexico City are free to ride," he said. "You're welcome to the horses you're riding, the saddles, rifles, and belt rigs, all courtesy of the Mexican army. I reckon you all have kin that don't know if you're alive or dead, and was I you, I'd be on my way to set their minds at ease."

"Whar be ye from originally?" asked one of the men.

"Missouri," said Gil.

"No more," said the other. "Yer a Texan, and a man to ride the river with. God bless ye!"

There were shouts of agreement from the others. They lined up, every man, to shake the hands of everybody in the outfit. Even young Rosa. They lingered longest with Clay and Angelina, and when they rode out, their Texas yells startled some of the grazing longhorns.

"Most of them," said Clay, "I didn't even learn their names, but now that they're ridin' out, I kinda hate to see 'em go."

"The frontier's as unpredictable as it is

violent," said Gil. "You may ride other trails with those hombres, where a friend with a fast gun is all that's standin' between you and a pine box."

"Now," said Van, with a look at Long John, "I reckon there's nothin' for us to do 'cept ride on to our Bandera range and see what kind of mood our bastard neighbors are in."

"Them Mex soldiers took m' *cuchillo*," said Long John. "Need t' git me another'n b'fore we show yer neighbors how the cow et the cabbage."

"*Si*," said Rosa. "Whack off pieces of carcass."

Only Gil understood why Van and Long John thought Rosa's words were so hilariously funny.

"We ought to shy away from San Antone," said Clay, "and come in to the Bandera range from the west."

"I think you're right," said Gil. "We can reach our range without crossing any of the other grants. Once we've spread these horses and longhorns out over seventy-seven thousand acres, nobody's going to know exactly how many we have."

"Damn good idee," said Long John. "Be jus' like yer neighbors t' take 'em a share, 'thout even askin'."

They moved out in a northwesterly direction under a sky the hue of blue bonnets, and they saw nobody. Gil called a halt an hour before sundown, and they bedded down the herds. They started the cook fire, taking their ease in a manner that hadn't been possible for long months.

"I have never seen the sky so blue, or so much of it," said Angelina. "It seems to go on forever. It is like another world here."

"*Si*," said Rosa. "No *soldados*."

"I almost miss the Mex soldiers," said Van. "After dodgin' 'em for most of a year, it seems like a bunch oughta come gallopin' over that ridge."

Then, as though materialized by the power of suggestion, five riders came galloping over that very ridge.

"Damn," yelped Long John, grabbing his pistol. "Now look what ye done did."

Gil, Van, and Clay got up, thumbs hooked in their pistol belts. Ramon and some of the other riders stood ready. The five horsemen reined up, one of them walking his horse a few yards ahead of the others.

"Howdy," he said. "Name's Wallace. Folks call me Big Foot, and I don't fault 'em for that."[1]

Gil relaxed. These were Texas Rangers.

"I'm Gil Austin, and this is my brother Van. This is our outfit."

"These other hombres," said Wallace, "is Bell,

---

[1] A. A. (Big Foot) Wallace participated in the fight at Bandera Pass in 1842. He, along with Ben McCulloch, P. H. Bell, and Creed Taylor were all Rangers who survived the ambush, and went on to become well-known in Texas history.

Taylor, Gannon, and Wood. I knowed Steve Austin. Texas owes him plenty."

"He was our uncle," said Gil, "and we have grants near Bandera Pass. It was some fight you gents had with the Comanches there last year."

"God," said Wallace, "don't remind me. It was a nightmare. Forty of us, and near a hundred of them. We lost five good men, every one a friend. But we got a bunch of them, includin' their chief. You must be the gents Ben McCulloch was talkin' about. Said a pair of his boys that fought Santa Anna at San Jacinto was goin' into Mejicano land, to give Santa Anna a chance to get even."

"Bad timing, for him," said Gil. "Somebody kicked him out before he got a shot at us. Cool your saddles, gents, and we'll share bacon and beans. Sorry we got no coffee."

"*Mucho gracias*," said Wallace. The Rangers dismounted, shucked their saddles, and allowed their horses to roll.

"*Soldados*?" Rosa asked, suspicious.

"No," said Gil. "Texas Rangers. They're with us. They fight with the *soldados*."

Wallace had introduced his men, and Gil had almost forgotten to introduce his outfit. He did so, dwelling on the fact that they were once the riders for the Mendoza ranch.

"I've heard of the Mendoza horses," said Wallace. "My God, with a bloodline like that, you can build a horse ranch that'll be the envy of the whole frontier."

"We aim to," said Gil. "We purely went

through hell, gettin' 'em out of Mexico. What's the situation between the United States and Texas, and between Texas and Mexico?"

"Damn Yankees in the Congress are trying to keep us out of the Union," said Wallace, "but they can't do it. Time's soon comin' when the Republic of Texas will be no more. We'll be part of the United States.[1] As for Mexico, they still won't recognize our independence. I look for war, especially now that Texas is about to become a state. We'll have to give the Mex army a few more doses of what we give it at San Jacinto, and by the Eternal, we'll do it. With or without the help of the United States. Sam Houston's had about enough, and that's the sentiments of every Texan."

Gil, Van, and Clay were hungry for news, and they enjoyed the exchange with the Rangers. In return, they found Wallace and his men intensely interested in a firsthand account of what they had experienced in Mexico. The

---

[1] Northern senators opposed Texas becoming part of the Union, lest it enter as a "slave" state. Politicians saw it as a ploy by the South to gain seats in the Senate. In despair, fearing invasion by Mexico, Texas turned to England, which offered to make the Republic of Texas a British protectorate. President James K. Polk, aghast at such a possibility, drove Congress to immediately annex Texas, or risk enforcing the Monroe Doctrine against England.

Rangers listened in awe as the trio of Texans told of leaving afoot the very general who had overthrown Santa Anna, of the daring escape from the Matamoros outpost, and finally, the glorious stampede through the soldier camp and across the Rio Grande.

"By the Almighty!" shouted Wallace in glee, "Sam Houston's got to hear this!"

Clay, Gil, and Van filled in the rest of the story, telling of the lack of soldiers and the unpopularity of Mexico's continual strife with Texas.

"It's not the will of the Mexican people," said Gil, "but the greed of the politicians in Mexico City. Santa Anna's spent millions on parties and lavish living; that's why the country's broke. I believe he's kept this war talk going as an excuse to tax the people and pillage the treasury. The Mexican people think of us as they thought of themselves before they finally got Spain off their backs."

"I like the way you gents kept your eyes and ears open," said Wallace. "You got a good handle on all this. I believe Sam Houston will want to talk to all three of you. Will you go to Austin to meet with him?"

"We'll go," said Gil. "Get word to us."

"*Bueno*," said Wallace. "Now, since you're going to be driving through South Texas for the next few days, there's a problem you need to be aware of. God knows, the constant trouble with Mexico is a thorn in our side, but we're here for another reason. With the Mex soldiers snipin' at us, and us throwin' lead at them, the damn Comancheros are taking advantage of us all. There's one bunch — a good dozen of the bastards — that's led by a pair of no-account *Mejicano* brothers, Manuel and Miguel Torres."

"I heard some talk of them in Mexico," said Clay. "They're not well thought of."

"Nor should they be," said Wallace. "It's one thing to drive Texas horses to Mexico, and Mex horses to Texas, but it takes real scum to steal human captives from their families."

"For ransom?" Gil asked.

"Not necessarily," said Wallace. "Some of the families have paid the ransom, but none of the captives have been released. Of course, they don't limit themselves to any particular crime. I mentioned the human victims so you can see them for the sorry lot they are. They'll be drawn to your herd of horses like flies to a honey jug, and I don't mean just while you're on the trail. Last few months, they've raised hell in and around San Antone, and your place won't be that far away. Even after these horses are on your range, you'd best keep your powder dry. And that especially is true while you're out here in the open. They won't hesitate to come into your camp at night and slit your throats, or shoot you in the back from ambush at any time."

"Thanks," said Gil. "My riders are partial to these horses, and have been through a lot for them. If this Torres bunch shows up on our range with ideas of takin' our horses, you won't be troubled with 'em. Just ride in, and we'll show you the remains, whatever the buzzards and coyotes didn't want."

"We'd be obliged," said Wallace, with a chuckle.

★ ★ ★

September 16, 1843. The Republic of Texas, south of San Antonio.

The Rangers stayed the night and rode out after breakfast. Gil moved out the herds, heading them northwest. Now that they were in Texas, without the constant threat of danger, Angelina set about making friends with Rosa. She made little progress. Rosa followed Gil everywhere, and when she wasn't with him, she was tagging after Long John. She liked Van and Ramon, but she wasn't all that fond of anybody else. To his regret, Clay tried teasing her. She became angry and said some things to him in rapid Spanish that left him embarrassed and the rest of the riders laughing. Gil had no idea what he was going to do with her. So far as he knew, she hadn't had a bath, or her hair washed, since he'd found her at that desolate cabin. Angelina had said she wanted him for a friend; when they reached the Bandera range, he was going to test that friendship.

When they found good water and graze and settled down for the night, they also found ashes from a recent fire. There were tracks of eleven horses, all shod, and they led north, toward San Antonio. Estanzio looked at the ashes and the tracks.

436

"Hoy," he said.

"They spent the night here," said Clay, "so that means they must have come a ways, with a ways to go."

"Them Comancheros, goin' t' San Antone t' raise hell," said Long John.

"From what the Rangers told us," said Gil, "the numbers are right. It's late in the day, but come mornin' I want to know for sure that this bunch kept goin' the way they were headed when they left here. For tonight we'll divide the outfit into two watches."

But they saw nobody, and heard only the distant cries of coyotes. At dawn, during breakfast, Gil told them what he had in mind.

"We'll take the trail as usual," he said, "but I want Mariposa to trail those eleven horsemen. They could have doubled back, and be layin' for us."

"I go," said Solano.

"Next time," said Gil.

"Mariposa looks as much Mexican as he does Indian," said Van, "and in Texas that can get a man shot. It ain't a good idea, sending Mariposa, Solano, or Estanzio out alone. From a distance they could be gunned down for Mexicans."

"He may have somethin'," said Clay. "We've been in Mexico so long, we're overlookin' the obvious."

"I reckon you're both right," said Gil. "Van, go with Mariposa, and if you meet any Texans, you do the talking."

Gil got the herds moving, while Mariposa

and Van rode north. While Gil hadn't set any limit on how far they should trail these riders, Van had set one of his own. When the sun was noon-high, if these riders had not changed direction, he and Mariposa would return to the trail drive. They had dismounted in a stand of cottonwoods to rest the horses when they saw the two riders. They were riding hard toward them. The front rider rode with a desperation that said his cause was lost. The pursuer gained rapidly, shaking out his loop as he rode. The front rider hit the end of the rope and was jerked brutally out of the saddle. Van wouldn't have gotten involved, but the fallen rider was dragged to his feet and then knocked to the ground.

"Stay here, Mariposa," said Van.

The rider who had done the roping was so involved in the beating of his lesser opponent, he didn't immediately see Van. When he did, he was stooped over the second rider, who lay facedown.

"That's enough," said Van.

The man's hand was on the butt of his pistol when he changed his mind. Van had drawn and had him covered. He was Mexican, with a knife scar that ran from the corner of his mouth along his left jaw, so that he wore a permanent lopsided grin. He wore a two-gun rig, and the haft of a knife was visible above his belt. He had cruel eyes, and he shuffled his feet like an angry bull. He looked as though he was working himself into a state where he might draw one or both pistols, and Van dared not take his eyes off the man. Finally the Mexican spoke.

"Senor, this is none of your business."

"For the love of God!" cried the rider on the ground, "please help me!"

A slender, dark-haired girl was on her hands and knees, blood dripping from her smashed nose and mouth. It was a distraction that almost cost Van his life. He still had his pistol in his hand, and it was all that saved him. A slug burned its way along his ribs, just under his left arm, and he shot the Mexican twice, just above the haft of the knife in his belt. The man flopped on his back and didn't move. Van holstered his pistol and knelt beside the girl. He took the rope off and helped her to her feet. He saw Mariposa coming on the run, leading Van's horse and the one the girl had been riding. With his help, she got shakily to her feet.

"The others will be coming!" she cried, her voice shaking. "You just killed Manuel Torres. When I got loose, he came after me, because they — he — said I belonged to him."

"You're not with him by choice, then."

"Dear God, no!" she cried. "I am Dorinda Jabez. They stole me from my home on the Atascosa River, south of San Antonio."

Without a word Van led her to her horse and helped her to mount. He swung into his saddle, following the girl as they galloped to catch up to Mariposa. The girl kept looking back, searching with fearful eyes for the expected pursuit. Mariposa set the pace, his horse at a slow gallop. They couldn't travel as far as fast, but it was an enduring gait. Any faster and their horses would be spent and lathered in half an hour. Van studied the girl. She didn't look a day older than Angelina, and she wore her hair short. From a distance that was why he hadn't known she was female. The old shirt she wore was too large, but as he helped her mount, he discovered that beneath it she was very much a girl. She wore tight-legged riding breeches, like a Mexican. She had blue eyes, and but for the bruises, a fair complexion. He grinned. Ten damn Mexican outlaws on his trail, and he had taken the time to notice the color of her eyes.

"They're coming," cried the girl desperately. "They're after us!"

He looked back, and they sure as hell *were* coming. But at a gallop that would soon have their horses lathered and spent. The question was, did he, the girl, and Mariposa have enough of a lead to stay out of rifle range until these renegades had exhausted their horses? He began looking ahead, seeking some cover, if they had to make a stand. Not much of a stand, he thought grimly, two rifles against ten. They might get close enough for the outfit to hear the gunfire, but could he and Mariposa hold them off until help came? He could hear the distant popping of rifles. They were still out of range, but their eagerness was getting the best of them. Wallace and his Rangers were looking for these bastards along the border, and they had, that very night, reached San Antonio. Just when he thought the situation couldn't possibly get any worse, it did. The girl's horse stepped in a hole, and she again was flung to the ground. Van didn't even have to examine the

440

horse. Eventually it would be all right, but now it limped. He leaned out of his saddle and gave her a hand up behind him. Mariposa had reined up, waiting. He seemed calm, in no hurry. Van reflected on all the months he had known Mariposa and Estanzio, and not once had he seen any evidence of fear, or even alarm. This very moment Mariposa might be only minutes from death, yet he waited patiently until they caught up. The girl was slender, trim, but it was still a double load for the horse. Van leaned forward, listening. He prayed he wouldn't hear the animal heaving for air, but he would if they continued at this pace. He was only delaying the inevitable. Already Mariposa was holding his horse in check, so that they could keep up to him. Van urged the horse ahead until they were riding alongside the Indian. Wordlessly, Van pointed to some rock outcroppings ahead, and there they reined up. Van dismounted, taking his rifle from the boot.

"Ride," he told the girl. "Mariposa will take you to our outfit and send some help. I'll stand them off and buy you some time."

"No," she said, sliding off the horse. "The horse is already tired from carrying the two of us. I won't leave you to . . . to their mercy, after you saved me. I can shoot. Ask your friend to let me use his rifle, and we'll both stand them off. Then he can ride for help without me slowing him down on a tired horse."

It was a magnificent thing to do, and it made perfect sense. Mariposa snatched his rifle from the boot and handed it to her. He plucked off

441

Van's hat and dropped his extra ammunition into it. He passed the hat to Van and without a word kicked his horse into a fast gallop. From his own saddlebags Van added to their ammunition and passed the hat to the girl. Looping the reins around the saddle horn, he sent the tired horse trotting away, out of the possible line of fire. There it could cool off while he and the girl fought for their lives. Following her to the fortress that had to secure them until help arrived, he found there wasn't as much cover as he had hoped. They could fire from their knees, but that was all. Once the outlaws worked their way around behind, there would be even less cover. It would force them belly down, just to avoid being hit, with little or no chance to return the fire. Her nose had stopped bleeding, and despite their perilous situation, she possessed a calmness that he lacked.

"Have they harmed you?" he asked. "I mean . . . besides the times I saw him hit you."

"No," she said. "The — That would have come later. That's why I ran; I'd rather be dead than violated by that beast. That hurt, when he roped me off the horse. My rump feels like it's been beaten with a singletree."

There was no pretense about her, and he grinned at her frankness. He was brought swiftly back to the present when lead sang off the rock face that shielded them. It was only to get their attention.

"Listen to me, gringo. I am Miguel Torres, and you have murdered my *hermano*. For that you are going to die. Surrender and we will

442

spare the girl. If you do not, then she will die with you."

Before Van could respond, the girl took matters into her own hands.

"I'd die," she shouted, "before I'd live with dogs like you!"

"Torres," Van yelled, "if you're the *malo hombre* you think you are, then prove it. Just you and me, without your *perras* to protect you. I will kill you with a knife, with a gun, or with my hands. It is your choice."

"You are the fool, gringo. You take the chance because you have nothing to lose. I prefer to kill you at my leisure, without risk to myself."

There it was. They'd be given no quarter, and taking his lead from the girl's response, Van wouldn't ask any.

★ ★ ★

Mariposa rode at a fast gallop, a thing he seldom did because it soon exhausted a horse. But this was an emergency. Normally squaws said or did little that impressed him, but when the dark-haired one had taken his rifle to side Van against the outlaws, Mariposa had been touched by her courage. It was the only way in which she could have gotten to him, and he vowed she wouldn't die. He listened for shots, knowing that when the shooting began, he had little time. When he judged he was near enough that his own shots might be heard by the trail-drive riders, he drew his pistol and fired three times, deliberately spacing the shots. His heart leaped when somewhere ahead three quick shots answered him.

★ ★ ★

"Trouble," said Gil. "Clay, pick four men and ride."

"Estanzio, Solano, Ramon, and Long John," said Clay.

Clay led out, and they rode hard. By the time they met Mariposa, they could hear the rattle of gunfire somewhere ahead of them.

★ ★ ★

"Torres," said Mariposa. It was enough.

Clay and his riders rode at a fast gallop. Mariposa slowed his tired horse and rode on. He would get fresh horses for Van and the girl, and return.

The Torres gang fired their first volley, and then a second, accomplishing nothing. It was a standoff the outlaws wouldn't allow to continue, and their silent rifles told Van that he and the girl were about to be caught in a deadly cross fire. But it didn't happen. When the rifles cut loose again, somewhere to the rear of their position, Van heard the horses running hard. The riders were well out of range, headed northwest. The outlaws had found themselves in a potential cross fire between Van and the girl and riders coming from the south. When Clay and his riders reined up, Van and the girl stepped out to meet them. Clay looked at the dark-haired girl and then at Van.

"Well, now," he grinned, "like I always said, you Austins are brighter than you look. Don't just stand there like a dumb cowboy, introduce us to the beautiful lady."

Van did. They rested the horses, and while they waited, Estanzio found Van's horse. The animal was rested, dry, and cropping grass. Van and the girl again rode double, this time at a slower gait. Eventually they met Mariposa with fresh horses, and with Van's horse on a lead rope, Van and the girl rode the fresh mounts. Shorthanded, unsure of what brand of trouble Van and Mariposa had encountered, Gil had halted the drive until he knew what the problem was. When the riders returned, Van included, Gil sighed with relief. Van dismounted and helped the girl.

"This is Dorinda Jabez," said Van. "The Torres boys had plans for her, but she got loose. When I tried to help her, Manuel objected, and I had to shoot him. That upset the others a mite, and they got mean."

The trail drive moved on, and Dorinda Jabez rode with it. While Gil was aware that her family should know she was well. He was reluctant to send her home immediately. The Torres gang was out there somewhere, probably seeking revenge, and it made sense to take her with them. Once they were on the Bandera range, Gil reckoned Van would jump at the chance to take her home.

26

SEPTEMBER 20, 1843. Cotulla, Republic of Texas.

South of the village of Cotulla, Gil headed the trail drive due north. It would take them almost fifty miles west of San Antonio. Cotulla consisted of a general store, a saloon, and a blacksmith shop.

"We can get some coffee beans here," said Van.

"No, we can't," said Gil. "We got no money."

"We'll swap them a cow," said Van, "or a horse."

"I don't think so," said Gil. "We're not more than a hundred miles south of our Bandera range. I want these horses and cows settled on our graze, without drawin' unnecessary attention to them. We didn't leave owing anybody, so we'll have a line of credit in San Antone. We'll ride there for the supplies we'll need."

They passed to the west of Cotulla, making their camp twenty miles north, on the Frio River. When it came Van's turn to night-hawk, he had begun taking the second watch, and Dorinda Jabez was riding with him. Gil had raised no objection, nor had he more than spoken to her since her arrival. She had been friendly to them all, especially so to Angelina and Rosa. But there were nights when she walked her horse alongside Van's, circling the herd for an hour or more, neither of them speaking. She had told Van little about herself, except that she came from a farm, rather than a ranch. Van knew she had some feeling for him beyond mere gratitude. When he helped her mount or dismount, her hand always clung to his a little longer than it needed to. Van had begun to think beyond these nights on the trail drive, beyond the time she would return to her home. Tonight, she seemed closer to him than ever.

"This is so peaceful," she said. "If only Mama and Daddy knew I am alive and well, I could ride like this forever. I think I would like a change of clothes too," she added.

"The next decent river where we bed down for the night," said Van, "we can find a private place for you to take a bath. I'll stay back a ways," he added hastily, "and see that nobody bothers you."

"I'll do that," she said, "on one condition. I don't want you too far away; I wouldn't feel safe." She spoke softly, almost in a whisper.

She reined up her horse. When he moved his near and leaned toward her, she met him halfway . . .

★ ★ ★

Another day's drive took them to the confluence of the Frio River and Hondo Creek. For two days they followed Hondo Creek for forty miles, until it veered west, toward the little town of Hondo.

"If my memory's anywhere close to right," said Gil, "we're thirty miles south of Bandera range. If we get an early start and push hard, we'll be home tomorrow night."

★ ★ ★

September 24, 1843. The Bandera range.

"Ramon," said Gil, "we're on our range, and there's plenty of it. Just anywhere ahead you can turn the longhorns loose. The horses too. Startin' in the morning, we'll work from can till can't, branding the longhorns. Van will take Dorinda home. He'll be taking two packhorses with him, and on the way back he can stop in San Antone and load up on supplies. We've got a blessed plenty to do, but once these longhorns are wearin' brands, we'll let our next project be the building of a bunkhouse."

"Am I to live in the bunkhouse?" Angelina asked innocently.

"I reckon," said Gil, just as innocently, "unless Clay had some other arrangement in mind."

"Looks like we'll *all* be living in the bunkhouse," said Van.

They had come within sight of their cabin, and smoke spiraled from the chimney. Ramon and the riders had begun scattering the longhorns on the new range, and the horses were already grazing.

"Come on, Van," said Gil. "The rest of you hold back until we find out who's squattin' in

448

our place." They dismounted and approached on foot.

Before they reached the house, the door opened and a man stood there with a shotgun in the crook of his arm. A pistol belt sagged low on his right hip, the weapon's shiny walnut grips attesting to frequent use. The man raised the muzzle of the shotgun. Gil reined up, Van following suit. The wielder of the shotgun had shaggy black hair, many days' growth of matching whiskers, and the nondescript clothes he wore looked as though they hadn't been washed — or changed — since the flood. His eyes were cruel, and he spoke through clenched teeth.

"Git offa our place," he grunted. "You ain't welcome here."

"Friend," said Gil coldly, "you got that turned around all wrong. This is *our* place, and it's *you* that's not welcome here. You have fifteen minutes to get out of our house and off our grant."

A second man had moved in behind the first, and the newcomer presented no better appearance than his companion.

"You aim to make us go, I reckon," said the man with the shotgun.

"No," said Gil, "we're giving you a choice. You can leave here, alive and breathing, or you can stay, graveyard dead and not breathing."

"We been here eight months," said the second man, in a whining voice.

Van had moved to Gil's right, and stood with his thumbs hooked in his pistol belt.

"You quit yer claim," the second man continued. "You got no right . . . "

But Gil wasn't listening to him. His eyes were on the man with the shotgun. It was coming, and he was ready. When the shotgun roared, throwing its deadly charge where he had been standing, Gil was belly down, his pistol smoking. The shotgun fell clattering down the steps, and the second man was driven back by the body of the first. Gil got to his feet, moved to the side of the door and waited. He had holstered his pistol. Van had not moved.

"Don't shoot no more," cried the voice from inside the cabin. "I — I'm comin' out."

He stepped out slowly, his bedroll under his arm, his right hand up shoulder high.

"You have ten minutes," said Gil, "to saddle and ride."

Gil and Van watched him run to the log barn, three hundred yards away. When he rode out, he led a second saddled horse. Some of the other riders had advanced, Clay Duval leading Gil's and Van's horses.

"While it's still light," said Gil, "some of you take that skunk somewhere and plant him. There's shovels in the barn."

Cautiously, Gil made his way into the cabin. It was a mess, as he had expected. Some of their meticulously made furniture had been broken up and used for firewood. He found the other four rooms in no better condition. When he again reached the front door, the body of one of the former tenants was gone.

"I reckon," said Van, "we'll be rollin' in our blankets on the ground another night or two. They been keepin' hogs in there?"

"It would be cleaner if they had," said Gil.

★ ★ ★

That first night on the Bandera range, they dropped their bedrolls between the house and the barn. There would be long, hard days ahead, as they laid out the anticipated horse ranch and branded the longhorn cows. But before any of that was done, Gil intended to resolve the ownership of the Mendoza horses. He began by repeating the offer he had made Ramon Alcaraz and the Mendoza riders, promising them working shares in the proposed horse ranch.

"I reckon," said Gil, "I promised Ramon and his *bueno* vaqueros something that don't rightfully belong to me. While Victoria Mendoza is dead, Angelina Ruiz is alive and well. In Victoria's words, Van and me would get the horses we rode, some breeding stock, and the longhorn herd, once we reached Texas. Now, we can't honestly claim any more than that. Angelina, do you understand what I'm saying?"

"Yes," she said, "I understand. Clay and I have talked about it, and I will allow him to explain my feelings."

"I told her an Austin would give up the shirt on his back," Clay grinned, "if he wasn't sure he was entitled to it. Now, think on what I'm about to tell you, and save the bullyraggin' for later.

Once things are shaped up around here and the cows are branded, me and Angelina are going to San Antone and stand before a preacher. She knows more about me than anybody alive, and she's still willing; I got to hog-tie her permanent, before she changes her mind. Now, in view of that, Angelina wants to go ahead with the original plan, with every Mendoza rider getting wages *and* a working partnership in the new ranch. We want a piece of it ourselves, and Angelina has just one other wish. In memory of all that was, so that nobody forgets the origin of the bloodline, she wants us to register and continue the Winged M brand."

Gil grabbed the startled Angelina and kissed her long and hard.

"Whoa," shouted Clay, "we're only sharin' the horse ranch!"

They yelled, pumped Clay's hand, slapped him on the back, and Dorinda caught Angelina in a sincere embrace. Everybody got into the spirit except Rosa, and when most of the excitement had subsided, she took one of Angelina's hands to get her attention.

"*Bebe?*" she asked. "*Nino? Baptizar?*"

Rosa thought they were going before a priest to baptize a child! The uproar started all over again, and even Clay was embarrassed. Angelina took it in good humor, and caught up Rosa before she could say anything else.

"Senor Clay and I are going to marry, Rosa. I will cut your hair, give you a bath, and make you a new dress."

"No!" shouted Rosa, kicking to get loose. "No

452

want cut hair, no want bath, like britches! Why Rosa be punish when you marry?"

"By God," said Long John admiringly, "a genoowine Texas cowpuncher in the makin'!"

When the merriment had died down to a dull roar, Van spoke.

"I still aim to take Dorinda home tomorrow; if everybody's going to San Antone in a few days, is there any reason why I have to take more than one packhorse? Nobody's goin' to miss seein' old Clay get a ring put through his nose, so why don't I just bring enough supplies to last maybe two weeks?"

"I reckon we can live with that," said Gil, "but there's some things we must have. We all look like we come up dry after nine months on the grub line. I'll get with Ramon, and we'll make a list of what the riders need. Angelina, you make up a list of what you'll need for yourself and for Rosa."

"I ain't doubtin' our credit's good," said Van, "but we don't have two bits among us. Why don't I ask around and see if we can get a decent price for some of these longhorns?"

"Good idea," said Gil. "I reckon we can cull two or three hundred head, and we can drive them in when we go to see Clay and Angelina get tangled up in double harness."

★ ★ ★

At dawn Van saddled a horse for himself and one for Dorinda Jabez. From what the girl had told him, Van figured it at about a sixty-mile

453

ride. Dorinda already seemed like one of them, and it was difficult for them to let her go. Angelina hugged her and invited her to the wedding. Rosa wept, and Gil invited her to return as often as she could. They rode out, Van leading a packhorse and doubting it could carry all the goods that Gil and Angelina had requested.

"You didn't need to bring an extra horse," said Dorinda. "You could have used the one I'm riding for a packhorse."

"No," said Van, "the horse you're riding is yours. The saddle too."

He half expected her to object, but she accepted it in the spirit in which it had been offered.

"Thank you," she said. "I've never owned a horse before; we have mules."

"You ride well," he said.

"We're from Kentucky," she said, "and we had friends who raised horses. Beautiful horses. That's where I learned to ride, and I have missed them."

"You have a way with them; I've seen you with the Mendoza herd."

"If I had — or was near — such a herd," she laughed, "I'd be tempted to get myself a blanket and sleep with them."

They were three hours reaching San Antonio, and by-passed it to the west.

"I may be making a big mistake," said Van, "by not stopping in town and gettin' myself some new clothes. I look like a saddle tramp. I'd like to make a good enough impression on your mama and daddy, so they'll allow me to see you again."

"When I tell them what you did for me, they may not let you leave. Besides, I'll have something to say about that. I'll be twenty-two on my next birthday. I can't go to Angelina's wedding unless you come and get me. I doubt Daddy will let me out of the house alone after this."

"He shouldn't," said Van. "This Miguel Torres didn't get a look at me, won't know who I am or where to find me. But he knows where they found you. I think he'll want somebody to pay for his skunk of a brother, and I'm almost afraid to leave you here without protection."

"I can't tell you how much it means, having you feel that way, but you have so much to do on your ranch, I'd feel guilty if I kept you here too long. But I do want you to stay the night. You can start early in the morning, stop in San Antonio, and still be home before dark."

They reached the Jabez farm with three hours of daylight remaining, and the place seemed deserted.

"It's early," said Dorinda, "and they're still in the fields. Perhaps you'd better wait here and let me find them. I've been gone so long, I know they've given me up for dead. I'd like a little while alone with them."

"I understand," said Van. "I'll take the other two horses to the barn and rub them down."

He watched her ride away toward the fields he could see in the distance. The house and the barn had been constructed of logs, and one

455

looked as roomy as the other. The barn had a full loft partially filled with hay, and above the open end an iron pulley hung from the roof's extended ridge pole. From somewhere a cow bawled, and he could hear the distinctive prattling of hens. He looked everything over with appreciation, his mind's eye recalling the glorious days when Grandpa Austin had been alive. His had been just such a place as this, and the memory that swept over Van brought a lump to his throat. Finally he saw them coming across the fields. Leading the horse, Dorinda walked beside her mother. The plow — or whatever the mules had been hitched to — had been left in the field. The mules were still in harness, and a big man walked behind them, the reins looped around his neck. When they were close enough, Dorinda dropped the horse's reins and ran to Van.

"Van," she cried, "this is my daddy and my mama."

Without a word the big man grasped Van's hand and almost wrung it off. There was gray in his hair and in his moustache, and the Texas sun had burned him brown as a Mexican. There were traces of tears on his dusty cheeks, and he had to swallow hard before he could speak.

"May God bless you for bringing her home to us," he said in a husky voice. "I'm Eben, and this is Matilda."

Despite the graying hair that crept out beneath Matilda's bonnet, Van could see an older version of Dorinda. He offered her his hand, but she seemed not to see it. She flung her arms around him in silent gratitude.

"Matilda," said Eben, "you and Dorinda go on to the house. We got a horse to look after, and the mules to unharness. We'll be along."

Following Eben, Van led Dorinda's horse on to the barn. He shucked the saddle, and while he rubbed the animal down, Eben unharnessed and tended to his mules. Finished, they paused in the dim interior of the barn.

"Sir," said Van, "I'm sorry we kept her so long, but we were winding up a trail drive from Mexico. From where I found her, it wasn't safe, taking her across South Texas, with the Torres gang still on the loose."

"Thank God you *did* keep her. Three times in the past week or so, there's been a rider here. He always came late at night, and I didn't know what more they wanted from us. I dared not speak to Matilda. Now I know they've come back for her, to steal her away again."

His voice trembled with a mix of emotion and anger. Van made a quick decision, and his hand gripped the arm of the older man.

"Mr. Jabez — Eben — I promise you they won't take her again, if I have to gun them down to the last man."

"You care for her very much," he said, "and she cares for you. I saw it in her eyes when she spoke of you."

"Yes, sir," said Van. "I aimed to talk to you. I'll be callin' on her."

"Young man, in affairs of the heart, do not delay. On the frontier, in this land which is not even part of the United States, a woman needs a strong man. The Rangers are few and scattered. The *alcalde* in San Antonio is no lawman. I am a farmer, and no gunman. They took Dorinda — eleven of them — and I did not resist. Had I done so, I would have died without saving her. I feel less a man, a coward, and I tell you this for my daughter's sake. They must not take her again."

"You have my word," said Van, "and this is no longer your fight. I had to shoot Manuel Torres, and it's me that his vindictive brother wants. But my outfit rode out to help me and Dorinda, and the Torres gang was forced to run. In Miguel Torres's twisted mind, he just wants somebody to pay, and Dorinda's the only one he can get to. Now, what do you know of this rider, the man who comes here at night?"

"Twice," said Jabez, "I found the tracks of his horse behind the barn, and the third time a fresh boot print beneath Dorinda's window."

"He's likely watching the house," said Van, "and by now he'd know Dorinda's here. Trouble is, he knows I'm here too. That means I'll have to ride out while it's light enough for him to see me go. When it's good dark, I'll circle back, picket my horse well away from here, and watch for him from the barn loft."

"Dorinda and Matilda will have to know, then."

"Yes," said Van, "and we might as well go tell them."

There were new tears from Matilda, and an alternate solution from Dorinda. She took

Van's hands in her own, and he saw the fear in her eyes.

"Stay the night," she said, "and ride out in the morning."

"He'd just follow me," Van said. "Revenge killers are a little crazy, and I'd just be taking the problem with me. I'd have a crazy bushwhacker camped on Bandera range. Let him come to me, and let it end here."

They had supper early, so Van could ride out well before dark. Matilda and Dorinda set a table such as Van hadn't seen since leaving Missouri. There was ham, fried chicken, and every vegetable Texas soil was capable of producing. It was all topped off with apple pie and fresh layer cake.

"Dorinda," said Van, a twinkle in his eye, "is all this your mama's doing, or can you do as well on your own?"

"All Mama's doing," said Dorinda, with a smile. "I only made the coffee. For the rest, you'll just have to wait and see."

While there was still an hour of daylight, Van rode out, leading the packhorse, heading north. Soon as it was dark, he rode east and doubled back, approaching the Jabez farm from a different direction. Once he was within a mile of the place, he tied the horses to a cottonwood with a slipknot. Taking his lariat, he walked the rest of the way. He approached the barn from the rear, keeping its bulk between him and the house. There were slats up the outside of a stall, and he climbed swiftly to the loft. Finding a strong roof beam, he tied one end of the lariat to it. From there he could grab the rope and be on the ground in seconds. With both ends of the barn loft open, he could see the house from one end, and to the south — toward the border — from the other.

The moon rose, and still Van waited. He doubted Torres would approach until after moonset, and it wasn't far off when he heard the chink of a horse's shod hoof against stone. Someone was coming! Van held his breath until he saw the dark bulk of horse and rider. He waited for the man to dismount and for his silent shadow to disappear around the corner of the barn. Quietly Van moved to the front of the loft and watched the man approach the house. Whatever Torres had in mind, he wouldn't have time to attempt it. Van slid down the rope and checked his pistol. Then he loosed the reins of the horse and slapped it on the flank. Startled, the horse ran nickering away. Van moved to the corner of the barn and waited until he heard running footsteps. It was time. He stepped past the corner of the barn.

"Torres!"

Torres drew and fired, but he'd been caught offstride, and the slug sang over Van's head. Van drew and fired twice; once at the muzzle flash, and again to the right of it. Torres fired again by reflex, but the muzzle of the gun had sagged, and the lead tore into the ground at his feet. His shadowy form tumbled backward, fell to the ground, and didn't move again.

"Van!" Dorinda cried from the porch. "Van!"

"Here," said Van.

Avoiding the huddled shadow on the ground, Dorinda ran to him. Eben Jabez followed with a lantern. Van pulled away from Dorinda to look at the fallen man.

"He looks some like Manuel Torres," said Van, "but I can't be sure. Dorinda, can you stand lookin' at him long enough to tell us for sure?"

She took a quick look, then turned away.

"Yes," she said, "that's him. That's the other one."

Van gratefully accepted the bed they offered him, and then lay there for an hour, wide-awake. He got up, minus only his boots, and crept back to the parlor. Dorinda was already there, and he sat down beside her.

"I couldn't sleep either," she said.

"Let's talk, then," said Van. "I already asked your daddy if I can come callin' on you, and he welcomed me. Will you?"

"You know I will. Come on Saturday and stay the night."

"It'll be maybe two weeks before Clay and Angelina stand before the preacher," Van said. "Do you reckon your mama and daddy would like to go? It'll give 'em a chance to meet Gil, Clay, and the rest of the outfit."

"Yes," she said, "I think they'd like that, especially if the invitation comes from you. Ask them in the morning."

When Van returned to the ranch, he had arranged for the sale of three hundred longhorns, and the packhorse couldn't have carried one more thing. Behind his saddle was a bulging sack

461

that contained a ham, onions, potatoes, turnips, and a variety of other vegetables. Gil and Clay ragged him some about Dorinda, and Angelina was pleased that the girl and her parents would be attending the wedding. Angelina took it upon herself to begin preparing Rosa for the occasion. Rosa got her first hair cut, her first bath with soap, her first dress, and her first spanking.

"I reckon," said Gil, "with this knot-tyin' ahead of us, we'd better split up the work. Clay, you'll need a house, and the rest of the outfit will need a bunkhouse."

"Angelina and me can take the house that's already here," Clay said, "and the rest of you can sleep in the bunkhouse."

"I sleep in bunkhouse," said Rosa.

"You'll have a room in the house with Van and me," Gil said. "Clay, pick three men to help you cut logs and get your house started. Everybody else will continue branding cattle. When that's done we'll start on the bunkhouse."

★ ★ ★

October 15, 1843. San Antonio, Republic of Texas.

Somewhere, somehow, Clay Duval found a Baptist preacher. Everybody from the Bandera ranch was there except Solano, Mariposa, and Estanzio. They had refused to come, but Solano had made Rosa a new pair of deerskin moccasins for the occasion. Rosa had accepted the bright new pink dress, but had stubbornly resisted the

462

underlying, restrictive pantaloons that went with it. As a result she wore only the dress, being stark naked beneath it. With a sigh, Angelina had agreed, but only when Rosa had promised not to sit down. Later, Angelina would tell her why.

Van had found and borrowed a fancy surrey, using it to drive Dorinda and her parents to San Antonio. Big Foot Wallace and his Rangers were on hand, as was Ranger captain Ben McCulloch and his men.

"I reckon you finished the Torres gang," said Wallace, when Van told him of his encounter with the infamous brothers.

"By the Eternal," said Captain McCulloch, as he congratulated Clay, "I never expected this young hellion to live long enough to marry."

Never had there been such an event. It took place in Overmeyer's wagon yard, for nowhere else was there room enough. The three hundred longhorns had been bought by a stock dealer and were all safely in his cattle pens. But during the ceremony, pranksters let down the rails, and all three hundred longhorns stampeded through the town. Horning their way into a bath house, they drove the patrons out stark naked, most of the men wearing only their hats. Not until the Republic was finally granted statehood would there be an occasion so widely remembered, so well attended, or so grand a reason for men to get roaring drunk.

★ ★ ★

February 19, 1846. Austin, the Republic of Texas.

Almost ten years to the day since Stephen Austin had died, Gil and Van were on hand for the transition, as the Republic of Texas surrendered the reins of government to the new state's first governor, J. Pinckney Henderson. The retiring president of the Republic, Anson Jones, loosed the lines on the flagstaff, and the Lone Star flag of the Republic of Texas was lowered for the last time. As the flag descended, Sam Houston stepped forward and took it. The Republic of Texas was no more.

"Thank God," said Angelina to Clay. "Perhaps this foolish conflict with Mexico can now be resolved."

"It will be," said Clay. "Now President Polk can send enough soldiers to give Santa Anna the beating he's been needin' for so long."

"Soldiers will need horses," said Gil, "and why shouldn't the government buy them from us?"

Dorinda kept a tight rein on Rosa, whose low opinion of *"soldados"* had not changed. She kept trying to get closer to a company of Union bluecoats who were there for show.

"I'm all for selling horses to our new government," said Van, "but why don't we sell 'em some cattle too? If we don't move some of those longhorn brutes, another two or three years of natural increase and our range will be over-grazed."

While their Winged M brand flourished and Indian-gentled Mendoza horses went at

464

a premium, longhorn cattle sales languished. There was no means of transportation to northern and eastern markets, and getting the herd there cost more than its eventual sale brought. The Austins even tried selling breeding stock, but to no avail. Why breed critters nobody wanted? Other Texans raised horses, hogs, fruits, and vegetables. But Gil and Van Austin were stubborn men.

"Someday, somewhere," said Gil, "there'll be a market for Texas beef, and our AA brand will be ready for the long trail."

History would prove him right. In 1849 gold would be discovered in California, and the miners would need beef. In the spring of 1850 Gil and Van Austin would move out a herd of Texas longhorns bound for the gold fields. Theirs would be the perilous route the Butterfield stages would follow almost a dozen years later — from the Bandera range to the Pecos River at Horsehead crossing, across southern New Mexico and Arizona territories, to southern California. Eighteen hundred miles of treacherous rivers, hostile Indians, border outlaws, desert, and rattlesnakes.

It was a stretch right out of Hell, which few men lived to talk about.

Those who did — Texans tough as whang leather, slow to run, and quick on the draw — called it the California Trail . . .

Epilogue

FOR all Stephen Austin's efforts on behalf of the American colony, he died disillusioned and broke. He had been authorized by the Mexican government to collect 12½ cents an acre to cover the cost of surveying and other expenses. While he had been awarded thousands of acres for his own use, he had no time to work the land, and was not permitted to sell it. The colonists accused him of 'gouging,' since he also had land, and refused to pay the small fee to which Austin was entitled. Many of those seeking land had registered as 'ranchers,' but farmed, raising corn and cotton. For many years, as a result, there would be a cattle shortage in the Republic. In 1836, still a young man, Stephen Austin died. Several times the capital was moved, and not until 1850, by statewide vote, did the State of Texas choose Austin as its permanent capital. Only after his death was Stephen Austin granted a place in history as the father of Texas.

Santa Anna became military dictator of Mexico three different times between 1833 and 1855, no small accomplishment, since he appears to have been one of the most hated and extravagant men in Mexican history.

The Texas Rangers led the U.S. Army into Mexico during the Mexican War. So fierce and elusive were these Texans, the Mexicans referred to them as los Tejanos Diablos — the Texas Devils. The effectiveness of the Rangers in Mexico with Colt revolvers resulted in the Walker Colt being adopted as the sidearm for the U.S. Army cavalrymen. The war with Mexico was short and bitter, and the Texas Rangers played a dual role. They operated as cavalry and as long-range recon men for the U.S. Army. They penetrated Mexican defenses with a stealth and skill that army brass could scarcely believe. A Tennessean, Ranger captain Ben McCulloch, led forty Texas Rangers through Mexican lines, seeking a route from Matamoros west to Monterrey for the invading U.S. Army. In ten days McCulloch and his men covered more than 250 miles, raiding villages as they went. Not once were they challenged — or even sighted — by Mexican soldiers.

Announcing . . .

Niagara Large Print!

A brand new series of Large Print books
by *American* authors
— on topics of special interest
to *American Large Print readers*!

- **All guaranteed great reads . . .**

  Niagara selections are guaranteed to be of special interest or well-reviewed in journals respected in American libraries — unlike the no-name filler titles that come with many standing order plans.

- **Richly appointed editions . . .**

  These deluxe hardcovers will be presented in a dual-jacketed format — a traditional dust jacket over a full-color laminated hardcover, with decorative end pages and top- and tail-bands.

- **A Multi-purpose collection —
  a well-rounded, eclectic mix . . .**

Offering a range of high-quality, best-selling titles usually ignored by Large Print publishers, Niagara has everything to delight the widest possible spectrum of Large Print readers. Unlike genre-restricted lines, Niagara is a multi-use collection geared to the walk-in Large Print patron but equally suited to the homebound Large Print reader.

- **Instant book recognition —
  original covers . . .**

Niagara Large Print editions feature original cover art, which will trigger instant recognition by Large Print patrons who've seen the small-print hardcover and paperback versions on display in bookstores and malls.

- **Customer Service and
  the Ulverscroft Guarantee . . .**

We take pride in our customer service — always prompt, professional, and personal. If you have a question about a book or shipment, an editorial suggestion, or any problem we may be able to help solve, just give us a call. If you are ever dissatisfied with any book — for any reason at all — you always have the option of replacement, credit to your account, or a full refund.

SISTERS & LOVERS

Connie Briscoe

On *Publishers Weekly* Bestseller List for four weeks.

Doubleday Book Club and Literary Guild Alternate.

A literary work to which readers of any ethnicity will be able to relate, this is the warm, often humorous story of three African-American sisters who are faced with situations that many women must deal with every day.

Charmaine, Beverly, and Evelyn are three sisters. They live in the same city, but in different worlds . . .

'*Destined to become a keeper, this is recommended for all fiction collections and for libraries supporting African American collections.*'

— **Library Journal**

BARBARA BUSH:
A MEMOIR

'Intriguing . . . wickedly funny. Mrs Bush's dry wit is often in evidence.'
— **New York Times Book Review**

No. 1 *New York Times* Bestseller — on *NY Times* Bestseller List 19 weeks.

For the first time, Mrs Bush gives readers a very private look at a life lived in the public eye for more than twenty-five years. Drawing upon excerpts from her diary, Mrs Bush takes us behind the scenes of the Persian Gulf conflict and the end of the Cold War. Through her reminiscences, we get to know the Gorbachevs, the Thatchers, the Mitterrands, the Mubaraks, and many others.

'The fun of Barbara Bush is reading past all the expected gracious, diplomatic stuff . . . and looking for the moments when the claws come out. In fact, they come out pretty early.'
— ***Entertainment Weekly***

FIRE HORSE

Bill Shoemaker

'*Shoemaker continues to show a broader streak of fun than Dick Francis, and a more pronounced taste for intrigue.*'
— **Kirkus Reviews**

To repay a debt, banned rider Coley Killebrew agrees to tail the beautiful daughter of an ultraconservative talk-show host, only to become entangled in a web of fraud, blackmail and murder. Horses are being killed for insurance money — and so are snoops who find out too much!

'*Superb . . . Devotees of fast-paced, intricately plotted mysteries will find Shoemaker's latest offering immensely entertaining.*'
— *Booklist*

'*Another compelling, intricately plotted tale . . . Once again displaying racetrack expertise to fine advantage, Shoemaker solidifies his position in the winner's circle.*'
— *Publishers Weekly*

RED INK
Greg Dinallo

'The chemistry between Scotto and Katkov — sexual but unconsummated — gradually proves memorable. Suspenseful, fast-paced throughout, a surprising entertainment and a riveting read.'

— **Kirkus Reviews**

Named a 'Notable Book of the Year' by *NY Times Book Review*.

Also featured as a Reader's Digest Book Club selection.

Dissident journalist Nikolai Katkov stumbles upon an international money-laundering racket involving the Moscow 'mafiya'. Their discovery of a hidden government document propels Katkov and his US Treasury agent friend and partner on a dangerous ride through the international underworld — Moscow, Washington, Miami, Havana . . .

'Insightful and entertaining . . . fast-paced, amusing, and scintillating. Highly recommended . . .'

— ***Library Journal***

BODY OF A CRIME
Michael C. Eberhardt

'*A tense, taut, terrific legal thriller.*'
— **Booklist**

In a case that's both a lawyer's dream and a lawyer's nightmare, Chad Curtis, a young ex-pro athlete, is booked for the murder of his gorgeous ex-high school sweetheart. An overwhelming array of evidence points to his guilt, but one vital piece of proof is missing: Robin's body. For defense attorney Sean Barrett, a 'no body' murder case is a legal plum he cannot resist.

'*The courtroom finale is worthy of Perry Mason.*'
— **LA Times Book Review**

'*Gripping plot . . . taut pacing . . . prose energized and graced with wit.*'
— **Atlanta Journal-Constitution**

'*Stands with Turow and Grisham.*'
— **Library Journal**

MIDNIGHT BLUE

Dorothy Garlock

'*Dorothy Garlock is the undisputed grand mistress of the frontier novel.*'
— **Romantic Times**

With a shuddering wave of desire she knew he was a champion who could fight by her side against the outlaws on her land and a soulmate who could share her deepest secrets.

With a derringer in her pocket and her heart beating wildly in her breast, she rode toward the home she barely remembered — only to find a wounded man lying across the rugged trail. He was beaten and bloody, but he was unmistakably a fighter — a handsome Irish brawler with shoulders a yard wide, hands as hard as steel, and midnight-blue eyes as proud and passionate as Mara's own.

'*Dorothy Garlock writes about love in such a way that one would almost believe she coined the word.*'
— **Affaire de Coeur**

LAST MAN OUT

Donald Honig

'Tinker is tough, sharp, and determined as hell. Honig, best known as a baseball historian, is in full stride with this fine second entry in the Tinker series.'
— **Booklist**

Sportswriter Joe Tinker can hardly wait. The was is over. The old Dodger stars are back but with a fantastic rookie, Harvey Tipper, who's a sure bet to put the icing on a pennant cakewalk. But when a New York heiress turns up dead, Harvey is the prime suspect. Only Tinker can save the future superstar. By the time he learns that even his street smarts leave him with a lot to learn about the cynical sophistication of café society, Tinker is already down to his final out — against a killer who keeps mowing 'em down.

'The author's sure-handed but light touch expertly re-creates a postwar ethos. Recommended.'
— **Library Journal**